Final Friends

VOLUME TWO

The Dance
PART 2

The Graduation

CHRISTOPHER PIKE

A division of Hachette Children's Books

First published in the USA in 1988/9 as two separate books by Archway Paperbacks,
a division of Simon & Schuster

First published in Great Britain in a single volume in 1991
by Hodder Children's Books

This edition published in 2011 by Hodder Children's Books

1

A Catalogue record for this book is available from the British Library

ISBN: 978 1 444 90128 3

Typeset in Berkeley by Avon DataSet Ltd,
Bidford-on-Avon, Warwickshire

Printed and bound in Great Britain by
Bookmarque Ltd, Croydon, Surrey

The paper and board used in this paperback by Hodder Children's Books
are natural reyclable products made from wood grown in
sustainable forests. The manufacturing processes conform to the
environmental regulations of the country of origin.

Hodder Children's Books
a division of Hachette Children's Books
338 Euston Road, London NW1 3BH
An Hachette UK company
www.hachette.co.uk

For Ashley

THE DANCE

part two

CHAPTER 1

On the Thursday before homecoming, Nick Grutler stayed after practice to work on his free throws. In the game with Holden, he had been fouled every other time he'd gone to the basket. The free-throw line, only fifteen feet from the hoop, was well within his range; the problem was, he was supposed to stand relatively still while taking a foul shot, and he had trouble hitting even the backboard when he couldn't move.

Nick put up a hundred practice shots and made half – not bad, but not great, either. He finally decided that when he was sent to the line during the game, he would just pretend he was taking an ordinary jump shot, and not mind what the people in the crowd thought.

Another reason Nick had stayed after practice was because he didn't want to take his shower with the rest of the team. When the coach was around, and they were working on plays, the guys treated him fair enough. But if Sellers was not present and The Rock – or the other two leftovers from the football team, Jason and Kirk – were in a bad mood, which they generally were, then he got razzed. If only Michael were around, Nick thought. The week before, when Michael had been coming to practice, no one had said so much as boo to him.

Putting away his basketball. Nick briefly wondered if it was all worth it. Here it was four o'clock, and he had to be at the warehouse by five to work an eight-hour shift, and he was already exhausted. Michael had told him he had to take the long view, but that was hard to do when he could barely see where he was going late at night while riding home on his bike. He couldn't see how all this was going to get him into college on a scholarship.

And he had thought being on the team would impress Maria. Yet as far as he knew, Maria didn't even go to basketball games. Even if she did, and he scored a hundred points every night, she wasn't going to talk to him. Why should she risk it? She was afraid he might kill her.

But that doesn't matter. None of that matters.

Maria's own words. They applied to his situation now. He had discovered something last Friday night during the game, the one thing that was giving him the strength to persevere. It had happened four minutes into the first quarter. Michael had passed the ball to him down in low. It was the first time he had handled the ball on offence. He had two guys on him, and probably shouldn't have put it up. He just did it on impulse, without looking for anyone to pass to. He missed, but managed to get the rebound. Stuffing it home an instant later, hearing the roar of the crowd – roaring for *him* – he felt an intoxicating power flow through his limbs. It was then the realisation hit him; he *loved* to play. And it was strange, in the midst of all the hoopla, in a very quiet way, he had felt at home on the court.

He was not going to quit.

Nor was he going to accept the situation lying down. The Rock was sitting on the bench tying his shoes when Nick entered the shower room.

Nick silently laughed when he saw how quick The Rock tried to finish with his shoes, how he put his head down and tried to disappear. It occurred to Nick that, since their first encounter in the weight room, they had never been alone together.

'Hi, Rocky,' he said. 'Waiting for me?'

The Rock's finger stuck in the lace. He was not so brave when he had no one at his back. 'No,' he mumbled.

'What?'

'No.'

'That's what I thought you said. But I asked twice because, well, you're always asking me the same question twice. It can be annoying, can't it?'

'Yeah.'

'What?'

'I said, yeah.' The Rock gave up on his shoes, stood and closed his locker. He started to step by. Nick blocked his way.

'I want to talk to you.'

'About what?' He was scared, a bit, but still cocky.

'Sit down and I'll tell you.'

The Rock thought about it a moment. Then he sat down. Nick remained standing, propping his foot on the locker at his back so that his knee stuck out close to The Rock's face.

'I never thought,' Nick began, 'that we would ever work together on anything, so I never cared why you despised me. But now we're on the same team, and I don't want it to be a losing team. I don't think you do either. What do you say?'

The Rock grunted, uninterested.

'What does that mean?'

'Go to hell, Grutler.' The Rock started to stand up.

Nick grabbed him by the collar. The Rock's eyes widened. Gently but firmly, Nick sat him back down.

'Now I've put it politely,' Nick said, still holding him by the neck of his shirt. 'But you're being rude. And that makes me mad. And the last time I got mad at you, I almost killed you. I'm asking you again, are you going to lay off me or am I going to have to finish what I started two months ago?'

Now The Rock was really afraid, and more arrogant than ever. 'You would kill me, wouldn't you?'

'I just might.'

The Rock sneered. 'And you've got the nerve to ask why I hate your guts? Scum like you doesn't give a damn about anybody.'

Because The Rock had jumped him twice for absolutely no reason, Nick found his response hard to fathom. He didn't know how to answer. He let go of him and backed off a step. 'Are you serious?' he asked finally.

The Rock rubbed at his tender throat, not taking his eyes off Nick now. 'You know what I'm talking about,' he said bitterly.

'I don't.'

'Get off it, Grutler.'

'I swear, I don't. Tell me.'

'You're a pusher.'

Nick couldn't help but laugh. 'You think I sell drugs? Man, you are one misinformed slob. I don't even smoke pot. Who told you I'm a pusher?'

The Rock was not impressed with his denial. 'I know the neighbourhood you come from. I work there as a Big Brother. Before you showed up here, I used to see you at a crack house on a corner. No one had to tell me nothing about you. And none of your lies is going to keep me from wanting to spit in your face.'

Nick stopped laughing and went through a five-second period of total confusion. The Rock a Big Brother to black kids? The corner crack house? But then, in a single flash he understood *everything*. He pointed a finger at The Rock. 'You stay here. I'm going to get dressed and then we're going for a drive in your car.'

'To where?'

'My old neighbourhood.'

'Why?' The Rock asked.

'You'll see when we get there.'

Nick dressed quickly. It was half past four. It would be dark soon. He would be late to work. If Stanley was at *his* work, however, it would be worth it to clear up this case of mistaken identity.

The Rock had a blue four-wheel-drive truck. Nick gave him directions. Getting on the freeway, they listened to the radio, and hardly spoke. The Rock drove like a goddamn maniac.

They ended up on dumpy narrow streets Nick knew all too well. The sun had said goodnight. They could wait a long time for the broken streetlights to come on. Nick could feel the darkness inside as well as out. Yet he did so from a rather detached perspective. He had grown up in this neighbourhood, but he did not feel as though he had ever belonged in this slum. He didn't know anyone who did.

'Park here,' he said, turning off the music. 'Under that tree.' The Rock did so. Nick glanced back up the street towards the house on the corner. 'Is that the place you saw me?'

The Rock twisted his head around, nodded. 'There's no use denying it, Grutler.'

Nick pulled out his wallet and removed a twenty dollar bill. He gave it to The Rock. 'Go to the house and knock on the door,' he said.

The Rock fingered the bill. 'What's this for?'

'To keep you from getting knifed.' Nick smiled at the alarm on The Rock's face. 'Don't worry, they'll be as afraid of you as you are of them. They'll think you're with the cops. They won't want to sell you anything. But ask for Stanley. Say you're an old buddy. Be sure to say Stanley, not Stan. Have the bill out where they can see it.'

'What am I supposed to say to this Stanley?'

'Whatever you want, except don't mention my name. You're not afraid, are you?'

The Rock scowled at him, put the keys in his pocket. 'You wait here,' he said reaching for the door. He had a hard time getting out. He was shaking.

Nick readjusted the rearview mirror, following The Rock's slow nervous walk towards the house. A stab of guilt touched him. He tried to rationalise that Stanley would not purposely create a messy situation that could not possibly profit him. On the other hand, Stanley might be bored and just looking for something to piss him off.

That moron had better have the sense to know when to run.

The plain white house had two qualities that distinguished it from the others on the block. It had no bushes or trees in the yard, not even grass. And the front door was split in half at the waist. They could open the top and look at you, but you couldn't go barging in. It was so obviously a drug den, Nick didn't know why the police hadn't bombed the place.

Nick suddenly wished The Rock had left him the keys or, better yet, had left the car running. They might want to make a quick getaway. He watched The Rock lumber up to the porch. He was fifty yards away at this point, and Nick could see the twenty trembling in his clenched fingers. He was going to say something stupid; it was practically a foregone conclusion. Nick leaned over and pulled the wiring from beneath the dashboard. He had known how to hot-wire a car since he was twelve.

When he had the truck running and looked back up, The Rock was at the door talking to someone. Nick couldn't see who the person inside was, but he appeared to be a young black kid with a shaved head.

Dammit!

The Rock was arguing with the boy, obviously throwing his weight around. The kid disappeared, and The Rock glanced towards the truck and smiled. It was the smile – arrogant, as usual – that pushed the red alarm inside Nick. Cursing himself for trusting the imbecile not to alienate the neighbourhood in a minute's time, he jumped into the driver's seat and put the truck in gear.

He had turned the truck around and was approaching the house when he saw a long black arm thrust out and grab The Rock by the throat.

The Rock tried to scream. A strangled whimper was all he got out. Nick remembered how strong Stanley was. The long black arm shook The Rock, pulling him off the ground and closer to the door. Nick floored the accelerator, then slammed on the brakes, jumping out on to the street in front of the house. He needed something, anything to distract Stanley for a second. Nick couldn't quite see his old enemy, but he didn't have to. The Rock was toppling into the door like prime surfer beef into the maw of a shark.

Nick spotted a Coke bottle in the gutter. The top had been cracked off, and Nick briefly wondered as he scooped it out of the dust if the last person to hold it had used it to keep someone with a knife at bay.

There was a narrow window to the right of the front door. Winding up, Nick let go with a wicked pitch. Glass shattered glass. The long arm snapped back inside. The Rock crashed to the porch floor.

'Get in the truck!' Nick yelled, leaping into the driver's seat again. The Rock had never moved so fast on either the football field or the basketball court. Although starting from flat on his ass, he was diving into the back of the truck even as the tall black dude appeared on the porch. Nick revved first gear, leaving a trail of burned rubber. One look at Stanley had been enough to remind him why he had gone down on his knees and thanked God the day his dad had moved him to the other side of town.

If I look half as scary as that bastard when I'm mad, no wonder people are afraid of me.

The Rock started banging on the rear windscreen so Nick would stop and let him in, but Nick left him in the howling wind all the way home on the freeway. It did his heart good to see The Rock go from shaking with fear to shivering with cold. Besides, he was having a great time driving the truck.

The school parking lot was deserted when Nick finally brought the pickup to a halt, turning off the engine. He half expected The Rock to leap out of the back and start cursing. Instead, the guy got up and opened the truck door for him.

'You drive like a goddamn maniac,' The Rock said. 'How did you start the truck without the keys?'

'A pusher's trade secret,' Nick said, climbing down.

'Oh, that.' The Rock turned away. 'You've got to admit, he did look a lot like you.'

'The only things Stanley and I have in common are that we are both tall and we are both black.'

'Then how did you know I was talking about him?'

'Cops have mistaken me for him in the past. White cops. Now, I guess, you're going to tell me we all look alike to you.'

'I wasn't going to say that.' Finally The Rock was beginning to show signs of shame, faint signs. Sticking his fat hands in his pockets, he shifted uneasily on his feet. 'I suppose I owe you an apology.'

'Especially if you lost my twenty dollars.'

The Rock glanced up, pulled out the money. 'I held on to it. He didn't scare me that bad.'

Nick chuckled as he accepted the money. 'Then do you have a bladder infection or something?'

The Rock started to speak, then quickly removed his hands from his soggy pockets. He had peed his pants. 'He was a crazy dude. He could have cut my throat. Why did you send me to the door?'

'I just wanted you to see him. I didn't expect you to make him reach for his switchblade. What did you say to him?'

'I said I was a friend of yours.'

Nick groaned. 'I told you not to bring me up. You're lucky to be alive.'

'Why? What did you do to him?'

Nick sighed. The truth of the matter was, he *had* been irresponsible taking The Rock to that house. Stanley was bad news. It was upsetting to Nick to remember exactly how bad, to remember how Tommy had died. It was weird; they had been such close friends for such a long time and now he hardly ever thought of Tommy. The last time had been . . .

When Alice had died.

No, it had been *before* Alice died, minutes before, when he had gone into that last bedroom on the left. What had been in that room that reminded him of Tommy? The only thing Alice had in common with Tommy was that they'd both died violent deaths.

'It's a long story,' Nick said finally. 'Can I ask you something?'

The Rock shrugged. 'Sure.'

'The night of Alice's party – you told the police you came back to the house to thank Mike for saving your eyes. Is that true?'

'No. I came back to kick the crap out of you.'

'Why didn't you?' Nick already knew one reason. The Rock had chickened out when he had discovered all his buddies were gone.

'My eyes started to burn again. I didn't totally trust what the doctor at the hospital had said. I thought I might go blind. I jumped in the shower to wash them out some more.'

'You really were in the shower when Alice was killed?'

'Yeah. Anyway, I heard she killed herself.'

Nick had never been able to understand Michael's conviction that Alice had been murdered. The facts spoke for themselves, and no one had been closer to the facts than Nick. But now, the more he thought of Tommy . . .

There is something connecting those two deaths.

He would have to talk to Michael about the sense of déjà vu he'd had in that dark bedroom. And he'd better tell him the truth about how he hadn't run straightaway to the bedroom – as he had told the police – but had dashed down the stairs first. All of a sudden, Nick had the uneasy feeling these things might be important.

'I heard she killed herself, too,' Nick said finally. 'But I changed the subject. You were starting to apologise?'

The Rock shifted on his feet again. 'I'm sorry. What else can I say? I thought you had come here to mess up everyone's mind. You can see why I was always on your case, can't you?'

'But you jumped me without any proof I was selling drugs?'

'I told you, I thought I saw you at that crack house.' He added, somewhat embarrassed, 'I did try to get proof.'

'It was you who set that narc, Randy Meisser, after me?'

'You know about him?'

Nick nodded, checked his watch. 'Hey, I've got to get to work. You give me a ride and I'll think about accepting your apology. I'll have to put my bike in the back.'

'It's a deal.' The Rock offered his hand. 'No hard feelings, Nick?'

Nick hesitated. 'Are you really a Big Brother?'

'I am.'

'What's your real name?'

'Theodore.'

Nick laughed, shook his head. 'God help those kids.'

CHAPTER 2

Sara started her car as she saw Russ jog down Polly's long driveway and turn on to the deserted pavement. She let the engine idle for a minute while he headed away from her.

He is living with Polly. I should run him over.

She was cold. She was tired. She had been sitting in her car in the dark for over an hour waiting for Russ to appear, thinking of the way Bubba was brushing her off every time she demanded an update on the money she had given him, fretting over whether the homecoming tent was going to collapse and smother the whole school, and remembering the good old days when she'd had only herself to worry about. She had been a different person then. She had been happy.

No, I wasn't happy. I was bored out of my mind.

Which had been a lot more fun, she decided, than

being downright miserable. She flipped on her headlights and started the car, rolling after Russ.

CIF is in two days, Saturday morning. He won't run far.

Nor, did it seem, was he going to run very fast. She followed him for two miles, out of the housing tract and on to a path that circled the park across the street from the school. He never broke his leisurely jog. He also gave no sign that he knew she was following him. But when he made a sudden U-turn and began to head back towards Polly's house, she momentarily panicked and put her foot on the accelerator, racing past him. She probably would have kept going if he hadn't waved. Slamming on the brakes, she pulled over to the side of the road and got out. His breath came out white as he walked towards her.

'Have you been following me?' he asked.

'No.' She wished more than anything else in the universe that she didn't feel this way when she was with him, that she didn't need him. 'Yes,' she said. 'Aren't you going to say "Hi, Sara?"'

He wiped the sweat from his face with the arm of his shirt. 'Hi, Sara.'

'Hi, Russ. How are you?'

'Fine. How are you?'

'I feel like an idiot. How did you know I was following you?'

'I don't go into a coma when I'm running.' He came up beside her, gestured to the unlit park, the silent rolling grass hills. 'It's late,' he said.

'I remember you told me you liked to run late at night.'

'Yeah, it's cooler. And you don't have to run into people.'

'Not as cool as a freezer, though,' she said. He tried to brush off her remark, but she spoke quickly. 'I'm sorry I locked you in there. I didn't mean to. I mean, I meant to, but I didn't know you'd have such a hard time getting out.' She reached for her car door. 'That's all I wanted to say.'

'Where are you going?' he asked, surprised.

'You don't like to run into people.' She opened the car door. 'That's what you just said.'

'I wasn't talking about you. Hey, don't go.' He closed the door, touching her hand in the process. 'Come on, Sara, let's not fight.'

She couldn't look at him, not when he was living with one of her best friends and sending that friend out to buy contraceptives in public clinics. 'I just don't want to bother you,' she said.

He put his hand on her arm. 'You're not bothering me.'

'I'm not?'

'No.'

She whirled on him, throwing off his hand. 'Well, you're bothering me! You got yourself fired. You've stopped coming to school. You've got this big race you've got to win if you're going to do anything with yourself. And you're—'

'I'm just sleeping there, that's all,' he interrupted.

'Did I say anything? Did I say a word about you having sex with Polly and the whole school talking about it when they're not talking about Clair's abortion?'

'Clair had an abortion?'

'Yeah, and it wouldn't surprise me if you're the one who got her pregnant!'

He scratched his head, confused. 'There you go yelling at me again when I'm trying to be nice to you.'

'I'm not yelling at you!' she yelled. Then she stopped. 'Why are you trying to be nice to me?'

'I don't know. I guess I like you.'

'You don't like me.'

He was beginning to get annoyed. 'All right, I don't like you.'

'I know you don't. Why did you say that you do?'

Russ sighed, sat down on the kerb. 'Never mind.'

She sat beside him, studying his face for a full minute. He looked about as miserable as she felt, but it gave her no satisfaction. A chilly damp layer of air began to creep towards them from the dark park. 'You're going to catch cold,' she said.

'I don't care.'

'I care.'

'What do you care about?'

'That you're going to get cold.' She hesitated. 'And I care about you, you know?'

'No you don't.'

It was her turn to be annoyed. 'Are you calling me a liar?'

'No.'

'Then what are you doing?'

He rested his head in his hands. 'I think I'm beginning to get a headache.'

'Oh, swell, thanks a lot. Sorry I had to be born and mess up your evening.' She started to get up. He stopped her.

'Would you please stop doing that?'

She brushed off his hand but kept her place beside him on the kerb. Her butt was beginning to freeze. 'I'm not doing anything. I tell you I care about you and you don't believe me.'

'Well, I told you I like you and you don't believe me.'

Sara paused. 'You're right.' Then she smiled. 'Do you really like me?'

'No.'

She pushed him. 'Yes, you do! You're crazy about me. You're just afraid to admit it.'

He laughed. 'I wouldn't go that far. Stop pushing me!' He grabbed her hands, pinning them together, hard, impressing on her again how strong he was. Then their eyes met. She didn't think she had ever looked him straight in the eye before. They were dark, intense. They even scared her, a bit. Still holding on to her, he leaned over and kissed her on the lips. She kissed him back.

Oh, my.

He wasn't cold at all. No one had ever kissed her before.

A minute later – or maybe longer, her sense of time went straight to hell the instant they had made contact – he pulled back.

'What's the matter?' she asked, opening her eyes with a start. She couldn't remember closing them. Nor could she remember him releasing her hands and wrapping his arm around her shoulders. Like his mouth, it, too, felt warm.

'Nothing. I can't kiss you all night. You're new at this, aren't you?'

'No. Why do you say that?' She had a rush of anxiety. 'Am I a lousy kisser?'

'Fair.'

She started to shove him again. But when he started to stop her, she let him. Unfortunately, he didn't pin her hands or kiss her again. He just stared at her, and she found herself blushing.

'What are you thinking?' she asked finally.

'About something you said.'

'What?'

'That I am a drunk,' he said.

'I didn't mean—'

'No you're right.' He took back his arm, rested his elbows on his thighs, his head hanging down. Even in the dark, she could see the gooseflesh forming on his legs. She should let him go, or give him a ride home, back to Polly's house. 'I've got to stop the beer,' he said.

She nodded. 'I wish you would. You'd run a lot faster. The race is Saturday, isn't it?'

'Yeah.'

He had kissed her, she thought, so her next question shouldn't be hard to ask. Yet it was. 'Do you want me to come?'

He glanced up. 'Do you want to?'

She spoke carefully. 'Will I be the only one there?'

He shook his head, serious. 'I'm only staying with Polly because I have nowhere else to stay.'

'That's not what she says.'

'Then she's crazy.'

Sara couldn't argue with that. 'Yeah, but she's also my friend. And she just lost her sister.' The mention of Alice made her pause. She had all these problems and, somehow, they all seemed connected to that night.

When Alice was alive, it was easy to be tough.

Suddenly she was close to crying. It was true, what people said about how when someone close to you died, a part of you also died. Two months ago she would simply have told Bubba to take a hike. She would never have lost the money in the first place. She wiped at her eyes, fighting for control.

'What's wrong?' he asked.

'Nothing. Yeah, I want to come. I'll be there.' She shoved him in the side. 'You'd better win.'

CHAPTER 3

The following afternoon, Friday, Jessica left school at lunch to go home. She had called the SAT test office in the morning looking for her scores. When they told her they would have to search for the information, she had asked them to call back and leave the scores on her answering machine. Naturally she was anxious to check the machine's tape. The big event of the day was over, anyway. Voting for homecoming queen had taken place during fourth period. She had intended to vote for Maria but, at the last minute, had checked the box beside her own name. Clair hadn't been in all week and the gossip going around about her was vicious; nevertheless, Jessica did not want to lose by one vote.

At home, Jessica found both her test score and Clair. She did not, however, notice her rival until after she had run upstairs and listened to the bad news on her answering machine.

'Jessica Hart,' a brisk-voiced lady said. 'This is Jill Stewart at the test office. Your scores are as follows: three hundred and seventy on the verbal section, and three hundred and twenty on the maths section. If you have any further questions, please feel free to call me back.'

Sixteen hundred total was a perfect score. If you got less than four hundred on either the maths or verbal section, your counsellor usually recommended a community college with a strong tutorial programme. Jessica trudged back downstairs and outside and plopped down on the front porch steps. She thought of all the Stanford yearbooks she had browsed through while growing up. Her father was going to kill her.

'Bad news?' a voice asked. Jessica looked up and stood quickly. Dressed in old, faded blue jeans and a plain red blouse, not wearing a speck of make-up, Clair strolled up the walkway.

'Clair, you surprised me. How did you know I'd be here?'

'Bubba told me.' Clair stopped at a distance of approximately ten feet, gave the house a cursory inspection, then fused on Jessica, her blue eyes cold. 'He told me a few things. All about your filthy mouth.'

She swallowed. 'What?'

'Don't deny it. You started the rumour about me having an abortion.'

'That's not true. All I know is what Polly told me.'

'Polly nothing. You made her talk. You did it because you're afraid of me. You're afraid I'll beat you out for homecoming queen, and that I'll take Bill away from you.' Clair took a big step closer. 'But like I told you before, dearie. I can't lose. And as far as Bill is concerned, you can have him. For all the good he'll do you.'

Jessica shook her head weakly, as weak as her lies. 'I don't know what you're talking about.'

Clair drew closer still, pointing a long nail at her face. 'When I first met you with Mike I thought you had class. I thought we could become friends. Now I'm glad I kept my distance. I hope Mike does the same.' She flicked her nail at the end of Jessica's nose, scratching it. 'You'll get what you deserve, bitch.'

Clair turned then, leaving, and Jessica went inside and collapsed on the couch. It was hard to remember when she had felt worse.

'Alice, where are you?' she moaned to the ceiling. Her little friend had always looked up to her, and perhaps because of that, she had always strived to do what she knew was right. Now that Alice was gone it seemed she didn't care who she stepped on.

Oh, I care. But I do it anyway.

That morning Bill had asked her to the homecoming dance, and she had said yes. Although talk continued to fly about how he had knocked Clair up, he appeared unaffected by it. Indeed, he hadn't even gone to the trouble of denying it, which confused her; she had recently learned from Polly that it had been Bubba, and not Bill, who had picked Clair up at the clinic.

Once upon a time, Bill's asking her to the dance would have meant everything. And she had agreed to go with him because he still had a body that wouldn't quit. But she was no longer infatuated with him. He had virtually no personality, she finally realised. More important, she was interested in someone else.

She was in love with Michael Olson.

When he had told her about the different tests, and in one stroke shattered her lifelong plans, she wanted to die. What she had done instead was sit in the shade of a tree at the back of the Sanders campus. Afraid to leave her in her fragile condition, Michael had sat with her. With the realisation that she wasn't going anywhere special after graduation, the Valium had begun to sock it to her. Lying on the grass, Michael sitting quietly at her side, she had wandered in and out of consciousness for what had seemed ages. But each time she had resurfaced, she opened her eyes to find Michael still waiting for her, sometimes writing in a notebook, other times just staring up into the sky. And each time he had looked different to her, as if she were seeing him through different eyes. Each time he had looked more beautiful, more perfect. Each time she woke hoping to find his fingers stroking her hair, or catch his eyes fixed on her face.

But he was just being the way he is, kind. I can't expect anything from him.

She kept taking advantage of him. Surely by now he must know why she had stood him up. Bubba knew everything, and Bubba must have told him. Yet he had treated her nicely all week, repeatedly apologising for giving her the wrong answers on the test, wishing her well on the homecoming queen vote, apparently oblivious to the self-serving gossip floating around that she had set in motion. He had treated her as Alice always had, as if she were special.

Not for the first time, Jessica wondered what he really thought of her. She would have given almost anything to know.

The mountains owned half the sky. Had the school been any closer to the slopes, it would have had to have been built perpendicular to the ground. Temple High was his best bet and, for that reason, Michael had saved it for the last. Parking in front of the administration building, he climbed out of his car and headed up the steps.

The receptionist-secretary was young and Hawaiian, with braided black hair and a dazzling set of teeth that made Michael think of South Pacific islands and warm green swells. It had been cold the past night and, from the forecast, would be colder still the next night for their outdoor homecoming dance. He hadn't made up his mind whether he'd go or not. All week he had been trying to psych himself up to ask Jessica. With the SAT fiasco, though, he felt the timing would be lousy. On the other hand, she had given no indication she had a date. Bubba hadn't heard anything about Bill having asked her, and that probably meant she needed an escort. Maybe he could give her a call, work the conversation around to the dance and see what happened.

'Can I help you?' the young lady asked, wheeling her swivel chair back from her desk.

'Yes, I'd like to buy a copy of your yearbook.' He had learned at the previous two schools he had visited that people would immediately get suspicious if he asked for a list of all the students named Clark. That's confidential information, they would say, and where are you from, and all that jive. All he needed was a picture with a name.

'The due date of ordering yearbooks was last month,' she said.

'A copy of last year's yearbook would be fine.' He had the lie ready. 'You see, I don't actually go here. I'm on the yearbook staff at another school. I'm doing format research for our annual.' He spoke sincerely. 'I've heard Temple's got one of the best yearbooks in Southern California.'

Never underestimate the power of school pride. The lady smiled at the compliment and immediately went looking for a book. When she returned a few minutes later with the annual in her hand, and he asked what the charge would be, she said it was a complimentary copy. He thanked her and hurried to his car.

Twenty minutes later, after a thorough search of the senior, junior and sophomore classes, he slammed the book shut in disgust. There wasn't a single Clark in the whole school, much less one with ugly red hair and green cat eyes. Tossing the yearbook on to the passenger seat, he rolled down the window and stared at the mountains. Far above, on a high-altitude breeze, the matchstick trees swayed in the hard blue sky.

He must have been stoned. He must have been rambling.

Michael had a couple of hours before he had to go to work. He wasn't sure what to do next. His mom had said she would be getting off work early that day, and he debated swinging by the house to see how she was doing. She had told her boyfriend, Daniel, about the baby, and the man was excited. Yet he hadn't proposed, not yet. He needed to digest the news, he said. Michael could understand that. He was still digesting the idea of having a dad. At least there was no chance of the baby telling him what he could and couldn't do. His mom appeared to be taking everything in her stride.

Not making any progress proving Alice had been murdered had frustrated him. He decided to go by the school and check with Bubba on the coroner's files.

When he arrived back at Tabb, sixth period was over and the campus was almost deserted. Crossing the courtyard, he caught a glimpse between the buildings of the huge tent being erected for the dance on the practice basketball courts. It looked like Sara had been talking to a circus.

He didn't enter the computer room from the outside, but through the central utility room that connected all the science classes. Just before opening the door, however, he overheard Bubba talking to Clair. Because it was Bubba, and because Bubba had more power than any teenager had a right to, Michael felt it was his moral responsibility to eavesdrop. He put his ear to the door.

'I can't do it,' Bubba was saying. 'It'll be too obvious.'

'Obvious to who?' Clair demanded.

'Mike for one. He knows what I can do. And he likes Jessie.'

'Would he talk?'

'He might. And even though the votes haven't been tabulated, the word around town has you way off the mark. If you suddenly won, it could get ugly.'

'For who? You?'

'As a matter of fact, yes.'

Clair growled. 'You're always bragging about your ability to get anything you want. And here I ask you one tiny favour and you say no. I'm sick of it, Bubba. I tell you, I won't stand on that stage and see her crowned.'

'I know.'

'You know? Then do something about it!'

'I can't.'

There was a long pause. Michael could readily imagine the expression on Clair's face and was glad it was not glaring down on him. 'You think of something,' she said finally, soft and deadly. 'Or *I'll* think of something.'

Bubba did not respond, or did not have a chance to. Michael listened as Clair stalked out of the room, slamming the door in the process. He waited a respectable length of time before entering. Bubba glanced up from his terminal.

'Hi, Mike. Did you discover Clark Kent's secret identity?'

Michael shook his head, sat down. 'The more I chase this guy, the more I think he must be some kind of superman to disappear the way he has.' He nodded towards the screen. Bubba was presently in an administrative file he had no right to be in. It could very well be the file where the votes for the homecoming queen had been stored. 'What are you working on?' he asked.

'Nothing important.' Bubba turned off the screen, thoughtful. 'Going to the dance tomorrow?'

'I'd like to see how Nick does in the game. I don't know, I might hang around afterwards. Sara's got the price for the dance down to five bucks.'

'I don't know how she does it.'

'Still no word on Bill asking Jessie?'

'It just came in. Bill nabbed her this morning after political science. The slut was flattered.'

'Don't call her that.'

'Sorry. A slip of the tongue.'

Michael decided he wasn't going to the dance after all.

He couldn't bear the thought of watching them moving hand in hand across the floor. He should have asked her himself! He honestly thought she might have said yes. Even though he had messed her up on the SAT test, she hadn't directed one word of blame at him. She had style.

Even when unconscious.

He remembered sitting beside her while she slept off the effect of the drugs, her shiny brown hair spread over her tucked-in arm, her lips pursed like those of a dreaming child, her long, thick eyelashes flickering slightly as her chest slowly rose and fell. If he hadn't fallen completely in love with her before, he had toppled the final distance that afternoon. He had been tempted to kiss her while she slept.

Then he thought of Alice. He always thought of Alice whenever Jessica appeared to be slipping further from his grasp. It was as if he substituted a fresh pain for one locked in memory, some kind of perverted reflex.

'When are you going to try for the autopsy report?' he asked.

'Tomorrow. But I warn you, it'll take a while to copy all the medical group's files over, twelve hours minimum. That's going to cost a couple of hundred at least.'

'I'll pay it. Can you start it in the morning?'

'For you, Mike, anything.'

'Thanks.' Michael almost made him promise to leave Jessica as homecoming queen if she had been elected to the position. He couldn't believe she had anything to do with the slanderous gossip going around about Clair. But it wouldn't do to hassle Bubba, he decided, until he had that report in his hand. And he remembered Bubba's words to Clair, that nothing could be done to change the outcome of the vote, and he was reassured.

CHAPTER 4

That night, the night before the dance and the ruin of a princess, Polly returned to her big house to find a message from Tony Foulton on her answering machine and a note from Russ taped to the mirror in her downstairs bathroom. She had stopped at the hospital after school to check on Philip Bart – the foreman who had got knocked on the head during the dynamite blast – and was late getting home. Poor Phil, initially he'd made good progress, but he'd lapsed back into a coma the previous night, and now the doctors were saying he wasn't going to make it. Polly had run into his wife in the intensive care waiting room and the woman had depressed the hell out of her, crying and carrying on.

But everyone's got to die, sooner or later.

Polly got to Tony's message first, playing it while she grabbed a carrot from the refrigerator.

'Polly, this is Tony. Just called to let you know the float will be ready tomorrow morning if you want to swing by the plant for an inspection before we tow it to the school. I'll be at home this evening if you want to reach me.'

Then she discovered the note.

Polly,

I've found a new place to stay. Thanks for the hospitality. I won't forget it.

Russ

A tidal wave of emotion began to rush over Polly, and then, as if the wave had suddenly run into a mountain of granite, there was nothing. She stood holding the note in one hand, the carrot in the other, staring at her reflection in the mirror and thinking about absolutely nothing for an indeterminate length of time. During this time, she wasn't the least bit mad or the least bit depressed. She simply wasn't there. Even when she began to think again, she didn't feel much of anything, except an abrupt, intense hunger.

She blinked at her reflection. She hardly recognised herself. She was much too skinny. No wonder Russ hadn't wanted to have sex with her!

Throwing both the carrot and the note into the toilet and flushing them out of existence, she hurried back to the kitchen. There was a two-pound box of chocolates in the cupboard above the refrigerator that some bleeding soul had given her after Alice's funeral. Love and chocolate, she'd once read, were practically interchangeable from a hormonal point of view.

Polly found the box and began to eat, one candy after another. They were truffles: raspberry, strawberry, mint, all her favourite flavours. She couldn't believe how hungry she was! She finished off the top layer and started on the bottom, checking the time. It was late, but maybe a shop would be open, and she could get another box.

'These are good, these are wonderful,' she said out loud to herself. 'These are just what the doctor ordered. And a little drink. When you eat candies you have to drink, Polly, or the sugar will make you thirsty. Yes, Mommy, I remember. Where is a glass? Here is a glass. Now let me get you a little drink, Pretty Polly.'

Polly did get down a glass and did grab a can of Pepsi from the cupboard beneath the sink. But then she thought of the paper cups she had told Alice to fetch from her parents' closet the night of the party. She looked down at her can of Pepsi, also thinking of how soda should always be drunk out of a paper cup and not a real glass, because then it tasted like you were at a party. Then you could pretend the party wasn't really over.

Setting down the glass and the box of chocolates, Polly ran up the stairs and dashed to her parents' old bedroom, where Alice had died. She flipped the switch, but of course the light didn't go on because it was still broken. She didn't care. She didn't need it. She just wanted the cups! Those stupid paper cups. And she knew where they were. She remembered exactly where her mommy had put them. At the top of the closet. And here was Mr Ladder, behind Mr Door.

Polly had set up the ladder in the dark room beside the closet and was on the third step going on to the fourth when the black figure came up at her back and shoved her hard in the rear, sending her toppling towards the hard wooden floor. For an instant, caught completely by surprise, she didn't throw out her hands to brace her fall. Actually, it seemed far longer than an instant; it seemed as if she fell for ever, and had all the time in the world to decide how she wanted to hit the floor, which angle would cause her the least harm. For some reason, the fact she had the opportunity to decide made her furious. In the end she did throw out her hands, her wrists absorbing the brunt – but not all – of the impact. Her right ankle took a nasty bang. Pain shot up her leg and she let out a cry.

'What is this supposed to be?' Clark demanded,

towering over her, a shadow, except for the yellow hall light filtering through his messy red hair. In his hands was Russ's note, torn and dripping wet. For a moment, Polly had the horrible idea that Clark had been hiding deep inside the toilet when she had come home, waiting for her beneath the house with the worms and slimy things in the black smelly pipes. Then she realised the carrot and the paper must have got tangled together, and not flushed properly. He had never been one to knock. He must have entered through the garage and gone straight to the bathroom, and found the evidence.

'He's just a friend who stayed here a few days,' she cried.

'You're a liar. You've been unfaithful to me.'

'No!'

'You've been sleeping with him.' He crouched down beside her, grabbing her shirt at the neck. 'Now I know why you pushed me away last time. You'd already had your fill.'

'He's just a friend,' she said, weeping. She could feel his breath, cold and damp, on the side of her face. The pain in her ankle was making her nauseated. She feared at any second he would step on it with his hard black boot.

He paused, his fury momentarily frozen on his face, then he appeared to relax a notch. He leaned forward, draping the dripping letter over her face. 'Tell me the truth, Polly,' he said softly, tightening his grip on her shirt. 'And I will set you free.'

'I told you.' The water spilled over her eyes, around her nose. It stank.

'Don't tell me, and I will break your ankle.'

Polly stopped fighting him. He was serious. 'I slept with him,' she said quietly.

'Honestly?'

'I swear.' It was the truth, the literal truth. It didn't matter that Russ had never been awake to begin with.

'I believe you. Do you want me to set you free?'

'Yes.'

'Very good.' Clark let go of her shirt, lifted the veil from her eyes. 'I can forgive anything, except dishonesty,' he said, the anger gone from his face.

'I'm sorry,' she whimpered, wiping the gook off her face and rubbing her ankle; it felt as if it might already be broken. 'I won't do it again.'

'I know you won't.' He stood, not offering her a hand, and stepped to the east-facing windows. She was surprised to see they were open, the shades up. She thought she had pulled them down. Clark took a breath of the cold air coming through the screens. 'Do you know what will happen if you do?' he asked.

'You'll leave me?'

He turned, his face serious. 'I can never do that. If I leave you, I die.'

Despite her pain, she smiled. 'You don't care that much about me, do you?' she asked hopefully.

'That's not what I said.'

'What do you mean?'

He nodded, as if she had answered a question and not asked one, turning back towards the outside, pointing a long bony finger at a damaged wooden shingle a few feet beyond the window. 'That's what I will do to you,' he said.

She lost her smile. 'I don't know what you're talking about.'

'You see it, don't you?'

'See what? You're not making any sense.' Suddenly it wasn't her ankle that was hurting, but her head – a thick pressure was building inside. 'Never mind. I said I won't do it again.'

He lowered his finger and almost instantly her head began to feel better. 'How is your foot?' he asked in an offhand fashion.

'It's fine,' she lied, before remembering what he had

said about honesty. 'It hurts.' Now it was her turn to be angry. 'Why did you push me off the ladder?'

'I didn't push you. You slipped.' He grinned. 'You won't be able to dance tomorrow. You have the perfect excuse.' He took a step towards her. 'Jessie and Sara will be at the dance, won't they? They'll be on the stage – up there beneath the lights while you'll still be lying here on the floor in the dark. Do you know why that is, Polly?'

'No,' she said, defiant. She wished he would help her up, and she wished he wouldn't talk this way. Yet, at the same time, she felt an obligation to listen. Clark had a certain perspective on things that most people didn't have. She supposed that was one of the reasons she liked him.

'It's because of what's in this room,' he said, lowering his voice, standing over her again, the windows at his back. 'What's *inside* it.' He shut his eyes briefly, and it seemed to Polly he was suddenly uneasy; he trembled slightly, and his breathing was heavy. When he opened his eyes again, he was staring, not at her, but at the spot on the floor near the windows where they had found Alice. He added, 'What's inside for now. It could escape.'

'Clark?'

He dropped his head back and looked at the ceiling,

and then stared again at the spot on the floor. Polly couldn't be sure, but it seemed he was mentally drawing a line from high above to far below. 'Your aunt's asleep beneath us,' he said finally.

'So?'

He tapped the floor with the heel of his right boot. 'What's beneath us feels solid. People always think that way. The fools! The ground can drop out from beneath you at any moment, and leave you falling for ever. Nothing's real.' He nodded towards the floor, and Polly thought she could see the stains in the wood, even though she knew they had been washed away long ago. 'Drops of her blood seeped through the floor,' he said. 'They escaped.'

'No.'

'Yes. Alice's dead blood. The drops seeped through the wood and dirt, and now one of them has finally landed on your aunt's face, on her lips.' He wiped the back of his hand across his nose and glanced down at her. 'Do you know what that means?'

She was afraid she might. 'She's not going to die!'

'But she is. She's going to smother to death on Alice's blood.' He moved towards the door, past her. Desperate, Polly reached out and grabbed his leg.

'No! *You're* going to smother her!'

He regarded her with calm indifference as she clung to his smooth black boot. 'It has to be done. Let me go and I can do it now, and it will be over. I'll use a soft pillow.'

Holding on to his leg, Polly tried to get up, to put weight on her foot. She screamed in agony when it gave out beneath her. She fell to her knees, her head banging against his knee. Any moment she expected him to shake her off. Yet he continued to stand above her, at ease, watching her crawl at his feet.

'You can't do this to me,' she said, weeping. 'I'll be alone in this house. There'll be no one to talk to. They'll all be gone. Leave Polly. Who cares about Polly? Please don't do it. I don't mind taking care of her. I really don't, I swear.'

'But she won't let you live until she's dead. Besides, she smells.' He shook his leg. 'Let go, Polly, and I'll set you free of her like I promised.'

'No!' she pleaded, tightening her grip, her tears smearing the leather hide of his trouser leg. 'No promises! Nothing! You don't have to do anything for me! I can do it myself!'

She hadn't meant to say that.

Clark began to chuckle, soft and steady. Reaching down and undoing her grasp, he helped her to her feet, setting her against a wall where she hobbled on one foot. 'All right,' he said.

She stopped her crying. 'All right, what?'

'All right, it's your show.'

She didn't like the sound of that. 'No.'

He nodded, smiling. 'Keep your promise, Polly, or I'll be back to keep it for you.'

Then he was gone, down the stairs and out of her sight. It seemed like a long time to her before the front door opened, but then she definitely heard him leaving; his motorcycle starting, its motor fading into the distance.

Bastard. Alice was right about him.

Polly crawled downstairs – moaning the whole way – straight to her aunt's bedroom. With relief bordering on hysteria, she found the lady snoring peacefully, undisturbed by all the commotion, her face clean and old.

Only later did Polly discover the message from Tony Foulton on her answering machine had been replayed.

That night there was a lightning storm, and Polly slept poorly, and had a bad dream that went on until dawn. An axe was chopping somewhere above her bed, cutting holes into the ceiling, narrow splintered holes from which drops of fresh red blood dripped into her open mouth.

CHAPTER 5

A strong wind was blowing off the nearby grey ocean as Sara helped Russ out of his sweats minutes before the start of the Four-A CIF Championship Cross-Country Race. The storm was over, but a few scattered clouds were hanging around, and the grass beneath their feet was still soggy. It would take a few days to dry out before it would qualify as a halfway decent running surface.

They were standing on the high point of the course, a hill located near the centre of Hill Park, a place that more than deserved its name. The spot afforded an excellent view of most of the three-mile course. A gold trail of chalk wound near each corner of the park, under trees and among horse paths crowded with spectators. To Sara, scanning the route, it seemed Russ would be running uphill more than downhill. But since the finish line was right next to the starting line, she decided that must be impossible.

'How do you feel?' she asked, folding his sweats and draping them over her left arm.

'You just asked me that,' Russ said, spreading his legs and stretching. He had incredible hamstrings, simply incredible.

'What did you say?'

'I feel all right.'

'Your back's OK?' she asked.

'Why would my back hurt?'

'The mattress in the guest room is worse than a leaky waterbed,' she said. The mere reminder of the fact he was now living at her house – with her parents' reluctant and soon to be revoked consent – made her embryonic ulcer take another big step towards adulthood. She couldn't understand how he could stay so cool. Then again, he hadn't been awake most of the night setting up for the dance.

Where was Jessie when I really needed her?

There was a ton of preparations left to complete.

'My back's OK,' he said.

'How about your feet? Never mind, we can't go through your whole body. As long as you feel strong.'

'I feel strong.'

'That's all I want to know.'

Tabb's cross-country coach, and a number of Russ's teammates, came over to wish Russ well. The team as a whole had not qualified for the finals. Russ would be the only one from the school running.

The announcer called out that there were five minutes to the gun. The colourful collection of athletes began to converge on the starting line. Sara followed Russ as he left his teammates and coach behind and made his way through the crowd. Having won his semi-final last week on a different course, Russ had a low number and was given a position at the privileged front of the pack.

'There're so many people to beat,' she said, getting depressed.

'There're only three,' Russ said. 'I know who they are. They know who I am. You'll see them at the finish.' He turned, stopping her from following him further, smiling at her gloom. 'You'll see me in front of them.'

She chewed on her lip. 'I hope so.' Poor words to inspire a man going into battle. She could do better. 'I mean, I know you'll beat them.' She wanted to give him a send-off hug, but was afraid she would accidentally knee him or something stupid like that. She just stood there feeling dumb and nervous while he completed a few last-second stretches. 'Well,' she said finally, 'good luck.'

He glanced up as the announcer gave the one-minute warning. 'You know what I would like more than anything right now?'

A kiss from sweet Sara.

'What?' she asked.

'A beer.'

'Swell,' she muttered, turning away in disgust. He stood straight and grabbed her by the shoulders before she could leave. 'Wait, Sara. But I'm not going to have one even if I do win. You know what I'm saying?'

'That you don't like beer any more?' Behind him, beyond the assembled runners, the starter was giving out final instructions. She suddenly had the horrible thought that they would be off without him. 'Hey, you better get going.'

'I'm saying that you're more important to me.'

'That's good, that's great, but they're really getting ready to go,' she said, hardly hearing him, shooing him towards the start. Hadn't she done something like this two centuries ago when he had collided with her the first week of school? Why was he comparing her to beer?

'Sara, you're not listening to me,' he complained.

'Everybody get ready!' the starter shouted out.

'Russ!' she cried. He waved his hand indifferently. 'That guy always gets everybody set then spends a couple of minutes loading his gun. I have time.'

She would just as soon he didn't count on the guy's past habits. 'Time for what?' she asked.

Now he was disgusted. 'Never mind.'

'Well, this really isn't a time to talk. What did you say?'

'Do you want to go to the dance with me tonight?'

Her heart skipped. 'Only if you win.'

'What if I don't?'

'Then you're out of luck.' She leaned over and kissed him quickly on the lips. 'Go. Run. Win.' She shoved him in the chest. 'Now!'

He went, slowly making his way through the runners. But he knew his starters. It was another couple of minutes before the gun finally sounded and the herd stampeded forward. Sara retreated to a spot at the top of the hill. The clouds flew overhead, chased by the wind. She watched as Russ let a quarter of the runners pass him. She was shaking like a leaf.

He warned me he likes to start slow and build momentum.

Nevertheless, it was disconcerting to see so many people in front of him. His buddies on the team had brought a pair of binoculars and they passed them on to her. The mile marker was in the low south corner of the park, close to the choppy sea. Watching through the binoculars, Sara estimated three dozen guys reached it before Russ did. She wished he would begin to make his move soon.

He did, finally, although at first it was almost imperceptible. The midway point was marked by a yellow flag near the entrance to the park. The runners were about half a mile from Sara as they went by it, and this time – she was monopolising the binoculars, but no one seemed to mind – she counted only two dozen guys in front of Russ.

Faster.

Between the midpoint and the two-mile mark he really began to turn it on. Heading into the last mile, turning back towards the starting line – and the finish line – he had drawn even with the leaders, a pack of three kids. Sara could actually see their expressions in the binoculars. Each one looked determined to win. But she hesitated to check Russ's face, afraid she would find him whistling to himself.

Pounding into the far end of the valley that lay beneath the hill on which she stood, Russ accelerated sharply, drawing away from the others.

'Go!' she yelled.

Ten yards, fifteen yards, twenty yards – his lead grew almost as if by magic. Sara was beside herself with excitement. She forgot about being ASB president, about homecoming, about being cool. She started to cheer like a maniac.

'Russ!'

Coming up the hill, running right past her, he twisted his head around and looked at her. His breathing was laboured and his red brow dripped with sweat. He smiled, anyway.

Then he slipped on the wet grass, and went down.

'Get up!' she screamed, leaping forward to help him. He had only fallen to his knees, and because he had been coming up the steep hill, his speed had not been that great. He was all right. He brushed off her hands and was on his way again before his lead disintegrated altogether.

He won by ten yards. Sara had about ten seconds to savour the victory before learning he had been disqualified. The coach told her while Russ was recovering in the chute.

'What?' she cried. 'What did he do wrong? This isn't gymnastics! Since when do they take off points for slipping?'

The coach's disappointment was obvious. 'He wasn't disqualified for slipping, but for receiving outside help during the course of the race.'

She was aghast. 'Outside help? You're not talking about *me*?'

'I'm afraid so, Sara,' he said sympathetically.

'But I didn't help him. If anything, I just got in his way. Where's the race director? We have to talk to him.'

The coach stopped her. 'It will do no good.'

'But it wasn't his fault that I helped him!'

'It doesn't matter. Because Russ won by such a narrow margin, he might have lost if you hadn't helped him. Disqualification is therefore automatic.' The coach glanced towards Russ, who had begun to catch his breath. He was shaking the hand of the fellow behind him in the chute. 'It's a real shame,' the coach said. 'He ran a brilliant race.'

Sara's voice cracked. 'Does he know?'

'He knows.'

This is not fair. This is not right. This is not happening.

Sara was afraid to go near Russ. The coach was being cool, but Russ's teammates were looking at her and shaking their heads. Russ would probably want to rip her head off. Had the positions been reversed, she would have wanted blood. She didn't know what to do. She wished she could simply leave, but they had come in the same car. She decided to go to the car anyway. Maybe he would think she had left or forget she existed and get another ride.

To where? He's staying at my house!

She was as furious as she was hurt. Once inside her car, his sweats lying across her lap, she began to pound the steering wheel with her fists. She still couldn't believe how strict they were. You'd think she'd given him an injection of speed or steroids or something! If they'd covered the course with plastic before it rained, he wouldn't have slipped in the first place. It was all their fault. She was going to write a nasty letter to somebody. She was the president of the school. She was going to . . .

'Hey, I need my sweats,' Russ said, standing outside the car door. She jumped in her seat, smacking her head on the roof. 'It's cold out here.'

Keeping her eyes fixed on the ground, Sara slowly got out of the car and gave him his sweats. She stared at his feet while he put them on. There was mud on the bottom of his shoes, and no doubt it would mess up her car, but she wasn't going to ask him to scrape it off if he still wanted to ride home with her. She was afraid she was going to start crying.

'Hey, aren't you going to congratulate me?' he asked.

She glanced up and was suprised to discover he looked very much as he had before the start of the race; a little more tired perhaps, and certainly more sweaty, but far from devastated. 'But you lost,' she mumbled. 'I got you disqualified.'

He waved away the remark as he had waved away her concerns about the starter. 'Everybody knows I won, I just don't get the trophy. Big deal. This way we don't have to wait around for the award ceremony. Come on, let's go to that McDonald's we ate at when we went out that night. I'm starving.'

'You're crazy,' she said, her voice incredulous.

He frowned. 'What's wrong with McDonald's? They use the same hamburger a fancy restaurant does. They just don't charge you an arm and a leg. You know what your problem is, Sara? You don't know how to find a bargain. Take that can of Spam you bought . . . hey, what are you laughing at?'

'You!' she burst out. 'You idiot!'

He scratched his head, his frown deepening. 'If I'm such an idiot, how come I know how to save money using coupons?'

Sara had to catch her breath to speak. Although from the outside she appeared in much better spirits than a minute ago, she was still upset. 'Russ, that's not what I'm talking about. Because of me, you're not the champion. It's not going to go in the records that you won today.

College coaches across the country won't know you won. It won't even go down that you placed.'

'So?'

'So you probably won't get offered a scholarship.'

'Who cares?'

'I care! I care about your future. That you have one. Russ, we're not going to be in high school for the rest of our lives.'

He didn't answer right away, but leaned against the car instead, looking out to the sea. The seagulls were having a great time in the wind, soaring hundreds of feet into the air on powerful updraughts and then diving down at breathtaking speeds to within inches of the choppy water. Russ reached out his arm and hugged her to his side.

'I don't run to win scholarships,' he said seriously. 'I run because it makes me feel alive. School doesn't do that for me. School isn't where I belong. Sure, I'll graduate and everything, but that's it.'

'But don't you want to get ahead?'

'I can get ahead without a fancy diploma.' He glanced towards the hill from where she had watched the race. 'When I broke away from the pack, I felt something. I felt powerful, like I could do anything.' He squeezed her shoulder. 'Remember what you said when we were fighting in the store freezer? That I could be in the Olympics? Well, Sara, I think you were right.'

She chuckled, not sure what to think, brushing his hair out of his eyes. 'You idiot,' she repeated quietly. Then she wrinkled her nose. 'McDonald's?'

'I like their food. And then, tonight, I'll take you to that dance.'

She shook her head. 'I'm afraid not, pal.'

'Huh?'

'You didn't win.'

CHAPTER 6

Half-time had just begun and Jessica was doing pretty much what she had done the week before at the start of half-time: changing the memory card in her camera, wondering if all her pictures were out of focus, watching Clair out of the corners of her out-of-focus eyes and listening to Sara complain.

There were, however, a couple of differences. First of all this game was a lot more exciting. It counted in the league standing, and the score was tied. Nick was tearing up the floor rebounding, blocking shots, slamdunking the ball. The most amazing thing, though, was he was doing all this with the earnest co-operation of his teammates. The Rock and Nick had been high-fiving it all night. Amazing.

There were also about four times the number of people present. Tabb's gymnasium was far larger than Holden

High's, but it was obvious the main reason for the extra numbers was because the dance followed the game. Judging by the clothes of the majority of the crowd, it appeared that practically everyone had come for both events. Like Maria and Clair – and probably Cindy Fosmeyer, wherever she was – Jessica had yet to change into her princess gown. Jessica had had her hair curled and teased, however, and could not believe the abandon with which Clair had led the cheers throughout the first half. Clair did not appear concerned about looking perfect. Indeed, she had seemed quite happy all night.

'You may as well know, dearie, I can't lose.'

That worried Jessica.

'Then this idiot with a camera stepped in front of Russ and tripped him,' Sara was saying. 'Naturally, I grabbed the guy by the arm and pulled him aside. And they called that interference! They disqualified Russ for that! Can you believe it?'

'No,' Jessica said, bending over for a drink from the fountain in the corner of the gym. The two of them were down on the floor. The team had left moments ago for the locker room and most of the crowd was heading for the refreshment stand or a breath of air outside. Her date for the dance, Bill Skater, was sitting with his football buddies a couple of rows above where the cheerleaders had performed. Jessica had been searching for Michael all night but hadn't seen him.

'What do you mean?' Sara asked, indignantly.

'I don't believe you,' Jessica said, finishing her drink and slipping a lens cap over her camera. 'What really happened?'

Sara put a hand on her hip, which she often did when her credibility was being questioned. 'I bet you think *I* tripped him?'

'Well, you locked him in a freezer once.'

'You didn't have to bring that up. That was an accident. And what does it matter how he got disqualified? The fact remains he won the goddamn race and they didn't give him the goddamn trophy.'

'Does he care?'

'No.'

'Then what's the problem?' Jessica asked.

'There isn't a problem. I'm just making conversation. What a stupid question. The biggest social event of the school year is about to take place and if it bombs it will be totally my fault.'

'What about me? I have a shot at the biggest social title of the year, and if I don't win I'll . . . I'll go out and get bombed.'

'You're going to win.'

'How do you know? You don't know anything.' Jessica glared in the direction of the cheerleaders. 'She shouldn't look so goddamn confident.' Clair was little more than a blonde blur to her at this distance.

'Quit swearing,' Sara said.

'Go to hell.'

They stared at each other a moment and then laughed.

'Bitch of a night,' Sara said.

'It's going to get worse. Hey, I've got to check on Maria and her folks.'

Sara nodded. 'I'll catch you in the dressing room after the game. Remember, room HB-22.'

'Good, yeah. Go light the tent on fire.'

'Don't tempt me,' Sara said.

Crossing the basketball court, her photo equipment stuffed in a bag hanging over her shoulder, Jessica again searched the stands for Michael. She thought he probably wouldn't attend the dance – he had never struck her as the type that went in for big phoney get-togethers – but Nick was his friend, he should have come to the game. Maybe if she put on her glasses she'd find him. She didn't just want to talk to him, she wanted to have a talk with him. All day long, from the instant she had woken up this morning, a frightening conviction had been growing inside her. She felt she absolutely had to get him alone and confess how she had stood him up, and then tell him how she really felt about him. What made this conviction so frightening – besides the usual reason that she would be risking outright rejection, which was nothing to sneeze at – was that she *knew* if she didn't do it now, she wouldn't be able to do it later. She didn't know how or why she felt this way. She certainly didn't feel lightning was going to strike him or her down. But there was something – something in the air.

What would Alice have wanted?

Alice had known Michael almost a year before her death and had never mentioned him. It still bothered her.

Did Alice feel Michael was too good for me?

That was nonsense. Alice had loved her. And yet, according to Polly, Alice had *worshipped* Michael. Jessica would have given a lot to be able to ask Alice how she really felt.

Bill waved to her as she came up the steps but did not stand or otherwise show any sign that he wanted her to join him amid the herd of jocks. She didn't mind. Besides wanting to speak to Maria, she needed to check on Polly. Poor Polly was limping around like a deer with its foot caught in a bear trap. She had fallen off a ladder the night before, she said. Jessica wished Polly had a date. She was worried how Polly would feel when Russ and Sara danced together.

Maria's parents made a handsome couple. Jessica had been particularly taken by Mrs Gonzales. The woman had Maria's soft-spoken manner, only to a much greater degree. Jessica wasn't sure how much English she knew. She so resembled her daughter, but was considerably more beautiful, with finer features and wide red lips.

Jessica took a seat on the bleachers between Maria and Polly; Maria's parents were sitting to her far right, speaking quietly to each other. Jessica hadn't told her own parents what tonight was. She didn't want them present if she should lose.

But if I win, I might have the guts to tell Dad about the SAT. 'What do your parents think of Nick now?' Jessica whispered in Maria's ear.

'My dad says he's unstoppable,' she whispered back.

'Does that mean he likes him?'

Maria smiled and nodded. 'I think so.'

'What does your mom say?'

'That he's tall.'

'That sounds positive. Ask him to the dance.'

Maria looked terrified. 'We'll see.'

Jessica turned her attention to Polly, who had brought

a sketch pad and a number of pencils. This was sort of odd because Polly drew about as well as your average alligator. The pad had belonged to Alice. As far as Jessica could tell, Polly hadn't done anything with it all night. At the moment she was staring off into the distance, her eyes dark.

'Are you all right?' Jessica asked.

Polly blinked and slowly looked at Jessica. 'I'm tired. I had a bad night. The lightning.' She gestured feebly. 'Everything.'

The reference to lightning made Jessica pause and remember the days Polly had spent in the hospital after her parents had died. Those had been dark times, almost as dark as when Alice had died. To this day, Jessica occasionally wondered if the doctors hadn't compounded the situation by using electroshock therapy to alleviate Polly's depression.

A lightning bolt across the brain.

Polly wouldn't remember. They knocked you out – so Jessica had read – before they taped on the wires.

'How's your aunt?' Jessica asked.

'Dying.'

'Are you sure you're all right? I could give you a ride home?'

'I'm fine, I have my own car. I don't want to go home,

anyway. I don't want to use my ankle as an excuse not to dance.'

'What? Surely you're not going to dance on that foot?'

'I don't mind the pain.' Polly turned away and added wearily, 'It's better than lying on a floor in the dark.'

Michael was bent over a CRT with Bubba in the computer room when they heard the cheer in the gym. That day, all day, Bubba had run a pipeline – via a modem between Dr Gin Kawati's ARC Medical Group and Tabb High. The end result was a packed hard disc and a ton of files they couldn't directly read.

'The second half must be about to start,' Bubba said.

'I don't know if I'll watch it. I'd like to look at that autopsy report tonight.'

'Tonight might be asking too much.' Bubba pointed to the data on the screen. 'These are binary files, not text. Our word processor can't access them.'

'We can use the sector editor and read them manually.'

'Yeah, but we're talking about forty megabytes of data. There must be sixty or seventy files here. You'll have to load in each file individually, do an "Alice McCoy" search, delete the file, then load in the next one until you find her. That could take a long time.'

'I have time,' Michael said.

'If that's how you feel,' Bubba said, surrendering his seat in front of the screen. Michael sat down and called up the sector editor while Bubba took down a fresh-from-the-cleaners suit of clothes hanging in the corner of the room. Naturally, it was not an ordinary suit Bubba had selected for the big night. A bright yellow, it came with a green hat. Bubba liked hats. 'Will you be coming to the dance?' he asked casually, pulling off the plastic and inspecting the material.

'I doubt it.'

'Not even for the crowning?'

Michael glanced at him. 'Why don't you just tell me who's going to win?'

Bubba smiled. 'I don't know everything, you know.' He held out his green tie. 'Is this too Irish or what?'

'No one can ever be too Irish. You're changing the subject.'

Bubba set aside his suit, spoke seriously. 'I knew you were standing outside the room when Clair was complaining to me about Jessie.'

'How?'

Bubba shrugged, indicating it wasn't important.

'Clair should be homecoming queen. She's prettier than Jessie.'

'In your opinion. Anyway, pretty isn't everything. All I'm asking for is a fair vote.'

'Why ask now? The name has already been recorded and placed in a sealed envelope. If I'm not mistaken, Mr Bark has it in his pocket at this exact moment.'

'Whose name is inside?'

'You put me on the spot, Mike. Clair did that to me, too.'

'Then you did arrange for Clair to win?'

'I didn't say that. What I said was she deserves to win. Jessie resorted to low-level tactics in this campaign.'

Bubba wouldn't look at him, and ordinarily Bubba wouldn't mind looking you in the eye while telling you he was sleeping with your girlfriend. '*Did* Clair have an abortion?' Michael asked, remembering how she had come to Bubba the afternoon she had been elected to the court, her eyes red.

'A vile and vicious rumour started by the vile and vicious Jessica Hart. No, she didn't.'

'Was it yours?'

Bubba snapped his head up. 'No.' Then he relaxed, adding with a chuckle, 'You know how careful I am about such matters.'

'Yeah, you're careful,' Michael muttered, confused at Bubba's behaviour. He wasn't simply being evasive –

Bubba never actually told the precise truth, except when it benefited him to do so, which was rarely – he was uneasy. And ordinarily he would not have been worried about having knocked Clair up any more than he would have been concerned about having knocked Jessica down.

Someone banged at the door. 'Yeah,' Bubba called out.

Kats walked in, surprising Michael. Kats had changed from his usual crusty jeans and oily army fatigue jacket into a pair of black slacks, a white shirt and a red tie. It was remarkable – he looked greasier than ever.

'What are you doing here?' Michael asked.

Kats grinned. 'I'm the man tonight. I'm taking care of the princesses.'

'Kats is driving the float into the tent before the crowning,' Bubba explained.

'Why did Sara pick you?' Michael asked.

Kats scowled. 'Is there something wrong with me, Mikey?'

Obviously Kats was still mad at him from the last time they had talked at the petrol station. 'Kats is a great driver,' Bubba said. 'Sara chose him as a favour to me.'

'What favour does Sara owe you?' Michael asked.

Bubba brightened at the question and picked up his

yellow suit and green hat. 'Honestly, Mike, you know I'm a gentleman.'

Bubba and Kats left together, leaving Michael's last question unanswered. Michael turned back to the computer screen. Hopefully, somewhere in all this data, was the answer to more important questions.

Michael set the computer to search for the McCoy name, sat back and waited. He wished he knew how the files were organised, which ones he should concentrate on. He heard another loud cheer come from the gym and checked his watch. The second half was definitely under way. He had been pleased to see Nick doing so well, particularly with the co-operation of The Rock. Michael had not had a chance to talk to Nick the last couple of days; he didn't know what had changed between the two. But it had clearly been a change for the better. At least somebody was making progress somewhere.

I can't complain.

His mother's boyfriend had finally come to a decision. He had proposed marriage, and his mom had accepted. Michael had to admit she had never seemed happier.

I'm going to have a father. I have a sister on the way, a comet in the sky that belongs to me. What else can I expect? Nothing. And yet, he was lonely, desperately lonely. Jessica – crazy as it sounded even to him – he sometimes believed he needed her simply to go on living. And he hadn't felt that way even in the depths of his despair over Alice. He kept remembering sitting beside her while she slept under the tree after the SAT. He should have lain down and slept beside her. Then maybe he could have met her in a dream and told her all the things he couldn't tell her when he was awake.

Go forward, I will follow.

That was a dream he hadn't had in a while.

Alice wasn't in the first file. She wasn't in the second or the third. He began to worry that he would go through all the files and discover Dr Kawati hadn't bothered to put the autopsy reports he did for the county into his business computer.

The fourth file turned out to be huge. Michael prowled the room while the name search went on and on, listening to the sporadic roar of the gymnasium crowd, thinking of how cute Jessica had looked during the first half crouched at the end of the court, her camera balanced on her knee, her long brown hair hanging loose and wonderful. He glanced again at the computer screen, the endless succession of numbers and text creeping by, and decided a quick stop inside the gym wouldn't make any difference.

He felt the tension the moment he entered the building. A glance at the scoreboard said it all: Tabb 56, Troy 57. Seven seconds left. Tabb had the ball. Nick had just called time out, and the team was huddling around Coach Sellers. The man would probably advise them to dribble out the clock.

Everybody was standing. Everybody except Jessica. Michael spotted her kneeling alone on the court floor behind Tabb's basket, doing a trial focus with her camera. He wondered if he should accidentally try to bump into her when the game was over. But he could imagine Bill coming up if he tried to talk to her, taking her hand and leading her away to the dance.

I'll just see who wins, and then go back to the room.

Sitting down, Nick grabbed a towel and wiped the sweat from his brow, trying to block out the noise of the cheerleaders at his back while listening to what the coach was saying. He was running on adrenaline, hyped up. He had played hard all night, but with each passing minute, he felt himself growing stronger. He was ready to take the last shot.

'Go Tabb! Go team! Take the ball and stuff it mean!'

To his disappointment, however, he quickly realised Sellers had other ideas.

'Troy will collapse on Nick the second we inbound the ball,' the coach was saying, sketching shaky *X*s and *O*s with a marking pen on a white board on the floor at the centre of the huddle. 'For that reason, Nick, I want you to line up on the baseline off the key on the left side. Stewart will take the ball into The Rock, here, who will dribble towards you, but then suddenly whip a pass over to Ted, here, beside the free-throw line. Ted, you'll take the last shot.'

Ted didn't know if he liked that idea. He was their best outside shooter – after Nick, of course – but he'd been having an off night, hitting four of fourteen from the field. He stared at the *X*s and *O*s as if they were part of a ticktacktoe game he had just lost. 'What if they don't collapse on Nick?' he asked, standing beside The Rock. 'Then I could have both their guards in my face.'

'Go Nick! Set the pick! Let your best shot rip!'

'Their guards should fall back,' Coach Sellers said, not sounding very sure of himself. 'But if they don't, you'll have to take the ball higher up and take a longer shot.'

'What if I miss?' Ted asked.

'Then we lose the game and you're the goat,' The Rock said.

'That's enough of that,' Coach Sellers said.

'Go Ted! Use your head! Make the Trojans drop dead!'

'I wish to God they'd shut up,' Ted said. 'Don't we have another play?'

'Don't you want to take the last shot?' Coach Sellers asked.

'Sure,' Ted said. 'I just don't want to miss it.'

Coach Sellers glanced at each of them, clenching and unclenching his fingers. '*Do* we have another play?' he asked.

'Let me pass the ball down to Nick,' The Rock said.

'It's too obvious a move,' Coach Sellers said. 'He'll have someone in front of him, someone behind him. You'd never get him the ball.'

'Ted will never get the ball in the basket,' The Rock said.

'Hey, I could make it,' Ted said. 'Maybe.'

'Go Rock! Be a jock! Catch the ball and give 'em a sock!'

'Who writes those bloody things?' The Rock growled.

Nick felt he should speak up. He could line up a couple of feet closer to the basket than the coach wanted, catch the ball on the leap and spin around and bank it in. The Rock had improved two hundred per cent as a passer in the last week. It would be a sound play. The coach was looking at him. They were all looking at him, waiting. Nick glanced behind him, at the jammed bleachers. He'd seen Maria up there when he'd been warming up before the second half. And her parents. He remembered them from Alice's party.

What if I *miss*?

Suddenly, although he had enjoyed their support all night, he could feel the weight of the crowd. This week, for the first time since his move to this part of town, walking around campus had not been an ordeal. Rather than jumping out of his way, people had been stopping him to wish him luck. But would these same people laugh behind his back next week if he blew the team's last chance? He had already had a great game. Prudence dictated he play it safe.

'Whatever you say, coach,' he mumbled finally, taking the easy way out and hating himself for it.

Coach Sellers nodded nervously, glanced at Ted. 'You'll make it,' he said.

Ted swallowed. 'Christ.'

The time-out ended. Wiping the last beads of perspiration from his hands with his towel, Nick followed his teammates back on to the court, positioning himself near the baseline, to the left of the basket. A moment later Troy's centre came and stood at his back, while Troy's power forward placed himself a few feet in front, between him and Stewart. Nick knew Troy's forward would drop back and lean on him, try to box him in, the moment the referee handed Stewart the ball. Both their centre and power forward – in fact their whole team – were strong, very physical.

Oh, no! We forgot to tell Ted to get off his shot early enough for me to stand a chance at a rebound.

Nick went to speak to Ted precisely when the referee tossed the ball to Stewart and blew the whistle. That settled that. Stewart now had five seconds to inbound the ball. Ted would have to follow the cheerleaders' advice and use his head.

Troy's power forward immediately jumped back and sagged into Nick. Their centre put a hand on his shoulder, a hand that might have had a hold on his jersey. Nick did not struggle to get free, deciding to wait a moment to see which way – figuratively and literally – the ball bounced.

Free of defensive pressure, Stewart easily inbounded the ball to The Rock. Unfortunately, as The Rock dribbled towards Nick, only one of Troy's guards moved to block his path. The other kept his position near the top of the key, near Ted. The seven on the clock slipped to five.

Putting forth a faked shot that probably didn't fake a person in the building, The Rock whizzed the ball over to Ted, who caught it a solid twenty feet from the basket.

Then Ted did the strangest thing. He paused to study the ball, as if he were checking to see if it were the brand name he would willingly have chosen to use while risking his athletic reputation. He did this for a grand total of perhaps one second. Given the situation, that was an extremely long time. Never give the ball to someone who's afraid of it, Nick thought. Michael was right, Sellers should coach checkers.

The clock went to three seconds. Ted finally emerged from his important study, but with no clear idea of what he wanted to do next, whether to dribble closer or shoot. The crowd screamed, clearly wishing he would make up his mind. Ted glanced at Troy's advancing guard, decided to put the ball up. Nick knew it wasn't going to go down before it left his hands. Ted launched it towards the backboard as if he were throwing a stone at an attacking dinosaur.

Nick pivoted to his left, slapping off the hold on him with his elbow, crashing into the key, into perfect position to grab the rebound. Ted's shot didn't even hit the rim, however, and had so much behind it that it ricocheted high off the backboard. Nick not only had to leap as he had never leaped before to catch it, but he had to twist back so that his midsection stretched directly across the face of Troy's big centre.

Time did not slow down for Nick as he had often heard it did in moments of crisis. Indeed, as he rolled prone off the centre's nose, the ball balanced precariously in his right hand, the floor five foot beneath the back of his head and getting closer fast, he caught a glimpse of the big red letters on the clock going from two to one. He acted instinctively. He scooped the ball towards the basket, feeling a painful slap to his right arm in the process. The slap, though, didn't hurt nearly so much as his butt did when he hit the floor.

Go in! Go in!

From flat on his back on the floor, Nick watched the ball roll lazily around the inside of the rim. The crowd gasped. The buzzer sounded. The ball rolled out.

We lost.

The disappointment soaked through him like a bitter drink, draining away his energy. He couldn't even be bothered getting up. But there was The Rock, his fat hand out, insisting he do so.

'You can do it, buddy,' The Rock said, clasping Nick's wrist and yanking him to his feet. 'Two free throws and this baby's wrapped.'

'What are you talking about? It's over.'

'You were fouled, man.'

The Rock's comment was slightly premature. The

refs – and the coaches – were still arguing about it. Nick had never seen Coach Sellers so alive; all that blood in his cheeks.

Standing with his teammates, waiting anxiously for the decision, Nick spotted someone that almost caused him to faint.

His father was standing at the top of the bleachers.

A moment later the crowd cheered. Coach Sellers returned to his seat and began to twitch. Ted and The Rock patted Nick on the butt. The referee handed him the ball. Nick stared at it a moment.

It's a Spalding, Ted. A fine brand.

Nick had trouble locating the free-throw line. It seemed to him someone had moved it back a few feet. He had shot about sixty-five per cent from the field tonight, but had taken six free throws and made only two. Standing at the line, alone on the floor – time had officially expired – he bounced the ball a couple of times and listened as the ear-busting din dropped to a heart-stopping silence. This wasn't pressure. This was murder.

Nick glanced up at his father. His father had only remarked on his going out for the team once; that had been to tell him it had better not interfere with his bringing home his weekly cheque.

Why is he here?

Nick tried to focus on his grip on the ball, the position of his feet behind the line, the basket, trying to envision the ball sailing through the air and swishing through the net. He dribbled twice more, took a deep breath and closed his eyes. But he felt himself beginning to sway and quickly opened them. Yet the dizziness did not leave.

I am going to miss.

As it was, feeling the way he did, he would be putting up a couple of shots reminiscent of Ted's last attempt. The problem was, he couldn't jump, pivot or fly away. Custom said he had to stand there relatively still and either make it or miss it. His decision after practice on Thursday notwithstanding, this was not his world. He was but a visitor. He had to obey custom.

He glanced again to his father. Although far away – two hundred feet, at least – it seemed to Nick their eyes met. His dad did a little jump where he stood, pumping with his arms and nodding.

Do it your own way, but do it.

Nick turned and took a fifteen-foot jump shot.

He made it.

The crowd cheered.

He took another jump shot. *Swish.* Game over: Tabb 58, Troy 57. The crowd freaked.

Like a wave bursting a dam, people flooded the

court. Nick felt his own wave breaking inside. He felt, without a speck of worry or pain to blemish it, a clear white euphoria.

He got touched more in the next few minutes than he had been touched in his entire life; guys and girls pumping his hands, slapping him on the back, telling him how great he was. He drank it up like a man dying of thirst would have drunk down a barrel of Gatorade, which, by the way, was exactly what The Rock had decided to pour over Nick's head.

Then his dad was congratulating him, along with Mr Gonzales. Nick introduced them, sounding to his own ears as if he were babbling in a foreign language, but making enough sense to get them shaking hands and talking basketball strategy.

And somewhere in all this, Maria appeared. Climbing to her tiptoes, she asked if she could speak to him outside. He let himself be led into the cold and the dark, down a hallway and behind a tree. Here she didn't compliment him on his defence or his lay-ups. She had never been one to talk a lot.

'I'm sorry,' she said. 'Can you forgive me?'

'No problem,' Nick said. In that instant, he honestly felt all his problems were behind him. He kissed her.

* * *

Jessica had taken her pictures and stowed her camera when she spotted Michael slipping away from the jubilant crowd out the corner doorway. She jumped after him, but had a few hundred people in her way, and didn't catch him until he was far down a black empty covered walkway outdoors. He didn't stop to see who was following him until she called his name.

'Hi, Jessie,' he said pleasantly, turning. 'Great game wasn't it?'

'It was fantastic. But I wish you could have played.'

'I'm busy enough these days. Going to change for the dance now?'

'Yeah, I have this long yellow dress I bought.' She forced a laugh. 'I'll probably be tripping over it all night.'

'Yellow suits you. I'm sure you'll look very beautiful.'

She wished she could see his face better, see if he was just being polite, or if she really was beautiful to him. She needed courage. There was so much she wanted to say. 'You're coming, aren't you?' she asked.

'No, I don't think so. I'm not much of a dancer. And I have work to do.'

That must mean he was leaving the campus. Yet he had not been walking towards the parking lot. Her heart was breaking. More than anything, she had wanted to dance with him. 'But you can't work on a night like this. It can't be that important?'

'To me it is.' He paused. 'Did you call and get your SAT scores?'

'Not yet,' she lied. And one lie always led to another, and suddenly she realised she didn't have the strength to confess how weak she was, or how strong she could be if he would come with her.

'Let's hope for the best,' he said.

'Yeah.'

He touched her arm. 'It's cold out here. You'd better get inside.' He smiled. 'Have lots of fun for me.'

She nodded sadly. 'I will.' Letting go of her arm, he turned and walked away.

'Michael?' she called.

He stopped. 'Yeah.'

I would love to love you.

'Nothing,' she said, knowing as she watched him walk away that the moment had come and gone. Gone for good.

CHAPTER 7

As planned, the four girls – Maria, Jessica, Sara and Polly – met in room HB-22 to dress for the dance. A number of rooms had been unlocked for girls to change in. The game had ended at eight and Sara had already warned the student body via an announcement in homeroom that morning that no one would be allowed into the tent before nine. Parents of the girls on the court, the announcement had further stated, would be welcome to stop by at ten-thirty for the crowning. Sara's own mother had wanted to come to the dance but Sara had told her not to dare. She hadn't been getting along with her parents since Russ had moved in. They were probably worried he was having sex with her in the middle of the night. But so far, she'd had no such luck.

'How do I look?' Jessica asked, a yellow ribbon in her hair to match her yellow gown.

'Wonderful,' Maria said, excited, wearing a relatively plain white dress, no ribbon.

'Great,' Polly said, still in the clothes she had worn to the game and showing no signs of getting out of them.

'You look like Jessie dressed up,' Sara said, thinking that it was Jessica's night, that no one was going to touch her. She glanced down at her own orange dress, which had squeezed her father's credit card for a tidy two hundred and sixteen dollars plus tax. 'How about me?'

'Real pretty,' Maria said.

'Pretty as a pumpkin pie before you put it in the oven,' Jessica said.

'Shut up,' Sara said.

They finished with their make-up, gave up trying to convince Polly to go home and put on something nice and tumbled out of the room for the tent.

'Maria, Jessie,' Sara said as they walked down the outside walkway, freezing to death without their sweaters, Polly struggling to keep up with her bad foot. 'Check on the band and the servers for me. I want to take Polly and have a look at the float.'

'What exactly are we checking with them about?' Jessica asked.

'It doesn't matter. That they're ready. Just talk to them, Jessie.'

They split up when they reached the tent, Jessica and Maria disappearing inside. By this time Polly was really dragging. Sara felt a twinge of guilt that she'd swiped Russ from the McCoy mansion when Polly wasn't looking. Yet Polly appeared unconcerned about Russ's whereabouts and determined to enjoy the night.

A number of students were milling around outside the tent as Sara and Polly circled to the back. Several called out to Sara complaining about the cold and asking why she didn't let them in.

'Go wait in the gym,' she said. 'And quit hassling me.'

The float surpassed Sara's expectations. That Tony Foulton had some imagination. Although she had given him a general idea of what she wanted – 'a castle look to go with our queen and princesses' – it was very much his creation. A blue-carnation moat circled the entire float. Lying across the front was a fake drawbridge – a wide sheet of board, cleverly painted with black and grey stripes to resemble whatever it was drawbridges were supposed to be made of. In the centre of the drawbridge stood the microphone. The plan was for Sara to announce the new queen after receiving the sealed envelope from Mr Bark, who would emerge from inside the castle proper. It was a fond dream of Sara's that he would hand her the envelope and not feel compelled to make a speech.

Last year's homecoming queen had flown in specially for the occasion from an Ivy League college back east. The latest word, however, had her at home sick from a crash fast she had undertaken to lose the forty pounds she needed to lose to get into the dress she had worn when she had been elected queen. On top of everything else, Sara would now be doing the actual crowning.

The castle had four battlement towers, all at the front, interconnected by a plank that would be invisible to the audience. They were approximately five feet higher than the moat, decorated primarily with chrysanthemums, each a different colour: gold, red, green, yellow. Four towers for four princesses.

At the back, inside the castle walls – another six feet higher than the battlement tower – stood the queen's throne. Whoever had her name in the envelope would ascend a hidden ladder behind the castle after the announcement and take up her rightful seat. (Sara had swiped the chair from her own living room.) With the lights flashing and the band playing, Sara thought they could do one better than the MTV video she had stolen the concept from.

'This thing isn't going to fall over?' Sara asked Polly.

'It's possible,' Polly said. 'Anything is possible.'

'Swell,' Sara said. Yet she trusted Tony's skill.

Kats appeared from beneath the float. Bubba had explained to Sara that Kats bore Tabb High a measure of resentment for the way everybody had treated him while he had been in high school. Playing an essential role in the homecoming festivities, Bubba had thought, would help dispel the resentment. Sara would have preferred a driver who had a positive outlook, but she had decided to be diplomatic about the issue, hoping Bubba would forget the sex contingency he had tied to his assistance. She still didn't know what was going on with the money she had given him.

'It's dark in there,' Kats said.

'Will you be able to see where you're going?' Sara asked.

Kats pointed to Polly. 'Hey, Alice was your sister, right?'

Polly lowered her head. 'Yes.'

'I asked you a question?' Sara said, annoyed at his lack of tact.

Kats grinned. 'I'll take care of you ladies, never fear.'

They left Kats and slipped inside through the folds in the tent. The band was ready on the stage. The food, the glasses, the plates, the silverware – everything was laid out. Ringing the entire canvas dance floor were four dozen electric heaters, glowing orange and warm. The temperature inside the tent was variable, with draughts and cold spots, but Sara believed it would even out when the people were crammed together.

Polly collapsed into a seat near the punch. Jessica came up to Sara. 'They're beginning to jam up outside,' she said.

Sara glanced at her watch. 'It's fifteen minutes early. Oh, what the hell, let's strike up the band and let them in.'

'But you don't have anyone stationed to collect tickets.'

Sara realised Jessica was right. She had forgotten all about that. 'Let them all in.' She laughed. 'Who cares? Let's party.'

Michael had gone through nineteen files and was initiating a search on the twentieth when he began to believe he was wasting his time. So far, the name *McCoy* had not rung a bell with any of ARC's records.

He could hear the music from the dance, the laughter and jeers of people having fun. He tried to remember when he'd last had a good time through a whole night, and couldn't. He would've liked to have seen Jessica in her yellow dress. Michael started the search on the file and got up and walked about the room, stretching. Half the overhead fluorescent lights had died moments after he returned to the computer room at the end of the game. His eyes were aching from staring at the CRT letters and numbers. Earlier in the day, someone must have spilled something in the biology room next door. There was a foul smell in the air. He felt vaguely claustrophobic, as if he were being forced to labour in a morgue.

Now that it had come down to it, he almost hoped he didn't find the autopsy report. He felt as if he were trying to dig up Alice's body.

Are these the days everyone says we'll remember as the happiest days of our lives? Jessica wondered. *God.*

Bill had just brought her a drink. Jessica wished he had brought her a real drink. Something to numb the pain. Yet she really shouldn't have been drinking at all. As it was, shaking from nerves over the upcoming announcement, she was running to the bathroom in the gym every twenty minutes to pee. And her stomach was upset. She had tried to eat something, thinking it would help, but had accidentally bitten her tongue, soaking her mouthful of chicken sandwich with blood and grossing out her stomach further. Luckily, Bill had not tried to kiss her so far. She imagined she wouldn't taste very good.

'How's your drink?' Bill asked.

Jessica sipped it without enthusiasm. 'Great.'

They were standing with a group of football players and their girlfriends at the edge of the dance floor not far from the band. The music was excellent: present-day pop and sixties rock classics. But the volume was way too high; it was giving her a headache. Bill and she had danced once, to 'Surfer Girl', slow and close. In his dark blue suit, his blond hair short and clean, he had to be the cutest guy under the tent. He'd put his arms around her and held her to his chest, where she found herself living a fantasy from the early days of the school year, but which now brought her no pleasure.

'Having a good time?' Bill asked.

Jessica smiled. 'Super.'

It was a night of firsts for Nick. He had never been a hero before, or a boyfriend. Now he was both, and although he couldn't say which brought him more satisfaction, he hoped he was to enjoy the two roles for a long time.

Like Maria in his arms, the music was soft as they slowly danced over the dimly lit floor. He had never danced before either, but he had been delighted to find it a lot easier than attempting to shoot a basketball with three guys hanging on to him. The feeling of warmth where Maria's body touched his was flowing straight to his brain, sending his blood and thoughts swimming. His only concern was that she was getting a crick in her neck trying to look up at him.

'I can't believe my father went off with your parents,' Nick said, his big hands resting on top of her black hair.

'He's usually not very sociable?'

'Sort of. He hates almost everybody.'

Maria chuckled. 'Does he speak much Spanish?'

'Some. Do your parents speak much English?'

'A little.' Maria smiled up at him. 'They'll be all right. They have things in common.'

'Basketball?'

'Us.'

'Oh.' He liked the sound of that little word. It gave him confidence. Yet, remembering she was an illegal immigrant, he hesitated before asking his next question. 'So, Maria, you no longer feel afraid to be seen by people?'

She chuckled again. 'I haven't been wearing a bag over my head at school.' Then she was serious. 'I have Jessica to thank for tonight. She told me to bring my parents to the game. She's the one who put my name on the homecoming-court ballot.'

'I feel the same way about Mike. He forced me to go

out for the team.' Nick laughed. 'He forced me to ask you out on our date.'

Maria stepped back and lightly socked him, but he grabbed her hand and pulled her closer and they went right on dancing. He rested his chin on top of her head. 'Are you worried about winning tonight?' he asked after a while.

She poked his chest with her nose. 'I've already won.'

Not long after Maria socked Nick, Russ tried to kiss Sara in the middle of a dance. Sara held her head back.

'What's wrong?' he demanded. 'You kissed me the other night?'

'There're people here.' She glanced to the chair on the other side of the floor where Polly had sat the whole night, Alice's sketchpad balanced on her knees, drawing. Sara had brought her some punch half an hour ago and glanced at her work, a rather poor – though elaborate – drawing of the float and the four princesses. Sara had not known what Polly was trying to say by putting a big clock about to strike twelve on the front of the queen's tower.

Does she think all the princesses are going to turn into pumpkins?

'So?' Russ said, annoyed.

'So, I'm ASB president, I can't be seen kissing a boy in

front of everybody like an ordinary girl.'

'If you don't kiss me right now, I'll fondle your breasts in front of everybody.'

Why doesn't he get urges like this when we're alone?

'You wouldn't dare!'

'No?'

He went to grab her chest with both his paws. She jumped back and scurried past him.

'Excuse me, Russ, I've got to go beat the bank.'

She had spotted Bubba, alone, taking a break from tearing up the floor on every song with Clair. One thing you had to hand Clair, she didn't give a hoot – unlike Jessica – about being seen with a fashionable guy. Personally, Sara thought Jessica would have done a lot better with Michael Olson instead of Bill Skater. You could talk to Michael. From watching Bill in political science, Sara had decided he was essentially a blank sheet.

'Where's the money?' she asked, tapping Bubba on the shoulder. He turned to face her, smiling serenely, alcohol on his breath. Obviously he had brought his own private punch.

'Where's your body?' he asked.

'Why is it that all of a sudden everyone wants my body?'

'Did you sell it to someone else?'

She glared. 'That isn't funny. Do you have the money to pay for this dance or not? And don't give me any BS.'

'Why the harsh tone?' Bubba gestured to the rest of the tent. 'None of this would have been possible without my assistance. Look about you and be grateful.'

Sara had to admit he was right; the dance was a stunning success. Three-quarters of the student body must have come, as opposed to last year's homecoming when less than three hundred tickets had been sold. The music, the food, the colourful ribbons and ornaments hanging across the tent – everything was perfect. Everybody seemed to be having a great time. Already tonight, she'd been stopped a dozen times and congratulated on what a fantastic job she'd done.

But he's still trying to screw me.

'It is me who should be disappointed with you,' Bubba continued, leaning closer. 'I've done all this and received nothing in return. But, I must say, you do seem in a frisky mood tonight, Sara, dear. Why don't we get together at my place after I drop—'

'Can it. You've done nothing for me. I spoke to the caterer and the band. They say we still owe them half their money.'

'Then repay me fifty per cent tonight. You know what

really turns me on and doesn't take a lot of time? Later, in my bedroom, if you could take off your dress and—'

'Stop it. Where's the money?'

Bubba belched. 'I lost it.'

'You lost it!' she screamed. People – probably more than would have bothered to look had Russ actually succeeded in fondling her breasts – turned their heads. 'How could you lose it?' she hissed.

He shrugged. 'Money comes and goes, just like girls and bad weather. It's the way of things.'

It was a frightening thing, feeling this close to wanting to murder someone. 'If you lost it all, how did you pay for any of this?' she demanded.

'Oh, I had to borrow some more.'

'From who?'

'Friends of the family.'

She had heard rumours about his family. 'Are you talking about loan sharks?'

'Shh. They don't like that word. Never use it around them. They might get angry.'

She grabbed him by his bright green tie. 'You don't know the meaning of the word *angry*! I am not going to pay loan shark interest rates on a loan you had no right to take out!'

He laughed. 'You sure are a feisty little girl.'

She yanked on the tie, choking him. 'I mean it!'

He calmly reached up and removed her hand, straightening his tie and the green hat on his fat head. 'I'm afraid you have no choice, Sara. I told you at the beginning, I'm not going to bring my own personal funds into this matter. But don't despair. I borrowed enough to make the first couple of payments. And it's six months till June, a long time before you'll need big money for another big event. I'll think of something between now and then.' He added slyly, 'If you're nice to me, that is.'

She sneered, absolutely disgusted. 'I hate you.'

He beamed. 'Not as much as I love you, Sara.'

Stalking back to Russ, she was apprehended by Mr Bark. He wanted her to gather the princesses outside behind the float. It was time to crown the queen.

If it had been cold outside before, it was freezing now. Jessica didn't know if she could stand to wait any longer in her short sleeves with the other girls on the basketball courts. A wind had begun to blow; it kept picking at the hem of her dress, sending gooseflesh up her legs. Maria was the only smart one among them. She had on Nick's jacket, and on Maria it was as good as a full-length coat.

'Won't the truck under the float start?' Maria asked.

Sara had raved to Jessica about how great the float was,

but looking at it waiting in the dark fifty yards to the rear of the tent, its numerous towers reminding her more of an obstacle course than a castle, Jessica wished the announcement were taking place on stage in front of the band. What a joke; Sara was always calling her a snob, and here Sara had obviously put together this float solely for the purpose of being remembered as the greatest president Tabb High had ever had.

'It starts fine; it just keeps stalling,' Jessica said. She could hear Kats and Sara arguing inside. It seemed Sara had rigged a hose to the exhaust tail of the truck so the fumes could be funnelled away from the float. Kats wanted the hose removed. The fumes kept backing up inside the tail pipe, he said, and were choking the engine.

'Do what he says and let's get this thing over with,' Clair called out, standing near the front of the float with Cindy Fosmeyer. Clair had selected blue for the colour of her gown, but even if she'd chosen bright stripes and polka dots, Jessica thought, she still would have been beautiful. But Jessica was finding it difficult to understand how Cindy Fosmeyer had been selected to the court. The girl had lost several pounds in the past week – perhaps as much as half a pound directly off her massive chest – but her large nose had not shrunk in the interim and the ton of make-up she had chosen to plaster over her face had failed to bury it. It was a sad fact, but a fact nevertheless: Cindy was a dog.

After a few more encouraging remarks from Clair – each one containing a few more cuss words – Sara finally relented and did what Kats wanted. She removed the hose, but muttered that they had better hold their breath for the duration of the ride into the tent.

Mr Bark appeared. An envelope in his right hand, he crouched down behind the queen's castle, while Sara stationed herself inside the moat up front. Clair and Cindy got on to the battle towers on the left. Jessica was the last one up, taking the tower on the far right – facing the float – off to Maria's left. Beneath them, Kats turned over the truck's engine.

'Go slow,' Sara called down to Kats, who was invisible beneath their feet. Sara raised a walkie-talkie to her mouth. 'We're coming,' she said, telling whoever it was inside to start the music and raise the curtains.

What followed next irritated Jessica's finer sensibilities, yet at the same time gave her a big rush. In reality, she was as much a sap for flash and glitter as the next teenage girl.

The float rocked forward. In front, the tent walls began to part, slowly revealing row upon row of couples waiting within a spell of pulsing synthesised rhythms and whirling strobe lights, looking like a futuristic gang of kids partying aboard a huge spaceship.

They passed beneath the ceiling of the tent. A searchlight caught the tip of the float. The true colours of the castle flooded Jessica's eyes, dazzling her. The searchlight rolled over her face and practically blinded her. She could smell the fumes Sara had spoken of, could hear the eerie sci-fi music. But the next thing she actually saw was the float swaying – as Kats brought it to a halt – and Sara stepping up to the microphone.

Heavy stuff.

Kats shut off the truck. The canvas closed at their back, and the temperature leaped into the comfort zone.

'Having a good time?' Sara asked the crowd, getting an immediate earsplitting 'Yeah!'

'That's good, that's great,' she went on. 'I know it's been a while since I last spoke to all of you at once. And there's something I said that day I'd like to take back. Getting ready for this dance with the help of the whole ASB council, I've learned a high school really does need class officers. I've also discovered that you'd have to be out of your mind to want to be one.' The audience laughed and Sara continued smoothly. 'But let's get down to business. Let's crown our new queen. I'll start by introducing the members of the court.' Sara gestured to her right. 'Over here, at a hundred and ten pounds and undefeated in all her previous fights, we have blonde and blue-eyed Clair Hilrey!'

Clair – much to Jessica's displeasure – accepted the silly introduction by raising both her arms high like a prizefighter, showing everyone that – besides being able to take a joke – she had the best body on the float. The audience loved it.

Her reputation sure has bounced back.

'Ooh, baby!' Bubba's voice howled from somewhere at the rear.

'Next,' Sara said. 'Beloved of the entire male population of Tabb High for her forward reaching expression and her twin mounds of feminine excellence – Cindy Fosmeyer!'

I cannot believe she said that.

Cindy didn't seem to mind the compliments, no doubt because she didn't understand them. Politely applauding, Jessica wondered what Sara would say about her. But not half so much as she wondered what name was written in the envelope Mr Bark carried.

Sara nodded to her left. 'And now we come to the smallest girl in the group. Small in size, but big in heart. Ladies and gentlemen, Maria Gonzales!'

The applause for Maria was warm but lacked the

enthusiasm the previous two girls had enjoyed; understandable, since Maria was all but unknown on campus outside a tiny circle of friends. Her election to the court made less sense than Cindy's.

The applause died down. Sara grinned wickedly. Jessica lowered her head and began to squirm, feeling sweat forming beneath the layer of deodorant she had rolled on earlier. Sara had just better remember, she swore to herself, that they were best friends.

Oh, no.

'As most of you know,' Sara began, 'our final princess and I have been best friends for many years. Now I know somebody out there must be asking him or herself the question "Can we trust good old Sara to read out anybody's name but that of her best friend?"' Sara paused, then giggled. 'We'll see, won't we?' She spread out her left arm. 'Wish Jessica Hart lots of luck, folks!'

Her heart pounding so hard it was close to skipping, Jessica rated her applause the loudest of the lot.

I'm in. It's me. It's got to be me!

'The envelope, please,' Sara said, turning to welcome Mr Bark as he emerged from behind the queen's tower. The chatter in the audience halted. Jessica raised her head. Sara took the envelope from Mr Bark – snatched it from him actually – and quickly began to tear it open.

Before she could finish, however, Mr Bark wedged himself between her and the microphone.

'If I may say a few words before the crowning,' Mr Bark began.

'Damn,' Sara mumbled under her breath – soft enough so that no one in the crowd seemed to hear – trying to get the slip of paper out of the envelope while trying to maintain her position behind the mike. Mr Bark gave her an uncertain glance before continuing.

'I am happy so many of you were able to make it tonight,' he said, stretching his head in front of Sara's face. 'Homecoming is an important event, not only as a social occasion, but as a time to reflect on our bigger home, the world we live in. It is a beautiful world but a fragile one. At any instant, on either side of the ocean, a button could be pushed and—'

'How many here are against nuclear war?' Sara suddenly broke in, raising her hand holding the torn envelope. The whole assembly threw their fists into the air and cheered. 'Wow, we're convinced!' she exclaimed. 'We'll have the petition at the door, and no one leaves here tonight without signing it. A big hand for Mr Bark, please! Thank you!'

More clapping. Mr Bark scowled down at Sara, and she smiled up at him. He must have realised he had nowhere to go with his speech now that she had stolen his thunder. He climbed down from the float.

The silence settled again on the audience, quicker this time, and deeper. Sara, alone behind the microphone – a beam of light bright on her orange dress – finished opening the envelope and took out the slip of paper. Jessica did not have on her glasses, naturally, and therefore did not have a clear view of Sara's face. Yet Sara was only a few feet away, and it seemed to Jessica she froze as she unfolded the tiny white paper. But only for an instant.

Jessica Hart! Way to go Jessie! Let's hear it for Jessie!

Then Sara turned towards her, catching her eye. Beyond Sara, on the other side of the float, Clair leaned forward. The crowd waited. Everybody on the float waited.

Everybody – except Jessica. Because as Sara had looked at Jessica, Sara's lower lip trembled slightly. Jessica saw it, and knew it was the one thing Sara did to show disappointment.

I can't believe it. I lost.

Jessica lowered her head again, her hair covering her face. She didn't see Sara turn back to the microphone, though she heard her clearly enough.

'Ladies and gentlemen, please welcome Tabb High's new homecoming queen – Maria Gonzales!'

The rest was a blur for Jessica. Maria reached for her

first, and Jessica hugged her. She kissed Maria, laughed and cried with her, telling herself she was happy for her. But she cried more than the occasion deserved.

Then the other princesses were congratulating Maria, and Sara was placing the crown on top of her head and wrapping the royal robe around her frail shoulders. Music played, lights flickered. The applause went on and on. Sara directed Maria towards the back of the float. Ascending the hidden ladder, a bouquet of red roses in her arms, Maria reached the top of the tower. There she stood radiant and tall.

But even the small have far to fall.

The thought flickered past the lowest edge of Jessica's conscious mind, disappearing almost before she knew she'd had it.

Maria waved her flowers, wrapped safe in the audience's adulation.

Clair leaned over and whispered to Jessica. 'As long as it wasn't you, sweetie.'

'I feel the same way,' Jessica replied.

Michael had found the file; he had reached the cemetery. The computerised search was now leading him through data that clearly made up Dr Gin Kawati's autopsy reports. Her tombstone was close. Any second now, he knew, he would have to take up the shovel and dig. He was literally trembling with excitement, with horror. He glanced at his watch: a quarter after one. Alice had died just after one in the morning.

Michael stood and again paced the room, as he had done so many times during the course of the night. He no longer felt simply claustrophobic; he felt as if he were smothering. His eyes burned; he hated to think what he would look like in a mirror. Part of it was from exhaustion, but the stink from the biology room had continued to assault his senses all night. He had only identified the smell – formaldehyde. But he had not gone to wipe it up. For some reason, he was afraid to leave the computer, afraid the information on the disc might suddenly vanish.

He hadn't heard anything from the direction of the tent in the last hour. No music, no laughter. He was surprised Bubba had not dropped by after the dance to check on how the search was progressing. But Michael couldn't blame him. Clair had probably invited him back to her place. Michael would have liked to have known who the new queen was. He hoped it was Jessica, although he realised that would make her even more unattainable.

He was about to return to his seat at the terminal when he became aware of an unusual sound outside. He paused, standing in the middle of the room, and listened. He thought someone must be knocking hard on a nearby door. Then he dismissed that possibility. Whoever it was would have had to have been knocking with a battering ram. The door – if that was what it was – sounded as if it were disintegrating.

Michael reached for the door to investigate further. A beep at his back stopped him. Turning, he saw the word *Found* flashing at the top of the computer screen. He jumped to his feet.

Subject: Alice McCoy. Age 15. Coroner: Dr Gin Kawati.

Forgetting all about the sound, Michael began to read.

The dance was history. The clean-up had begun. Jessica and Sara had changed from their gowns back into the clothes they had worn to the basketball game. Along with Maria, they were trying to undo in a couple of hours what had taken weeks to put together. It was a hopeless task. If the amount of fun had by all was proportional to the amount of mess they had made, then Sara's place in Tabb's history as the best ASB president was already secure.

Polly had hung around at first and tried to lend a hand, but watching her hop pathetically about with plates and glasses balanced in her arms, Jessica and Sara had sent her home. Maria was almost as useless. She had *not* changed out of her dress. She continued to float about beneath the deserted tent as if the crowds were still cheering her to the top of the float, a stoned smile on her lips.

All right, I'm envious. That doesn't mean I'll hate Maria from now on.

Jessica couldn't figure out how the girl had won.

'I'm tired,' she complained, stuffing red ribbon in a green plastic trash bag and wiping the sweat from her eyes.

'You can't quit,' Sara said, standing on a ladder above her. 'This tent has to be ready to take down by tomorrow at noon or I'll have to pay for another day's rental.'

'Let them take it down the way it is,' Jessica said.

'Sure, right, and leave this pile of garbage out in the open where everybody can see it.'

'Ask me if I care, Sara.' Jessica threw down her bag. 'I've had enough. I'm going to my locker, getting my books and I'm not coming back.'

'Some friend you are.' Then Sara stopped, surveying the tons of junk. 'Well, I guess you're right. There is too much to do. Go home and rest.' She lowered her voice, nodded to the other side of the tent where Maria was gathering the carnations from the tables, smelling each one as if it were a gift from a boyfriend. 'But on your way out, ask our little brown butterfly to give me a hand with the last of these ribbons.'

'Will do.'

Sara stared at her a moment. 'You know, Jessie, you looked awful pretty tonight. It should have been you.'

Jessica smiled, touched. 'Wasn't in the cards, I guess.'

Maria hugged Jessica when she told her she was leaving.

'I owe all this to you,' Maria said, holding her tight.

'You did it yourself,' Jessica said, embarrassed by the twinge of jealousy that was still there.

Maria let go, shook her head. 'I lived in a box until you came along. I never went out. I never talked to boys. If it wasn't for you, I wouldn't even know Nick.'

Jessica squeezed her arm. 'We all get what we deserve, Maria. I really believe that.'

Except for Alice, our sweet Alice.

Jessica grabbed her coat and left.

The wind had died. The cold had deepened. She had to get her homework from her locker before she could go home. Outside the tent, striding across the empty basketball courts towards the silent black buildings, Jessica looked up at the clear sky punctured with stars.

Thoughts of Alice had come and now they would not leave. Jessica decided not to fight them. Sometimes when she was sad, she would remember everything in her life that had ever brought her unhappiness, and then whatever was depressing her at the moment would appear less significant, and she would feel better.

She spotted the red star she had been wondering about the night she had gone out with Bill. Again she wished she had Michael by her side to tell her its name.

Strange how she could not remember Alice without thinking of Michael. He was always there, deep in her mind, standing beside Alice, as he had been in the painting her lost friend had been working on before she died.

I'll have to find that picture and hang it above my bed.

Lowering her gaze, Jessica quickened her pace. Soon she was under the exterior covered walkway, her sneakers squeaking on the smooth concrete, cursing again the fact that Tabb was too cheap to keep a few lights burning throughout the night. With the roof from the class wing above her head and the branches of some of Tabb's oldest trees off to her side, she was in a dark place, so dark she could barely see her hand in front of her face.

As a child, the dark had both fascinated and frightened her. During the day, when the sun was bright, she had loved nothing better than to go exploring with Polly in a big sewer that was the sole source and inspiration for a creek that ran through a jungle of a lot not far from their houses. The lot was later to become a park, and then the site of another housing tract, but in those days it had been the big outdoors. They must have been five or six at the time. The last time Jessica could remember exploring the tunnel with Polly – their legs spread wide so they wouldn't step in the smelly water that ran down the centre, their heads bent low, flashlights swiped from Polly's garage gripped tightly in each of their tiny grubby hands – had been the time they had brought Alice with them. *That* had been a mistake.

They were further into the tunnel than they had ever been before. They had been walking for ever. They were excited. Of course it was a big dream of theirs to get to the other end of the thing. They had this idea that if they could get that far, then the dimensions of the world – or at least of their neighbourhood – would make more sense. Then they would know where they stood in the scheme of things.

They could see no light up ahead. But a noise had begun to throb around them, a slow thumping sound that reminded Jessica of a giant heart – not the heart of a person, but the heart of a huge machine, a machine that she imagined made all the cars and buildings and sewers. When they got to that noise, she thought, they would really know what was happening.

She never did find out what the noise was.

Alice slipped, smack into the slime in the centre of the sewer. Turning to rescue her, Polly dropped her flashlight and broke it. And naturally, in the heat of the moment, Jessica imagined that her flashlight was beginning to fail too. She told the others it was, and the thought of what it would be like to be trapped in the sewer without any light was enough to send them racing back at warp speed.

Oddly enough, however, once they were out, Alice had begged them to try again to reach the other end. But Alice's stinking clothes alerted their parents to what they had been doing. Their subterranean exploration days were over.

The heart of a machine.

Jessica stopped in midstride in the black walkway. There was a noise coming from up ahead. Not the noise she had heard in the tunnel a dozen years ago. That had been deep and rhythmic. This one sounded like someone chopping wood. Yet as she listened more closely in the dark, holding her breath, her heart pounding steadily harder and harder, the gap between the chops seemed to shorten, to almost disappear altogether, to blur with her heartbeat, until they were practically a single sound, until she was feeling smaller and smaller, and standing, not in a school outdoor walkway, but far beneath the ground, with a machine over her head that made *everything* – maybe even little girls.

The sound stopped. Silence. Her heart could have stopped.

Then Jessica heard the crash. Glass, metal and wood exploding.

Help!

She turned and ran back the way she had come. But this was not a tunnel, with only two ways to go. Suddenly it was a maze, and she didn't even have a failing flashlight to show her the way. She went right, she went left. She didn't know which way she was going. It was insane; she spent five hours, five days a week at this school. And now she was lost!

Then she froze, holding on to the corner of an exterior wall, on to the tunnel wall. When she was a child, this had never happened to her. Although as a child, she had, like every other child in the world, dreamed it a million times.

Footsteps. Rapidly approaching footsteps.

Someone was chasing her!

Jessica let out a soft moan, remembering how when the three of them had escaped from the sewer into the wonderful sunlight, they'd discovered Alice had skinned her head. How the blood had trickled from the side of Alice's head through her bright blonde hair.

And how the blood had *flowed* out the back of Alice's head as she lay dead on her back on the hard floor in her parents' bedroom.

And Michael said she'd been murdered.

Jessica bolted away from the footsteps, around the corner, back down a walkway she had the terrible feeling she had run up a moment ago.

God help me. God save me.

Apparently God only helped those who helped themselves. Or those who had a better sense of direction.

She ran smack into her pursuer.

He grabbed her. She screamed.

Michael was confused, and all because of a paragraph Dr Kawati had added to the end of the autopsy report. The other ninety-five per cent of the information had been much as he had expected.

The coroner had detailed how a twenty-two calibre bullet had entered through the roof of Alice's mouth, torn through her cerebral cortex, ricocheted off the top of her skull and finally exited via the base of the skull. In his notes, the doctor referred several times to a sketch he had drawn tracing the path of the bullet, and to X-rays he had apparently taken during the examination – neither of which was available in the data Bubba had swiped. But the absence of the sketch and the X-rays was not what had Michael stumped. Nor was the analysis of her blood out of line. Alice had had no unusual chemicals in her system at the time of her death, not even alcohol. There had also been no sign that she had undergone a struggle immediately prior to her death: no flesh under her fingernails, which might have been scraped from an assailant; no scratches on her face or arms; and, at first glance, no bruises anywhere on her body.

In conclusion, the doctor had stated that the cause of death was a severe cerebral haemorrhage brought about by a self-inflicted gunshot wound.

Then he had added a note at the end.

> Because the bullet travelled a complex path before exiting the head, the girl's brain was left in extremely poor shape. It is, therefore, difficult to know if the haemorrhage found in the region of the hypothalamus and thalamus was brought about by the course of the bullet or by the force of the blow to her nasal cartilage.

> The cartilage has a significant fracture across its entire width, which could not have been a result of the bullet's trajectory. It is the opinion of this coroner that Alice McCoy must have fractured her nasal cartilage upon hitting the floor with her face after shooting herself. As she was found lying on her back, I must assume that someone rolled her over before the police arrived. It is suggested to the investigating officers they pay specific attention to this point when questioning all those involved.

A fractured nasal cartilage? That was a fancy way of saying Alice had a broken nose in addition to a hole in her head. Michael was angry – but not the least surprised – that Lieutenant Keller had withheld this information. But Michael did remember the detective repeatedly asking if anyone moved Alice after they had found her. The lieutenant had obviously been anxious to clear up the discrepancy; and yet he had closed the case without doing so.

There were two possibilities. Either someone had moved Alice's body before they reached the room, or else something other than the fall had broken her nose.

Did someone break it for her?

The bullet had clearly snaked around inside her skull

before exiting at the base; nevertheless, the bullet hole in the wall had been at best only three feet off the floor. And straight into the plaster. The chances remained that Alice had been sitting when she was shot. And if that were true, it would be almost impossible for her to have broken her nose in a fall.

Did someone hit her hard, in the face?

The coroner had also referred to an area of haemorrhage that was possibly unconnected to that caused by the bullet. That raised another question, one that was in many ways far more confusing than the others.

What?

Something large and loud crashed outside.

Michael leaped to his feet. He was out the door before he could finish asking himself the hard question.

The dark caught him off guard. For a moment he couldn't see far enough to know in which direction to run. He paused, straining to listen. It was then he heard the footsteps, racing along the hallway on the other side of the wing that housed the computer lab. He assumed the footsteps belonged to the person who had caused the crash. He set off after him.

Whoever this individual was, he couldn't make up his mind which way he was headed. He was fast, though. Michael chased him up one hallway, down another, without catching so much as a glimpse of him. But the idiot was going in circles. Michael finally decided on a different approach. He stopped and silently jogged the *other* way, away from the guy. The strategy proved effective. A minute later he ran right into him.

'Hold on there, buddy,' he shouted, grabbing him by the wrists. The fellow – he wasn't that tall – struggled furiously.

'Let me go! Help!'

Michael let her go in a hurry. 'Jessie?'

'Oh, thank God,' she whispered, collapsing against his chest, sobbing. 'Someone's chasing me, Michael.'

'*I* was chasing you.' He held her in his arms. He never would have believed a person could shake so much and still remain earthbound. He could hardly see her face, but he could feel her hot panting breath on his neck. He brushed her sweaty hair from her eyes, hugged her tight. 'Shh, you're OK. You're safe. No one's going to hurt you.'

'There was this strange sound,' she said, weeping. 'It was like in the tunnel, and then it just blew up, and I started running, and I . . . I don't know.' She pulled back, wiped at her eyes, dazed. 'What was it, Michael?'

'Let's go see. I think the crash came from the courtyard.'

Jessica grabbed his hand. 'Do you think it's all right?'

He spoke calmly, although inside he was not exactly coasting along himself. 'We'll be fine.' He didn't want to leave her alone, even back in the computer room.

They found the varsity tree – it was lying across the snack bar. The trunk had caved in one entire wall of the building. Branches poked out dozens of glass windows. It was quite simple; someone had chopped it down. They discovered the axe resting in the grass on top of a pile of wood chips scattered beside the splintered stump. Jessica knelt to touch it. Michael stopped her.

'There could be fingerprints,' he warned. He glanced about, but didn't see anybody. 'Why are you here by yourself this late?'

'I was helping Sara and Maria clean up the mess from the dance. Then I was going to my locker to get my homework. Michael, why would anyone want to kill this tree?'

'I don't know. Are Sara and Maria still at the tent?'

'Yes. I think so.'

The tree had not fallen in a random fashion. The angle had been purposely chosen to cause the most destruction possible. Only a crazy person could have been behind this. In the wake of reading the conflicting details surrounding Alice's death, the thought sent a shiver through Michael. 'Let's get the girls and get out of here,' he said.

Before they left the scene of the crime, however, Michael changed his mind about the axe. Getting a handkerchief from Jessica, he grabbed it by the blade and took it with them.

Sara yawned. She was as beat as Jessica had complained about being. The day had gone on for ever. But she was sort of sad it was all over. Russ had been disqualified in his race, Jessica had not been crowned queen, and yet many good things had happened. Ten years from now, she imagined, if she was still alive and the world was still here, she would have fond memories of homecoming.

'Maria, I'm stacking these trash bags together and then I'm out of here,' Sara called.

Maria was wandering about on the float, her royal flowers in her hands. Sara had to chuckle. There was someone who was definitely unhappy to see the evening end. No doubt Maria would find it hard to fall asleep, remembering what it had been like to hear her name called out, how it had felt to ascend to the top of the queen's tower with the whole school cheering her on.

'OK,' Maria said, disappearing into the back of the float.

She's doing it all over! But can I blame her?

Thoroughly amused, Sara watched as Maria slowly wound her way up the tower steps. Once at the top, Maria set down her flowers and picked up her crown, holding it high above her head in both her hands.

'We should do this every week!' Maria called.

'Somehow, I don't think it would be the same,' Sara said, glancing down, twisting the tie on the trash bag in her hands. As a result – with her attention divided – she had only a vague idea of what happened next.

Out of the corner of her eye, Sara received the impression that Maria had placed the crown on her head and did a little skip into the air. That was it. Then Maria appeared to dematerialise. The illusion persisted for a fraction of a second. Until Sara heard the scream and the crash, and knew the top level of the float had caved in and taken Maria with it.

She can't be dead. Please God.

Sara scarcely remembered crossing the tent and leaping on to the float. The next thing she knew, she was staring down into a deep, mangled hole. There was sufficient light to see the worst. Maria lay sprawled over the truck's shattered windshield, her body bent at a grotesque angle. There was blood on the glass and glass in her face. She was not moving.

'I'm coming, Maria,' Sara said. 'I'm coming.'

It was just as well that Michael and Jessica showed up at that moment and that Michael had an axe in his hands. Sara had no idea how to help Maria without doing more damage. Shouting for Sara to get down, Michael peeped through a crack in the tower wall, and then began to hack away with the blade. Apparently he did not feel it would be wise to attempt to free Maria by coming in from beneath the float. Sara trusted his judgment. Hanging on to Jessica in the middle of the drawbridge, Sara felt more helpless than she had ever felt in her entire life.

Michael was through the wall in a couple of minutes. Pulling away the cracked boards, he stepped down on top of the hood of the truck. Jessica and Sara crouched beside his chopped opening.

'Is she alive?' Jessica whispered, staring in horror. There was not a great deal of blood. It was the way Maria was lying – her torso twisted like a Gumby; her chest and face pressed into the roof; her legs jammed into the steering wheel – that filled her with dread.

'She's breathing,' Michael said, taking her pale wrist in his hand and feeling for a pulse. 'She's alive.'

'Let's get her out!' Jessica exclaimed.

'No,' Michael said firmly. 'We can't move her. She could have a spinal injury.' He pointed to Jessica. 'Use your phone. Dial nine-one-one. Describe the situation and our location.' He nodded. 'Hurry.'

With Jessica gone, Sara carefully stepped on to the hood beside Michael. 'It's just like the party,' she said bitterly.

He sighed. 'It doesn't surprise me.'

Pulling her Mercedes on to her street, Polly spotted Clark swinging a leg over his motorcycle parked at the foot of her driveway. Before she could reach the house, however, he had gunned the engine and roared off in the opposite direction. For a moment she contemplated going after him. But even if she had been in a Ferrari, she knew she would never have caught him. He was like a witch on a broom.

Heading up her driveway, she noticed that the front door was wide open. The house was black, and she never left for the evening without turning on at least a couple of lamps.

'Aunty,' she whispered to herself, leaping out of her car. Inside, she couldn't get a light to go on. Either Clark had fiddled with the circuit breakers or else he had broken every bulb in the house. She stumbled into the kitchen, found a candle in a drawer and lit it on the pilot light of the stove. Creeping down the hall towards her aunt's bedroom, shadows following her along both walls, she started to cry.

Her aunt was lying on her back and staring at the ceiling. Staring without blinking. Polly set the candle down on the nearby bed stand and sat on the bed. Aunty's pupils had clouded over, like cheap marbles that had been left too long in the bright sun. Polly couldn't even tell what colour her eyes had been, and this disturbed her a great deal, that she couldn't remember.

Polly picked up the old lady's mottled hand. It was soft, softer than it had been in life, and it was still warm. She had not been dead long.

She was alive when Clark was here.

Polly glanced at the ceiling and didn't see the blood dripping down that he had spoken of; nevertheless, she felt herself smothering, a black panic rising.

She fainted on top of the dead woman.

EPILOGUE

Jessica drifted in and out of reality trying to sleep on the hard brown vinyl couch in the deserted hospital waiting room. When she was awake, she watched Michael and Nick sitting in the hallway outside the room. Sometimes they would be talking quietly to each other. Other times Nick's head would be slumped back on the wall and he would be snoring softly. But always Michael would be sitting upright, and always he looked as if he were thinking. Not once, however, did she catch him looking her way. And this simple fact filled her with a sadness that went beyond reason. It made her anguish about Maria almost unbearable. There was only pain in waking.

In being alive.

Then there were her dreams. They were mostly dark thundering things without shape or reason. But there was one that had sent a knife through her heart when she had awakened from it; for it had been beautiful and filled with a joyfulness that made her chest ache to recall it.

She was in the tunnel of her childhood. Only now Michael was with her, and they were both fully grown. Alice was there also, and another blonde-haired girl Jessica did not recognise. But the two girls were younger, only three or four years old. Together, with Michael leading the way with the aid of an old-fashioned lantern, they were approaching what they knew to be the end of the tunnel.

A warm yellow light began to stream over them from up ahead, making their eyes shine and their hearts quicken. Then the walls of the tunnel started to dissolve, until they could see through them. Suddenly Michael smiled and extinguished the lantern. And they were standing on a sloping desert plain, with a sparkling clear sky overhead and a breeze, sweet with the fragrance of honey, wafting through their hair. In the distance were a cool green ocean and people, old friends of theirs they could hardly wait to meet again.

Behind them, Jessica caught the faint roar of a churning river and realised that the now invisible tunnel had been a bridge over the icy water. It was, however, only a passing thought, of something that had once concerned her but which she now understood to be of no importance. Michael took her hand – Alice and her friend were dancing ahead of them and they walked towards the place by the ocean where the day was only beginning.

She felt as if she had just been born.

A bright spot in a dreary night. Fits of reality and nightmares chased her from then on. Until she felt a hand on her arm, shaking her gently.

'Jessie, wake up. Time to get up.'

Jessica opened her eyes and discovered Sara sitting beside her on the couch. Sara had begun the vigil with Jessica outside the operating room at two in the morning, but had rushed home after receiving an emergency call from her mother. It hadn't been clear exactly what the problem was.

'What time is it?' She yawned, pushing herself up with an effort, her neck stiff as a board.

'Eight-thirty,' a voice said at her back. It was Michael, standing in the hazy sunlight of the waiting room window. 'The doctors say Maria's operation went well. Her parents are with her now.'

'But is she going to be all right?' Jessica asked anxiously. 'What did they operate on?'

'Her back,' Michael said, coming over and sitting on the chair beside them. 'It was broken.'

'Is she – paralysed?' Jessica asked.

Michael shook his head, tired. 'I don't know. I don't think the doctors like to use that word. One of us might be allowed in to see her in a few minutes. Nick's gone to talk to the surgeon who performed the operation.'

'At least she's alive,' Sara said.

'Yeah,' Michael said. 'She was lucky.'

'What did your mom want?' Jessica asked Sara. Her old friend grimaced.

'Bad news. The police identified the axe you guys found as the axe taken from the store where Russ used to work. They found his fingerprints on the handle. They've arrested him!'

'You can't be serious?' Jessica said.

'Can't your parents verify where Russ was at one o'clock in the morning?' Michael asked.

'No,' Sara said. 'He didn't go straight home after the dance.'

'Where did he go?' Jessica asked.

Sara hesitated. 'He says he went to a bar. But the idiot – he can't remember which one.'

'That's bad,' Michael said.

'You don't think he chopped down the tree, do you?' Jessica asked.

'Of course he didn't!' Sara snapped. 'But while questioning him, the police learned that he'd stayed at Polly's house for a few days. They called her, and she said that she'd had the axe in the trunk of her car until last week, when it disappeared.'

'What was Polly doing with the axe?' Jessica asked.

'She says she took it from Russ one night when he was drunk and trying to chop down the varsity tree.'

'They believed her?' Jessica asked, amazed.

'Russ agreed with her! Except he says *I* was the one who stopped him back then and took his axe. He's incriminated himself left and right. They're going to lock him up, I swear it.'

'No way,' Jessica said.

'They might,' Michael said. 'When that tree fell, it caused a lot of damage.'

'He should have kept his mouth shut,' Sara said. 'Polly should have kept her mouth shut.' She sighed rubbing her head. 'I guess we can't blame her, though. Her night was as lousy as Maria's. Her aunt passed away.'

Jessica groaned. 'It never stops.'

Sara nodded. 'And to top it off, an old-time employee of her parents' company died yesterday from a work-related accident. She's got two more funerals to go to. I hope they won't be plugging her into the socket again.'

tood. 'I have to get back to the police station. I'm to get Russ out on bail.'

'Will your parents lend you the money?' Jessica asked.'

'No,' Sara said. 'They're being total jerks about the whole thing.' She patted Jessica on the shoulder. 'I'll be back later to check on Maria. I guess we should be glad things can't get any worse. See you, Mike.'

When Sara was gone, Michael sat beside her on the couch. 'Can I get you anything from the snack bar?' he asked.

'Thanks, I'm not hungry. Have you been up all night?'

'Yeah.'

'And you don't think it was an accident?'

Her question surprised him. 'It's hard to tell from what's left of the tower. Clearing a path to Maria, I messed up the evidence something awful. We may never know if someone tampered with the float.'

'But you think someone did, don't you?'

He shrugged. 'I'm not sure of anything these days.' He glanced at her. He needed a shave. She needed a hug. 'What did Sara mean when she made that remark about plugging Polly into the socket again?'

'When we were twelve, Polly's parents died. Alice must have told you. They drove off a road in the desert and their car burst into flames. Polly was with them, but was thrown free. She didn't get so much as a scratch. But she suffered from severe depression afterwards and was in the hospital for a long time. The doctors treated her with electroshock therapy.'

'What!' Michael exclaimed. 'They used electroshock on a twelve-year-old girl?'

'Is that unusual?' she asked uneasily. 'She had the best doctors money could buy. It seemed to help.'

Michael shook his head angrily. 'Electroshock therapy has got to be the greatest evil modern psychiatry ever spawned. It alleviates people's depression by causing irreversible brain damage. The patient is no longer unhappy because he can hardly remember what was making him unhappy.'

'Then why do they use it?'

'You said it: "the best doctors money could buy." It costs the hospital a few cents in electricity, produces superficial improvement and makes MDs tons of cash.' He nodded to himself. '"The man with the electricity". Makes sense.'

'What?'

'Just something Polly said to me when I was at her house.'

'Why did you go to her house?'

He realised he'd made a slip. 'You know why.'

'I suppose I do.' She touched his arm. 'Michael, you've got to let it go.'

He looked away. 'I can't.'

'But it's tearing you apart.'

'Not like it tore Maria apart,' he muttered.

'What?'

'Nothing.' He rested his head in his hands, his eyes on the floor. He was thinking again. 'She was outside when the gun went off. We're sure of that, aren't we?'

'Who?'

'Polly. The night of the party.'

'Yes, she was outside, *alone* in the backyard. And Alice was upstairs, *alone* in her parents' bedroom. Polly didn't kill her. She loved Alice.'

Michael sat up. 'But a crazy person could love someone and still kill her. She wouldn't need a reason why.'

'You think Polly's crazy?'

'I think she's close enough not to make much difference.'

'You're wrong. She may be a bit off, but she gets by. I've known her a lot longer than you.'

He softened his tone. 'I appreciate that, Jessie – that she's your friend. And I realise you knew her before they attached electrodes to her brain. But tell me honestly, was it the same Polly who came out of the hospital that went in?'

'Of course she wasn't the same,' she said, wondering if she wasn't trying to convince herself. 'She was a young girl, and she'd lost both her parents.'

'I wonder if that's all there was to it.'

'But you saw Polly go out to the backyard, same as me,' she said, her voice growing constricted with emotion. 'And you saw her come running inside when the gun went off. Believe me, I know that house. There's no way up to the master bedroom except the stairs we took. There're no trapdoors, no hidden stairways. It's physically impossible that she shot Alice. It's impossible anyone did.'

Michael looked unconvinced; nevertheless, he nodded. 'I can't argue with what you say. I'm sorry I brought it up. I didn't mean to upset you.'

He was still feeling guilty, she knew, about the time he had yelled at her in Alice's studio after the funeral. She smiled, squeezed his arm. 'You never have to apologise to me, Michael.'

He blushed, or frowned, or both. 'Yeah?'

'It's true. And I'll tell you why it's true.'

Because you're the only one I know who's striving

for perfection. Who's completely noble and totally unselfish. The only one who's always there when I need rescuing from myself.

The words did not come out, not right away, and not so much because she was embarrassed to say them, but because she was ashamed that she had stood him up on their date, that she had purposely started the rumour of Clair's abortion and accepted his help on the SAT. That she was unworthy of him.

'Jessie?' he said, waiting for her.

I can still tell him, and let him decide. About me. Us.

'Because, Michael Olson, old locker buddy—'

'Jessie,' Nick called, striding into the waiting room, a different person from the guy who had led Tabb to victory the night before. He had huge bags under his eyes. He stuttered when he spoke. 'The d-doctor said you can see M-Maria for a couple of minutes.'

'Have you seen her?' Jessica asked, jumping up with Michael.

'She wants to see you first,' Nick said, tense.

'But how is she?' Jessica asked. 'Will she be able to walk again?'

'I don't know,' Nick complained. 'Nobody will tell me nothing. And her parents have left already.'

Jessica followed Nick's directions and ended up in an

aggressively green intensive care ward. The medicine smell made her empty stomach uneasy. The patients' rooms were tiny glass cubicles arranged around a nurses' station packed with enough electronic equipment to pilot a Trident submarine. The RN on duty pointed out Maria's cubicle and reminded her that her visit was not to exceed three minutes.

A white sheet loosely covered Maria's body; it wasn't much whiter than the colour of her skin. Quietly closing the door, Jessica noted through an opening in the sheet that a plastic and metal brace was locked over Maria's bare hips. It reached all the way up her side, embracing her slim shoulders. It could not have looked more uncomfortable. Maria had her eyes open – one eye, rather; the other was swollen shut and was staring at the ceiling.

Where else can she look?

'It's me,' Jessica said.

Maria cleared her throat. 'I know.'

Jessica moved closer to the bed. A bandage covered the right side of Maria's face; out of the bottom of it peeped a stitched cut. She would be scarred as well.

But did she sever her spinal cord?

Jessica walked over to take Maria's hand and bumped into her IV. Wires led from beneath the sheet to monitors overhead. She had to fight to keep her voice calm. 'How are you, Maria?'

Her single black eye turned towards Jessica. 'How do I look?'

She forced a smile. 'A little under the weather. But you'll be better soon. This is a great hospital.'

'Is it?'

'Oh, yeah. I had my appendix out here when I was thirteen years old. They have the best doctors. Wonderful nurses.'

Maria closed her eye. 'Since you love it here so much, it's too bad it wasn't you who broke her back.'

'Huh?' Jessica had to force air into her lungs in order to speak. 'You don't mean that.'

Maria smiled, and with her cuts and swollen face, it was truly gruesome. 'I remember when you talked me into putting my name on the ballot for the homecoming court. You told me this was America, that anything could happen, that I might even be nominated queen. But you didn't believe it. Had you thought I stood a chance in a million, you wouldn't have let me get within a mile of that ballot.'

'You've been through a terrible ordeal,' Jessica said, struggling to keep her composure. 'You need to rest, to heal. And you're going to heal, Maria.'

Maria looked at her again, her one eye a single accusing finger. 'It should have been you standing at the top of that float. You wanted to be homecoming queen more than anything. You schemed to go out with the popular boys so you'd be popular. You told lies about Clair. You told me lies.'

'Stop it. You don't know what you're saying.'

'It should be you lying here instead of me!'

The tears burst from Jessica then and she had to turn away. She went to the huge window by the door. Hanging from a white thread close to the glass was a silver angel – a Christmas decoration. With everything else going on, she had forgotten that Christmas was only a couple of weeks away. She had got so caught up in the fantasy of being the most desired girl on campus that she had almost overlooked what had always been for her the most precious time of the year, and the realisation made her feel there must be some justice in what Maria said.

I'm no longer a little girl. I've grown up. I'm a bitch.

Searching for a handkerchief in her pocket to wipe away her tears, her fingers ran into a bobby pin. An idea occurred to her. Pulling out the pin, her back to Maria, she scraped off the rubbery black stuff at the ends. Then she stepped to the foot of the bed.

'They'll only let me stay a minute longer,' she said,

carefully lifting the sheet from Maria's toes. Maria, her eyes again closed, didn't seem to notice.

'A pity.'

'I'm still your friend, no matter what you may think right now. I'll be back tomorrow to visit.' Holding the pin between her thumb and index finger, she poked it gently into Maria's heel.

She should have jumped. If she could feel . . .

'Don't put yourself out.'

She poked Maria harder, again and again. But the girl just lay there. She was paralysed. Jessica began to back away from the bed, trembling. She *had* lied to her. Maria was never going to heal. Never.

'It's no trouble,' she said, her voice choking. 'If I can bring you anything, anything at all?'

'There is one thing I would like.'

'What?'

'A promise.' Maria opened her eye, but Jessica did not believe she could actually see her this close to the door.

'Yes?'

'Promise me I will never have to see you again.'

Jessica swallowed hard, tasting her friend's bitterness, her own worthlessness. 'Goodbye, Maria. I hope you feel better soon.'

* * *

Michael was waiting with Nick by the coffee machine in the hall next to the waiting room when Jessica reappeared. Ordinarily Michael did not drink coffee; it gave him heartburn. But since he had been staying awake all night worrying whether a girl was going to lose her life or not, he had considered it sort of absurd to be concerned about minor gastric upset. This was his eighth cup since three o'clock in the morning. Nick had just downed his tenth.

Jessica was crying. Nick grabbed her as she tried to pass them by without stopping. 'What's wrong with Maria?' he demanded. 'Did she die?'

Jessica stared at him, her eyes big and red. She shook her head weakly. 'She wants to see you now.'

Nick let go of her and dashed down the hall. Jessica took a couple of feeble steps forward and then sagged against the wall. Michael put down his coffee and placed his palms on her back, over her soft brown hair, feeling her shiver. 'Tell me, Jessie?'

'The fall cut her spinal cord.'

'You're sure?'

'Yes.'

He had feared as much. 'That's very sad. But it's not the end of the world for her. She can live a full life. But she's going to need a lot of support. I know you have a lot to give her.'

Jessica stood upright, looked at him, her face a mess with tears. 'She hates me.'

'What? No.'

'She told me she wishes it was me who was crippled instead of her.'

'She didn't mean it. She's just upset. Tomorrow—'

'There won't be any tomorrow!' Jessica cried. 'I told you, she hates me! She doesn't want to see me again. She blames me for what happened to her.'

'She came out of surgery two hours ago. You can't take what she says seriously. You didn't do anything to her. You're her friend.'

'Like I'm your friend, Michael?' She shook loose of his hands. 'You don't know who I am. I screw you left and right and you think I'm Miss Pretty Perfect. Well, I'm not. I don't give a damn about anybody except myself.'

'We all watch out for ourselves. We have to because most of the time it seems no one is watching out for us. I know how you feel. You're not a bad person.' He took a breath. 'If you were, I wouldn't care about you the way—'

'No!' she interrupted. 'It's all true. Everything I touch gets ruined. Alice and Maria and Clair – I do it on purpose I think!'

'Stop it. You're carrying on exactly like I did after the funeral.' He lowered his voice, tried to hold her. 'Jessie, listen to me, I need to tell you something.'

'No,' she moaned, pushing him away. 'Don't touch me. Don't get near me. I'm no good, Michael. I'm not.'

'Jessie?'

She wouldn't listen. She turned and fled down the hall. He didn't go after her. Had people chased after him during the days following Alice's party, he might have killed them. He would leave her alone, maybe for ever. He would remain alone.

Nick returned a few minutes later. He was pale as a ghost. 'Does she hate you, too?' Michael asked wearily.

Nick fell down in a chair. 'She wants the person who tampered with the float,' he said. 'She's flipped out. She thinks there's a plot against her.'

'Anything else?'

Nick nodded heavily. 'She told me to find those responsible. She threatened me if I didn't.'

'How?'

Nick bowed his head. 'She said if I didn't do what she wanted, she would tell the police I was running down the stairs, away from the bedroom, right after the gun was fired at the party.'

'That's true?'

'Yeah,' he croaked. 'I lied to you before. I was afraid the police would hear that and think I'd killed Alice.'

It was Michael's turn to use the wall for support. 'Why were you running downstairs?'

'I thought the gunshot came from there.' He shook his head miserably. 'I don't know, I was scared. I'm sorry, Mike.'

Kats also thought the shot came from downstairs.

Michael pulled himself off the wall and slapped Nick on the back. 'Stay with her, buddy. Love her. It's the best anybody can do. I'm going home.'

Nick nodded pitifully, beginning to weep. 'She can't feel anything in her legs. Nothing from the waist down.'

'I know. I wish—' He wished a thousand wishes, but it didn't make any difference. There was nothing he could say. He left Nick and headed for the parking lot, where he climbed into his car. About to start the engine, he noticed Temple High's yearbook on the passenger seat. On impulse, he reached over and began to browse through it again. He hadn't really searched the book thoroughly the first time. Perhaps . . .

It could have been coincidence, like Kats and Nick both running the wrong way towards a gunshot they were closer to than anyone else.

Michael found Clark in a group photo on the lower

right-hand corner of the first page he turned to. It was a black-and-white, and the bright green eyes and red hair were not in evidence. But it was the bastard; there was no mistaking that twisted grin.

The picture had several people in it. None of them were identified at the bottom by name. Michael flipped to the end of the junior class and studied the list of names of kids who hadn't posed for pictures. There was only one Clark.

Clark Halley.

We're going to have a talk, guy. A long talk.

THE GRADUATION

CHAPTER 1

The last day of school began early for Sara Cantrell. As ASB president, she had inherited the job of passing out the yearbooks. No one else had wanted to do it. The task called for a crack-of-dawn rising. The books had only arrived the night before and had to be unpacked and sorted into alphabetical order. The yearbook club had been late sending the book to the printers. There had been some concern – so the rumour went – about the quality of the athletic photographs.

The price of vanity. Did I not say it months ago?

Sara smiled with glee as she squatted on the floor of the recently reconstructed snack bar and tore open one of the boxes and pulled out a copy of the annual. The cover was dark blue, featureless except for a silver name tag on the top and a tiny gold rope emblem in the lower right corner, which Sara had to assume bore some relationship to Tabb High's bronco-bull mascot. Quickly she turned to the sports section. A moment later she was laughing her head off.

'Where are your glasses, Jessie?' 'Bug off, Sara.'

In the basketball section in particular, and to a lesser extent throughout the football and wrestling pages, every other picture looked as if it had been shot underwater. There was a blurred photograph of Nick Grutler going to the basket with what could have been a swollen pumpkin in his hand.

'I love it,' Sara said aloud, noting something else unusual about the basketball section. Michael Olson, who had been dropped from the team at the start of the season, was in more pictures than anyone else. And a couple of those were remarkably sharp. Jessica must have slipped on her glasses for a second here and there during the game against Holden High, Sara decided. No doubt there was going to be talk when the rest of the basketball players saw how he had been favoured.

They'll talk all day, and talk all night. Then nobody will see anybody again.

The graduation ceremony was to be held at three in the afternoon in the football stadium. The time had been moved up to accommodate nearby Sanders High's ceremony. Sanders's stadium was undergoing major renovations. Sara thought it was a bum rap that Sanders's ceremony wasn't first. She would have the sun directly in her eyes when she addressed the stands. She still hadn't figured out exactly what she was going to say in her speech, although she had stayed up half the night worrying about it. She simply had too much on her mind. There was the all-night party aboard the cruise ship she still had to pay for, and then there was Russ Desmond. Last Christmas he had been sent to a juvenile hall in northern California for chopping down the varsity tree, which fell on the snack bar. He was being released – temporarily – to attend graduation and receive his diploma. She was supposed to pick him up in downtown LA at the bus station at one o'clock. She hadn't seen him in over five months.

He's probably forgotten what I look like.

Sara set aside the yearbook and, with a razor blade, began to cut open the boxes. Although the books had not been packed alphabetically, she was pleased to see they had been grouped according to class, simplifying her job somewhat. But there was still a lot to do. Tabb High had a student body of over two thousand, and more than half had ordered annuals. She wished she had Jessica to help her, the new clear-sighted Jessie who now wore her glasses wherever she went. But her best friend, bless her lazy hide, was getting her full measure of beauty sleep this morning.

The first knock at the window came two hours later, an hour earlier than Sara had anticipated – she had less than half the annuals unpacked. Two junior girls wanted their books *now*. Sara had no sooner found them than two more students arrived. It must have been because it was the last day – no one came to school this early usually. From that time on she was running. She quickly gave up checking receipts and IDs. If anyone felt he needed to steal a yearbook to be happy, she wasn't going to stand in the way.

Fortunately, before the big rush started around eight-thirty, three sophomores on the student council came to her rescue. Now she was able to take people's names and call them out to her helpers, who would hand her the right book a moment later.

Michael Olson and Clair Hilrey appeared at eight forty-five.

Sara had seen neither of them since January. Both had chosen to leave school at the semester. Apparently both had had enough units; and that was all that mattered, although Michael's GPA must have been about twice Clair's. The word going around was that Clair was making big bucks modelling and Michael was working for the government on some top-secret space laser. But, Sara knew, you couldn't believe everything you heard, although Clair had been on the cover of the May issue of *Seventeen*. Looked pretty damn good, too, and hadn't Jessica scowled when she had seen *that* magazine.

Clair had on baggy white shorts and a thin red blouse, perfect for the weather – the temperature was already close to eighty. She'd always had a tan, even in December, but now she was chestnut brown. It went without saying she was gorgeous.

Michael looked different. It was possible he hadn't cut his hair once since he'd left school. Black as night, and now curly, it hung way past his collar, practically on to his shoulders. He had lost weight, especially in his face. He appeared more handsome than she remembered, less a boy, more serious.

'Hi, Mike,' Sara said. 'Hi, Clair. Been a long time. How are you both doing?'

'We're just as happy as can be.' Clair giggled, squeezing Michael's arm. Michael smiled faintly and nodded.

'It's good to see you, Sara,' he said. 'Busy?'

She glanced past them at the line. 'Yeah, but I can take a minute off.' She called behind her, 'Michael Olson and Clair Hilrey. They're both seniors. And, Lori, take the window for a second.' She had their books a few seconds later and carried them with her as she slipped out the side door of the snack bar. The carpenters were still working on the building's south wall; it was covered with plastic instead of stucco. The varsity tree had been awfully heavy.

Clair immediately opened her yearbook to the homecoming court pictures. Michael peered at the page over her shoulder. Clair made a face.

'That photographer – what an amateur,' she complained.

'You look fine to me,' Michael said.

'I'm supposed to look sexy, not fine,' Clair said. She studied the page a little more, then added reluctantly, 'But that is a nice picture of Jessica.'

'Very nice,' Michael agreed.

'Have you seen Jessie, Mike?' Sara asked. Clair quickly glanced over her shoulder at Michael.

'I've got to go,' she said, suddenly closing the book. 'I've got to find Bubba. Nice to see you Sara.'

'Catch you at graduation,' Sara said.

'I'll be along in a minute,' Michael told Clair. When she was gone, he said, 'No, I just got here. How's she been?'

'Great,' Sara said, which was something of an exaggeration. After Maria Gonzales's crippling accident the night of the homecoming dance, Jessica had gone into as deep a depression as she had when Alice died. She hadn't even returned to school after Christmas vacation to finish the semester. If Sara hadn't brought her work to her, Jessica might have flunked out. Her spirits had improved somewhat when she finally returned at the start of the new semester. Yet Sara continued to worry about her. Jessica wasn't interested in going to the movies, going shopping – hardly anything any more. Sara had had to use every bit of her considerable persuasive skills to talk her into going to the senior prom in May with Bill Skater. Afterwards Jessica told her she'd had a wonderful time, but Sara didn't quite believe her. Jessica hadn't gone out with Bill since.

Not returning to school until the beginning of February, Jessica had missed Michael Olson's last days at Tabb. Sara remembered how Jessica's face fell when she had heard Michael was gone. To this day, however, Jessica denied they were close or that she cared one way or the other about him.

'She's doing real good,' Sara continued. 'She should be here any minute. Why don't you wait for her?'

He looked doubtful. 'I have a lot to do today.'

'But you're coming to the ceremony this afternoon, aren't you? I heard you're valedictorian?'

He smiled faintly at the mention of the word. 'Yeah, it looks like I am. I have to give a speech.'

'You're not the only one. Well, that's great. I'll get to introduce you. But I wish you could stay now. She should be here any sec. I know she'd love to see you.'

He glanced down at the closed yearbook in his hands. 'I really can't wait. But say hello to her for me.'

'I will.' She was trying to get rid of the habit of talking people into stuff. Russ had told her – before they had locked him up – that it was one of her least desirable personality traits. On the other hand, she didn't believe Michael couldn't wait a few minutes, any more than she believed Jessica when she had said it was no big deal that Michael had left school early. 'She's as pretty as ever,' she added.

Michael smiled politely. 'I don't doubt it.' He turned to leave. 'I'll be back this afternoon for the ceremony.'

'Hey, hold on. Let me sign your yearbook.'

'Sure.' He handed it over. 'Where's yours?'

'I've been so busy with everybody else's, I haven't had a chance to look for my own. You can sign it later on the boat. You're coming to the all-night party, aren't you?'

He hesitated, spoke under his breath. 'If need be.'

'Huh?'

'I don't know. I didn't buy a ticket.'

She pulled a ticket from her back pocket and gave it to him. 'It's on the house. The party won't be complete without our class genius.' She clicked out her ballpoint pen and turned to one of the blank pages at the back of his yearbook. 'I promise not to write anything disgusting,' she said.

'Don't let me stop you,' he remarked, stuffing the ticket into his back pocket and scanning the half-filled courtyard. Sara thought for a moment and then wrote.

Mike,

Of all the people in the school, you're the only one I wish I knew better. All the rest, I wish I could forget. Just kidding! What I really mean is, I'll never forget you. You're so smart! Figure out how to be happy and then tell the rest of us miserable slobs. We're counting on you.

Luv, Sara

She returned his yearbook, saying, 'Read it later tonight, preferably when you're drunk.'

He nodded. 'Thanks for the free ticket.'

Sara hugged him briefly. 'I'm so glad you're here. I think we're going to have a wild time today.'

'I think so, too.'

Michael left and Sara returned to distributing the

yearbooks at the snack bar window. Bubba put in a typical annoying appearance ten minutes later. He didn't have to say or do anything. Just the sight of him irritated Sara. It had been Bubba who had talked her into renting the cruise ship for the all-night party, even when he had known it was way beyond their means. She was beginning to believe he was purposely prolonging her personal crisis with the school funds to keep her dependent on him. After the homecoming dance, he had continued to pay her creditors just enough to keep them from suing, but not enough to make them go away. Lately he had been hinting at a scheme that would clear up all her money worries. Of course he hadn't said what it was.

'Come for your book?' she asked wearily. The predicted temperature for the day was a muggy ninety-five and Bubba had on an immaculate pair of light blue slacks, a navy-blue sports jacket and a red and white striped tie. His choice of hat that day was a wide-brimmed straw sombrero. He looked positively ridiculous and was loving every minute of it.

'No, I've come for you to sign it,' he replied, lifting up his yearbook from beneath the counter. The silver name tag on the top read – in unusually big letters – BUBBA.

'Where did you get that?' she demanded. 'I didn't give you that.'

'I was sent an advance copy.' He produced a feathered quill pen. 'While you're signing mine, may I have the pleasure of brightening yours with a few words of love?'

'No. Go away, I'm busy.'

Bubba glanced at the line behind him, smiled. 'No time for Bubba on this, our last day of school? No time to share a precious moment to express our unspoken feeling for each other? Surely you must realise that an occasion such as this—'

'Stop it! I'll sign your stupid book. Lori, fetch my annual, and then do me a favour and take the window again. Thanks.'

She met Bubba outside in the same spot she had spoken to Michael and Clair. Before handing over her annual, she said, 'I talked the captain of the ship into taking a postdated cheque like you told me to. Now I want to know if the cheque will clear?'

'It should.'

'What? Two days ago you told me it definitely would!'

'I do not believe I used the word "definite". The only things definite in this world are death, taxes and my good humour.'

'But my name's on that cheque!'

'Better your name than mine.'

'Why are you doing this to me? What have I ever done to you?'

Bubba chuckled. 'I've done nothing you haven't asked me to. You wanted a party the class wouldn't forget, and I told you how to give them one. I'm only here to serve, Sara.'

She started to yell at him again, but couldn't think of anything to say. To her immense horror, she realised it was because what he said was partially true. He'd had no trouble putting her out on another financial limb. All he'd had to do was dangle before her nose another way to impress the school with what a fantastic president Sara Cantrell was.

'How are you serving me this week?' she asked. 'Where's the school money?'

'I'd prefer not to say at this moment.'

'Why not?'

'I'd rather not make you more nervous than you already are.'

'What kind of answer is that? Where's the money?' Sara asked again.

'Do you like basketball?'

'Yeah, it's all right.'

'The seventh game of the NBA finals is tonight. The Lakers versus the Celtics. A classic matchup. I grew up with the Lakers. They're my team. I know them better than their own coach.'

'Wait a second. You didn't bet our money on a basketball game?'

'I was given excellent odds. We'll double our investment if we win.'

'What if we lose?' she screamed.

He shrugged. 'We'll still have our good looks.' He held up his yearbook and offered her a regular ballpoint pen. 'You don't have to go overboard. A few paragraphs and a poem or two will suffice to let me know you care.'

Bubba came very close at that moment to losing whatever good looks he believed he might have. Sara almost poked his eyes out. Only because she was essentially a non-violent person did she grab his yearbook and pen instead. Inadvertently she let him get hold of her annual in the process. She plopped down on a nearby bench and began to scribble furiously on a back page.

Bubba,

Words, even the filthiest, cannot convey what I think of you. You are a liar, a thief and a pervert. You are also the most unattractive slob to ever abuse my eyesight. I consider it the greatest misfortune of my adolescence that I had a chance to get to know you. You will not go far. You will end up in the mud – where you belong – with the rest of the world's slime.

Get There As Soon As Possible,
Sara

When she looked up, Bubba had vanished. He reappeared a couple of minutes later, her annual in his hand, a beatific smile on his lips. She snatched her book back and tossed him his. He read her inscription with obvious pleasure.

'You have beautiful handwriting,' he said. 'Very sensual.'

'Go to hell.'

'Later.' He grinned as he walked away. 'Later, Sara.'

She was back inside the snack bar when she opened her yearbook. Her scream frightened everyone. Bubba had covered the entire inside cover with fat black marking-pen letters. There was no way to tear out the page. She shook as she read it.

My Dearest Sara,

My heart patters at the thought of us making love tonight above the deep ocean swells, our bodies locked in passion, the salty sweat on the burning flesh of our entangled limbs mingling like oil and wine, ready to burst into flaming ecstasy. My head swoons. Tonight, Sara, I promise you, will be our night. The gods will envy our joy.

But we mustn't be foolish. We mustn't forget, in our carnal hunger for each other, certain responsibilities. You would rather float on love-intoxicated perfumed clouds, I realise, ignoring the practical demands the world places upon us, only fantasising about the pleasure I will send throbbing through your body. Yet we have to be careful. We can have our cake and eat it, too, but only if we don't let the ice cream melt. We have to get some condoms.

As you have probably guessed, anything that will heighten our delight is fine with me. I prefer the natural to the artificial, the tight to the loose, blue to red. Keep this in mind when you visit the pharmacy, Sara, and you will be thanked a thousand times over when the time comes.

Love You Always,

In So Many Different Positions,

Bubba

P.S. Or, if you'd like, I can pick up something on the way to the boat?

'What is it?' Lori asked, standing beside her.

If the Lakers should win, would he keep the money if I don't come across?

Stupid question.

Sara slammed the book shut and answered Lori. 'Don't ask.'

CHAPTER 2

Michael had never seen Clair so happy. As they walked the familiar hallways searching for Bubba, she kept glancing over at him and giggling.

'What is it?' he asked finally.

'I have a secret I want tell you, but I can't.'

'What if I promise to tell no one else?'

'I still can't tell you. Bubba would kill me.'

'He knows the secret?'

'He knows everything.' Clair giggled again and grabbed his arm. 'Everything!'

'How come he doesn't know we're looking for him?'

She smiled, her blue eyes clear and bright. 'Maybe he's trying to avoid us.'

'That's probably the truth. How's the modelling coming? Is Bubba really acting as your agent?'

'Yeah, and he's doing a great job. I'm shooting an ad

for Nabisco next Monday, and on Wednesday I'm starring in a video with Killer Kids.'

'Is that a heavy metal group?'

'Punk. Their music stinks but the pay's great. I'm making so much money! Bubba's investing it for me.'

'Legally, I hope.'

She laughed easily, still holding on to him. He didn't understand why she liked him so much, unless it had to do with stuff Bubba had told her, which was hard to imagine. He regretted his initial low opinion of her. She was really very sweet.

'How about you?' she asked. 'I hear you're working at JPL?'

He had not planned to leave school in January. But after Maria's accident and Jessica's subsequent disappearance, he began to feel that Tabb High had lost whatever charm it had once possessed. From his freshman year on he had taken a heavy load. He had more than enough units to call it quits. Plus Mr Gregory, his MGM (Mentally Gifted Minors) adviser, had helped him land another workstudy position at Jet Propulsion Laboratory. The job was only twenty hours a week, so he hadn't quit his job at the 7-Eleven to take it – much to the relief of the store owners. The JPL job came with the impressive title aeronautics intern, but it amounted to little more than errand boy to the engineers. It was not that he wasn't learning. Often he was allowed to sit in on discussions relating to the design of future spacecraft, both manned and unmanned. The problem was, the experience was boring him.

Throughout his school days, he had seen himself as a budding scientist. Now he was finding out that the entire analytic approach to the universe left him feeling cold and unsatisfied. This was a critical discovery; it completely threw off his future plans. He no longer knew what he should study in college, or even *if* he should go to college. Looking around at the other kids in his class hanging out in the hallway, signing one another's yearbooks and gossiping about how loaded they were going to get on the ship, he wondered if he was the only one who felt confused. He often wondered that – why he felt so different from everybody else.

'Yeah. The rocket and space business is OK,' he replied. 'But I've been thinking of starting my own rock-and-roll band. Would you like to front it for me?'

Clair was amused. 'I'm totally tone deaf.'

'But you can dance. That's all that matters.'

'You should get Jessie. She's got a great voice. She's singing at the ceremony this afternoon.' She stopped, obviously afraid she might have offended him somehow. 'I'm sorry, Mike.'

'No problem. That's neat, she'll be in the ceremony and all.'

Clair was watching him. 'You never talk to her any more, do you?'

He shrugged, feeling uncomfortable. Bubba must have told Clair how he felt about Jessica. 'I never see her.'

'You'll see her today.'

'I guess.'

'Look, I'm being nosy.'

'No.'

'Well, then, talk to her today. Hey, I said a lot of nasty things about her before – and I still think she deserved them – but she *is* a classy chick. She really likes you.'

Curiosity got the best of him 'What makes you say that? You haven't seen her in six months.'

'I can tell.' She leaned closer. 'Do you want me to tell her?'

'Tell her what?'

Clair reconsidered. 'Nothing.'

'What?' he insisted.

She grinned mischievously. 'Nothing.'

'Clair.'

She shook her head. 'I won't say anything.' But she had

to add, 'As long as you say something.'

'You've been hanging around Bubba too long. That sounds like a threat.'

She gave him a quick kiss on the cheek and began to bounce away. 'I've got to talk to my pals on the cheerleading squad. If you run into him before me, tell him I went to look for them in the gym. Think about what I said!'

'You remember what *I* said,' he called after her, embarrassed.

He continued to search for Bubba. The first period bell would ring in a few minutes, but he doubted that many kids would be heading to class. As usual on the last day of school, there was a party atmosphere all over campus. He observed it without feeling it. The hot weather contributed to his mood. He remembered how it had been hot the day he had met Jessica.

Am I looking for Bubba or trying to hide from Jessie?

He bumped into Nick Grutler next outside. They had kept in touch: regular telephone calls, occasional one-on-one basketball games. Tabb High had finished first in the league for the second straight year. Some people were saying Coach Sellers was a genius. None of those people had been on the team. The title belonged to Nick. Come next fall, he would be attending UCLA on a full athletic scholarship. Michael was proud of him.

'Does the old school still look the same?' Nick asked.

'Hey, I haven't been gone that long.' Nick had been heading in the direction of the parking lot. 'Where you going?'

Nick averted his eyes. He had gained a great deal of confidence since he had stumbled stuttering into the 7-Eleven at the end of the first week of school, but when he was troubled, he reverted to his old habit and looked away. 'Maria's coming to the graduation ceremony,' he said. 'I'm picking her up at the rehabilitation clinic in San Diego.'

'How is she?' He knew Nick hadn't seen Maria since she had been discharged from the hospital in February to the spinal injury clinic to begin rebuilding her body. But Nick had talked to her on the phone, although he wouldn't say what they talked about.

'I don't know,' Nick said.

'Does Jessie or Sara know she's coming?'

'No.'

'I wonder if someone should tell them?'

'I think Maria wants it to be a surprise.'

'Why?'

Nick shook his head. 'I guess none of us can know what it feels like to be suddenly crippled.'

Michael knew he was trying to make excuses for her ahead of time, and felt bad for him. 'Tell her I'm looking forward to seeing her again.'

Nick nodded. 'I will, Mike.' He glanced at his watch. He had one now – and a car. His dad had begun to let him hold on to his money, or else the college recruiters had been very generous. 'I better go.'

They exchanged goodbyes. Michael decided he might find Bubba in the computer room. He spotted Polly McCoy as he was on his way there. A talk with Polly was on his list of things to do.

She was sitting by herself on a bench outside on the far side of the girls' shower room. Her dark hair hung long, straighter than before. The weight she had lost following Alice's death had not returned; if anything, she was thinner. She glanced up as he approached, her eyes dark and uncertain. She had been studying her palm.

'Hi,' she said.

'Hi, Polly. How are you?'

'Fine . . .' The word trailed from her lips. Then she blinked. 'Mike, it's you. Where have you been?'

He sat beside her on the green wooden bench. Her blue jeans were old, skintight, her white lace blouse long and loose. She had bitten her nails down a fraction too far. The only make-up she wore was lipstick, thick and red.

'I finished school at the semester,' he said. 'Didn't you know?'

'Jessie didn't tell me. She never tells me anything.'

He forced a smile. 'I don't think *I* told Jessie. What are you doing way over here in the middle of nowhere?'

'I have a headache.'

'Oh, that's a shame. Is it bad?'

'No. It's long.'

'Long?' Mike asked.

'I've had it a couple of months.' She paused. 'I've missed seeing you. I'm glad you've come back to school.'

'She was outside when the gun went off. We're sure of that, aren't we?'

He had asked Jessica that question six months ago. The answer was still yes. That was a fact. But he still didn't trust Polly. 'Just for the day. You must be excited about graduating?'

'I'm glad it's almost over.' She glanced down at her hands and wove her fingers together. She answered his initial question again. 'I like to be alone.'

'Do you want me to go?'

'No. But why do you want to talk to me?'

'I like talking to you.'

'Did you find him?'

'Find who?' He knew who she was talking about.

'Clark.'

'No,' he lied. He had found him, he just hadn't spoken to him. He planned to do so today. 'Does he know I'm looking for him?' he asked carefully, his heartbeat accelerating.

'I think so,' she said, her expression dreamy.

'So you've seen him?'

'Not in a long time.'

'When was the last time, Polly?'

'A long time ago.'

'You don't remember?'

She jerked slightly, then frowned, concentrating. 'It was the night Aunty died. It was raining.'

The sun shone bright in their faces, rebounding off the light brown wall at their backs. Michael realised that he was sweating.

Her aunt had died the night of homecoming, but there had been no storm. And since then, Polly had been alone. The court had not appointed her another guardian; apparently she was over eighteen.

'What did he do?' Michael asked, referring to Clark.

'The doctor said she died of natural causes.'

'Your aunt?'

'You don't think he killed her, do you?' She could have been talking to herself. 'I know you think he killed Alice. That's why you're looking for him. But he says he didn't.'

'He told you that?' Michael asked.

'Yes.'

'Do you believe him?' She looked him straight in the eye. Her dreaminess lessened. Indeed, she seemed suddenly cautious. 'I do.'

'But was he there, the night of the party?'

'He said something about coming at the end.'

Michael could hardly contain his excitement. 'Was he up in the bedroom when Alice died?'

She became slightly annoyed. 'Why are you asking all these questions? I told you, I have a headache.'

'I'm sorry, I was sort of pushy. Let me ask just a couple more and then I'll help you find an aspirin.'

'I don't take aspirin. They make your stomach bleed. I have to save my blood to donate to the hospital.'

'Was Clark in the room with Alice just before she died?'

'No. He left when I left.' She put a hand to her temple – as she had done when he visited her last winter – and paled. 'I wish you'd stop. Please stop.'

It drove him nuts, to be so close and yet so far. 'I have

to ask you, Polly, if I'm ever to clear Alice's name.'

'She's dead. She doesn't care about her name. The dead don't care about anything. The only one who cares is me.'

'That's not true. I care.'

She paused, surprised. 'You do?'

'I really do, Polly.'

She thought for a moment, then looked away. 'Don't go to the all-night party, Mike.'

'Why not?'

'Clark might come,' she answered.

'Did he tell you he was coming?'

'No.'

'Then why do you think he will?'

'I . . . I feel it. It's a bad feeling.'

'But I want to talk to him.'

Polly shook her head. 'He won't talk to you.'

'What will he do?'

'I don't know,' she said, standing, obviously upset. 'Excuse me, but I have to go to the bathroom.' She looked right and left, confused. 'I hate this school. I come here and Alice shoots herself and then Aunty chokes on a pillow. It's an awful place. It makes me want to throw up.'

'Polly,' he began.

'Just don't get too close,' she cried, running away.

Michael wondered if anything she had told him had been accurate.

Bubba appeared a minute later, dressed to kill, except for an oversize sombrero that bobbled around on his head. Michael had not seen him in over a month. Bubba had lost a few pounds. Must be Clair's doing. He sat beside Michael on the bench, a brown paper bag in his right hand, his yearbook in the left. Michael knew what was in the bag. He immediately glanced all around.

'We're alone,' Bubba said.

Michael nodded at the sack. 'You got it?'

'I got it. Are you sure you want it?'

'Where did you get it?'

'Kats,' Bubba said.

'Bubba! I told you no one is supposed to know.'

'You only gave me a few days. Besides, I fed Kats a good story. Don't worry.' Bubba glanced at the bag, appearing a tad worried himself. 'You know, Mike, you're a smart guy, but I know a lot of smart guys who have done stupid things with one of these.'

'I'll be fine.'

'If you'd tell me what you want it for, I might be able to give you some sage advice to keep you out of jail.'

Michael held out his hand. 'The less you know, the better for you.'

Bubba reluctantly gave him the package. 'Everything's inside. The keys, too.'

Earlier in the week Michael had asked Bubba to slip into Polly's school locker, borrow her purse and make a copy of her house keys. Michael wanted another look at the bedroom where Alice had died, but wasn't fond of the idea of breaking into the McCoy residence. 'I appreciate it.'

'What are Bubbas for? I hear Maria's coming to the ceremony.'

'Did Nick tell you?'

'No. A confidential source. Do you have your speech ready?'

'I haven't given it a moment's thought. Hey, what am I doing as valedictorian anyway? What happened to Dale Jensen? Did he get a C in a class or what?'

'He got busted.'

'When? How?'

'Tuesday night. Remember that narc that was hassling Nick before Christmas? Randy Meisser?'

'Yeah. You said you were going to run him off campus.'

'I changed my mind. Thought he might come in useful. He busted Dale snorting coke in a bathroom.' Bubba took off his hat and fanned himself. 'We can't have an ill-mannered druggie giving any long-winded speeches on graduation day. Not when it's hot like this.'

Michael sighed. 'You set Dale up.'

'I may have put the white powder beneath his nose, but I did not force him to inhale.'

'Were his parents able to bail him out?'

'Yes, and weren't they embarrassed. Relatives flying in from the Midwest and all. Would you like me to write your speech for you?'

'No, thank you.' Michael stood up, gripping the bag, testing its weight. 'Clair's in the gym. She wants to talk to you. You probably know that, right?'

'Of course.' Bubba got up, too, brushing off the seat of his trousers.

'She said she had a secret to tell me.'

Bubba raised an eyebrow. 'Did she tell you?'

'No.'

He nodded. 'She's a good girl. Did you know Kats will be receiving a diploma today?'

'He mentioned something like that once.'

'He's also coming with us on our cruise to Catalina.'

'Wonderful.'

Bubba smiled. 'He might surprise you. He might just be the life of the party.'

Michael had what he had come for. He had a great deal to accomplish before he returned to the campus at three. He bade Bubba goodbye and hurried towards the parking lot. Crossing the courtyard, extremely conscious of the sack in his hand, he spotted Jessica talking to Sara outside the snack bar. He practically dropped the sack. He stepped behind a tree, peeping around like a frightened lowlife.

'No. Don't touch me. Don't get near me. I'm no good, Michael. I'm not.'

Her brown hair and brown eyes. He always saw them first. Long and silky, big and round. Then would come her smile. Yet she was not smiling now. She was as pretty as ever, but it seemed to him, even at a glance, that she didn't smile as often as she had. She was no longer the young girl who had almost wept over the grape juice he had spilled on her sweater.

Her clothes were seductive now – as was her body. She had on a short green skirt and thin yellow blouse. Her legs were every bit as tanned as Clair's. He had dreamed about them the last few months, along with the rest of her body.

Love would not care. It should not care.

Yet Michael did not feel guilt over his sexual desire for Jessica. It was natural, he realised. He could not separate who she was from her body. He didn't want to.

I just want her.

But she did not want him. Bill came up to talk to her then. He put a hand on her shoulder. Now she smiled.

Michael left quickly for the parking lot. In his car he removed the gun from the brown paper bag and opened the box of shells. Pressing the bullets into the clip of the automatic weapon, he wondered if maybe he should have waited for Jessica as Sara had suggested. If maybe Bubba was right, and he was stupid.

He put the loaded automatic in the glove compartment and drove away.

CHAPTER 3

Jessica Hart was thinking of winning and losing. She had begun the year at Tabb optimistically. She had figured she would earn outstanding grades, be nominated homecoming queen, get accepted to Stanford, fall in love with a cute boy and enjoy the respect and goodwill of all she met. She hadn't thought she was asking for more than her fair share.

And none of those things came to me. Not one.

She had received a C in chemistry, the same grade she would receive on her report card. She hadn't been able to find a lab partner after Maria got hurt. Her overall grade-point average for the year was a C-plus. In a class of four hundred and sixty-four, she was graduating somewhere in the mid-two hundreds. The ranking would have been lower if they'd averaged in her SAT score.

Her father had held back her application for Stanford.

Maybe after a couple of years at a local junior college, he said. Junior college – it would be like going to summer camp after expecting to climb Mount Everest. Her father had been so disappointed in her. Sara was heading to Princeton.

She had found a boy she sort of liked – good old Bill. But he wasn't a real boyfriend. They'd only been out three times. She didn't love him and she seriously doubted he loved her. She was beginning to doubt there really was such a thing as love. Sex, yeah – she was as horny as anybody else. But where were the couples who cared more for each other than for themselves? She couldn't find them. All she saw around her were boys and girls struggling to boost their egos at the expense of those they supposedly adored. She despised it, particularly since she wanted to do the same thing.

The year died when Alice died. I should have written it off right then and quit.

'I love this material,' Jessica said to Bill, feeling the upper sleeve of his red shirt. 'It feels like silk.'

'It is,' he replied. 'My mother bought it for me.'

'For a graduation present?' she asked.

He nodded. 'Yeah, and I got a car. A Corvette.'

'I hope to God it matches your shirt,' Sara said. Sara had just given them each a copy of the new yearbook.

Jessica had no desire to open it; she knew all too well what most of her photographs looked like. The yearbook club had been very disappointed in her. Had they not been so desperately short of football and basketball pictures, they probably would have trashed all her 'pre-glasses material'. She didn't care, she told herself, but it did bother her. So, maybe, she really did care. Letting go of Bill's shirt, she pushed her glasses back on her nose. She was never going to get used to wearing them. She hoped the sun burned out soon and everyone could walk around blind with her in the dark.

'It's black,' Bill said seriously. 'It goes with everything.'

Sara winked at Jessica and patted her hair. 'My colour co-ordinator says I absolutely should never be seen in a black car.'

'That's too bad,' Bill said.

'Our parents are sending us to Hawaii next week for our graduation presents,' Jessica said, wanting to stop Sara before she got started. Because Polly was now off-limits, Sara got her kicks out of ridiculing Bill. Jessica hated it that he never even knew it was happening. 'Isn't that neat?'

'They've got great surfing there,' Bill said.

'It's the waves,' Sara said confidentially. 'Something to do with the waves.'

'Yeah, that has a lot to do with it,' Bill agreed.

'Bill, could you do me a favour?' Jessica said, clearing her throat and looking pointedly at Sara. 'Could you get me a book from my locker?'

'Sure. Did you want one in particular?'

No, any old book will do. Just make sure it has pages, a cover, words in it – the usual.

In reality, she didn't care what book he got. She just wanted to talk to Sara alone.

'My political science book,' she said.

'We handed those in to Mr Bark yesterday,' Sara said. 'Get her something else. Get her a brush.'

'Do you want a brush?' Bill asked, and now even he was beginning to wonder.

But Jessica kept a straight face. 'Yeah, I'd appreciate it,' she said.

When Bill was gone, Sara said, 'He's lucky he's so good-looking or we'd have to have him stuffed.'

'Leave him alone, he's all right.'

'Oh, I think he's great. I love him. I can see why you love him.'

'Right, my feelings go real deep.'

Sara laughed. 'Hope it goes plenty deep tonight.' She leaned close, her excitement barely concealed. 'You know how I told you the captain wanted the passenger suites on the ship kept locked and off-limits? Well, last night I had a long talk with him and arranged for the use of a couple of adjacent rooms. I've got the keys. Isn't that great? Everything's set.'

Jessica was not sure why she was doing this. She supposed that like anything else, virginity got old after a while and – like a hundred per cent of the young ladies in her present situation – she'd been a virgin since she was born. Once she had imagined that when she finally did give herself to a guy, it would be to someone she really cared about. She guessed hormones and biology had finally caught up with her. Now all she wanted was to have a good time.

It's all I can hope for at this point.

That was closer to the truth. She wanted a lot more than a roll in the hay, but she felt – until something better came along – that this would give her life spark. The flatness of each day was becoming almost unbearable.

Yet she hoped boredom was all there was to it. She hoped she wasn't attempting to seduce Bill in an effort to prove to herself beyond a shadow of a doubt that she really didn't care about anything.

That was a frightening thought.

And what was even more frightening was that she recognised her self-destructive streak, and its source, and still wasn't able to free herself from it. She had not killed Alice. She had not crippled Maria. She had not chased Michael from school. But somehow she felt as if she had *allowed* all those terrible things to happen. As if she should have known ahead of time. As if someone had been trying to warn her of the dangers and she had not been listening.

Someone . . .

'Everything's set like hell,' Jessica said, forcing her thoughts back to Sara and trying to shake off her melancholy mood. 'We don't even know if we've got ingredient A.'

'Russ will be down. Bill's coming to the party. What's the problem? You think we can't seduce two eighteen-year-old boys?'

Jessica remembered back to senior prom night. Bill had kissed her long and hard in his car before dropping her off home, yet she couldn't have sworn they had been passionate kisses. He had made no move to grab her or even touch her. It had left her feeling frustrated and with all sorts of doubts about her own sexuality.

'I don't know if the shower routine is what we want,' Jessica said.

'What's wrong with it? We have every reason to be in the shower when they get to our rooms. People are dirty creatures – they're always taking showers. It won't look like a set-up. They'll see us naked, we'll squeal and the rest will be history.'

'Don't give me that confident BS. You're scared to death Russ will take one look at your bare ass and bust up laughing.'

Sara was insulted. 'What's wrong with my ass?'

'I don't know. I've never looked at it that closely. Christ, this is beginning to sound ridiculous. You would think we were hard up or something.'

'Yeah, isn't that a ridiculous thought.'

Then they laughed at how far past ridiculous they already were. Jessica began to feel a bit better. If nothing else, she had her best friend to share her misery with. Jessica nodded at Sara's yearbook.

'Let me sign it,' she said. 'And you can be the first person to sign mine.'

But Sara held her book back. 'Later. On the boat.'

'No, let's do it now.' Jessica reached out for it, and when Sara held it further away, Jessica naturally snatched it out of her hands. 'What's the problem with you. What's—' She stopped. Sara's yearbook had a crudely cut rectangle of brown paper pasted over the inside front cover. 'What is this?'

Sara grabbed her book back. 'I got a defective copy.'

'How can you get a defective yearbook for God sakes?'

'All of them are defective, Miss Fuzzy-Film Face.'

'Haven't you insulted me enough times about that already this year? I know what's wrong with your book. Somebody wrote something nasty in it.'

'Sure, yeah, who would do that?'

'Bubba. That's who. I know that's it.'

'I wouldn't let that slime touch my book if he didn't have any hands.'

'What did he write?'

'He didn't write anything!'

'Forget Russ and the shower. Bubba will do it with you no matter how many clothes you have on and no matter how flabby your ass is. What did he say?'

Sara sucked in a breath. 'I wish, Jessie, for the sake of our long and warm association that you would please change the goddamn subject.'

'OK. But you're right – the grease just sweats off that guy. Can you imagine why any girl would go to bed with him?'

'I try not to think about it.' Sara stared at the ground, thinking, chewing on her lower lip.

'What's the matter?'

'Nothing.'

'What?' Jessica persisted.

'I was wondering if I should tell you this.'

'Don't tell me. Play it safe. Keep it to yourself.'

'All right.'

'Sara?' she said, getting exasperated.

'Mike was here about half an hour ago.'

'Michael?' The strength went out of her. She had not been thinking of winning and losing. Only of losing. 'Why didn't you tell me?'

'You just got here.'

'But where is he?' She quickly scanned the courtyard, almost afraid to find him. 'Where did he go?'

'I don't know,' Sara said.

'What do you mean, you don't know? Which direction was he heading when he left you?'

'He went after Clair.'

'Clair's here, too?'

'Yeah.'

She swallowed. 'I don't care.'

'Jessie, of course you care.'

'I don't. So she's got her stupid face on the cover of some stupid magazine?'

'We're talking about Mike. You might be able to find him if you go look.'

'First period's going to start in a minute. I don't have time.' She shielded her eyes from the bright sun – it was going to be a cooker of an afternoon – searching harder. 'Why was he here?'

'He came to pick up his yearbook. He's going to be at the ceremony. He's valedictorian.'

'*What?* When did this happen? What happened to Jensen?'

'All I know is Mike is going to be giving the speech.'

'Since when have you known this?' Jessica pressed.

'Since yesterday,' Sara said.

'Why didn't you tell me?'

'You didn't ask me.'

'Why should I have to ask you?'

'Because you keep telling me you don't care.'

'I don't care. I mean, what's there to care about? He left school early. He didn't even say goodbye. I hardly knew him. How did he look?'

'Great.'

Jessica smiled. 'Did he?'

Sara smiled, too. 'Yeah. His hair's longer. He's got a tan.'

'I always wanted him to grow his hair.' She scratched her own hair. 'He wasn't with Clair, like in *with* her, was he?'

'No.'

Jessica bounced on her feet. 'I've got to find him. Talk to you later.'

'Good luck.'

Unfortunately, she had no luck at all. She was hurrying down the first hallway when she ran into Bubba. He had on a straw hat so huge it was causing traffic jams.

'Bubba, have you seen Michael?' she asked casually.

'He left already.'

'But he's coming back, right?'

Bubba showed a flicker of uncertainty. 'I hope so.' Then he grinned and reached out his hand. 'May I sign your yearbook, my dear?'

'Yeah.' She clasped it to her chest and looked at his fat ink-stained fingers. 'Later.'

CHAPTER 4

Ray Bradbury had written a short story called 'Rocket Man'. Michael had read it in junior high. It told of a man who piloted a rocket for a living. Most of the time he worked alone in space, but occasionally he returned home to earth. He had a wife and son, and although the story was largely told through the son's eyes, it was the wife's point of view that had stayed with Michael. It came to him as he stood in the cemetery at the foot of Alice McCoy's grave.

The wife always worried that her husband would crash into the moon, or die on Mars, or Venus, or on any other planet in the solar system. Then she would never again be able to look up when the moon was in the sky, or when the particular planet was close to the earth. For that reason, she tried to keep distance between herself and her husband. She knew that one day she would lose him, and that from then on there would always be a light in the heavens to remind her of him, and break her heart.

Of course the husband's rocket fell into the sun. It had been a sad story. Yet the Western custom of pumping dead people's veins with preserving fluids, Michael realised, and sealing the bodies in airtight coffins to bury them in concrete-lined holes, affected him in much the same way. One of the reasons he couldn't get over Alice, no matter how often he told himself her soul was free,.was that her decaying body was always, in a sense, beneath his feet. He wished they'd had her cremated and thrown her ashes into the ocean, or tossed them on to the wind.

At the same time, he wondered if it would have made any difference.

He had not intended to visit the cemetery. He had many things to do. He had to question the coroner who had performed Alice's autopsy, examine the bedroom again, speak to Clark and give that silly speech. The fact that he had so many things to investigate all on one day caused him to wonder about his convictions. He could have made his appointment with the coroner months ago. He could have had Bubba duplicate Polly's keys any time. And he had found Clark three weeks ago, but still hadn't approached him. There was really no two ways about it – he had postponed the investigation. The question was, had he done it because he was afraid to discover a fact that proved she had pulled the trigger?

But why would she kill herself?

Even Jessica had not attempted to address that point. Maybe Clark would. Michael glanced back towards his car and the gun safely stowed there. More questions came to mind. Why had he postponed his investigation until this particular day, the last day of school? And why did he feel he could no longer postpone it?

'I feel it. It's a bad feeling.'

It was hard to stand beside her grave, but harder still to leave it. He wished he had brought flowers. This was the first time he had been to the cemetery since the funeral. He glanced at the two graves on either side of Alice: Martha McCoy and Philip Bart, Alice's aunt and an employee of McCoy Construction who had died from an on-site accident. The grass was not quite as green around their tombstones. They had been in the ground less time, but perhaps it would always be greenest near Alice.

It was just a thought. He turned and left the cemetery.

Michael had obtained his appointment with Dr Gin Kawati under false pretences. He had called the doctor the previous week and explained he was an assistant editor at a local paper in need of technical information on modern forensic techniques for an article his boss was doing on how modern murders were sometimes solved. Michael had given the doctor the impression the name Dr Kawati would figure prominently in the article if he would help him out. The doctor had sounded interested.

Michael drove to downtown Los Angeles and parked across the street from the ARC Medical Group. This was his first visit to the office, but Bubba had been there before when he swiped certain codes from the physician's secretary. It was those codes that had allowed Bubba and Michael to dump the medical group's files on to Tabb High's computers homecoming day.

The receptionist showed him directly into the doctor's office. Dr Kawati was of Japanese descent – which was no big surprise given his last name – short and moustached. He was not old – thirty-five at most – and appeared at first glance to be friendly. He gave Michael a firm handshake and offered him a seat beside his cluttered desk. But Michael couldn't help glancing at the man's hands and thinking to himself that here were hands that spent their days dissecting people. Michael couldn't understand how anyone could willingly go into such a gruesome field.

'I wear gloves,' Dr Kawati said. Michael glanced up.

'Pardon?'

'I wear gloves when I perform an autopsy.' The doctor smiled. 'I have yet to be at a party or any social occasion and not have someone stare at my hands. Don't be embarrassed, I am proud of what I do.'

'You read minds?' Michael asked, shaken at his own transparency.

'I read mysteries. The human body is the most mysterious of all God's creations, and when it ceases to work, for whatever reason, it often leaves behind a puzzle more complex than anything you can find in a movie or a book.' He nodded towards the tape player Michael had brought. 'That would be a fine opening for your piece. You might want to turn on your cassette machine.'

On the spur of the moment, Michael decided to take a big chance. Perhaps the doctor's obviously keen perception gave him the inspiration. 'I lied,' he said. 'I don't work for a paper.'

The doctor raised an eyebrow, not fazed. 'I'm intrigued. What is your real name and why are you here?'

'My name *is* Mike, and I wanted to question you about an autopsy you performed last fall on a friend of mine. Her name was Alice McCoy.' He added, 'I realise I deserve to be kicked out, but I really would like to talk to you.'

'This Alice – she was a close friend of yours?'

Michael nodded. 'Yes.'

Dr Kawati turned to the computer on his desk. 'M – C – C – O – Y?'

'Yes.'

Kawati called up a file menu, then typed in the name. A moment later an autopsy report appeared on the screen. Michael recognised it; he had, after all, read it a dozen times. Kawati frowned. 'I remembered the name McCoy when you said it. A most interesting case.'

'Why?' Michael asked.

'A minute, please,' the doctor said, taking several minutes to read the report from start to finish. When he was done, he looked over at Michael. 'I believe you are a friend of hers, but why are you concerned about the results of her autopsy?'

'I have serious doubts about the police's investigation into her death.'

'Please be more specific.'

'I think Alice McCoy was murdered.'

'Why?'

Michael hesitated. 'I've read your report.'

'Did the police show it to you?'

'Not exactly.' The doctor smiled. 'You *are* an intriguing young man. I won't ask you how you managed that. I don't believe I want to know.' He glanced at the screen, frowned again. Michael spoke quickly.

'She didn't break her nose falling to the floor after firing the gun. She was sitting when she was shot. None of us rolled her body over when we found it.'

'You can't be certain she was sitting,' Kawati said.

'It is likely when you take into account where and at what angle the slug hit the wall. Also, she had the gun in her mouth, with her hand around it, when we found her. How could she fall and break her nose with that in the way?'

'How could someone have got close enough to put the gun in her mouth, wrap her fingers around the handle and then pull the trigger?'

'Before I answer that, why did you remember the name? What was so interesting about the case?'

'What you mentioned – the fracture to her nasal cartilage.'

'Then you don't think it was caused by a fall?'

'I didn't say that,' the doctor replied.

'How else could she have broken her nose?'

'Any number of ways. She could have been struck across the face, or rather, struck directly on the nose. There were no scratches on her cheeks, nor any other signs that she had been in a struggle.' Kawati paused, intent on the details, apparently not minding the exchange. 'You still have not answered my question.'

'In your report you mentioned brain haemorrhage that appeared unconnected to the path of the bullet.'

'It *may* have been unconnected. The bullet followed a twisted route before exiting at the back of the skull. The brain was in extremely poor condition. What are you getting at?'

'I have thought about this a great deal. I was there the night of the party.'

'Go on.'

Michael remembered back to another night, to homecoming, to the moment before the varsity tree toppled and destroyed the snack bar. The idea had begun to form in his mind even then. 'I think she was dead before she was shot,' he said.

The doctor thought a moment. 'It's possible.'

'Is it?' Michael asked, realising he had been holding his breath waiting to hear those exact words.

'Possible, but unlikely,' Kawati quickly added. 'Why would someone quietly and effectively kill her with a blow to the nose and then put a gun in her mouth and fire a shot that alerted everyone in the house?'

'To give the impression it had not been a murder, but a suicide.'

'Why?'

'To give the police an excuse not to investigate, which is precisely what has happened. They threw the file on the shelf and closed the case before they opened it.'

'You sound angry.'

Michael felt a tightness in his throat. 'She was very dear to me.' He started to get up. 'You've told me what I wanted to know. Thank you, doctor.'

Kawati glanced at the screen a last time. 'There is one other thing you might want to consider. If someone did strike her, cracking her nasal cartilage and giving her a cerebral haemorrhage in the process, then he must have done it with a baseball bat. Either that or he was a strong devil.' Kawati put a hand to his chin, nodded thoughtfully. 'Incredibly strong.'

CHAPTER 5

Nick Grutler drove fast down the coast, reaching San Diego in less than two hours. He had never been to the rehabilitation clinic before, but Maria's directions were precise and he found the huge modern, two-storey building without difficulty. Since her discharge from the local hospital three months ago, Nick had spoken to her on the phone every couple of weeks. Each time, *he* had called her. Each time, she had sounded much the same, quiet and withdrawn. Yet the bitterness that had unexpectedly arisen after her accident still remained. It had faded, true; nevertheless, it tore him apart to catch hints of it in her voice. Sometimes he felt as if he were talking to a stranger, that he was in love with someone who no longer existed.

She was sitting outside, waiting for him as he walked towards the front stairs. She had a red wool blanket over her legs and a battered suitcase by her side. Only she wasn't simply sitting; she was sitting in a wheelchair.

Oh, Jesus, please heal her.

He had prayed the same prayer a thousand times since last winter. Jesus was either keeping him in suspense or else He had already given him his answer. Nick was a big, strong young man but he almost broke down and cried at that moment.

'Hi, Maria,' he said. She had cut her hair, her beautiful hair. There was hardly any of it left. It was probably easier to take care of shorter, he reasoned. She smiled briefly, and rolled towards him. He wondered if it would be OK to hug her, if he would hurt her.

'Hello, Nick,' she said, glancing up at him before quickly looking down to make sure of her hold on the wheelchair handles. She still seemed to be learning how to get around. 'Thanks for coming.'

He stood above her, afraid to move. 'It was no problem. It's good to see you again.'

'It's good to see you.' She nodded to her bag. 'I'm already checked out. We can go.'

He stepped past her and picked up the suitcase. He knew it was all she had to her name. After the accident, her parents had been exposed as illegal immigrants in the United States. They had subsequently been deported to El Salvador. Maria's status was still questionable. As long as she needed medical attention that only the United States could provide, she was allowed to stay. She might be deported now that she was leaving the rehab clinic. Michael had helped Nick write a letter to their local congressman pleading her case. So far, there had been no reply.

Nick helped her into the front seat of his car – he could have picked her up with one hand, she was so light – and folded the wheelchair and put it in the trunk. It was a tight fit but he was able to close the lid. He climbed in beside her and started the engine.

'Nice car,' she said.

'Thanks. The Rock sold it to me cheap.'

'The Rock – I remember him.'

'I bumped into him in the parking lot when I was leaving school this morning. He told me to tell you he'd like to see you. Mike also said he was looking forward to seeing you again.'

'Good old Mike. Is he still searching for a murderer?'

There was an edge to her question, but not of sarcasm; she really wanted to know. 'He doesn't talk to me about it,' he said, feeling uncomfortable. He wanted to touch her, kiss her and comfort her, but he could have made the trip for nothing. She was still a hundred miles away, wrapped in a cool protective shell.

'I bet he is,' she said.

'Are you?' He hadn't shifted the car into gear yet. He hadn't intended to ask that question. Maria looked over at him. He noticed a faint two-inch scar near her right eye. She'd had some plastic surgery; she'd need more.

'Yes.'

'And you want me to help you find the murderer?'

'You'll help me,' she said, implying with her tone that he didn't understand what she was talking about, which was true.

'How?'

She smiled, slow and calculating. 'You'll know when the time comes.'

CHAPTER 6

Sara hated LA's downtown bus station, located in one of the worst parts of town. She always felt relieved to get in and out of it without being molested. The whole world was full of perverts. Society was sick. It still infuriated her how the courts locked Russ away for a crime he had not committed. She wished she'd sent him an aeroplane ticket. Then she could have driven to Los Angeles airport instead. She had suggested the idea in her last letter, but he hadn't answered her last letter, so that had been the end of that.

He didn't answer my letter before that either.

It didn't matter. He wasn't into writing letters. She couldn't stand writing them herself. The only reason she had sent him so many was that she'd had nothing else to do – only get good grades, keep her mother and father from killing each other and run the whole school.

Actually, she was going to give him hell for not answering her – immediately after she determined if he still liked her. She was worried he might have found someone else.

In a juvenile hall full of boys?

One could never tell. They probably had a buxom secretary or two working in the warden's office. She'd always had the impression Russ could go for an older woman, or a teenybopper for that matter. God help him if he had been unfaithful to her.

He was supposed to be on the one o'clock from Sacramento. She was on time and waiting at the right gate, but when all the people had passed by, there was no Russ. She couldn't believe it. The bastard had missed his bus and hadn't had the decency to call her house and leave word that he'd be on the next one arriving at – she glanced up at the schedule board – three o'clock. Three o'clock! She couldn't wait till then. She was ASB president and this was her last and most important day on the job. That insensitive son of a bitch had dragged her all the way down here *after* getting himself thrown in jail where she couldn't see him at all, and now he had stood her up.

She reached in her bag for her handkerchief. Life sucked. She hated this trying not to care when all she felt like doing was crying. She dabbed at her eyes. Well, that was the end of that. Jessica would get Bill tonight, and there would be no one there to save poor Sara from being raped by Bubba.

Sara blew her nose and headed for the exit. If she'd known for sure he'd be on the next bus, she would have waited, her important speech notwithstanding. But he had decided not to come, she realised, because he didn't want to see her. God, she hated him!

She ran into him the second she stepped outside. He was crouched on the kerb feeding a pigeon a piece of chocolate doughnut, his duffel bag propped against a nearby fire hydrant. They had cut his hair short. They must have been keeping him inside; he had lost his bronze sheen. It didn't matter. He looked incredible, simply incredible.

'Where have you been?' he asked, glancing up.

'Where have I been? You were supposed to be on that bus that just came in. You had me standing there waiting for you like some lost bag lady. You have a lot of nerve asking me where I've been.'

He gave the bird the remainder of the doughnut and checked his watch. 'It's five past one and you only just got here. I've been waiting around a couple of hours. I told you I was coming in at eleven.'

'No, you didn't.' She pulled his last letter from her bag – it was little more than a slip of paper – practically ripping the envelope in the process. 'See, it says one o'clock. You wrote it yourself.'

He stood and studied the paper. 'There're two ones there.'

'What? No, that's not another one. It's just a scratch.'

'No, I made it. It's a one.'

Now that he mentioned it, the scratch did bear a faint resemblance to a one. 'Why didn't you call, then?' she asked.

'I didn't have your number.'

'Why not? What did you do with it?'

'I didn't do anything with it. I never had it stored in my phone.'

'Is that why you haven't called me since you left?'

'I couldn't afford it.'

'You could have called collect,' she began to yell.

He stared at her a moment. 'You look great.'

'What do you mean? Do you mean my body or my face?'

He shook his head. 'Never mind.'

She pouted. 'How come you're not being nice to me?'

'How come you're yelling at me?'

'I'm not.' She wanted to reach over and brush a hair

from his eyes as she used to, but she couldn't see any hair long enough to give her an excuse. 'I'm sorry if I am.'

'It's all right.' He paused. 'Your body's all right.'

'It's not great?'

'No.'

She started to sock him, but he grabbed her hands and gave her a quick kiss on the lips. A little too quick. She had been hoping for a lot more. As he stepped back and picked up his duffel bag, he averted his eyes. He didn't want to talk, not about why he had been out drinking on homecoming night at a bar he couldn't remember. She had the feeling he didn't really want to talk about what he thought of her either.

'The car's over here,' she said. She wished she understood him better.

CHAPTER 7

The keys opened the door. Michael knew they would. Bubba was a master when it came to secretive preparations. Glancing down the McCoys' long driveway to make sure no one was watching, Michael quickly slipped into the house and closed the door.

I could get arrested for doing this.

That would be a joke. He could share the same cell with Dale Jensen and the local paper could do an article on the shortage of good valedictorians this year. In reality, he wasn't concerned about getting caught. The chances were against it, and even if someone did call the cops and he was carted down to the station, he didn't care. It would give him an excuse not to go to graduation. He still hadn't thought about what he was going to say. Not having gone to the rehearsal a couple of days earlier – he hadn't been valedictorian back then – he didn't even know when he was supposed to speak: first, last or what.

He had hit traffic returning from the coroner's office and was running behind schedule. He would have to go to Clark's house after the ceremony.

The house was silent in the manner empty houses are prone to be. Yet it was not a comforting silence. It reminded him of the silence that hung in the air following a major argument or an explosion. It seemed to him that acts of violence somehow transcended time. He remembered when he was a boy going with his mother to a bank where there had previously been a hold-up and a fatal shooting. He told his mother it was a 'bad place' before she had told him what had happened there. The McCoy house now felt like a 'bad place'.

He paused for a moment at the foot of the stairs, looking towards the kitchen. Standing in this spot, Nick had seen Bill with his head bent over the sink. Bill never explained why he had been standing there upset, before the gun went off.

Michael decided to retrace Nick's steps to the room where Alice had died. He climbed the double flight of stairs and paused at the first door on the left. It had been locked the night of the party, the room beyond silent, and it was the same now. The next door on the left led to the bathroom. The Rock had been there, showering and flushing out his chlorined eyes.

Michael opened the sole door on the right and peeped out on to the second-storey porch, where Kats had been getting a breath of fresh air and admiring the stars. It seemed to clear Michael's mind, going through this ritual. This hallway had one more door on the left. Nick had paused there, too, and listened at the door and heard snoring. Russ said he had been asleep inside. Then again, Russ couldn't remember where he had been when the varsity tree had toppled to the ground, or whether it had been Polly or Sara who had taken his axe away the first week of school.

The hallway turned to the right. There were two doors on the left. The first swung open easily, revealing a spacious bedroom with an adjoining bathroom. But it had been locked when Nick tried it, and there had been moans coming from inside. Bubba said he didn't know anything about it. No one seemed to know anything.

Michael came to the last room. The door was closed, and as he opened it, the hinges creaked loudly, doing wonders for his nerves. The room was bare except for an aluminium ladder set beside the closet. He remembered the ladder from his last inspection the day of the funeral.

The starkness of the wooden floor struck him, as it had

before. Every room in the house had carpeting except this one. He found the fact disturbing, although he wasn't sure why. He stepped inside.

The blinds on the windows – those facing east and south – were down. He raised them, letting in more light. The bullet hole in the wall beneath the east windows had not been plastered over. As he knelt beside it, his conviction that she had not broken her nose falling strengthened. It was less than three feet above the floor and straight as an arrow into plaster.

Yet all this was old news. He searched the room and the adjoining bathroom, and discovered nothing significant. The screens on the windows were all screwed down. There were no trapdoors, as Jessica had once pointed out. There was only one entrance into the room, one exit.

If she was dead before she was shot, was she dead long?

He found himself standing at the east windows, which faced the McCoy garden – as opposed to the south windows, which overlooked the pool – pondering what the coroner had said about the strength of her assailant. Clark was thin, thin as a rail. In a fight, Michael figured he could have taken him easily.

Then he looked up and noticed the broken shingle at the overhang of the eaves outside the east window. It appeared to Michael as it had before, as if someone had been on the roof and stepped too close to the edge and broken off a couple of inches of the dark brown wood with the heel of his shoe. When he thought about how steep the east slant of the roof appeared from the front, however, he began to doubt that the damage could have been caused by a misplaced foot. Only the original roofers, with the help of safety lines, would have been able to stand that close to the edge. Why wouldn't they have repaired the damage? It was the only shingle on the entire side of the house that was broken.

Michael wanted to have a closer look at it. But he didn't bother undoing the screws on the screens. The overhang was too far for him to reach, even if he were to hang out the window. He hurried downstairs to the garage instead, where he found a tall ladder. After assorted jostling and banging noises – and, thank God, Polly's nearest neighbours were more than a hundred yards away – he had the ladder situated beneath the bedroom window. Unfortunately, it wasn't tall enough for him to reach the shingle.

He had come down the ladder and was returning it to the garage, walking past the pool where Nick had almost drowned The Rock and beside the covered patio attached to the rear of the house, when he spotted the piece of yellowed paper lying in the grass next to the bushes. He set the ladder down and picked it up.

It was the permission form he had given Polly to have her aunt sign so that he could examine Alice's autopsy report. Polly had never returned it to him. It looked as if it had been sitting outside in the elements since that day. He stuffed it in his pocket.

He wasn't crazy about his next plan. He almost hoped, as he searched the garage after replacing the ladder on its hooks, that Polly didn't have any rope. Then he'd have an excuse not to play Mr Roofer. But in a cabinet above the workbench, he soon found a fifty-foot coil of one-inch cord.

He didn't return to the bedroom, but took the second-storey hallway door on to the porch that overlooked the backyard. The shingles came directly down on to the tar floor of the porch, giving him easy access to the roof. Climbing up towards the peak of the house, Michael felt the hot sun on the back of his head, the slickness of the wood beneath his feet. He was glad he had chosen to wear his tennis shoes that morning.

If I slip and break my neck, people will say I committed suicide.

At the ridge, he tied one end of the rope to the sturdiest vent he could find, the other end around his waist. With the life insurance in hand, creeping down towards the broken shingle was not nearly so intimidating as he had imagined it would be. He actually found it quite exhilarating. He wasn't even worried about the neighbours. Not many crooks climbed on to a victim's roof in the middle of the day and performed gymnastics.

A moment later he was kneeling beside the shingle, forty feet above the spot where Alice and he had had their last talk over the hot coals of the barbecue. He felt the damaged edge and was immediately taken by its smoothness. There were splinters, yes, but they –

They were turned *upwards*.

Strange, very strange. Did the roofers break the shingle while it was lying upside down on the ground, and then install it? He found that hard to believe.

It was fortunate that he had a safety line. His next discovery almost sent him reeling. Placing his head inches from the finely splintered edge, he noticed a number of tiny round metal pellets embedded in the wood. He dug them out with his nail, studied them in his palm.

They were from a shotgun blast.

CHAPTER 8

The stadium stands were packed, and the football field was jammed with grey folding chairs and blue-robed seniors. The ceremony would start in minutes. Sara still hadn't finished rewriting her speech. Jessica hadn't decided which song to sing. It was hot and getting hotter.

'Should I bring up the state of the environment?' Sara asked. 'People are always talking about pollution. Maybe I could work it into my overall theme.'

'What is your overall theme?' Jessica ask.

Sara glanced at her notes. 'Isn't it obvious from what I've told you so far?' she asked anxiously.

'No.'

'Jessie!'

'Well, I'm hardly listening to you. I have problems of my own. I can't sing the Beatles song I rehearsed.'

'Why not?'

'Mr Bark says it's too racist.'

'"All You Need Is Love" is racist?'

'That's what he says. He wants a song with more of a political message, like "Back in the USSR" or something.' She took off her cap and glasses and wiped the sweat from her forehead. Her tassel was blue. Sara had a gold one. Their parents were in the stands. The six of them were supposed to go for an early dinner to an expensive restaurant afterwards. Big thrill.

'What if I bring up the space programme?' Sara asked. 'Everyone likes astronauts.'

'What if I sang Bowie's "Starman"? I know the chords.'

'That's ridiculous. You can't sing about spacemen at my graduation.'

'Then you can't talk about astronauts at mine.' Jessica replaced her glasses and scanned the crowd for Michael. 'When is he going to speak?'

'After Mr Bark.'

'I forget, when do I sing?'

'After Mike speaks,' Sara said. 'It's all there in your programme.'

'Michael's not even listed in the programme.'

'Dale Jensen is. You know he's taking his place.'

'Yeah, you told me – as of this morning.'

'What are you complaining about? I can't even have notes with me when I go up there.'

'Why not?'

'I have no place to put them.'

'What's wrong with the podium?' Jessica asked, pointing to the stage in front of the folding chairs.

'It's been fixed.' Sara smiled suddenly. 'You'll see. Mr Bark wants to talk before me. He thinks he does. What grade did he give you?'

'A B-minus,' Jessica said angrily.

'He gave me an A-minus.'

'That's so unfair. You fell asleep the first day I was back.'

'Well, then, I was obviously most improved.'

'You are beginning to bore me. I think I'll leave.'

Jessica had another reason for splitting. She wanted to check out the piano – how it had been miked. She was a fair pianist; she'd had lessons since she was six years old and could play most popular songs if she had the music in front of her. She knew dozens of Beatles tunes by heart. Although many people complimented her on her voice, she didn't think of herself as a vocalist. Her voice was too similar to her speaking voice, which had always bothered her for some strange reason.

The school piano had a single microphone rigged above it – that was all. Yet the sound appeared to carry fine when she tapped out a few chords. She wondered if it would offend the older members of the audience if she played Alice Cooper's 'School's Out for Summer'. It annoyed her, being censored by Mr Bark, especially when he considered himself so liberal.

'Don't worry,' The Rock said, coming up at her side, a green plastic trash bag in his hand. 'The chance of there being a record producer in the audience is five hundred to one.'

She smiled. 'I'm not here to get signed. I just want my diploma. What's with the bag?'

She knew it without asking. Being a Big Brother wasn't enough for The Rock. A couple of weeks ago he had joined the Keep America Clean Society. He took his membership seriously. Tabb High was now the cleanest school in Orange County, or it should have been. Bubba had organised a counterorganisation; It's Biodegradable. Bubba had a lot of friends. The Rock could regularly be seen at break and lunch picking up half-eaten apples and banana peels. Nothing irritated Bubba like a social conscience.

'The gang's getting started early,' The Rock said. 'I've already collected a hundred beer cans at school today.' He sighed and shook his head. 'I hope no one falls overboard tonight.' He patted her on the shoulder. 'Stay sober.'

'I'll try.' Either that or she was going to get stinking drunk.

She was heading towards the stands to ask her mother for a throat lozenge – she wanted to keep her vocal chords well lubricated – when she caught sight of Michael standing alone by the equipment shed on the far end of the stadium. He had his head down and appeared deep in thought. She hesitated to disturb him. As Sara had mentioned earlier, his hair was a lot longer, and he looked so damn good to her that she felt her eyes water. She found herself jogging towards him before she knew what she was doing.

He did not see her coming. She trembled inside as she came to a halt a few feet from him and spoke his name. 'Michael?'

He glanced up with a start. Then he smiled. 'Jessie. I love your glasses.'

She laughed. She could have cried. She spread her arms wide and gave him a big hug. It might have been the best moment of her life when he hugged her back. Except he had to let her go. What a mush she had become.

'It's good to see you again,' he said casually.

'It's good to see you. Oh, God, these glasses. I hate them.'

'Why? You look like a scholar in them.'

'I do?' He was being serious. She should have worn them all along. She giggled, shaking on the outside as well as the inside. No one in the world made her feel this way. She hated it, but only because she knew, like his hug, that it would not last. He would go away again. He always did. 'So, how have you been? You look great. I hear you're building a spaceship at JPL?'

'Not exactly. I'm doing janitorial work.'

'Really? No! You're kidding. I know you. Our chemistry teacher told us one day he'd never had a student like you. He said you invented the carbon bond!'

He chuckled. 'Now I'm responsible for all the life on this planet. What a reputation. What have you been up to?'

She shrugged. 'Oh, the usual. I sleep all day in a velvet-lined coffin and then prowl the streets at night. Hey, Sara told me you're valedictorian. Congratulations! Your mom must be real proud.'

Michael nodded past her shoulder. 'Here she comes. You've never met her, have you?'

Oh, no, she's going to hate me. Mothers always hate me.

His mom was massively pregnant; she waddled as she walked. Jessica hadn't even known she was married. Michael indicated that they should meet her halfway. Jessica could not believe how nervous she was. One would think she was Michael's fiancée.

'She's due in a couple of weeks,' Michael remarked as they walked towards her. 'Did you know I have a stepfather now?'

'That's neat.'

'I never see him. They spend most of their time at his place by the beach. I'm still at the old house.'

That was not news to Jessica. She had driven by his place a couple of times and parked down the street to wait for him to come home. But each time he appeared, her nerve had failed and she'd driven away.

His mother had his black hair and dark eyes, but little or none of his seriousness. Jessica spotted that the moment she spoke; her voice was light, happy. Jessica could tell at a glance she was looking forward to the baby.

'Mom, this is Jessie. You remember her, don't you?'

'Sure, I do.' She offered her hand. 'I spoke to you on the phone once. Nice meeting you, Jessie.'

'Thank you. Nice meeting you.'

The woman turned to her son, handing him a letter.

'This came from the observatory this morning. Is it what I think it is?'

'Probably,' Michael said, slipping the envelope into his gown pocket.

'Aren't you going to open it?' his mother asked, slightly exasperated.

'Later. We know what it says.'

'What is it?' Jessica asked, curious.

'Nothing,' Michael said quickly, catching his mom's eye.

'All right,' his mother said. 'Be that way. Be rude.' She nodded to Jessica and laughed at Michael. 'She's pretty.'

'I know,' he said quietly.

Jessica quickly pulled off her glasses, embarrassed. 'I have to wear these stupid things all the time.'

'You look wonderful with them on,' his mother said.

'Like a philosopher,' Michael said.

'A professional woman,' the mother said, reaching out and fixing Jessica's cap.

'I don't even have a gold tassel,' Jessica muttered, trembling worse. Michael's mom brushed a hair from her cheek, then took the glasses from her hands and checked the lenses for dust.

'These are strong,' she remarked. 'You *do* have to wear them.'

'Come on, Mom,' Michael said. 'Give her a break.'

'I know,' Jessica said. The lady wiped them on her green dress and then carefully fixed them back on Jessica's nose, momentarily staring into her eyes.

She's checking me out.

'I hope we get to meet another time, Jessie.'

'So do I,' Jessica replied, a bit confused. Michael's mother turned back to him.

'Daniel and I are sitting near the bottom on the far right,' she said. 'In case you wanted to know. Be sure to thank your mother in your speech for being so wonderful.'

'I'll mention it several times,' he promised. She hugged him briefly, and then to Jessica's surprise gave her a hug, too. When she left, Michael tugged gently on Jessica's tassel.

'Would you like to trade caps?' he asked. 'I know you would have got an A in chemistry if I'd done a better job structuring the universe.'

'Yes, it's all your fault.' She added softly, 'No thanks.'

'I didn't mean—'

'No, it's me.' She shrugged. 'I really messed up this year. It was my own fault.' She smiled quickly. 'Your mom's great.'

'I'm glad you like her. I'll have to meet your parents.'

'That's right. You didn't see them when we went out.'

Hint. Hint. Hint. Ask me out again.

Of course he hadn't asked her out in the first place. He never had in all the time they had spent together. She must be crazy to think he liked her.

In the hospital, however, the morning after Maria's accident, he had begun to say something that had since given her cause to wonder.

'I know how you feel. You're not a bad person. If you were, I wouldn't care about you the way . . .'

She had been crying because Maria had been bitter to her. He had probably been trying to cheer her up. She would never know. She had run away from him. She would run away again. She didn't deserve him. She was going to seduce the football quarterback tonight. It was all she was good for.

She suddenly felt as if she were going to cry. Here it was her last day of school, a beautiful summer day. She had everything: rich and understanding parents, perfect health, a bright future. Yet she had nothing. She had no love. Alice was gone. Michael was going. And Maria hated her.

It was at that precise moment that she saw Maria. Had that not happened, she might have been able to push aside her self-recriminations long enough to invite

Michael and his parents to have dinner with her and her family after the ceremony. It was an idea, a good idea. But Nick guiding Maria across the track and on to the football field was bitter reality. She froze in midstride. Michael glanced at her face, then followed her eyes.

'I was going to tell you,' he said.

'I haven't spoken to her since that morning.' Jessica swallowed thickly. 'She's in a wheelchair.'

'It was a terrible accident.' He laid emphasis on the last word. She found that strange. He had always given her the impression that he didn't believe in accidents. He was trying to dispel her guilt. He might as well have tried to convince her she would gladly have traded places with Maria. But she wouldn't have, not for the world, and so her guilt remained.

'I'll talk to you later, OK?' she mumbled. 'I have to get in line.'

She walked off the field and hid in the crowd. Maria had asked Jessica never to make her see her again. It was the least she could do for her crippled friend, Jessica thought.

The ceremony began shortly afterwards. The huge audience had been seated when the chatty senior class marched in and took their seats. Mr Smith, Tabb's elderly principal, was the first speaker. Dressed in the same blue robe as the rest of them, he thanked the many parents, relatives and friends for coming, and then proceeded to praise the group of graduates as the most dynamic in his long academic career. Jessica found his choice of the word 'dynamic' appropriately vague. Hitler had been dynamic. Of course, she realised, it had not been a bad year for everyone.

The diplomas were to be presented alphabetically; for that reason, the seating followed roughly that order. But Jessica Hart had switched with someone so she could sit next to Polly McCoy rather than Larry Hay. Larry not only had a weird name, he also had such consistently bad breath that Sara once remarked that if at the end of his life he donated his body to medical science, he would probably be found posthumously guilty of involuntary manslaughter when the medic students cut open his cadaver and choked to death.

Jessica also wanted to be with her old friend at this special time. Polly had suffered far more than any of them, and Jessica had courageously helped her the last few months by avoiding her. Not entirely, naturally; they continued to talk at lunch and stuff. But they no longer hung out as real friends do. The reason was simple. They were both down, and Jessica had discovered that the truism that the depressed seek out the company of other depressed people to be entirely false. Being around Polly only made her feel worse.

Yet seeing Maria again made Jessica want to atone for her cowardly approach to the situation. Sitting to the far right of the stage, in the back row – twenty rows behind Maria's front-row wheelchair – Jessica leaned over to Polly as Mr Smith completed his talk.

'He's such a nice man,' she said.

'He must be to have put up with Sara all year,' Polly said.

'Who's that he's introducing?'

'A car company executive. He's here to inspire us to go out into the big wide world and get rich.' Polly winced slightly, took off her cap, and put her hand to her temple. 'I'm already rich.'

'Do you have a headache?'

'Yeah.'

Jessica wiped the sweat from her bow. 'It's this sun.'

'It's sunny every day.' Polly searched the stands.

'Looking for somebody?'

'No, nobody.'

The guest speaker did turn out to be a strong believer in capitalism. His name was James Vern and ten years ago he had swiped – his actual phrase was 'drew from the research of' – an invention that improved the efficiency of transmissions in large trucks, parlayed it into millions. He laughed when he recounted the lies he had told to get financing for his company. Jessica wondered if he knew what a jerk he was. He talked for forty-five long minutes.

Sara came next. People giggled as she made her way to the microphone. Jessica tossed around in her head the idea of singing 'Hey Jude'.

'Thank you, Mr Vern, for your enlightening words,' Sara said, the tiniest hint of tension in her voice as she adjusted the mike down to her height. 'The world of modern business really sounds like a jungle. But I suppose even a snake needs a place to live.'

The audience chuckled uneasily. The senior class cheered appreciatively. Sara smiled and went on more confidently, not using any notes. Jessica noticed for the first time that the top of the podium had been removed. As Sara had mentioned, there was no place to put papers.

'I have written several speeches this last week,' Sara said. 'I have one on this country's need to remain competitive in the world marketplace. I put a lot of time into it. Then I thought, haven't we been number one long enough? Shouldn't we give someone else a chance?

I decided it was all a question of whether we want to be greedy or cool about it. I also had this speech on *our* future. It is my understanding that ASB presidents across the country talk about this subject on graduation day. I really got into the idea myself – for a while. Then I realised that the best minds on Wall Street can't tell if the Dow Jones average is going to go up or down a couple of lousy points tomorrow, never mind where it's going to be ten years from now. The earth could get smashed by a huge meteorite this instant and vaporise us all, and then what would we do? Why worry about it? Why talk about it? I'm certainly not going to. Then, finally, I had this speech on the problems facing the youth of America: overindulgence in alcohol, lack of ambition, sexual promiscuity. But I had to ask myself, are these things really that bad? Think about it for a second.' Sara turned to the class and raised her voice. 'Do we really want to give them up?'

The class let out a resounding *no*! Then it burst out altogether. The audience – full of real-life parents – didn't know what to think. In the end, though, the crowd joined those on the field, and applauded Sara. She loved it.

'You know what I finally decided?' she said. 'Not even to give a speech. Let's get this thing over with as quickly as possible and get to the party.' She cleared her throat and glanced to the side as the class clapped and hooted. 'With that in mind, please welcome our senior faculty adviser, the wonderful Mr Bark!'

Their political science teacher, wearing a blue graduation gown and a dyed fringe of hair that was supposed to take ten years off his age, strode confidently to the microphone. Sara remained on the stage. Jessica leaned forward in anticipation.

'Mr Bark and I have had our disagreements this year,' Sara said pleasantly as the teacher stood nearby. 'But I like to think our trials have brought us closer together. I think, especially in the last month, I have only begun to understand his commitment to social causes, particularly his concern over the arms race.'

Mr Bark leaned forward and spoke into the mike. 'I am happy to hear that, Sara. It means a great deal to me.'

'I wanted to show you how much it means to me,' Sara said, nudging herself back behind the mike. 'I bought you a present, a very special present.' She gestured to someone on the left side of the stage. Jessica was surprised when Russ Desmond – Sara had not said a word about the progress of *their* relationship since she had picked him up at the bus station, and Jessica had been hesitant to ask – stood up and strode on to the stage, a small white package in his hands. He gave it to Sara, then hastily retreated. Sara presented it to Mr Bark.

'Open it,' she said.

Mr Bark beamed. 'This is so thoughtful of you, Sara.' He began to peel away the paper. 'I wonder what it could—' The crowd murmured expectantly. It took a minute to get through all the wrapping. When he had, he was left holding what appeared to be – from Jessica's admittedly poor vantage point – a black rectangular stone. 'Sara?' he said, uncertain.

'It's a paperweight,' Sara explained.

'Oh.' He grinned as he weighed it in his palm. 'It feels like it should be able to handle the job. Thank you.'

'Thank *you*, Mr Bark.' Sara muttered the next line under her breath as she turned away, but the mike caught it. 'It's a uranium paperweight.'

It was perfect. He obviously had a long speech prepared. Undoubtedly it was to be every bit as long as Mr Vern's. He would talk about how much he loved working with the kids this year, how sad he was to see them all leave, but how happy he was to know they were going on to bigger and greater things. Then he would bring up the nukes, the goddamn nukes that could destroy all of them at the push of a button.

Yet he had a uranium paperweight in his hand, and

though he probably understood intellectually that the level of radiation it was emitting was extremely small – probably one thousandth or one millionth of what he would absorb if he had a chest X-ray – he would not be able to stop thinking about it. Jessica watched as he began to speak and then glanced down at the thing in his hand and fidgeted. There was no place to put it, except on the ground. And he couldn't do that. No, that would be rude. He clearly didn't want to be rude.

'I am very happy to be here this afternoon with all you fine people,' he began uneasily. 'It is always an honour for me when I am given a chance to speak to – fine people.'

He paused and glanced again at the paperweight. For a moment, it appeared that he might actually drop it. Jessica could practically read his mind. He was thinking of gamma rays, beta rays and those always terrible cosmic rays – all those mean nasty things he read about every night in his literature about the mean nasty military industrialists.

'It's always a sad day, graduation day,' he mumbled. 'And a happy day.'

His voice faltered. He moved the paperweight from his right hand to his left, then moved it back. He was probably imagining the different rays penetrating his flesh, Jessica thought, mutating the DNA in his cells, setting him up for a hideous case of cancer five years down the line. His fear practically screamed out at the crowd.

This rock is killing me!

He couldn't take it any more. He took a step away, realised what he was doing, and then leaned back and spoke hastily into the mike. 'And all I'd like to say is, good luck, good luck to all of you kids. Thank you.'

He left the stage in a hurry, pausing at his seat only long enough to get rid of Sara's present, then strode towards the end of the folding chairs and off the football field. The audience watched quietly, reacting little. The class members whispered among themselves, relieved to have been spared another speech. Sara returned to the microphone.

'Our next speaker is the rarest of people,' Sara said seriously. 'He is the smartest individual I have ever met, and the nicest. He is Michael Olson, our class valedictorian.'

'You should have gone out with him instead of Bill,' Polly whispered as Michael stood up and walked to the microphone. The welcoming applause was the loudest of the afternoon.

'I know.' Jessica sighed. 'Do you think it's too late?'

'Yes.'

'Thank you, Sara, for the kind introduction,' Michael said, standing perfectly straight, his hands clasped in front of his gown below his waist, not as relaxed as he could have been but nevertheless in control of the situation. 'And thank you, ladies and gentlemen and fellow classmates, for inviting me to speak on this occasion. Like Sara, I will try to keep my talk brief. I, too, have written and discarded several speeches in the last couple of hours. None of the topics I chose seemed right. I suppose that is the problem with selecting any topic. It can only be about one thing, while our lives are about so many things. I finally decided I would simply talk about what is important to me as I prepare to graduate from school.'

He glanced down at a small white card he held in his hand, and Jessica looked down at her shiny white high heels, and the grass beneath them. She was sitting on the forty-yard line, directly above the hash mark. She remembered the first Tabb High football game she had attended, how the team had tried for a first down on this part of the field and failed. Bill had fumbled the ball. She had a picture of the fumble in her files at home. She smiled at the memory, especially at how Michael had inadvertently helped her take the picture when he was demonstrating to her how to fit the telephoto lens on to her camera.

But that had been a long time ago.

Polly's right. It's too late.

'In a way I'm five months late with my speech,' Michael went on. 'I left school in January, and today is my first day back. Since I've been gone, I've been rather busy, working and stuff. But I've often looked back and thought about what I learned at Tabb. The obvious thing that comes to mind is the science and maths and history I absorbed. The teachers here are really great, some of the best, and now, I think, would be a good time to thank them for their patience and dedication. They always praised me and gave me confidence. But maybe they did too good a job. One of the problems with people thinking you're smart is that you eventually begin to believe it. I remember all the times in class – how restless I would be for the teacher to get on with the lesson. I've grasped the concept, I used to think, why haven't the rest of the kids? What I didn't realise then is that learning something doesn't just mean figuring it out. It's also the pleasure you get from the knowledge. I didn't appreciate that the teacher would sometimes dwell on a particular subject because he or she loved it. I got mostly As but now I wish I'd had more fun doing it. I hope this is one lesson I won't forget.'

Michael paused and looked over the audience. When he spoke next it was in a lower voice, and Jessica found herself leaning forward, afraid she might miss something.

She knew he was going to bring up Alice.

'But there is something else high school taught me,' he said. 'Something I did not know until I was no longer here on a daily basis. Like everybody, I suppose, I knew certain people at school that I didn't really like. They bugged me for one reason or another, and I used to think I'd be glad when I didn't have to see them any more. Then again, I had friends I loved to be around, people that made it easy for me to get up in the morning and drive here. But the strange thing I've discovered since I've been gone is that I miss both groups of people. And I like to think I've been missed by both groups. I like to think we're all good friends. Maybe I've learned the importance of friendship. Mr Bark was right – today is a happy day, but it's also sad. We'll all promise to keep in touch, but realistically, many of us will never see one another again. Today is supposed to be the day we grow up, yet in a way, it's a shame any of us have to. Your high school friends – I think they're your best friends.'

Your final friends.

Jessica didn't know why she thought that. There was life after high school. There would be other boys besides Michael. There was only one problem. She didn't want any other boy.

Michael coughed once and looked down. 'In closing I would like to pay tribute to the memory of a very special friend who had her life taken suddenly from her. If possible, I would like her remembered with a minute of silence. Her name was Alice McCoy. She would have graduated in a couple of years.'

Michael lowered his head. Most of those present did the same. Jessica closed her eyes and felt a tear slide over her warm cheek. Just one tear. The minute lasted an eternity. Sara's voice made her sit up with a start.

'And now Jessica Hart will close the ceremony with a song.'

Jessica stood and glanced at Polly, who in turn stared up at her.

'Was he right about us not having any more friends?' Polly asked sadly. Jessica squeezed her shoulder.

'We'll always be friends, Polly.'

Jessica found the piano and sat down. The silence persisted, but a faint breeze had begun to cross the stadium. She felt it in her hair and on her damp cheek.

She had no music before her; she had to choose a Beatles song. That was OK. They had composed the perfect one for the occasion, especially since Michael had forgotten to thank his wonderful mother for having given birth to him.

Jessica began to sing.

'When I find myself in times of trouble, Mother Mary comes to me, speaking words of wisdom, let it be. And in my hour of darkness, she is standing right in front of me, speaking words of wisdom, let it be. Let it be, let it be, let it be, let it be, whisper words of wisdom, let it be . . .'

She went through the song alone, and when she came to the final chorus, no one in the stands or on the field joined her. That was OK, too. She may not have sung it as beautifully as Paul McCartney, but she sang it as if it were important to her, which it was. When she finished, the silence returned, deeper than before and just for a moment. Then the applause poured down on her from all sides and she smiled. It was the first time she had felt good all day.

The diplomas were handed out, one by one, with Mr Smith shaking everybody's hand and wishing each one well. When that was done, Sara squealed something ridiculous into the mike and the class sprang to its feet and cheered. Then five hundred caps sailed into the air, the largest of which was Bubba's huge straw sombrero, complete with gold tassel.

Jessica hugged Polly. They had made it. School was over, and if they wanted, it could be over for good. Sara burst through the crowd and embraced them both. And then they laughed and insulted one another, and it was just as it always had been between them and, she hoped, always would be. Michael didn't know everything after all. Jessica meant it when she had told Polly they would be friends for ever.

Jessica didn't find Michael in the crowd, though she looked long and hard. He seemed to have disappeared.

Michael had indeed left the school, but Carl Barber, better known as Kats, had not. He stood in the middle of the joyous crowd, watching everybody hug and kiss, a wide grin on his face, but a scowl in his heart. Nothing really changed, he thought bitterly. He had his diploma. He had earned it attending hours of tedious night classes. He was as good as the rest of them. But how many of them wanted to shake his hand? As many as had shaken his hand last June when he had failed to graduate because of a few lousy grades. Nobody cared about him. Nobody ever had and nobody ever would.

After tonight, though, they would remember him, if they remembered anything at all. Almost the entire senior class would be on that cruise ship when it left the dock for Catalina. But if he had his way – and he would, he swore it – not a single one of them would be on board when it reached its destination. That ship would be a ghost ship.

CHAPTER 9

Michael parked down the street from Clark Halley's house and removed the gun from the glove compartment. Checking again to be sure it was fully loaded, he stuffed it inside his sports jacket pocket. Clark's huge black Harley-Davidson sat at the end of the crumbling asphalt driveway, fuming in the boiling sun from recent exertion. Clark was home. If the place could be called a home. It looked more like a chicken coop, out at the far east end of San Bernardino Valley, where the desert began and the rents plummeted. The place stank, yet when Michael had finally located the house a month earlier – after a great deal of effort and an equal amount of luck – he had celebrated.

And then I did nothing but watch and wait.

A last name is not the same as an address. Michael discovered that soon after he had found Clark's ugly picture and full name in the Temple High yearbook. The Monday after Maria's accident, he had revisited Temple High and asked to speak to Clark Halley. Turned out the guy no longer went there. He should have been in the middle of his senior year, but he had unexpectedly dropped out at the beginning of October. He had, in fact, disappeared just after Alice had died.

No sweat to find him, Michael had figured. He would get Clark's family address and catch up with him there. Easier said than done. Clark didn't have a family. He lived alone. He was an orphan or something; the secretary at Temple High wasn't sure what the situation was. Using the best of his charm, and a couple of tricks Bubba had taught him, Michael was able to obtain from the secretary – the same woman who had given him the yearbook during his original visit – the address Clark had had his mail sent to while at the school. It proved to be phoney – a closed Laundromat.

Michael went back to Temple High at lunchtime, again and again. He mingled, made friends, asked questions and listened. He led the other kids to believe he went to Temple. He began to build up a picture of Clark Halley, and it matched the one he already had – the guy was a creep.

Clark had kept mostly to himself, but when he did

speak up, it had usually been to insult somebody. One girl recalled how he'd asked to sign her cast after she'd had a skiing accident. He'd drawn a tasteless sketch of her stepping into a bear trap, her foot being sliced off at the ankle and bleeding all over the ground. That was one thing everyone seemed to agree on – the dude could draw. He had talent. He might even be a genius.

What he didn't have, and what Michael desperately needed to find, was a friend. Clark didn't seem to have a single one. No one knew where he lived. No one had his phone number. He had attended the school for three years and no one could provide Michael with a single fact about his personal life. Did he have a job? Did he have any brothers or sisters? Did he have a favourite place to eat? Michael heard the same answer repeatedly – I don't know. At one point he began to feel he was chasing a phantom.

Then in mid-March he got a lead. He was on something like his twentieth visit to Temple High and talking to a guy who had gone motorcycle riding with Clark a couple of times. The guy's name was Fred Galanger, and although he appeared to be a pretty tough son of a bitch – he carried thick biceps and lurid tattoos beneath his biker jacket – he spoke of Clark reluctantly, as if he were afraid Clark's ghost might suddenly appear and rake him over with a steel chain. Fred probably knew Clark better than anyone at Temple, which, of course, was not saying much. Michael had cultivated his acquaintance carefully. Then he had tired of the game and offered Fred twenty bucks for a single slice of useful memory. Fred's brain cells had lit up.

'We were out that afternoon I told you about before,' Fred said carefully, sliding the crisp bill into his pocket and keeping his hand wrapped around it in case it somehow vanished while he spoke of the mysterious rider. 'We were hotdogging these turns in the foothills down from Big Bear. That's a dangerous place to be riding hard, but Clark, he'd have a smile on his face heading into the bonnet of an oncoming truck, if it came to that. He was crazy. It took guts to keep up with him. I was one of the few guys who could.

'Anyway, we came around this one turn near the bottom of the mountain and there was an oil spill on the road. Clark's front wheel caught the edge of it and he went flying, right off the embankment and into this ravine. I figured he'd bought it right then. But he didn't even have a scratch. Don't ask me how. He was already pushing his bike back up the hill and on to the road before I could get to him. He thought it was the funniest thing in the world. But his leather coat was torn to shreds and he'd crashed his shift lever. It was weird; I went to help him bend the lever back so we could get home, but he wouldn't let me touch it. He said he didn't let anyone near his bike except this Indian who works at a station in Sunnymead. He wouldn't even work on it himself, like it was sacred to him or something dumb like that.'

'What's the name of the station?' Michael interrupted.

'I don't know. It's an independent, right off the freeway, I think at Branch. Yeah, it's on Branch. We crawled there at ten miles an hour, Clark's bike stuck in first gear the whole way. The Indian's a mechanic at the station. I don't remember his name – Birdbeak or Crowfoot or something. He must have been in his nineties. You shouldn't have any trouble finding him. They seemed like old friends. He'll probably know where Clark lives.'

'Anything else?' Michael asked.

'No. Except if you do find him, don't mention my name. I mean it.'

'Why not?'

Fred Galanger wouldn't tell him why. He didn't have to. He was obviously afraid of Clark.

Fred was right about one thing – Michael did find the station without difficulty. He also met the Indian mechanic. His real name was Stormwatcher, and although he didn't have Clark's strange pale eyes, he had a similar otherworldly stare that made Michael uncomfortable. Michael figured it would be a mistake to approach him directly for Clark's address. He suspected that Clark was somehow involved with the occult, that he was in fact an apprentice of the Indian. The old guy might warn Clark he was being hunted.

It was the perfect time to go to the police. Michael didn't have the time or the inclination to stake out the station day after day, hoping Clark would show up. The police could demand that the Indian tell them what he knew of Clark. But Michael did not trust the police; in particular, he did not trust Lieutenant Keller's detective skills. Keller would question Clark, Clark would tell him about Alice's instability and Keller would go away satisfied, confident he'd got what he had come for.

A month later Michael was still debating how to make friends with one of the teenagers who worked part-time at the station – someone who could alert him by phone if Clark should arrive – when he got another big break. He was getting petrol at the station when Clark drove up.

Clark didn't see him – Michael was pretty sure of that. He was off again quickly after exchanging a few words with the old Indian. Michael followed him carefully, but not too closely. Clark drove very fast. Yet he didn't go far before he pulled into the driveway of a broken-down house in a decrepit neighbourhood.

And this was the same house Michael found himself sitting outside an hour after he had graduated valedictorian, a gun in his pocket, doubt in his mind. Yet he had sat here before – without a gun but with the same doubts – and he had done nothing.

Clark could say one word, and smash everything I believe.

Michael did not fear Clark so much as he feared Alice – feared who she might have been. When he got right down to it, he hadn't known her that long.

He got out of his car, the sweat sticking to him like a layer of deceit; surely Clark would be suspicious about his wearing a coat on such a hot day. Yet Michael had no intention of lying to Clark about the purpose of his visit.

A cat ran across Michael's path as he walked towards the door. It was brown, not black, but it had green eyes. Most cats did, he supposed. He wondered if he was going to die in the next few minutes.

Michael knocked on the door. Clark answered quickly. He had on a grey T-shirt and black trousers. His red hair was shorter than it had been last autumn, neater and he was not nearly so bony or pale. Indeed, Michael wondered briefly if he had the right house. He remembered Clark as fish dug from a foul swamp. This guy was not unattractive.

The eyes gave him away, however; they could have been plucked from the cat that had just crossed the yard. And the southern twang was still there.

'Can I help you?' he asked, standing behind a torn screen door.

'Maybe. I don't know if you remember me. My name's Mike. I met you at a football game at Tabb High? You were with Alice.'

'What do you want?' His voice was cautious, but not hostile.

'I'd like to come in and talk to you about Alice. If that would be all right?'

Clark considered a moment. 'All right.' He held open the screen door. 'The place is a mess. It always is.'

It was messy only because it was crammed with paintings and artistic paraphernalia: recently stretched canvases, tubes of oils, stained rags, dozens of brushes in various sizes and shapes standing upright in tin cans. Except for the supplies, the house, though claustrophobic, was not bad. There were no half-finished TV dinners or overfilled ashtrays. Clark was not a slob. His place was, in fact, neater than Alice's studio had been.

Michael had part of an answer to one of his questions even before he sat down on a stool beside the narrow kitchen counter. Art had been at the core of Alice's life.

Michael remembered how her bright blue eyes had constantly darted about wherever she was, as if she were eternally starved for visual input, of the beautiful or the unusual kind. Here, in Clark's place, she could have drunk up images to her heart's content. Maybe that, and that alone, had drawn her to Clark. The room was the inside of an LSD-gorged brain cell, despite the fact that the bulk of Clark's work was black-and-white sketches and not psychedelic paintings. Michael didn't know how he filled the colourless with colour. It was as if he used magic; the mind saw something the eye did not.

A phantom.

The subject matter of the sketches consisted largely of women and *creatures* relaxing together in barren desert scenes. The women were always beautiful. More than a few looked like Alice. The creatures had insect and reptile qualities. They smiled a lot. They obviously liked their women.

'Want a beer?' Clark asked, picking up a can of Coors from the floor beside his chair. Clark appeared to have been reading when Michael had knocked. The book lay face down on the thin green carpet, a hardback. Michael couldn't make out the title.

'No, thank you,' he said.

Clark sat down and crossed his long legs at the ankles.

'You were a friend of Alice's, weren't you?'

'Yeah. Do you remember me? We met at that football game I mentioned.'

'Sort of. I wasn't feeling so hot that night, if you know what I mean.'

'You seemed stoned,' Michael said. Clark didn't look stoned now. He appeared very alert. He was definitely watching Michael closely. Michael pulled his coat tighter, conscious of the weight of the automatic pistol in his inside pocket.

'I might have been. What did you want to ask me about Alice?'

'Well, she's dead, you know.'

'Yeah, I know,' Clark said, betraying no signs of grief. 'I read about it in the papers.'

'Did you come to the party that night?'

'No. Alice didn't invite me. Were you there?'

'Yeah. Why didn't Alice invite you?'

'I don't know. She was mad at me.'

'Why?'

Clark took a gulp of beer and set down the can. 'What is this?'

'What's what?'

'Why are you here? Who gave you my address?'

'I discovered your address by accident. As to your other

question – I have doubts about how she died. The police say it was suicide. I think they might be wrong.'

'You think she was murdered?'

'I think it's a possibility.'

Clark thought a moment. His eyes never left Michael. 'Go on,' he said finally.

'Do you think she killed herself?'

'I wasn't there.'

'But you were her boyfriend. Did she show any signs she was about to commit suicide?'

'No. When I read about it, I was surprised.'

'How come you didn't come to the funeral?'

'I don't believe in funerals.'

'That's not much of an answer.'

'I wasn't invited.' Clark stood slowly and moved towards the kitchen, stopping beside the wall, standing above Michael. 'Sure you don't want a beer?' he asked.

'I'll take one,' Michael said. Clark stepped into the kitchen, opened the refrigerator and handed him a can of Coors. Clark had left his own beer on the floor beside his chair. He returned to his seat beside the wall, only a few feet from Michael's stool. Michael opened the can and took a sip. 'It's cold,' he said.

I wish he wasn't so close.

'Tell me more about Alice's party,' Clark said, staring.

'It was big, with lots of people coming and going.' Michael felt uncomfortable under Clark's scrutinising gaze. The boy's eyes were not only bright, but penetrating; naturally an artist as talented as he would be visually perceptive. Michael wondered what he was giving away to Clark. He was getting nothing back from him. Clark was impossible to read. His expression – if it could be called that – was as flat as a dead man's.

'Yeah?' Clark said. He didn't appear overly interested in the details of the party.

'But there were only a few people there when Alice died.'

A painting sitting on the floor next to Clark caught Michael's attention. There was a creature and there was a girl – the usual. But this one was in a house, an ordinary room. It looked like an empty bedroom. The girl looked like Polly. The creature was a manfly. It was kissing the girl on the neck, probably sucking her blood. There was a real fly buzzing around the room. It landed on the wall near Clark's head. He took no notice of it.

I'm on fire.

The temperature inside the house had to be over a hundred. Michael was dying to remove his jacket. He thought of the gun, why he had brought it. He wasn't going to kill Clark. He had meant only to scare him into telling the truth. Now he was beginning to feel scared. He took another gulp of beer.

'Have you been to the McCoy house much?' Michael asked.

'No.'

'Have you been there lately?'

'No.'

'Oh.' The fly leaped on to the shoulder of Clark's grey T-shirt. Clark continued to ignore it. Michael felt off balance. He had plotted too long against Clark in his own mind. The physical presence of the guy was intimidating the hell out of him. And that stupid fly. He had always hated flies. 'Have you been to see Polly since Alice died?' he asked.

'No.'

'But I spoke to Polly this morning. She says you were at her house the night her aunt died.'

'She's wrong.'

The fly crawled towards Clark's neck, pausing beneath his Adam's apple. He mustn't be able to feel it. Or else he liked flies.

Of course he likes flies. He's always painting them.

'Polly also thought you were there the night of the party.' Michael said.

'She wanted me to come at the end, but I didn't.'

'So you were invited?'

'Why are you asking me all these questions?'

Michael desperately wanted to move. He wanted to brush away the fly from Clark's neck, and then put more space between the two of them. He also wanted to pull his coat closed tighter. Clark was staring at Michael's coat pocket now, the way it hung down slightly. Michael could feel the eyes of every creature in every sketch in the room watching him. He felt – knowing full well it was a hysterical thought – as if they were Clark's allies.

'I told you why,' Michael said.

'The paper I read said Alice died with a gun in her mouth?'

'That's right.'

'That doesn't sound like murder to me.'

'The gun in her mouth didn't kill her,' Michael said, straining to keep his voice steady. The fly crawled around the back of Clark's head and disappeared. But Michael knew it was still there. He could feel it as if it were crawling along the base of his own skull. 'She was killed by a blow to the nose.'

Clark showed a flicker of interest. He stood away from the wall, moving closer to Michael. 'Go on.'

He was committed. He would throw everything at Clark that he knew or suspected and see what happened.

He saw plenty happen, quicker than he thought he would.

'It was some kind of set-up,' he began. 'We were downstairs in the living room when we heard this shot. But the shot—'

The fly suddenly buzzed from behind Clark and went straight for Michael. It had chosen a bad time. Michael was in the middle of trying to readjust his coat. The fly made him jerk slightly, as if he were going for something *inside* his coat. Then again, maybe the fly made no difference. Clark obviously suspected Michael was carrying a weapon. Sooner or later, he would probably have lashed out.

Clark snapped his right foot up. He had on heavy black boots. The tip caught Michael in the lower right side of his ribcage, sending him and the stool he was sitting on toppling backwards. Michael hardly had a chance to react. Pain flared across his side. The back of his skull hit the wall hard. He fell to the floor at an awkward angle.

Oh, man, this is bad.

Clark loomed above, the manfly painting in his hands. This time Michael definitely reached for the gun. He had his fingers on the handle and was pulling it out when the canvas came crashing down on him. The frame tore into the top of his scalp, the canvas ripping down over his face. He felt the gun slip from his hand. Then another hand – this one had thick numbing fingers – reached inside his brain. He momentarily blacked out. The next thing he knew, Clark was leaning over him, the barrel of the automatic pressed to his cheek. Clark's hair seemed suddenly much redder. Then Michael realised he was seeing him through the film of his own blood.

'I didn't kill her, dude,' he hissed, showing some emotion at last. 'She was my girl. Maybe it was you who killed her. Maybe I should kill you and bury you in the backyard. What do you say to that, Mr Mike?'

'Go to hell,' Michael whispered.

Clark chuckled. Then he drew back the hand that held the gun and a freight train hit the side of Michael's head.

He came to an hour later. The fly was crawling around his ears. He waved it away, feeling nauseated. His hair and shirt were a mess with sticky, wet blood. Clark was gone. So was the gun. He sat up and groaned, the room spinning at odd angles. He suspected he had concussion. He noticed Clark's book still face down on the floor. He crawled towards it, throwing off the painting wrapped around his neck. *Shakespeare's Collected Works*. Clark had been reading *Romeo and Juliet*.

Michael stumbled outside on to the cracked drive. The

Harley-Davidson had gone for a ride. He checked his watch. The sun would be setting soon.

'Don't come to the all-night party, Mike.'

Michael climbed into his car. He had to get down to the dock.

CHAPTER 10

Jessica and Sara stopped at the first drugstore they saw when they got off the freeway in San Pedro, not far from Los Angeles Harbour. It was after six. The boat was set to sail at precisely seven. They had little time to purchase the contraceptives.

'So what are we going to get?' Sara asked as Jessica turned off the engine.

'Ask the pharmacist for his recommendation.'

'No way. I'd be too embarrassed.'

'What's the big deal?' Jessica asked. 'They're professionals.' She added, 'I'll wait for you here.'

'Hold on a second, sister. I'm not going in there alone. You go in.'

'Why me?' Jessica asked. 'You look more innocent.'

'All the more reason you should do it.' She grinned. 'You slut.'

Dinner with the parents had been far more enjoyable than Jessica had anticipated. First of all the food was fantastic. Both Sara and she had lobster. Then her mom and dad had been in good spirits. They hadn't brought up her future once. The conversation had revolved mainly around the ceremony. Mr and Mrs Cantrell had loved her song. Sara's various improvisations had been tactfully forgotten. Jessica's mom had fallen in love with Michael.

'He seems such a nice boy. How come you only went out with him one time, Jessie?'

One sticky spot during the entire meal wasn't bad. Russ and Bill were riding down to the boat with their buddies. Make that two different sets of buddies. Nobody on the football team would speak to Russ. He had, after all, supposedly wiped out their varsity tree. The situation didn't seem to bother him. During the brief time Jessica had spent talking to Russ after the ceremony, he'd appeared removed from the whole situation. Perhaps that was what came from being locked up too long. Sara and Russ had looked stiff together. Sara still wasn't talking about it.

Jessica's mood had continued to brighten since the applause for her song. But it could have been hormonal. The idea of a sleazy encounter on the high seas no longer depressed her. Indeed, she was now looking forward to it.

'I wish I had more slut in me,' Sara said, jolting Jessica back to the present situation.

'Is someone having second thoughts?'

'No,' Sara sad quickly. 'I was just wondering, you know, if it will hurt. I've heard that it can. Have you heard that?'

Jessica nodded solemnly. 'I read about this one girl – the first time she had sex, she bled so much she had to have a transfusion.'

Sara snorted. 'Get out of here.'

'Don't worry. I honestly believe we'll find it a deeply moving and fulfilling experience.'

'I hope not. I just want to have some fun. So what are we going to get?'

'What are our choices?' Jessica asked.

'In a drugstore, there're condoms, foam and sponges.'

'Guys aren't supposed to like to wear condoms.'

'I heard that, too,' Sara said. 'But they're safer.'

'You think Russ caught something at juvenile hall?'

'The place is full of guys.'

'That's worse,' Jessica teased.

'Please, we just ate.'

'Why don't we get all three? None of it can cost much.' Not to mention the fact that she wasn't hurting financially. Less than an hour ago, her father had given her an envelope stashed with ten crisp one hundred-dollar bills. The cash was supposed to be spending money for next week in Hawaii, but she was going shopping this week. Boy, was she going shopping.

'Great,' Sara said. 'And have Bill put on a wet suit while you're at it.'

'We just have to buy the stuff. We don't have to use it all at once. Come on, I'll go with you.'

The drugstore was empty except for the pharmacist and a helper. Unfortunately, the pharmacist appeared preoccupied in the back making up prescriptions. Worse, his sole employee was a total babe of around nineteen years old. He smiled as they entered.

'Can I help you find something?' he asked.

'No,' they said in unison, looking at each other. Jessica leaned over and whispered in Sara's ear, 'Let's go somewhere else!'

'We don't have time!' Sara whispered back.

'This is totally humiliating. I'd rather have a baby.'

'You're coming to the counter with me.'

'I'm just here to get a toothbrush.'

'Jessie!'

'Shh! Tell him our names why don't you.'

They huddled into a back row and inspected the store's G.I. Joes and Gumbies. Sara idly picked up a package of pink balloons. 'Those won't fit,' Jessica warned.

Sara threw the balloons down in disgust. 'I'm supposed to be the first one to the ship. I have to talk to the captain about a cheque I gave him.' She glanced towards the counter. 'I think I see them.'

'Where?'

'Near the cash register.'

'All right, here's what we'll do,' Jessica said. 'I'll call the guy over and get him to help me pick out a toy. You grab the stuff, get the pharmacist's attention and we'll be on our way.'

'Why can't I get help with the toy?'

'Because I thought of it first. Now get away from me.'

Sara sulked over to the laxative section. Jessica smiled and waved her hand. The guy saw her and hurried to her side. He had blond hair like Bill's, but was taller and thinner than Bill. She could tell he liked her, glasses and all.

I hope to God he doesn't ask me for my number.

'Looking for something?' he asked.

'Yeah,' she said, picking up a brown plastic horse. 'I wanted to ask you about this toy.'

'Yes?'

'Ah – how much is it?'

He checked the price, which was clearly marked on

the side. 'Two twenty-five.'

'Oh,' she said. Sara had reached the proper area and was quickly examining the boxes on the shelves. 'What kind of horse is it?' Jessica asked. He took it from her hands and fiddled with the cheap tiny hatch on the underbelly.

'It looks like the Trojan horse.'

'Trojans?' she whispered. *How did he know?* Then she realised he was *not* – thank God – referring to the popular brand of condoms. She giggled loudly. 'Yeah, that's what it is.'

He smiled uncertainly. 'Buying it for a nephew?'

'Yeah.'

'What's his name?'

'Michele.'

'Your nephew?'

'I mean Michael.'

Oh, no, no, no!

Sara had finished making her selection – it apparently didn't take long when one was willing to take everything the store had to offer – and signalled the pharmacist. Unfortunately, someone else had entered the store. No, not another person. An all-seeing, greasy butterball.

'Do you live around here?' the guy asked Jessica.

'Sara, my darling!' Bubba exclaimed, sauntering up to

the counter, still wearing his ridiculous gold-tasselled sombrero and blue graduation gown. He must have stolen it.

Sara turned a distinctly unhealthy shade of green and threw Jessica a look of pure misery. She wanted help, Jessica knew. But Jessica wasn't about to give it to her. Bubba hadn't seen her so far and Jessica had no intention of letting him see her. She pulled the young man with her towards the corner, using him as a shield.

'I'd really like to know more about this horse,' she said.

'What are you doing here?' Bubba asked, picking up one of the boxes. Devilish delight filled his face. 'Sponges! A girl who thinks more of her man's pleasure than her own. Bravo, Sara! Bravo!'

'How old is your nephew?' the guy asked.

'Who cares?' Jessica asked. 'I mean, what?'

'I was just wondering if another gift might be more appropriate,' the guy replied, not put off by her rudeness.

'Is this all?' the pharmacist asked Sara. Sara nodded stiffly, not looking at Bubba, even though she was obviously trying to dematerialise him by the sheer power of her thoughts. Bubba raised a hand.

'Wait,' he said. 'We would like a bottle of baby oil.'

Bubba spoke to Sara. 'Usually, after exerting myself in lovemaking, I enjoy a full body massage. It restores my vital energies that much quicker.'

The pharmacist somehow kept a straight face, but it was clear it was only because he had been a pharmacist for many years. 'Would you like the oil?' he asked Sara.

'No,' she said curtly.

'Is that guy hassling your friend?' the handsome young man asked Jessica.

'I don't know her,' Jessica said.

Bubba put his arm lovingly around Sara and spoke to the pharmacist. 'This is all new to her. She's embarrassed. Look, she's blushing. Give us the largest bottle of oil you carry.'

'My name's Dave,' the guy said to Jessica. 'What's yours?'

'Why?' she asked, terribly distracted.

'I don't want the oil,' Sara said, pushing forward her money. 'But I'll pay for this other stuff *now*.'

'I won't hear of it,' Bubba said, reaching for his wallet.

'I was just wondering if maybe we could get together later?' the handsome young man asked Jessica.

'I can't,' she said.

'Why not?'

'I'm busy,' Jessica said. 'I'm married.'

Sara kept shoving her own money on the pharmacist. He finally showed mercy on her and took it, ringing up the three different boxes of contraceptives, minus the oil. Bubba moved back a step.

'Modern women,' he told the pharmacist, shaking his head, not overly displeased. 'They think they know what they want, when they haven't a clue what they *need*.'

'Thank you,' Sara told the pharmacist, grabbing the bag and hurrying for the door. Bubba watched her leave, then turned towards the rear of the store. Jessica tried to duck behind Dave. Too late.

'Give my regards to Bill, Jessie,' Bubba called. 'But if I were you, I'd keep Sara's receipt.'

Jessica gave the Trojan horse back to Dave and chased after Sara. When they were back in the front seat of the car, trying to breathe and not groan at the same time, Sara glanced over at Jessica and remarked, 'That wasn't so bad.'

Jessica stuck the keys in the ignition, her hand trembling. 'We handled it like mature adults,' she agreed.

CHAPTER 11

Wrong and right. Dark and light. Polly was confused. She did not know what to do. The flowers in her hands were dying. She had just bought them. Roses – the day they bloomed they began to wilt. She didn't suppose it mattered. Alice wouldn't care.

Polly knelt beside the grave, the grass thick and wet beneath her bare knees. Her headache had returned. The voice at her back didn't surprise her. She'd heard the motorcycle approaching from far off.

'So she really is dead,' Clark said.

Polly turned. Clark was all in black. She couldn't remember when she had last seen him in the sunlight. It could have been the day they had met. It didn't make much difference, the time of day; he brought the night with him. He was the only guy she knew who stood in his own shadow. She had not seen him since the night her aunt had died.

'Hi,' she said.

'Hello.'

'Did you think I lied to you about her?' she asked.

'You lie to me all the time.' He turned back to the tombstone, annoyed. Alice Ann McCoy. Polly could have sworn Ann was her own middle name. 'Go away.'

'You're not happy to see me?'

'No,' Polly said.

'Then why did you call?'

'I didn't call.'

'Then why am I here?' Clark asked.

'I don't know.'

Clark stepped on to the neighbouring grave, her aunt's. He grinned as he looked down, and she thought that he might spit. A green canvas bag hung by a strap over his shoulder. 'She finally choked to death, I see,' he said.

'The doctor said she went peacefully in her sleep.'

'But doctors lie.'

'Did you smother her?' she asked angrily.

Clark shrugged. 'She was old and ugly.'

'I hate you.'

He chuckled. 'You hated her. You hated taking care of her.'

'That's not true! Get out of here and leave me alone!'

Clark circled Alice's grave. He did so carefully, almost as if he feared the spot. He moved to Philip Bart's grave. A rock from a dynamite blast had put him in the ground. Polly had donated the plot to his family. It was supposed to have been her own plot.

Clark slipped the bag from his shoulder and set the strap over Philip's tombstone. His middle name had been Michael. Her father's name had been Michael. But neither her father nor mother was buried in this cemetery. There hadn't been enough of them left to fill a coffin. Their car had burned for ever. Ashes and smoke. If she closed her eyes, Polly could still smell it, and hear her father shouting at her to behave in the backseat – right before he had driven off the road.

Polly liked the name Michael. It brought back warm memories. But she still hoped Michael Olson didn't come to the party. Clark knelt beside his bag and began to unzip it.

'I'm not leaving,' he said. 'Today's your last day of school. It's our last chance.'

'For what?'

'To even the score.'

'You're not doing anything. They won't let you on the boat.'

'You can get me on board.'

'Why should I?' she asked.

He let go of the bag. Anger filled his face. 'You're sitting on your why.'

'They didn't kill her! She killed herself!'

'That's a lie. You're lying to me again.'

'Then you killed her.'

His anger left suddenly. He grinned. He had ugly lips, like a fish. It made her sick to remember all the times they had kissed. 'Closer to the truth, Polly. But not close enough. Go on.'

'What?'

'Tell me how I killed Alice.'

She stared down at her roses. They'd scraped away the thorns at the florist; nevertheless, she felt a sharp prick – a band of thorns wrapped around her head like the crown of thorns Jesus wore. Bloody red roses. Funeral flowers. A waste of money. Her vision wavered at Clark's question. 'I was outside in the backyard,' she said.

'All right.' He appeared to sigh. He'd wanted her to say something else. He went back to his bag, pulling out a tiny metal clock, black and red wires and a lump of what could have been orange Play-Doh. 'We'll say the party killed her. If there hadn't been a party, there would still be an Alice.'

Polly nodded wearily. 'Yeah.'

'Most of the kids who were at the party will be on the boat.'

'What is that stuff?'

Clark tapped the tombstone at his back. 'Mr Bart could tell you.'

'You're not going to blow up the boat!'

'Of course not.'

'You better not.'

He laughed. 'I'm just going to put a hole in it.' He crawled towards her, his leather-clad legs slithering over the grass like twin snakes. She thought he was going to grab her, kiss her – she didn't want him to kiss her, not that much – but he halted, shy of Alice's grave.

'You remember the party? All the kiddies were in the pool. They know how to swim.'

'Not all of them,' Polly said.

'Who doesn't know?' he asked gleefully.

'Jessie.' That was a fact. Jessica had grown up with a pool in her backyard and was going to Hawaii next week, but she had never learned to swim. She had almost drowned as a child. She was terrified of the water.

'Who talked you into the party?' Clark asked.

'Jessie. And Sara.'

Clark glanced at his bag. There was something black

and muddy inside that he had not unpacked. 'Sara never did like you.'

Polly put her hand to her head. She could feel the blood pounding beneath the skin. She had given blood all year – to different hospitals, more times than she was supposed to – and there was still so much pressure inside. Sometimes she honestly felt the only real way to let it all out would be to take a gun and put a hole in her skull the way Alice had.

'How did you know Jessie couldn't swim?' she whispered.

Clark reached over with his bony left hand – he was left-handed, as Alice had been – and touched Polly's lips with the nail of his index finger. He touched her teeth. He probably would have stuck his finger inside her if she had let him. He was trying to get inside her. He had been trying from the beginning, though he had never wanted to make love to her. She had never been able to understand that. He was one way, and he was another way. She imagined his finger would have felt the same way the cold hard barrel of a gun would have felt inside her mouth. She knew it would have been just as deadly. But that might not be such a bad thing, not if it stopped the pain. Her head was killing her!

'If I tell you that,' he said. 'I will tell you everything.'

He was asking for her permission. 'No,' she said.

'Are you sure?'

'No.'

'I'll kill them. I'll kill them all.'

She set the roses down. *For my sister*. 'He'll stop you.'

'Who?'

'Michael.'

'I very much doubt it.' Clark stood and put the explosives back in his bag. He held out his left hand. 'Come along, Polly. It's time.'

She went with him.

CHAPTER 12

Haven was her name, and she was at the end of a long and fun-filled career. In the sixties and seventies, she had been a popular choice for vacationers looking for an intimate cruise ship to take to Mexico's Mazatlán, La Paz or Acapulco. But that had been before a new generation of vessels – larger and more sophisticated – had pushed *Haven* into an uneconomic no-man's-land; she was too plush to haul cargo, and she was too plain and small to attract parties of the rich and pretty. When Bubba had come to Sara in the spring with the idea of renting *Haven* for Tabb High's all-night senior party, he had never spoken so truthfully as he did when he said it was the chance of a lifetime. Her captain had just decided to rent her out as a party boat, making the trip between Catalina and the mainland. This class party was to be one of his first short cruises.

Bubba had caught Sara at an anxious moment. She had been thinking hard and without success for a way to blow everybody's extracurricular mind one last time, and thus for ever ensure their fond memories of her leadership skills. Because neither side was aware of how desperate the other was, the negotiations between the captain of the *Haven* and Sara proceeded with remarkable smoothness. The captain didn't even mind a postdated cheque.

Yet the cost for the all-night party was unusually high – forty dollars per student, and that didn't include a hotel room to recover in on Catalina. But you only graduated from high school once, Sara had thought. She figured the class should be able to stay awake until *Haven* returned them to the mainland the next evening. From the beginning, the idea of the class bumming around together on the island all day had struck her as the best part of the plan. When she had announced the extravaganza, practically every senior had bought a ticket.

It was only because Sara had taken extra pains to keep the price as low as it was that she found herself in desperate need of an LA Lakers victory over the Boston Celtics.

Jessica, however, was blissfully unaware of the financial complications surrounding the evening as she sat on the edge of the bed in 'her' cabin and watched as Sara split their drugstore bounty. It was just as well. Jessica already had plenty on her mind, not the least of which was the fact that, although *Haven* was still anchored to the dock, she was no longer on dry ground.

They don't have icebergs this far south, Jessica told herself. *The Titanic was one in a million.*

Maria's accident had been one in a million. It had been that kind of year. Jessica wished they had gone to Disneyland as a normal school class would. She was afraid to hold her breath and stick her head underwater in her own bath. The floor beneath her feet was swaying now, ever so slightly.

'I think we should put the stuff in the bathroom cabinets,' Sara said, dumping everything out of their boxes and on to the bed.

'Are you giving me the condoms and taking the foam or what?' Jessica asked.

'No, you take some of each.'

'Then I don't think we should put it in the cabinets. Imagine how Bill or Russ will feel if he sees we have a selection. We should make it look like we just happen to have something with us.'

'That's a good idea.'

'Another thing, don't throw away the boxes. I want

to read the directions.'

'The stuff is pretty self-explanatory, don't you think?'

'I don't know. I've never seen it before. Have you?'

'No.'

Jessica picked up the roll of condom packets. 'Let's look at one.'

Sara stopped her. 'No, we shouldn't waste any.'

'We won't waste it opening the corner and peeping inside.'

'Yeah, we will. Then it will be contaminated.'

'So what? We can just throw it out. What do we have here? A dozen. That's six each,' Jessica said.

'Is that a lot? I mean, how many times do people usually have sex when they have sex?'

Jessica laughed. 'What a stupid question.' Then she thought a moment. 'I'm not sure.'

'I don't think we should waste any.'

'All right. You know what just occurred to me?'

'What?'

'That we don't know what the hell we're doing.'

'Do you think they will?' Sara asked, serious.

'Oh, yeah. Bill and Russ have been around. Hasn't Russ?'

'I never asked him. Have you asked Bill?'

'No,' Jessica said.

'But you figure he did it with Clair, right?'

'What an awful thing to say! Now you have me worrying how I'll match up.'

'Sorry,' Sara said. Something outside the cabin's tiny round porthole caught her attention. 'Oh, no. Don't look.'

'What?'

'Nick's just appeared, and he's got Maria with him.' Jessica stood up from the bed and reached the window in one step. The dimensions of the cabin were going to take some getting used to. The whole room was not much larger than her walk-in cupboard at home. She could feel her heart pounding as she pressed her face to the circle of glass.

'She'll have trouble getting around the ship in that chair,' Jessica said. *Haven* sat between the dock and the western sky, throwing a deep shadow over the boarding ramp and the boardwalk beyond. Despite the fact that they were to set sail within minutes, a surprising number of kids continued to mill about the dock. Nick was having no trouble wheeling Maria's chair up the ramp. Jessica had forgotten how small she was.

Her lovely long hair. She cut it all off.

Hair meant nothing next to an injured spinal cord, and yet its loss deeply troubled Jessica.

'Not as long as she stays on deck,' Sara said, also peering out the window.

'I didn't know she was coming to the party.'

'Who did?'

'Well, she must have bought a ticket,' Jessica said in a slightly accusatory tone. She still hadn't forgiven Sara for not telling her Michael was to be valedictorian when Sara must have known way in advance. Jessica had been anxiously awaiting Michael's arrival. Sara swore she had *given* him a ticket.

'The tickets are tickets. They don't have names written on them.' Sara paused. 'You won't be able to avoid her all night.'

The ramp carried Nick and Maria out of sight around the curve of the ship. Jessica came to a decision. 'I'm not going to try.' She stood back from the window. 'Come on. We'll talk to her now, get it over with.'

'Whatever you say,' Sara replied without enthusiasm. She picked up the contraceptives on the bed and stuffed most of them under Jessica's pillow. Except for Polly, they were the only students who had rooms. Theirs were located towards the stern, adjacent to each other, but unconnected by a door. Jessica wasn't sure where Polly's was. Polly had asked when she had come on board if Sara could get her a place to crash. Sara had been quick to oblige; the evening had yet to begin and Polly already looked wasted.

The remainder of the passenger rooms were locked tight, and would remain so the whole night. Kids who wanted to sleep before they reached Catalina would have to do so outside on the top deck or on the floor in one of the main rooms.

'We'll take care of the stuff later,' Jessica said as Sara continued to stare at the label on one of the boxes.

'Do you think he was right?' Sara asked.

'Who?'

'Bubba. About using a sponge and a man's pleasure and all that?'

'Ask him. What did he write in your yearbook, anyway?'

Sara hid the box under Jessica's top sheet. 'Shut up.'

The corridor to the stairway, or companionway, was narrow. Jessica detected a faint odour of diesel in the air. No nuclear power aboard this vessel. Mr Bark would have been pleased. Too bad he was going to be unable to chaperone the party. Word had it that he had developed a sudden unbearable rash on his hands. Miss Fenway, a secretary in the administration building, was to take his place.

A bell rang as they climbed on to the upper deck. The

kids loitering on the dock began to walk up the boarding plank. The temperature was still warm, but Jessica could feel it dropping. Cool air over warm water – the fog would roll for sure. She hoped the captain didn't accidentally miss Catalina on the way out to sea.

'Aren't you going to check people's tickets?' Jessica asked, making a brief futile scan for Michael.

'Nope,' Sara said. 'If someone wants to come that bad, I ain't going to turn them away.'

Nick had parked Maria's chair near the bow of the ship. He was pointing out something of interest on a nearby tanker. Maria appeared to be listening closely.

'Promise me I will never have to see you again.'

'Do you want me to come with you?' Sara asked, watching her.

'Yeah,' Jessica said.

Nick noticed their approach and alerted Maria. Jessica saw one thing had not changed. Maria's eyes were still dark, still solemn. Yet a smile seemed to touch her lips as their eyes met. Jessica reached out both her hands. Maria took them after a slight hesitation. Their fingers squeezed together briefly, lightly.

'I'm glad you're here,' Jessica said.

'Thank you,' she said, her eyes fixed on Jessica's face.

'Hi, Maria,' Sara said, leaning over and giving her a

quick hug and kiss. Jessica wished she had done the same. Maria gently returned Sara's embrace.

'I liked your speech,' Maria said.

'I'm having it copyrighted,' Sara said. 'How are you?'

'Fine.'

'You look good.'

'Thank you.'

It was all too formal. Maria continued to watch Jessica with her dark eyes, and even though Jessica didn't detect a hint of hostility in them, the tension between them was still there.

Why can't we just talk?

A silly question. She could walk and Maria couldn't.

'You got us a big enough ship here, Sara,' Nick said.

'Hey, Nicky,' Jessica said.

'Hey, Jessie,' he replied, chuckling.

Sara moved to his side and wrapped an arm around his waist, saying, 'There is one thing I haven't told anybody about this boat.'

'What?' Nick asked.

Sara poked his powerful biceps. 'How are you at rowing?'

Sara went on flirting with Nick, and Jessica thought it was cute and everything, but she couldn't help wondering why Sara wasn't spending every available minute with Russ. He would be heading back up north come Sunday morning.

Jessica lightly squeezed Maria's hands again and asked if they could talk later. Maria hesitated before nodding. Jessica left her to go and stand by the boarding plank, and repeatedly checked her watch. A second bell rang. The last of the people on the dock boarded.

Please be here, Michael. Please God.

'Should be a fun night,' Bill said, appearing suddenly by her side. He had on a yellow turtleneck sweater and shiny black shoes. He looked good. He always looked good. The boxes of condoms and foam popped into her mind. She pushed them away. She tried instead to imagine the thrill of having his naked body lying beside hers. The picture wouldn't come. A third bell rang. One of the few crewmen appeared and began to withdraw the plank.

'Yeah, it's going to be great,' she said, her heart sinking.

'Is Michael here?' Bill asked.

'Who?'

'Olson?'

'No.' She spoke to the crewman. 'We're expecting someone.' The sailor went right on pulling in the plank. The end clanged off the dock and hung out limply from the faded white hull. 'That's a shame,' he said.

'Could I sign your yearbook?' Bill asked.

'Later,' Jessica said sadly. Then she spotted a figure striding briskly around a wall of stacked pallets. She almost lost her glasses jumping to her toes. 'He's here! He's here! Sir, our friend's come. Put down the plank, please, sir. Thank you. He's here.'

Michael was on board a minute later, his yearbook in his hand. Bill gave him a warm slap on the back and complimented him on his valedictorian speech. Jessica felt more than a little awkward welcoming Michael with Bill at her side. Michael didn't seem to mind. Her joy at his arrival surprised even her. Once she had thought she was in love with him. Now she knew she was.

Before the night is over, I have to tell him.

Michael shook her hand and thanked her for holding the boat for him. He seemed to have just taken a shower. His hair looked damp. He moved on to speak with Nick after talking to her for less than a minute.

Jessica left Bill a moment later to be alone at the stern of the boat. A breeze came up from the north and a fine mist rose up over the flat ocean. The anchor was lifted and the ship slipped away, the lights of the harbour blurring in the mist, growing fainter. The western sky went from orange to purple to black. The party kicked into high gear. Jessica felt little inclination to join in. She shivered, looking at the dark water beneath her feet. She had always had nightmares of drowning.

CHAPTER 13

Although he had been in a hurry to reach the harbour when he left Clark's house, Michael soon realised he could not board the ship with his hair and clothes full of blood. He made a quick stop at his house to wash and change. Fortunately, his mother and Daniel were not there to see what a mess he was. They had been disappointed when he hadn't let them take him out for a celebration meal after the ceremony. He had given them some feeble excuse about work he had to finish at JPL.

Michael was worried his mother would have the baby early. She hadn't said anything, but he noticed after the ceremony that her breathing was irregular, as if she were having pain. If he hadn't felt so close to solving the mystery of Alice's death, he wouldn't have left her.

Close does not count in life and death. Only in horseshoes.

When had the shotgun been fired that had torn

away part of the shingle outside the bedroom window? What did that shot have to do with the one that had been fired into Alice's head? Who had broken Alice's nose? Had Clark really been at the party? Why would Polly lie to him?

The endless stream of questions didn't frighten Michael as it might have another investigator. He, in fact, felt as if he had almost enough pieces of information to solve the puzzle; he simply had to arrange them properly and the picture would make sense. But as with a child's puzzle, he knew that one more piece – preferably a big corner piece – would help speed up the process immensely.

Showering at home, Michael had begun to take Polly's warning more seriously. He began to worry that if he didn't return from the all-night party, his efforts on Alice's behalf would be wasted. Cursing his shortage of time, he took a piece of paper and quickly jotted down everything he had discovered, including half a dozen different scenarios that might cover the facts. The problem was, all of his scenarios had at least one major hole.

But he *was* able to print Clark's full name and address on the bottom of the paper. If nothing else, Lieutenant Keller could follow up that lead.

Sealing his information in an envelope, he took it to the station. The lieutenant happened to be in his office.

'What can I do for you, Mike?' he asked politely, offering him a seat. Michael was not fooled by the seriousness with which the officer welcomed him. Keller may have respected his intelligence and persistence, but he also had doubts about his emotional stability. Michael did not take the offered seat.

'I'm sorry, I'm in a hurry,' he said, handing the policeman the envelope. 'I want you to hold this for me until next Monday. If I don't return for it by then, I want you to open it.'

Keller glanced from the envelope to Michael's face a couple of times and Michael could see the lieutenant's doubts about young Mr Olson's stability being replaced by something far worse – pity.

'What's inside?' Keller asked.

'Information.'

'About Alice McCoy's death?'

'Yes.'

Keller stood uneasily. Perhaps he was worried young Mr Olson was going to follow in Alice McCoy's footsteps and go out with a bang. 'Why wouldn't you be back to pick it up?'

Michael smiled to put him at ease. 'Who knows? I just graduated today. I might find a girl tonight and elope.' Then he got serious. 'Please hold it for me. And if, by chance, you still have it on Monday, give what I had to say some thought.'

'But where are you going tonight?' he asked.

'To our all-night senior party.'

The lieutenant relaxed slightly. 'Sounds like fun.'

'I think it's going to be a wild party,' Michael agreed.

Now he stood at the edge of the party and above the ocean. They were an hour out of dock and he had already searched *Haven* from the bow to the stern. Clark didn't appear to be on board. Yet Michael was far from convinced he wasn't there. He had been unable to persuade the captain to let him look in the thirty locked passenger rooms. Granted, if he couldn't get into the rooms, Clark shouldn't be able to. But with so many places to hide, Michael had to wonder. Even without access to the rooms, a sufficiently determined individual could probably have found some hidden corner to tuck into. It was a big ship. Michael was debating whether or not to give *Haven* another going-over when Nick came out of the main lounge and joined him by the rail.

'The game's going to start in a couple of minutes,' Nick said.

'I'll watch the second half,' Michael said.

Nick stared out over the calm water. The rise and fall of the ship was almost non-existent. The fog continued to gather. The coast was already invisible and their path through the night seemed to be taking them into a land of clouds.

'It's peaceful out here,' Nick said.

'You like the water?' Michael asked.

'I didn't know how much until tonight. Did you know, Mike, when I was growing up in the barrio, I never saw the ocean once?'

'That's amazing.'

Nick leaned on the rail. 'I hear they have a sailing class at UCLA. I think I might sign up for it.' He laughed softly at the thought. 'Imagine me on a yacht?'

'Who knows, with the salaries they pay in the NBA, you might be able to afford one some day.'

Nick shook his head. 'That's a one-in-a-million shot. I'll never play pro ball.'

Michael leaned on the rail beside him. He wondered how deep the water was. The thought nagged at him. He wasn't able to relax. 'Yeah, you'd be better off concentrating on your education. You sprain your ankle or twist your knee and you're out. But they can't take your degree away from you.'

'The day I get it, I'll have you to thank for it.'

'You get what you deserve. Good things are going to come to you.'

'I read that last book you gave me,' Nick said.

'Which one was that?'

'*The Hound of the Baskervilles* – Sherlock Holmes. It was great.'

'I'm glad you enjoyed it. I'll give you another one.'

'You remind me of him.'

'Me? I don't smoke a pipe.'

Nick looked at him closely. 'What's wrong?'

'Nothing.'

'You look kind of down.'

'I'm all right,' Michael said.

'Have you talked to Jessie today?'

'Not really. How's Maria?'

Nick frowned. 'Very quiet.'

'Has she told you why she wanted to come tonight?'

'No.'

'Has she threatened you again like she did at the hospital?'

'No, nothing like that. But she's got something on her mind. She seems to be *waiting*.'

Michael glanced about, feeling he couldn't wait. He tapped Nick on the shoulder. 'I'll catch up with you later, buddy.'

Above the main lounge, where the bulk of the class had gathered in front of the large screen TV to watch the final game of the NBA play-offs, sat *Haven*'s bridge. Michael looked up and spotted the helmsman – lit a faint blue and red by rows of luminescent dials – turning the wheel several degrees to port. That was another place the captain hadn't let him inspect.

Am I searching for Clark or Jessie?

He found Polly instead. She stood alone against the entrance to *Haven*'s galley. Michael could hear kids laughing and carrying on inside. Few were walking the deck. The temperature had dropped steadily since they had pulled out of the harbour. The salty breeze, however, continued to blow soft and easy.

'Is your headache better?' he asked cheerfully.

She jumped slightly at the sound of his voice. She had on a short-sleeved white blouse, a thin red skirt. Gooseflesh covered her arms. 'I'm all right,' she said.

He had told Nick the same thing a minute ago. He had lied. His head was throbbing from Clark's blow. Worse, his vision continued to blur off and on. It blurred now as he looked at Polly. She went back to playing with her dark hair, watching the fog.

'I'm sorry I ganged up on you this morning,' he said.

'That's OK.'

'Having fun?'

'I'm cold.'

'Why don't you go inside and have a hot drink? I'll have one with you.'

She stared at him. 'He likes me cold.'

'Come again?'

'He told me: "Stay alive babe and stay cold. It's the only way for the likes of us." That's what he said. He's weird.'

'I saw him today.'

It didn't surprise her. 'At the cemetery?' she asked.

'No, I went to his house. Did you see him at the cemetery?'

She nodded. 'Before I came to the harbour.'

'When was that?'

'Five o'clock, six o'clock?'

Clark must have gone straight to the cemetery after knocking him out. 'Did he have a gun with him?' Michael asked.

'I didn't see everything in his bag.' She chewed on her lower lip, looking exhausted.

'Is he on board?' he asked.

'Yes.'

He moved a step closer. 'Are you sure?'

'Yes.'

'Where?'

'I don't know.'

'You must have some idea?'

'I don't. He comes and goes, like lightning.'

The simile made him pause. Polly was the only one who even indirectly supported his belief that Alice hadn't committed suicide, and yet, whenever he spoke to her, he didn't believe her. 'Why is he here?' he asked.

'I can't tell you.'

'Why not?'

'He'll kill me.'

'Does he intend to kill me?'

'If you get in his way.'

She was doing it to him again – confusing him. He remembered the weather-beaten paper he had found in her backyard. 'Polly, back in November, I gave you a form for your aunt to sign. What did you do with it?'

'I gave it to Clark.'

'Why?'

'He wanted it.'

'Where and when did you give it to him?'

'In my backyard, during the storm.' She shivered. 'I have to take a warm bath now before it gets any later, Mike. I don't care what he says. I have to warm my blood.'

'I'll see you around,' he muttered, distracted, hardly caring how or where she would take her bath. As Polly turned and walked away, for an instant, everything in his immediate surroundings seemed to jump into the air, and land in reverse. He put his hand to his head and took it away and found blood on his fingers. No, it was not concussion that was making reality dance. She had given him the answer! For an instant, he'd had the entire solution to the night of the party, to the whole crazy year, in seed form in his mind. Not the details of the truth, but the essence of it. Unfortunately, it had gone as quickly as it had come, leaving him more confused than ever; leaving him cold, too, almost as if he had just fallen overboard.

It will come back.

CHAPTER 14

Either one person had sneaked fifty gallons of alcohol on board or else a fair percentage of the class had ignored the prohibition against mixing ocean cruises and intoxicating substances and had brought enough good cheer on to *Haven* to give themselves and their closest friends a respectable buzz. The air in the main lounge literally stank of booze. Sara was getting drunk just breathing. Unfortunately, the basketball game on the tube was keeping her more sober than she would have liked. Half-time had just begun and the Lakers were down by eight points.

'The Lakers are a great second-half team, aren't they?' she asked Nick, who, along with Maria, was sitting with her in the rear of the lounge. Maria appeared to be enjoying the game, although she hadn't said more than five words since it had begun.

'They are, yeah,' Nick said.

'That's good,' Sara said.

'But so are the Celtics,' Nick added.

A faint creaking sound went through the lounge as the floor dropped a few inches. It was a rare sign that they were far out at sea. The lounge could have been in a bar on the west side of town. It was loud enough.

'But an eight-point lead,' Sara said. 'That's nothing in a basketball game, is it?'

Nick nodded. 'It can disappear in a couple of minutes.'

'If you were to put money on this game right now, who would you bet on?' she asked.

'You'd have to be crazy to put money down on the Lakers versus the Celtics. It's always close.'

'But just suppose? Who do you think is going to win?'

'The Celtics.'

'What? I thought you were a Lakers fan?'

Nick smiled. 'Yeah, but you're talking about money.'

He was not very reassuring. Sara stood. 'I've got to find somebody,' she said.

Bubba was sitting on the bar on the far side of the room. Most of the kids who were drinking were doing so from brown-bagged pints barely hidden in their coat pockets. Bubba had a fifth of Jack Daniel's riding his left knee. Every time the Lakers scored, he toasted the room and the basket and took a chug. It really pissed her off that he was having such a good time.

Clair stood by his side. She was not drinking. In fact, she didn't seem all that happy about his flagrant consumption. She was trying to take the bottle away from him. She was a little late; the thing was three-quarters empty. Then again, it was always said that Bubba could drink a crew of sailors under the table.

Why are people always saying good things about this jackass?

'You've had enough,' Clair said, unwrapping one finger from the neck of the bottle only to see the finger before it wrap back around the neck. 'It's still early and you're already loaded.'

'I'm not loaded,' Bubba said, slurring his speech. 'I'm merely giving a few of my brain cells a much needed vacation.'

'You're going to end up falling overboard,' Clair said, getting annoyed. She gave up trying to be gentle about it and yanked the bottle from his hand. He laughed uproariously.

'That's why I've got to get my drinking done now!'

Sara poked him in the side. 'I need to talk to you.'

He turned, his jovial smile rolling around his fat face

like a goldfish in a bowl. 'Sara, how come you've left your post? Who's steering the ship?'

Clair gave her a sympathetic look. 'He's impossible when he's like this.'

Bubba reached out and grabbed Clair, putting his arm around her, snuggling the side of his head up to her smooth tanned cheek. 'But nothing is impossible when we're together, darling,' he said.

Sara half expected her to shove him away; he was, for all intents and purposes, slobbering on her. But Clair did nothing of the kind. She put her arm around him instead and hugged him back, blushing red and laughing as he turned and whispered something in her ear.

Sara just couldn't understand how such beauty could be attracted to such disgust.

Clair gave him a quick kiss on the forehead as she broke free a moment later, the bottle still in her hand. She began to walk towards the rear exit. 'I'm still dumping this poison, Bubba,' she called over her shoulder.

'There's plenty where that came from!' he called after her, giggling. He turned back to Sara. 'Isn't she wonderful?'

'The Lakers are losing,' she said flatly.

He sat back in mock surprise. 'No.'

'They're down by eight points. Nick says they're going to lose.'

'Does Nick want to play?'

'Huh.'

Bubba clapped his hands together. 'Yeah! The coach should put Nick in. He's a homegrown boy. It'll be legal.' Bubba went to jump off the bar. 'I'll radio for a helicopter.'

Sara grabbed his arm, keeping him on the bar. 'Stop carrying on like a lunatic. We've got a serious problem here.'

He eyed her as best he could with his eyes rolling around in a multitude of directions. 'We can't have a problem until the game's over.'

'But what if they lose?' she cried.

He leaned closer, his breath enough to anaesthetise a tubfull of clams, and raised a fat finger close to her nose. 'You know what your problem is, Sara?'

She paused. 'What?'

'You don't know how to dress.'

'What's wrong with the way I dress?'

He gestured to her orange dress. 'You're always in autumn colours.'

'So what?'

He turned his head and sneezed. She felt the spray. He

went on in a confidential tone. 'Autumn is a rotten time of year. School starts in autumn. Leaves fall off the trees in autumn. People hate autumn. They hate people who remind them of it.'

She sneered. 'Get off it.'

He belched loudly. 'It's a fact. You send out depressing vibes. Look at me. A minute ago, I was finishing my bottle and singing. Then you showed up.' He wiped at his eyes. 'Now I'm beginning to feel sad.'

'What are you sad about?'

'I feel so unhappy.'

'No, you don't.'

'I do. I can't bear it.'

'Well, what do you want me to do about it?'

He thought for a moment, looking as miserable as he would have her believe he was. Then a wild gleam entered his eyes, and he suddenly reached for her with his grubby paws. 'I want you to take your clothes off!'

She dodged him easily. He fell from the bar stool and landed on his face. She kicked him while he was down. He sat up and rubbed his head. 'Bubba, you're drunk,' she said, disgusted.

He rolled his eyes upwards and grinned. 'No, Sara. I'm just happy.'

She decided she would give him to the end of the game

– then she would kill him. She left him giggling on the floor.

Russ was bothering her as much as the game. He was acting like a stranger. No, stranger was too strong a word. He was being friendly and all – but that was the problem. He wasn't supposed to be her friend. He was supposed to be her boyfriend. At least that was her understanding. But she wondered if he knew. He had kissed her. He had told her he liked her. He had let her bail him out of jail. He had written to her while he was away; not so often as she might have wished, but a letter and a postcard should count for something. Yet they had never made any promises to each other. When she thought about it, they had never even *talked*, not really, not for any length of time. And now they were supposed to make love before the sun came up.

What the hell have I talked myself into?

It was a lonely thing, to suddenly realise that maybe she had been suckered all along, not by Russ, but by her own imagination.

He was watching the game with 'the boys'. That was fair enough. He hadn't seen his pals from the cross-country team since December. She didn't require every blessed second of his time. But eyeing him from across the room as he was sitting on the arm of a couch and laughing at some fool joke, a beer can in his hand, obviously having more fun than she was, she thought of all the trouble she had gone through to pick him up at the bus station. He owed her something. She strode up to him.

'Hi,' she said.

'Hi,' he said, glancing over briefly, before continuing with his wild tale of mystery and intrigue at the state's most exotic juvenile hall. 'Then I said to him, I said, "You hide that knife under my pillow again during a shakedown and I'll use it to shred every piece of clothing you've got." He called my bluff, the idiot. And a month later he was walking around with his—'

'Excuse me,' Sara interrupted. 'Russ?'

He looked at her again. 'What, Sara?'

She smiled. 'How are you doing?'

He glanced at the beer in his hand. The rest of his buddies were waiting for him to continue. 'I'm fine,' he said. 'What's wrong?'

'Nothing's wrong. I just wanted to, you know, say hi.'

'How about we talk in a few minutes?'

'The game starts in a few minutes.'

'Then we'll talk after the game. Would that be all right?'

'Sure. Yeah.'

He went to give the punchline of his story, then noticed she had made no move to leave. He smiled uneasily. 'I don't know if you want to hear this, Sara.'

'Why not?'

'It's kind of disgusting.'

'OK. Thanks. I'll take that as a compliment, being told to bug off because I'm not disgusting enough to listen to you.' She spun on her heel and stalked away. He called to her, but she didn't slow down till she was standing outside in the damp darkness beside the rail. The fog kept getting thicker. She kept getting more tense. She hadn't wanted to fight with him. She had promised herself she wouldn't. But whenever she was around him, she just wanted to strangle him!

Or kiss him. Why didn't he even kiss me after the ceremony when everybody was kissing everybody else?

She stood there for several minutes, catching her breath and trying to tell herself she was too cool to get upset about a boy. After a bit she began to notice her surroundings. It was a bizarre night. She could hear the splash of the water against the hull, could even smell it. But she could not see the ocean in any direction. *Haven* could have been ploughing through the sky above a storm.

'Hi,' a nearby voice said. It was that weird dude who

worked at the petrol station, the one with the greasy hair and moustache, the guy who had owned the gun that had killed Alice. He had come up so quietly that he had startled her.

'Hi,' she said.

He grinned. He had incredibly crooked teeth. 'You don't remember my name, do you?'

'No.'

'You're Sara, right?'

'Yeah. You go by a nickname – Rats?'

'Kats.'

'Yeah. Sorry. How are you doing?'

'Couldn't be better. How are you?'

'Fine.' He wasn't someone she would have chosen for a late-night ocean-cruise partner. The way he kept grinning at her – it was as if he was thinking about doing things to her she preferred not to know. His next question did not exactly put her at ease.

'Can you swim, Sara?'

'Yeah. Can you?'

He leaned over the rail and spat into the fog. How disgusting! Sara thought she heard the splash of the spit in the water. He must have grime in his saliva glands. 'I don't have to,' he said. 'I know how to float.'

'I think I'll go back inside.'

She heard him laughing to himself as she re-entered the lounge.

CHAPTER 15

Haven did not ordinarily require an entire night to reach Catalina. Usually the trip took only a couple of hours, but the captain was cruising slowly for the party; the engines were operating at only quarter power. Standing near the diesel-driven turbines, Michael was surprised at how quiet they were, especially since they must have been close to thirty years old. Michael always had a special admiration for machinery that performed its function year in and year out, and for the men who built it.

Clark was not in engineering. Michael had serious doubts that he was on board.

Haven's chief engineer had explained the fundamentals of the propulsion system to Michael earlier. He was now in the crew's galley having a cup of coffee. Michael had the engine room to himself. There was no wasted space.

The turbines were housed in huge, twin white-steel tunnels, out of which sprang a complex array of pipes that stretched about thirty feet to the ceiling and walls before disappearing into a massive black fuel tank. The tank was set in the middle of the floor; it neatly divided the rear of the ship's lowest deck from the front. It was amazing the amount of fuel a vessel like *Haven* consumed. Michael estimated the tank's capacity at over a thousand gallons. If fire ever got to it, the whole ship would blow.

Following the narrow passageway to the right of the tank, Michael left the rhythmic drone of the engines and headed for the storage area. He had been through the place once already, but decided to have another quick inspection before he headed topside.

The crew for the cruise was at a minimum; besides the captain, there were only eight men on duty. It was probably plenty. Although the ship seemed large to most of the class members, he knew it would be dwarfed by a modern cruise ship. Also, the trip out to Catalina was little more than a warm-up for *Haven*. Michael saw no one as he went through the various sections: the janitorial supply area, the linen department, the food stores, finishing with the machine shop. The latter was small but uncluttered. It occurred to him the place might be ideal for the meeting he was hoping to have later in the night.

Another invitation to Alice's party.

He surfaced into the night air at the ship's stern. He was surprised to find Jessica standing alone and staring back the way they had come, staring into nothing; the fog had cut visibility to practically zero. Thank God for radar. *Haven*'s horn blared once from the bridge, sounding lost as it faded and died over the invisible waters. Michael wondered why Jessica had been spending all her time by herself. He tactfully cleared his throat, and she turned around.

'Hi, Michael,' she said, smiling, quickly removing her glasses and slipping them in her back pocket.

He climbed the last treads of the companionway and stepped on to the deck. 'You should have a jacket on. It's getting chilly.' He moved up beside her, the water softly churning beneath their feet. Despite his remark, he liked the way she was dressed – in tight white trousers and a light blue sweater, her long brown hair reaching almost to her waist. He supposed she could have had on a canvas sack and he still would have found her perfectly presentable. She tugged at the arm of her sweater and looked at him expectantly.

'I had to wear this tonight,' she said. 'It's the last day of school.'

'Oh?'

'I had this same sweater with me my first day at Tabb. Don't you remember?'

'I do now, yeah. I still don't see how you got the grape juice out. I think you flew over to Switzerland and bought another one just so I wouldn't feel guilty.'

Her eyes lingered on him. 'Maybe I did.'

He laughed softly, feeling uneasy and happy. He was used to the contradictions she inspired in him. 'Why aren't you watching the game?' he asked.

'Why aren't you?'

'Not fair. I asked first.'

'It's so loud inside. It was giving me a headache.'

He nodded. 'I'm not a great party person myself.'

'I thought you weren't going to come. You cut it pretty tight.'

'Yeah, I had some business to take care of.'

'What was it?'

'Ah, nothing. Just stuff.'

They had a big wooden lifeboat and dull yellow light at their backs. Jessica was staring at his head strangely. She reached out to touch his hair. He stopped her. He knew his head was still bleeding. He wished he'd had time to get it stitched. He couldn't very well bandage it now. He had already wiped it several times with toilet paper.

'Your hair was wet when you came aboard, too,' she

said, pulling her hand back, her face falling slightly. 'You're the one who's going to catch cold. I should find you a towel.'

He could just imagine the colour he would turn the towel. Fortunately, in his black hair, the blood was hardly recognisable for what it really was, even under better lighting. No one else on board had even said anything about it.

Clark had struck him a nasty blow. Michael was looking forward to repaying the favour. He was still annoyed with himself for having been caught so easily. 'Don't bother,' he said.

'It's no bother.' She turned. 'Really, you must dry it.'

He stopped her again, this time grabbing her arm, perhaps a shade too hard. He released her quickly when he saw her startled expression. 'I know where a towel is, Jessie,' he said.

'OK.' She forced a smile. 'So, what's new? I loved your speech. It touched me.'

'I'm just glad I got to give it before you sang. You stole the show. How come you never told me you could sing like that?'

'You really like my voice?'

'I do. Have you ever thought of doing anything with it? Like getting in a band?'

She smiled, pleased. 'When I was younger, I used to fantasise about being on stage and having everyone chanting my name. Alice used to . . .' She paused. 'Alice used to encourage me to do something with it.'

'You should think about it.'

'Yeah? I don't know. I'll see.' An awkward silence followed, during which a disturbing warmth began to spread over the right side of Michael's scalp. He knew what it was. Jessica finally spoke. 'I broke the ice with Maria.'

'How was it?'

She sighed. 'Not horrible, not good. We only talked for a minute. But I felt like – this is going to sound weird – she'd like to talk more, but not yet.'

Nick had made a similar comment. Maria was waiting. Interesting. 'Give her time. The fact that she's here says a lot.'

'I hope you're right.' Jessica shook her head.

'What is it?'

'I was just thinking of that morning at the hospital. It was awful. I couldn't talk to her.' She peeped over at him. 'I couldn't talk to you.'

'You can always talk to me, Jessie,' he said, feeling a drop of blood trickle into his right ear. This was getting serious. He turned his head away from the water. He had better get to a bathroom. Jessica shook her head again.

'How? I never see you. You're never at school any more.'

'Well, from now on, you won't be at school either.' Here came another drop. He was lucky Clark hadn't done a lobotomy while he was at it.

'That's what's bothering me,' she said. 'We're together long enough to become friends, then we have to go our separate ways.'

'You'll meet a lot of people at Stanford.'

She chuckled sadly at the remark and brushed away a hair. 'I'm not going to Stanford.'

The blood was a distraction. He had momentarily forgotten the SAT disaster. She never had told him her scores. 'They didn't accept you?'

'There was no sense in even sending in my application.'

'I'm sorry,' he muttered.

'It's not your fault. I didn't mean to give you that impression. I shouldn't have brought it up.'

'I should have known they used different tests.'

She was getting upset at him. 'That's ridiculous. How could you . . .' She paused, staring. 'Are you bleeding?'

He practically leaped away from the rail. 'I scratched my ear. I think I'll go clean it up. It's nothing big. I'll talk to you later.'

'OK. Let's do that. Are you sure you're all right?'

'I'm fine, really.'

'I have to sign your yearbook.'

'Great.' He cupped his hand to his ear and backed away from her over the slippery deck. He had a regular vein pumping over his scalp from the feel of it.

'Michael?'

He stopped, for a second, caught by her eyes. She had the biggest eyes on the whole boat; he could have sworn it. 'What?'

She thought a moment. 'Nothing.'

The cramped and dimply lit bathroom behind the galley was empty. He was lucky, none of the blood had got on to the collar of his coat. Locking the door, he grabbed a whole roll of toilet paper and pressed it to the side of his head. The wound was deep and ragged. If he washed his hair in the sink, the bleeding would only worsen. When he had showered at home, the bath had been red as ketchup. He needed a hat. Maybe Bubba would lend him his.

Michael had stopped the bleeding and cleaned up as best he could when another spell of dizziness struck. He grabbed the edge of the sink, fighting to steady himself, his reflection in the mirror splitting into two. Before he could force his eyes back into focus, he thought he saw – in the mottled glass – Clark standing behind him. Not the Clark of this afternoon, but the one from last autumn, pale and drugged, arrogant and frightening. Michael jerked around frantically, his heart racing, then shook himself for being so foolish. Of course there was no one there.

The lounge was noisy as Jessica had said it would be. The fourth quarter had just begun. Celtics 82, Lakers 78. Ordinarily Michael would have enjoyed such a game, but tonight was far from ordinary. He was beginning to think the ship was haunted.

Bubba was standing on top of the bar, a half-empty bottle of Seagram 7 in his right hand, cheering on a Lakers comeback. Michael had once seen Bubba down a case of beer and a fifth of rum and an hour later ski off the top of Mammoth's most dangerous slope. Michael suspected that that was not Bubba's first bottle. Bubba was waving his sombrero around as if it were a pompom. Michael tapped him on the knee.

'You're going to kill yourself up there,' he said.

'Worry not for the royal Bubba, my dear Mike,' he said. 'If he should by chance fall, he will surely bounce.' Then he let out a howl and thrust his bottle into the air – spilling a few stinging drops of whisky over the top of Michael's head in the process – as the Lakers cut their deficit to two. 'My men!'

'I have to talk to you.'

'What?'

'I have to talk to you!'

'Go talk to Sara! She likes to talk!'

'Bubba.'

Michael probably would have got nowhere with him if the Celtics had not chosen that moment to call a timeout. Bubba apparently had a full bladder. As the players walked to the sidelines, he leaped off the bar, shouting, 'Show me to the captain's toilet!'

Michael led him to the bathroom he had used a moment ago. Bubba was not inside long, and when he came out, Michael grabbed him by the arm and dragged him into the galley, to a quiet table in the corner. The lighting in the dining area was low. There was no TV and few people were present. Bubba looked around in a daze.

'Where're my men in purple?' he asked.

'Give me two minutes and I'll let you get back to your game.'

'Where's my bottle?'

Michael had taken it from him on the way to the bathroom and thrown it into a garbage can. 'I'll get you a fresh one in a minute.'

Bubba pounded the table with his fist, satisfied.

'A kingly deal! Speak, Mike, and may your words be inspired.'

'I wanted to ask you about the night of Alice's party.'

Bubba's joyful demeanour faded. Michael also knew from experience that, although Bubba could drink like a sink, alcohol often brought out a hidden sensitivity. Bubba shook his head sadly. 'That poor girl. She was so beautiful. Had she lived, she might have got to know me better.' Then he paused and eyed Michael. 'You don't think I killed her?'

'Of course not.'

Bubba nodded, relaxing. 'That is good. The Bubba can be nasty, but he only wants to have fun.' He burped. 'I consider the killing of a beautiful girl to be a sin against the gods and the boys.' He glanced about. 'What's the score?'

'It hasn't changed. I have a problem about that night, Bubba. I want you to help me with it. The bedroom next to the one where Alice died – who was in there?'

'Was it not the exalted Bubba himself?'

'Was it?'

Bubba hesitated. 'Is this a trick question?'

'Were you in the room just before the shot was fired?'

He spoke reluctantly. 'It was me.'

'Were you with Clair?'

'The Bubba is well known for his discretion and his silence. This is a delicate subject.'

'Please, Bubba, I have to know the truth. I have to cross that room out of the equation before I can go on. Was Clair in there with you or not?'

'Yes.'

'How about anyone else?'

'No. Yes.'

'What does that mean?'

'Bill was in there before I got there.'

'With Clair?'

'Yes.'

'What were they doing?'

'Nothing. Absolutely nothing.'

'And then you entered the room? Right after Bill left?'

'Yes.'

'Why didn't you tell me this six months ago? Why did you lie to me?'

'The Bubba is well known for his—'

'Cut the crap.'

Bubba lowered his head and took a breath, a breath that seemed to sober him considerably. 'I was trying to protect Clair's reputation.'

Michael had to laugh. 'But you bragged in the car on the way to the party, in front of both Nick and me, how many condoms you used on her before you even went out with her.'

'I didn't.'

'Yes, you did.'

'No. I didn't have sex with Clair on our first date.'

'Why did you say you did?'

'At the time I thought the topic made for stimulating conversation.'

'If you didn't have sex with her, how did you keep her from killing you when she found out you didn't have any U2 tickets?'

'I gave her a gold necklace,' he admitted sheepishly.

'You bought her off?'

'I wouldn't put it in precisely those terms.'

'All right, back to the night of the party. How did you just happen to be upstairs and see Bill leaving the bedroom?'

'I was standing outside the bedroom door.'

'How's that?' Michael asked.

'I followed Bill up the stairs.'

'What were you doing outside the bedroom?'

'Listening.'

'Listening to what?'

'To what was going on inside,' Bubba said.

'And what was that?'

'Absolutely nothing.'

'That's the second time you've said that. What does it mean?' Michael insisted.

'I don't know. Nothing.'

'Did Bill see you when he left the room?'

'He bumped into me.'

'Was he mad at you?'

'He was upset.'

'At you?' Michael asked.

'No.'

'What was he upset about?'

'Clair and he weren't getting along.' He shrugged. 'I went inside to see how she was. I guess it was good timing on my part.'

Michael felt as if he were missing something obvious. 'Were you and Clair having sex when the gun was fired?'

'Mike! That is a very personal question. I do not feel legally or morally bound to answer it.'

'Did you hear anything coming from the adjacent room before the shot was fired?'

'No.'

'Are you sure?'

'Absolutely.'

'Dammit, Bubba.'

'Clair was moaning in my ear,' he admitted.

'You were having sex.'

'I didn't say that.'

'You two were having sex for the first time,' Michael said, finally understanding at least a part of the puzzle. 'And after doing it, you started to fall for her and feel protective of her.'

'Is there something wrong with that?'

'Not unless you have a huge stud reputation to maintain.'

Bubba sighed. 'It does demand a great deal of my energy.'

'Did you have condoms with you?'

'That's none of your business,' he snapped, showing a rare flash of anger. Then he showed something more rare, perhaps an emotion he had not displayed since before he had mastered the art of 'attitude' at the age of two. His face sagged into lines of deep pain. 'I didn't,' he said softly. 'I was careless.'

Michael leaned closer. 'She got pregnant?'

'Yes.'

'Well, that's all behind you now.'

'No, it's not.' Bubba took another deep breath; he was obviously struggling with intense feelings. 'She had an abortion, Mike. I talked her into it.'

Michael's instinctive distaste for the procedure rose up. He had to remind himself his views were not everybody's views. 'It must have been a difficult decision for both of you.'

'For Clair it was. For me it was just another problem to be handled.' The transformation was remarkable – he was close to tears. Michael thought an argument could be made for the beneficial effect of periodic alcoholic binges on Bubba's character. Bubba buried his head in his hands. 'But I couldn't forget what I'd done. The more I fell in love with Clair, the more I thought about the baby I'd killed.'

Fell in love?

'You made a mistake. Everybody makes mistakes.'

Bubba looked at him with red eyes. 'I murdered my son.'

'How do you know it was a boy?'

'Of course it was a boy,' he said, insulted. 'I would not have a female for a firstborn.'

Despite the serious nature of the discussion, Michael couldn't help but laugh. Bubba had finally begun to accept girls as people, but he was a long way from accepting them as equals. 'Bubba, promise me one thing. Ten years from now, when you're ruling the world, please try to remember that it was a woman who brought you into the world.'

Bubba was confused. 'What about Baby Bubba?'

'What about Clair?'

He brightened suddenly. 'We're getting married.'

Michael almost fell out of his chair. That was the big secret Clair had been afraid to tell him. '*What?*'

Bubba nodded solemnly. 'It's time I settled down. She's a good woman. She understands me.' He touched Michael's hand. 'I want you to do me a favour, Mike?'

'Anything.'

'I want you to be my maid of honour.'

'Your best man?'

'Yes. I want you to stand beside me on Sunday.'

'You're getting married this Sunday?'

'In Las Vegas.' Bubba sat back. 'I've thought about this a long time, Mike. It's nothing Clair has talked me into. I've made up my own mind.'

'I believe you.' Michael offered his hand. 'Congratulations.'

Bubba beamed. 'You're not going to try to talk me out of it?'

'Why should I? Like you said, she's a good girl. I hope you don't drive her crazy. You better not cheat on her.'

Bubba waved his hand. 'I've cancelled my subscription to *Playboy*, that's how serious I am about this.'

'Great. I suppose you want to get back to your game now?'

Bubba nodded enthusiastically, then furrowed his brow in concentration, worried. 'I haven't told you anything I wouldn't have ordinarily, have I?'

'You've been fine. Oh, there is one other thing. Now that school's over, how often did you use the computer codes to change stuff?'

Bubba scratched his head. 'I can't remember.'

'Did you make Sara president?'

'No, not that. Sara got elected by a landslide. But I did make Clair vice-president. Don't tell her, though. She doesn't know.'

'What about homecoming?'

Bubba looked unhappy. 'I don't know if I should talk about that.'

'Did Jessie get elected queen?'

He hesitated. 'Yes.'

'Why did you choose Maria?'

'I couldn't put in Clair. People were too down on her because of the abortion talk. And Clair wouldn't stand for Jessie being queen. Maria was neutral.'

'But Jessica should have been queen,' Michael insisted.

'Nah. Clair should have been queen.'

'Maybe, maybe not.'

'I'm glad neither of them won. They're both bigger than Maria. The float probably would have collapsed on them in the middle of the dance.'

Did someone tamper with the float thinking it would be Jessie?

'But what about Maria?' Michael asked.

He shrugged. 'What can I say? I'm only Bubba; I'm not God.'

'At least we've made some progress tonight.'

Michael accompanied Bubba back to the lounge. It was good that he did. Along the way, Bubba tried to tightrope-dance on the top of the rail. Had he fallen the wrong way, he would have disappeared into a hazy soup, probably disappeared for good.

Michael just couldn't get into the game, even though the score was close and the end was near. He went out to search for Polly. But he couldn't find her anywhere.

CHAPTER 16

Polly lay soaking in the steaming bath, staring at her naked body. Her figure was fabulous. She had large firm breasts, a narrow waist, smooth wrinkle-free thighs and soft creamy skin. Any normal guy, she thought miserably, would have been happy to climb into the tub with her.

The door to the bathroom lay wide open. Clark prowled the room beyond. In the last half hour, he hadn't so much as peeped in. She didn't understand it.

Polly was, however, grateful for the room. Sara had done her a good turn in that regard for once. Polly didn't know if she could have stood a whole night partying with people who didn't like her. She knew they didn't. She'd known it all along, actually, although she had never understood that either. She wasn't a bad person. She had been sort of fat once, but now she had a nice body. You'd think they'd want to talk to her more often. The last few months at school, hardly anyone had talked to her. They'd avoided her as if she'd had the plague. She'd had bad luck, true, but a lot of people had bad luck. She wasn't alone in that respect. In fact, a lot of people on this stupid boat were unlucky.

They couldn't have imagined how unlucky they were.

Polly had left the hot water in the bath running a trickle. A drain prevented the water from overflowing. It was an old trick; it kept the water always hot. She liked it that way, so hot her skin turned cardinal red whenever she took a bath. She'd first learned the trick in a book she had read on the Mafia. It seemed that whenever a mob member got thrown in jail for life, his buddies on the outside would provide for his family if he'd take a hot bath and slit his wrists. Those mob guys were always afraid that anybody in jail would eventually break down and talk. The hot water was important; supposedly when you bled to death, you got real cold, and then nauseated. A good bath made the whole experience much more comfortable. Leaving the water trickling was the key; if you sat all night in a tub with the hot water faucet turned on a little and your wrists slit, in the morning most of the blood would be gone. No vomit, no blood and naked as a babe. When Polly thought about it, she imagined it wasn't such a bad way to go. Much better than, say, being trapped in a room overflowing with icy sea water.

An open razor blade rested on the soap tray next to Polly's head. She picked it up and let the overhead light reflect off the sharp edge into her eyes. White light, star bright. Sitting up, she transferred the blade into her left hand. Like Alice, she was left-handed. Some things ran in the family.

Like bad luck.

'You should have got the paper cups when I told you the first time,' Polly whispered, taking the blade and pressing the tip into her right wrist. For a second nothing happened, and she wondered if she had a dull blade. Then a drop of blood drew a line down the pink flesh of her inner arm, dripping off her bent elbow into the clear water. It was interesting to watch how the red dissipated when it hit the water, how quickly her blood was lost. Maybe when she was through bleeding, her body would dissolve, too; it would be as if she had never been. She started to push the blade deeper.

'Polly,' Clark said. He stood outside the bathroom, a lamp at his back; she could clearly see his shadow on the bathroom door.

'What?' She set down the blade.

'What are you doing?'

'Nothing. What are you doing?'

'I'm waiting for you.'

'I'll be out in a few minutes.'

Clark thought a moment. 'Why are you taking so long?'

She had been hoping he would come in and join her, make love to her before he killed them all. It had really hurt her feelings that he'd had her pose nude all those times and not once stopped painting to touch her. The drops of her blood continued to drip off the end of her elbow. 'I don't know,' she said.

'I don't believe you.'

'Go, do what you're going to do without me. I want to stay here.'

'I can't do that.'

'Why not?'

'You know why.'

She felt a stab of pain across her temple. 'I'm not going.'

'If you don't come, Alice will have died for nothing.'

'I don't care about Alice.'

He entered the bathroom. At first she thought he was bleeding, too – from the head. His red hair was ablaze, as were his eyes. But it was only hate. 'And where do you think you're going?'

She crossed her arms over her breasts, trying to hide

her wrist. The red spilled over her nipples. 'I accidentally cut myself.'

He strode to the tub and leaned over, grabbing the razor blade and holding it inches from her face. 'I'll show you an accident. I'll cut your eyes out.'

'No,' she cried, suddenly terrified.

'I'll cut your tongue, make you eat it. Then you can bleed all you want.'

'I won't do it again, I swear. Stop it, Clark!'

He stood and threw the blade aside. Then he picked up her hair dryer and flipped it on. 'You're getting out of that water this instant. It's too hot for a bitch as cold as you.'

He threw the hair drier into the tub. The electric shock hit Polly's brain like a fistful of exploding dynamite, just as it had when she had been in the hospital as a child. She began to scream.

CHAPTER 17

The Lakers had called a timeout. There were ten seconds left on the clock. They had the ball. They were down by two points. Never in her wildest imagination could Sara have dreamed a stupid basketball game could make her feel so miserable.

'What if they don't make it?' she asked Nick, who stood beside her. With the exception of Maria, the whole room was standing. On the screen, the Lakers' coach drew diagrams on a big white sheet of paper while the players huddled in a semicircle at his back and nodded their exhausted, sweaty heads. On the left side of the lounge, Bubba paced along the top of the bar, shouting out encouragement.

'My men!'

'If they miss and don't rebound the ball, they're dead,' Nick said.

'But they don't get any points for a rebound, do they?' Sara asked.

'No. They'd have to put up another shot quick. And it would have to go in.'

Sara clasped her hands together. 'I'm going to kill him.'

'Who?' Nick asked.

'You'll know when you see the body.'

The timeout came to an end. Both teams walked on to the court. The noise in the Fabulous Forum and the lounge of *Haven* settled down. Sara bit her lower lip. The referee handed the ball to a Laker player and blew his whistle. Immediately the players of both teams scattered across half the court. A second went by, two seconds. The guy wasn't going to have time to inbound the ball!

'Shoot!' Sara yelled.

'He can't shoot from out of bounds,' Nick said.

The player inbounded the ball to a teammate at the top of the key. The guy fed to the right, dribbled to the left. Then he leaped; it was a magnificent leap. He floated through the air towards the basket. Green uniforms sprang up to block his way. Sara thought they were too late. The time on the corner of the screen went to six seconds.

'Shoot!' Sara yelled.

'He doesn't have the ball,' Nick said.

Nick was right. The player had passed the ball to a teammate in the left corner. The guy was all alone, far from the basket. He was going for a three-pointer! If he made it, the game would be over! There would be no need for an overtime!

'Shoot!' Sara yelled.

The clock went to three seconds.

He shot it. The ball sailed high through the air. It had beautiful arc, seemingly perfect touch.

'No!' Sara screamed along with the rest of the room.

It missed. A Celtic grabbed the rebound. The Lakers tried frantically to foul him. They were too late. Time expired. Sara collapsed into the chair behind her.

I will not kill him. He is fat and slimy, but he has a working heart, functional kidneys. I will force him to sell his organs to pay off the debt.

'Excuse me,' Sara said to Nick and Maria, standing and making her way through the crowd to the bar. The mood of the lounge was gloomy, but compared to Sara's mood, the place was in seventh heaven. Yet Sara wasn't exactly angry. The pure fullness of her anger had transformed it into something quite the opposite, into an almost perverse joy. Bubba no longer had a hold over her. She could say what she wanted to him, do what she wanted. There were so many things she would do to him.

Bubba sat on top of the bar, his head bowed in misery, an empty bottle loosely clasped in his chubby fingers. Clair was not around.

'Bubba,' she said sweetly. He looked up, rubbed his red eyes.

'It's you again?'

She nodded. 'Outside.'

He did not protest. They exited the lounge and stood on the deck. A lot of kids had just come out for a breath of fresh air, however, and Sara decided their 'talk' would go better in private. She steered Bubba down a companionway and into a deserted hall. The locked passenger staterooms stretched the length of the boat away from them on either side. Bubba slumped to the floor and leaned against a wall. Sara stood above him, her hands on her hips.

'They should have gone for the tie,' Bubba said sadly. He looked up at her as though he expected her to offer him comfort. 'I should be coaching that team.'

'I don't care about the Lakers.'

He was shocked. He was even more drunk than before. 'I've followed them since I was a little Bubba.'

She knelt in front of him. 'Bubba, do you know how close you are to having terrible things happen to you?'

He was interested. 'How close?'

She held her thumb and index finger up a quarter of an inch apart. Then she squeezed them together. 'This close.'

He was *very* interested. 'What are you going to do?'

She leaned closer. 'I *need* the money you promised me. I *need* you to get it for me. I don't care *where* you get it. Do you understand me?'

Now he was disappointed. He brushed off her remark with a sloppy wave of his hand. 'I bet your money on the Celtics.'

'What?' Sara fell back on her butt. 'I don't believe you.'

'You can have all the money you need tomorrow evening.' Bubba wasn't much interested in the discussion. He clenched his fist and pounded his knee. 'They should have gone for two points.'

'Why would you bet against the Lakers? They're your team. You just said it – you grew up with them.'

He nodded. 'I knew in my heart it was time for them to take a fall.'

Sara laughed. Then she did something that could have ruined her reputation for all time had there been anyone around to see it. She gave Bubba a big hug. 'I never will understand you.'

'My true nature is unfathomable,' he agreed.

Sara suddenly remembered the bargain she'd made. She quickly sat back. 'I suppose now you'll expect me to put out for you?'

He hesitated. 'Does it mean that much to you, Sara?'

'My body?'

He spoke in a regretful tone. 'I suppose I could make love to you, give you a night you could carry happily to your grave, but I'd hate to do that to Clair. Faith and trust and not screwing around mean so much to her. Do you understand, Sara?'

'Are you saying you *don't* want to have sex with me?'

'It's not you personally.'

Her usual distaste for him returned. 'But you've been dying to sleep with me all year! Or was that just an act?'

'Well . . .'

'You don't find me attractive?'

'Now I didn't say that.'

Sara leaped to her feet and paced in front of him. 'What about me don't you like? Is it my face? Is it my legs? Come on, don't worry about my feelings. I don't care what you say.'

He studied her a moment. 'I've never liked the way you walked.'

She stopped. 'I walk just like any other girl. Just like Clair does.'

He shook his head. 'No, you walk like you're in a hurry. A lady is never in a hurry. Good things come to a lady. She doesn't have to chase after them.'

'What else?'

'Your clothes—'

'You said that earlier. I'm getting new clothes for the summer. What else is wrong with my body?'

'Nothing. Your body's fine.'

'Fine? China and silk are fine. Come on, what don't you like? Is it my ass?'

'I'd have to see you naked before I would be willing to express an opinion in that area.'

'Hold it right there, slimeball. I'm not taking my clothes off for you. No way you're going to trick me into that.'

'All right.'

'What do you mean, all right? You don't want to see it?'

'Not at the moment.'

She sagged against the wall, feeling totally unwanted. 'You really don't think I'm very sexy, do you?'

Bubba gathered himself off the floor and put his arm around her shoulder, the odour of half a dozen of the world's most famous distilleries on his breath. 'Sara, if I had met you before I met Clair, I honestly believe things would have been different between us. Of course I think you're sexy. You have a great ass. A few private lessons and I'm sure you could have made me very happy.'

She realised he was feeding her a crock of pure BS. It was amazing – not to mention ridiculous – how much it meant to her. She kissed him on the cheek. 'I bet you're still a virgin.'

He reached around and pinched her butt. 'If I am, I was born with incredible natural talents.'

CHAPTER 18

If Nick had been told in his first week at Tabb High that he would end the school year as perhaps the most popular person on campus, he would have laughed. Yet, when the basketball game was over and the class gathered in groups to discuss it, the biggest group gathered around Nick. It was true, of course, they were talking about a subject he was an acknowledged master of; nevertheless, had they just watched a war movie, he still would have drawn the most people to him. He knew this without understanding it.

He was the best athlete in the school – he had no qualms about accepting *that* distinction – and he was no longer the shy mumbling ghetto exile he had been last September. He was, however, still soft-spoken and hesitant to express his opinion on any subject, including basketball. Also, his fearsome appearance had not changed with Tabb's capture of the league basketball title. But perhaps Michael had explained Nick's popularity best when he had said that Nick was the only one in the school who even vaguely fitted the definition of a hero.

'And people are always searching for a hero, Nick. Just look at who's big in Hollywood. It's usually the actor who can rescue the most prisoners of war in two hours or less. Enjoy it while it lasts. Someone's sure to come along soon and take your place.'

Nick did enjoy the adulation, although he found himself shying away from it at the same time. A few minutes of attention from a big group gave him a pleasant high. More than that made him anxious. As soon as was politely possible – after saying for the tenth time that he didn't like second-guessing the Lakers' coach for going for the win instead of the tie – he excused himself from the lounge and wheeled Maria on to the deck. Here there were fewer people; it was now cold and the fog had gone beyond thick to frightening. Nick had once seen a television show on the Bermuda Triangle – a place in the Atlantic Ocean where many ships had disappeared. Had those ships ended up in another dimension, he imagined, it might have resembled *Haven*'s present environment. Complete darkness would have seemed more natural. The damp greyness was spooky.

'Are you cold?' he asked Maria, parking her chair near the rail. The splash of the ocean against the hull could be heard beneath the fog. Maria pulled her shawl tighter.

'No.' She looked up at him. 'Are you?'

'The fresh air feels good.'

A period of silence went by. There had been a lot of those between them since he had picked her up at the rehabilitation clinic. 'They like you,' she said finally.

'I guess. They like my jump shot, that's for sure.'

'I wish I had got to see you play again.'

The remark warmed his spirits somewhat. Maybe she did still care about him. She had given few signs one way or the other. 'It was a fun season. Making the CIF play-offs was exciting. Track was fun, too. I ran the quarter-mile and did the long jump.'

'I was told they gave you a trophy at the awards banquet?'

He nodded. 'It's for having done well in more than one sport.' Coach Campbell had presented the award, the same man who had almost expelled him the first week of school when he had floored The Rock in the weight room. Coach Campbell had given him a big smile and a slap on the back with the trophy, but still no apology. Nick didn't feel any resentment. It was easy to forgive when you were winning. His father had been at the banquet. He had been the first one to stand and clap. The rest of the school had followed suit. Nick had never received a standing ovation before.

'Trophies, fans, scholarships,' she said. 'You must be happy?'

He looked down at her white tennis shoes lying still on the wheelchair's metal footrests. 'I'm not happy, Maria.'

'Why not?'

He turned away. 'Isn't it obvious?'

Another spell of silence. *Haven*'s foghorn broke this one. Maria touched his leg. 'Don't worry about me, Nick.'

He chuckled, staring into nothing. 'Sure. I'll just wheel you all over the place and forget that you used to walk. How can you tell me not to worry?'

'I don't want you to. I don't know why you do.'

A note of anger entered his voice. 'You know why.'

She took her hand back. 'I don't.'

He turned on her. 'How would you like it if *I* got crippled that night? What if I had gone up for a rebound and came down wrong and broke my neck? Would you even—' He stopped, realised what he was saying. Awful as it was for him to see her paralysed, it was nothing compared to *being* paralysed. She answered his unfinished question.

'I would care.'

'I'm sorry,' he said quickly. His apology had a strange effect on her. She seemed to take up his shame. She turned her chair as if about to leave, as if she were embarrassed to be with him.

'Nick, you don't have to—' she began, getting upset. 'I can take care of myself. Really I can.'

He touched the handle of her wheelchair instead of her arm, holding on to her just the same; the chair was a part of her now. 'What do you want me to do?' he asked, afraid she would respond by telling him to go away. He didn't understand till right then how much he loved her. Maria composed herself and looked in the direction of the lounge.

'Later, when things slow down,' she said, 'I want you to talk to everybody who was still at the party when Alice died: Bubba, Clair, Bill, The Rock, Kats, Russ, Sara, Polly, Michael and Jessica. I want you to gather them below, where we can be alone.'

'Why?'

'You'll see.'

CHAPTER 19

The night went on. The air grew colder. The fog grew thicker. Around midnight, *Haven* encountered four foot swells and began to rock uneasily, her hull softly groaning with each rise and fall, the stomachs of many of her passengers doing likewise. A few kids lost their dinners over the ship's rail. Yet the rough waters did little to slow the momentum of the party. Time took care of that. No matter that for many it was the most exciting night of their lives – passing the three o'clock hour, the bulk of the senior class could be found lying curled up in the lounge or the games room on sheets of foam someone had been thoughtful enough to provide. Those who were resting were smart. They would be fresh for the upcoming day on Catalina.

If they lived that long.

Once again, Jessica and Sara were in Jessica's cabin,

trying to decide about the contraceptives. Jessica was not enjoying the pitch and roll of the ship. It made it impossible for her to pretend – as she had done most of the night – that she was still on dry land. The way *Haven*'s hull kept creaking was particularly disturbing. Sara's reassurances that the sound was natural didn't ease Jessica's mind in the slightest. Sara knew as much about boats as she did, which was precisely nothing.

'I don't see how you can be worried about drowning at a time like this,' Sara said, the bottle of foam in her hand. 'You should be worrying about how you look.'

'Excuse me, but I've heard that when you drown it can affect your appearance,' Jessica said, sitting on the bed beside Sara. Jessica had already changed into her bathrobe. Sara was going to have to pop next door in a minute and get ready. Ten minutes ago they had told Bill and Russ – Jessica had told Bill and Sara had told Russ, to be precise – to meet them in their rooms in exactly twenty minutes. Bill and Russ thought they were being invited to a private party.

Just our luck they'll bring their buddies with them.

But it seemed unlikely. Jessica and Sara had both made it clear that they were to come alone.

'I don't think I like the ingredients in this stuff,' Sara said, studying the foam label. 'Nonoxynol nine, potassium hydroxide, benzoic acid – does that sound like something you want inside your body?'

'It sounds like it'll work.'

Sara handed her the foam. 'You take it then. If you explode, don't blame me.'

'Thanks,' Jessica muttered sarcastically. The room had a lamp hanging from a corner of the ceiling. The motion of the boat made it swing back and forth, sending shadows chasing its light, giving Jessica a headache.

'You don't look very excited.'

Jessica shrugged. 'I'll get excited when Bill gets here.'

Sara nodded, thoughtful, chewing on her lower lip. 'Can I ask you something, Jessie?'

'As long as it's not about your ass.'

'Well, I've been getting a lot of complaints about it lately. Come on, you've taken showers with me in PE.'

Jessica groaned. 'I just cannot believe you are asking me this. Who's complained about it?'

'Bubba.'

'Bubba! Bubba's screwed half the girls in the school.'

'Yeah. So he's a goddamn expert on the subject.'

'What did he say?'

'It's not what he said. It's what he didn't want to . . . Look, I'm asking for a vote of confidence here.'

'You have a great ass, Sara.'

'You're just saying that.'

'Please don't make me say it again. I'm changing the subject. How much light should we leave on?'

'I'm turning off all the lights.'

'You'll be in the shower when Russ gets there. How can you have all the lights off?'

Sara looked worried. 'I guess it would seem strange.'

Jessica realised Sara was more scared than she was. Actually, Jessica was surprised at her own lack of fear. She felt more resigned to the event than anything else. One thing had become clear: she was not giving up her virginity in joy. She just wanted to get it over with.

'How are you getting on with Russ?' she asked gently.

Sara snorted. 'Oh, we get along fine, as long as we don't talk. So far tonight, we've been doing *splendidly*. He's been with his buddies since he came on board.' Sara glanced at her watch. 'Well, I guess I've got him to myself now, for a few minutes, anyway.' She stood. 'You promise to tell me exactly what happens?'

'I'll record it.'

Sara smiled. 'I guess this is it.'

Jessica hugged her. 'I hope this is it for one of us at least.'

When Sara was gone, Jessica stood by the porthole for several minutes, staring out into the eerie night. Alice had loved the fog. Alice had loved everything. Jessica had been trying to tell Sara she had no hope for herself. Not for love.

'I'm going to the movies Saturday night. You won't believe it, I asked the guy. His name's Michael Olson . . . That reminds me, where's that fantastic guy you were going to introduce me to?'

'Ask me after your date.'

And then Alice had lain down to sleep.

'I could go to sleep here and never wake up,' Jessica whispered, remembering her exact words.

The bathroom was small but neat. Jessica removed her robe and got in the shower. The water came out hot and hard at first, and she jumped back, almost slipping and falling. She had left her hair down, though she didn't want to wash it; she looked a lot better with it down. Well, it was going to get wet, there was no helping that. She wondered how long Bill would be. The shower curtain was translucent; at least it would have been without all the steam. She had read somewhere that steam was supposed to be very sensual. She hoped she started to feel sexy soon.

Several minutes went by. During that time she scrubbed herself from neck to toe using her own soap – just to be sure. The spray of the shower waved up and down in rhythm to the ocean swells. Finally there came a knock at the door. Naturally, she had left the bathroom door open – it was part of the plan. The distance between the two doors couldn't have been more than eight feet.

'Bill?' she called, pulling the shower curtain to the edge of the tile, on the small chance he did have someone with him.

'Yeah.'

'Come in.'

He opened the door to the suite, paused. She could see his outline through the curtain, but that was all. He was alone. 'Jessie?'

'It's all right. I'll be out in a minute. Come in.'

He entered, closing the door, and then sat on the bed. She peeped around the edge of the curtain. He had his hands folded in his lap and was staring at his feet. He was being a gentleman. 'Where's the party?' he asked.

'It's in Sara's room.' She added, 'I've been running around all night. I thought I'd grab a quick shower. I won't be long.'

'I could go on ahead of you.'

'No.' He was still looking down. 'Just let me wash off this soap.'

'OK.'

Now what? Sara and she hadn't given this enough

thought. It would have been much easier had he come into the bathroom and tried to peep around the curtain or something. There was really no good excuse to invite him into the bathroom.

Fine, I'll give him a lousy excuse.

She turned off the water. 'Bill?'

'Yeah?'

'Could you hand me my towel?'

'Where is it?'

It was right outside the shower, on a hook on the back of the bathroom door. She could see it through her crack in the curtain, along with Bill, searching the bedroom. 'I don't know,' she said. 'Don't you see it?'

'No.'

'God, there's so much steam in here. Is it on the sink?'

He paused in the bathroom doorway. 'I don't see it, Jessie.'

She grabbed hold of the edge of the curtain and stuck her head around at him and smiled. He couldn't have been three feet away. He jumped slightly. She pointed to the towel with her wet and dripping arm. 'There it is,' she said sweetly.

He handed it to her, saving her a six-inch reach. 'You want me to come back?' he asked, his eyes down.

'That's all right.' She let go of the shower curtain and

began to dry her face. 'I'm almost done.'

'OK. I'll wait for you.' He closed the bathroom door and returned to the bedroom. She couldn't believe how proper he was being. In all the teen movies she'd ever seen, guys were always dying to get peeps at cute girls in showers. And she was cute. She had almost been voted homecoming queen for God's sake.

She quickly dried herself, climbing out of the shower and slipping into her bathrobe. Sara had given it to her last Christmas. It was pink, thin and it clung to her damp body in a number of important places. She glanced at herself in the foggy mirror. Wet, her hair appeared almost black, and the heat of the shower had flushed her face. In her totally unbiased opinion, she thought she looked pretty fantastic.

Just have to get him to kiss me. Just get him started.

She opened the bathroom door. Bill was standing by the window, admiring the fog. He jumped again when he saw her. She smiled to put him at his ease. 'I didn't know you'd get here so soon.'

'You said twenty minutes.'

'Oh, that's right, I did.' She gestured to the bed and reached for the towel around her neck. 'Have a seat, let me dry my hair.'

He sat on the bed. She stepped past his knees and sat

beside him, on his left. They had the bathroom and its diffusing steam in front of them, the door to the hallway on their right. Bill still had on his yellow turtleneck and brown trousers. She reached up as if to fix his collar. Too bad he didn't have a collar. She brushed a hair from his neck, playing the role of the seductress to the hilt.

'I haven't got to talk to you much tonight,' she said.

'Yeah, where have you been?'

'Oh, I went for a little swim.' She giggled. 'I wish you could have joined me.'

He frowned. 'What are you talking about?'

'Nothing.' She turned to face him, tucking her right knee under her left leg while pressing her knee against the side of his leg. She had made a similar move months ago on his parents' couch without much success. But now they knew each other a lot better, and her bathrobe was split open and my, didn't her wet legs look fine. 'I'm glad you're here,' she said.

His gaze strayed to her legs. She was not sure how far up he could see, not exactly, nor did she care. Suddenly she began to enjoy herself. 'You're going to catch a cold,' he said.

'I'm not cold.' She smiled her naughtiest smile and moved her hand into his hair. 'Are you?'

'No.'

'That's good.' She tugged lightly on the hair at the base of his neck. 'If you were, I don't know what I would do.'

'Jessie?'

'Yes Bill.'

'What about Sara's party?'

'It'll wait.' She leaned closer, her wet hair hanging over the arm of his yellow sweater. 'I'm not making you uncomfortable, am I?' she asked.

'No.'

She continued to play with his hair, continued to smile as if she couldn't wait for him to kiss her, which was the truth of the matter. 'That's good, because I feel real comfortable with you. I mean, I like you, Bill. Did I ever tell you that?'

'Yeah. I like you, Jessie. You're a nice girl.'

She gushed over the remark as if he had just sworn his undying love. 'Really? Oh, that's neat. I mean, I wasn't sure if you felt that way.' She let her right hand slip from his hair to the top of his right shoulder and caught his eyes. 'You know what I liked most about the prom?'

'What?'

'When you kissed me afterwards.'

He took the hint. He kissed her. He might not have intended for it to be a deep and passionate kiss, but the moment his lips touched hers, she tightened her arm around his neck and pulled him close. She had not kissed many guys in her life. She was unaware of the finer points that constituted a great kiss. Nevertheless, she didn't feel Bill was giving her his all. She felt that way very strongly when he suddenly pulled back.

'It's late,' he said.

She laughed, tugging him towards her. 'It's early.'

They started again and things began to pick up, possibly because they rolled back on to the bed. This had nothing to do with her; it just happened. He put his right hand on her robe near her left breast. The kissing got harder, deeper. Yet she still felt as if she was doing most of the digging. She wished he would touch her breast. His hand kept moving towards it, then pulling away. It was driving her nuts.

'Jessie?' he mumbled.

'What?' She was having trouble with other parts of their bodies as well. Her legs were up on the bed. His feet were still on the floor. She tried swinging her left leg over his hip, but it kept slipping loose. Surprisingly, her robe continued to hold together; she must have tied the belt too tightly coming out of the shower. She took his right hand and put it on the knot, hoping he would work on it.

'Why are we doing this?' he asked, between heavy

breathing and kissing.

'Because we want to.'

'I don't think it's right.'

'Don't think, Bill.'

He didn't loosen the knot. He put his hand on her hip instead. That would have been fine except his hand just stayed there, while his kisses became less and less passionate, until finally she began to feel as if she were chasing a strawberry around an empty bowl with a baseball bat. She had heard him when he said he didn't think what they were doing was right, but she hadn't *really* heard him. When she took his right hand and pressed it to her left breast, his reaction took her completely by surprise. He leaped off the bed and began to yell.

'What are you trying to do?'

She had never seen him mad before. 'Huh?'

'You're trying to seduce me!'

She sat up, very slowly. 'No. I was just, you know, being friendly.' There was something not quite right here. She still hadn't figured out where she had messed up. He looked positively livid.

'Look at you, Jessie. You're practically naked. And you're trying to undress me!'

'No. I was in the shower, and—'

'The shower! You knew I was coming. What kind of girl are you anyway?'

It hit her then – the humiliation. Her voice came out small and shaky. 'I'm a nice girl, like you said.'

He began to shout again, then suddenly balled his hands into tight fists and turned to face the wall, breathing heavily. She thought he wouldn't speak again, that he'd just leave. But finally he got hold of himself.

'I shouldn't have yelled at you like that, Jessie,' he whispered, reaching out and putting his hand on the doorknob. 'I shouldn't have come.'

'Why did you come?' It could have been a stupid question. She had, after all, given him a legitimate reason to visit her cabin. But she had been a fool to think he had been fooled. He was nodding as he turned and looked at her, nodding to himself, asking himself the same question.

'I wanted to see, I guess,' he said.

'See what? Me?'

'No.'

'Oh.' His remark did wonders for what was left of her ego. And here all these years she had thought she was pretty cute. Oh, well, half the point in this whole seduction had been to run what was left of her self-esteem into the ground. It was funny how she had got exactly what she had wanted.

She began to tremble.

'This has nothing to do with you,' he said.

She nodded weakly. Of course her being unattractive to him had nothing to do with her. She may as well not have been in the room. She still couldn't believe this was happening to her. He took a step towards the bed, stretched out his arm to touch the side of her face, then thought better of it and pulled his hand back to his side.

'I'd better go,' he said.

She nodded again. 'All right.'

But he didn't leave immediately. Ignoring her for a moment, he stepped into the bathroom and picked up her brush beside the sink. He ran it under the faucet and began to comb his hair. She had run her fingers through his hair while they'd been kissing, but since he always wore it short, she hadn't really messed it up. From his perspective, however, she must have messed him up bad. Her eyes began to burn. He set the brush down and stepped to the door.

'I won't say anything to anybody about this,' he said gently.

She bit her lip. 'Thanks.'

'Bye.'

'Bye.'

He left. She picked up her towel and buried her face in

it. She began to cry. A few minutes later someone knocked at her door.

CHAPTER 20

Sara almost froze to death waiting for Russ to appear. The captain must have been scrimping on fuel. There was no hot water, and never before in her life had Sara taken a cold shower. She understood that only monks took those, and that they did so mainly for reasons of celibacy. Just what she needed – a cold shower to make her as horny as a statue and as desirable as a fish.

Why is he taking so long?

She had said twenty minutes. At least forty minutes must have gone by since she had last seen him. Maybe he'd gone with Bill to Jessica's suite. Yeah, the three of them were probably having a great time about now. Disgusted, Sara grabbed her towel and tried to stand at the far end of the shower out of reach of the spray. But every time *Haven*'s bow went under, the water splashed her legs. She had gooseflesh on her thighs ready to sprout feathers.

Someone pounded on the door.

'Who is it?' she called, pulling the old grey shower curtain tight. She'd left the bathroom door open, but she was beginning to wonder if that had been a good idea. He might have brought the whole cross-country team with him.

'It's me,' he called.

'Are you alone?'

He opened the door. 'What?'

'Are you alone?' She was afraid to peep around the edge of the curtain.

'Yeah.' She heard the door close. 'What are you doing?'

'I'm taking a shower. What do you think I'm doing?'

'Do you want me to join you?' He sounded as if he could have been standing in the bathroom doorway. She couldn't stop shivering.

'No. Close the door.'

'Whatever you want.' He closed the bathroom door.

He had to choose this moment to do exactly what I said.

She turned off the water and dried herself furiously, trying to get some warmth back into her flesh. All was not lost. She had a cute orange bathrobe waiting to put on. Jessica said she looked like a doll in it, even if autumn colours depressed Bubba. Sara knew as soon as Russ saw her in it, he would want to kiss her.

When she came out of the bathroom a few minutes later, he was lying flat on his back on the bed and staring at the ceiling. He had on blue jeans, a blue Pendleton shirt and looked so masculine it made her legs weak. He hardly glanced over.

'Are you ready?' he asked.

'Sure, I'm going to go dressed like this.' She sat on the bed by his feet. The soles of his running shoes were dirty and he wasn't going out of his way to keep them off the sheets. She had to remind herself that she couldn't fight with him when she wanted him to make love to her. 'How are you doing?' she asked.

He yawned. 'Tired. I wish I could just stay here and sleep.'

'You can.'

'What about your friend's party?'

'We don't have to go.'

He sat up suddenly. 'No. I'll go. Hurry up and get dressed.'

She smiled. 'Don't you want to talk for a few minutes? I haven't really had a chance to talk to you all night.'

'We can talk at the party.' He glanced about restlessly. 'How come you and Jessie are the only ones to get your own rooms?'

'I'm ASB president.'

'So?'

She stopped smiling. 'It's me who rented this stupid boat. Why shouldn't I get my own room?'

He shrugged, doing an excellent job of not looking at her. 'I guess you're right. Come on, put on your clothes. Let's go.'

'No, I want to talk.'

'About what?'

She reached over and began to fiddle with the lace on his left shoe. 'Have you been able to train up there?'

'They have a track.' He was watching her hands. 'I run laps.'

'But you told me you never liked to run on the track?'

'They don't let you out, Sara.'

His saying her name – she didn't know why it touched her so. She squeezed his toes through his shoe and glanced up. He was looking at her now. 'It must be hard on you?' she said.

'I can take it.'

She was still cold from the shower. The thinness of her robe and the temperature of the cabin were not helping matters. She could have used a long hug. 'How come you never wrote to me?' she asked.

'I wrote.'

'Not really.'

'I didn't have anything to say. Every day there is the same.'

'But I wrote. You could have answered my letters.' She loosened his lace all the way and started to pull off his shoe.

'Don't,' he said, jerking his foot away.

'You're messing up the sheets.' She hadn't meant the remark to sound harsh. He got up.

'Let's go to the party.'

'No,' she said, watching as he leaned against the wall beside the bathroom door. His expression was inscrutable, and it depressed her; she'd always believed she could read his mind simply by looking at his face. He had changed while he was away. 'What's wrong?' she asked.

'Nothing.'

'Then why are you acting this way?'

'I'm not acting any way. You told me you wanted me to go to a private party with you. I'm here to go to the party. Let's go.'

'I can't go. I'm not dressed.'

'Get dressed.'

'You didn't really want to get in the shower with me.'

'What?'

'You just said that. You don't really like me.'

'What are you talking about?'

She began to speak, but found a lump in her throat. 'Nothing. Forget it. Forget the party, too. I don't want to go.'

'What do you mean, you don't want to go?'

'I don't want to go!'

'What?'

'And quit asking me what I mean. Isn't it obvious what I mean?'

'No. What do you mean?'

She put her face in her hands. 'Get out of here.'

Time went by. It could have been a whole minute. He finally sat beside her on the bed. 'I'm sorry,' he said.

'What are you sorry about?'

He hesitated. 'I'm sorry I don't know.'

She burst out laughing, although she knew he hadn't meant the remark to be humourous. She laughed until her sides were ready to burst, until she was ready to cry. Of course, she had felt like crying before she had started laughing. 'Oh, Russ,' she said, trying to catch her breath. 'You are a prince.'

He didn't respond to her raving, just sat looking at her. 'I know I'm not good enough for you,' he said without bitterness.

Sara stopped laughing. 'What do you mean?'

He glanced down at the dirty shoes she had criticised. 'You're ASB president. I'm just a beer-drinking bum out on a weekend pass from juvenile hall.'

She stared at him as if she were seeing him for the first time and discovering that he had two heads instead of the one she remembered. It sure was another side of him. 'How come you went to a bar after the homecoming dance and got drunk?' she asked. She had always wanted to know.

'Because you didn't want to kiss me.'

She knew instantly what he was referring to. Before the homecoming queen announcement, they had been dancing together and he tried to kiss her. She had stopped him because she felt uncomfortable with any public display of affection. At the time she figured he understood. He hadn't seemed upset. 'I was joking,' she said.

'After my race that morning, you said you didn't want me taking you to the dance.'

'I went to the dance with you!'

'We went in separate cars.'

'I had to get there early. I had to . . . You knew I was joking.'

He glanced at her. She wished again they hadn't cut his hair so short. 'Were you?'

'Yeah!'

'Oh. I didn't know.' He started to get up. 'It doesn't matter.'

She pulled him back down. 'It does matter, Russ. You didn't have to go out drinking that night.'

Now she could read his face. It was filled with regret. 'I wish I hadn't.'

'You do hate it up there, don't you?'

'It's a cage.'

'But you didn't cut down the tree?'

'No.' He showed a trace of annoyance. 'How could I when you took away my axe.'

'I didn't take your axe. Polly took it.'

'Polly took it? I thought that was you.'

'No.' She giggled. 'Does this mean you're in love with Polly now?'

He was insulted. 'Who says I'm in love with you?'

'Of course you're in love with me. Why else would you get all upset because I rejected you? And why would you go out drinking all night and try to kill yourself?'

'I didn't try to kill myself.'

'Anyone who drinks so much he can't remember where he drank is trying to kill himself. Don't be embarrassed. You can love me. You're an incredible person. I'm an incredible person. And I love you.' She stopped. 'I can't believe I said that. Never mind, I didn't say that.'

He kissed her. She didn't see it coming. She quickly decided those were the best kind of kisses. They fell back on the bed and she felt his hands on her body. It was incredible. She couldn't even count the number of places he touched her. It was absolutely the most exciting thing ever! She didn't mind in the least that his twelve-hour beard was scratching the hell out of her face. She was just about to slip out of her robe and give him a night in heaven to make up for all his days in hell when he suddenly stopped and sat up.

'I shouldn't be doing this, Sara,' he said.

I shouldn't? She'd thought she'd been doing a few things of her own. 'What's wrong?' It was her ass, she knew it. He didn't like it, and he hadn't even seen it yet.

'I'm taking advantage of you. You're not even dressed.' He shook his head, ashamed. 'I can't treat you like you were just any old girl.'

She got up on her elbow, wishing she was a little older. 'You've slept with girls before?'

'Oh, yeah, loads of times. But they didn't mean anything to me.'

'Not like I do?'

'Well, yeah.'

'Do you love me?' she asked.

'Do you love me?'

She thought a moment. 'Maybe we should quit while we're both ahead.'

He laughed, hard and loud, as he used to laugh a long time ago. 'Come on, get dressed. Let's go to that party.'

She sat up. 'Oh, I forgot to tell you. It's been cancelled.'

He seemed disappointed. 'What are we going to do? Today and tomorrow are my only days out. I shouldn't waste them sleeping.'

She had this great idea. On the other hand, she didn't want to be one of *those* girls who meant nothing. She stood, heading for the bathroom and her clothes. 'Let's jog around the deck a few times.'

She'd have to do some creative thinking about what it had been like. She couldn't possibly tell Jessica she was still a virgin.

CHAPTER 21

The late-night hours were hard on Michael. After questioning Bubba and searching unsuccessfully for Polly, he got trapped in a chess game with Dale Jensen – Tabb's first valedictorian ever to be impeached. Dale had not attended the graduation ceremony, but he had boarded the boat with a vengeance. He had sent out the challenge via Bubba: 'Meet me in the galley, twelve midnight. We'll see who's so smart.'

Michael didn't want to play. He had a lot on his mind and the pain in his head, rather than diminishing as the night wore on, kept getting worse. But Bubba, sobering at a truly phenomenal pace – insisted that Michael play, and Bubba could be incredibly persuasive. He had always despised Dale. He even lent Michael an extra hat to hide his head wound. Michael had finally told Bubba about his run-in with Clark. He hadn't planned to, but Bubba had started to ask about the gun. Seemed Kats was worried about it. Michael hadn't talked to Kats directly about the gun, of course, but as he searched the boat after the basketball game, he felt Kats was following him. Every time he turned a corner, Kats was there.

The galley was packed when Michael arrived with Bubba and Clair at his side. Dale had brought a chess set and cigarettes. Dale chain-smoked, and like everything else he did, he used the habit to irritate people. Michael knew he would have smoke in his face until one of them was checkmated.

Although he had a despicable personality, Dale was not bad looking. Besides Bill Skater, and possibly Russ Desmond, he might have been the most handsome boy in the school. He was half Italian, with thick black hair, dark olive skin and a wide insolent mouth Clair had once admitted looked mighty tasty. Dale was extremely slim, however, and he also had a chronic cough. He didn't care in which direction he coughed.

Bubba had warned Michael not to underestimate Dale, but Michael thought he would win easily. He had been playing chess regularly on his home computer since leaving school in January. He could beat the most sophisticated programs at the highest levels of complexity. He thought the contest would be over in less than twenty minutes.

He was still playing at one-thirty in the morning. Dale threw him off balance in the first few moves with a strategy Michael had never seen before. That was one of the weaknesses about honing chess skills against a computer; the programs had an almost endless supply of complicated attacks, yet they were often quite predictable. During the first hour of play, Michael had to use all his skill simply to defend his position. And then, when he finally did take command of the board, and his victory appeared certain, he allowed his mind to wander and made a disastrous mistake. He lost his only remaining rook, while getting nothing in return.

'Mike!' Bubba yelled, pounding the table beside the board and upsetting several of the pieces.

'I wanted to make it interesting,' Michael muttered, knowing that unless Dale made an equally careless blunder, the best he could hope for was a draw. Dale blew a cloud of smoke in his face.

'You won't be making a speech after this game,' he said.

Michael got his draw, but it took him until two, and left him feeling weak and drained. Dale surprised him afterwards by shaking his hand and complimenting him on an excellent game. Bubba did not approve of the result or the sportsmanlike gesture.

'Play him again and kick his ass,' Bubba whispered in Michael's ear as Dale got up to leave. Michael shook his head. He had to have another talk with Polly.

Unfortunately, once again, he could not find the girl. He decided to search *Haven*'s engine rooms one more time. He was seriously beginning to worry that Polly had jumped overboard. Before he started down, however, he stopped in the tiny bathroom he had used earlier. He needed a gulp of water.

That was the last he remembered for a while.

He regained consciousness on the floor of the bathroom in a pool of red, his heart thumping in his brain, his thoughts a grey fuzz. He must have knocked his cut open again. His watch said he had lost an hour. He was fortunate he had automatically locked the door on entering. He sat up and stared in the grey-speckled mirror. The ghost image of Clark did not jump out to scare him as it had before, but his own appearance was frightening enough. A vampire could have got hold of him. His coat had blood all over it and he had to stuff it in the wastebasket, leaving him shivering in the damp night air.

The effect of the blackout went deep. After cleaning up, he stumbled outside and found he was trembling inside as well as out. He felt defeated, lonely. He had spent the whole year chasing an unseen enemy who might not exist, and running away from a girl who hardly knew he existed. He suddenly felt so weak he wanted to cry.

He had hit rock bottom.

It was precisely then he decided to tell Jessica he loved her.

He went searching for her. He brought his yearbook with him. She had said she wanted to sign it; it would give him an excuse to talk to her. But he couldn't find her either. He couldn't even locate Sara to ask where Jessica could be. He decided to go to Bubba for help. Bubba was supposed to know everything.

Except who killed Alice.

Michael found Bubba and Clair entwined in blissful slumber on a piece of foam on top of the bar. If they were to roll to the right or the left a couple of inches, they would surely get a rude awakening. Michael shook Bubba gently. Bubba half opened his eyes and smiled.

'Cabin forty-five,' he said.

'Jessie?' Michael asked.

Bubba closed his eyes. 'Forty-five.'

'Thanks.' Clair touched him with a warm hand as he was leaving.

'Tell her,' she mumbled, not raising her head or opening her eyes.

'I'll try,' Michael said.

Walking down the long hall that led to Jessica's cabin, Michael bumped into Bill. They had the space to themselves. Bill smiled broadly.

'I loved that speech you gave,' Bill said for the second time that evening.

'Thanks.'

Bill laughed. He appeared sort of jittery. 'So, where's our scholar off to now? Harvard? Yale? Stanford?'

'No place like that. I can't afford it.'

'No shooting, Mike? Did you apply for any scholarships?'

'No.'

'Why not?'

'I didn't feel like it.' And he sure didn't feel like talking to Bill at this very moment. He had to wonder where Bill had just come from. The neck of his yellow sweater was damp and he had water spots all over the arms.

'Does that mean you'll be around for a while?' Bill asked.

'I guess.'

Bill nodded to his yearbook. 'Hey, let me sign that. I'll give you my number. Maybe we can get together sometimes for a movie or something. Just 'cause we're graduating doesn't mean we can't keep in touch. Right?'

'Sure.' Michael handed him the book. Bill whipped out a pen and scribbled something on the inside cover. Michael glanced down the hallway. Jessica's room must be at the end. Bill gave him back the book.

'I can run and get mine if you'd like to sign it,' Bill said. 'It'll just take me a minute.'

'That's OK, I'll sign it later.'

'You sure?'

'Yeah.' Bill followed Michael's glance down the hall. 'Looking for someone?'

'No.'

Bill smiled again. 'Catch up with you later, Mike.' He disappeared up the companionway.

Michael found cabin forty-five three-quarters of the way down the hall. He stared at the number for a long time, remembering how he had felt when he had gone to Jessica's house to pick her up for their date. He had been scared then, but he'd had hope. He realised, suddenly, he didn't have a shred of hope now.

'I love you, Jessie.'

'That's sweet, Michael. I think you're a very special person, too.'

He knocked on the door, waited. No one answered.

Maybe she was asleep. He was turning away when he heard a feeble, 'Who is it?'

'It's Mike.'

There followed a long pause. 'Come in.'

He opened the door slowly. She was sitting on the bed, wearing a pink bathrobe, a white towel resting on her lap, her hair wet. The air in the room was moist with steam. She must have taken a shower recently. Her eyes, however, were puffy, as if she had just awakened from sleep. She did not smile in welcome.

'I didn't wake you, did I?' he asked.

'No.' She glanced towards the bathroom and touched her head as if it hurt. 'What are you doing here?'

'I'm sorry. I thought . . . I'll leave you alone.'

'No,' she said quickly. 'Come in, have a seat.' She picked up her towel and began to dry her hair, her attention obviously elsewhere. 'Please excuse the mess.'

The bed sheets were rumpled; otherwise the room appeared neat. A ceiling lamp in the corner swung back and forth with each rise and fall of the ship. It reminded Michael of a hangman's rope. 'I could come back later,' he said, closing the door.

'No, it's fine. I was just drying my hair. Have a seat.'

There was nowhere to sit except on the bed. He did not believe she had anything on beneath her robe. As it was, he could see more of her legs than he had ever seen before. He did not want to sit on the bed. He leaned against the wall near the bathroom doorway. 'You said you wanted to sign my yearbook?' He held it up. 'I have it here.'

'Oh.' She set down her towel and glanced around for her own yearbook. It was sitting on the stand three feet from her nose, but it took her several seconds to spot it. They exchanged books. 'Do you need a pen?' she asked, reaching for her purse.

'I have one.'

She found something to write with and flipped open his book, sitting cross-legged in the centre of the bed with her head down, her long hair hiding much of her face. She appeared to be having a hard time thinking of something to say. Michael took his pen out of his shirt pocket. For a moment, he considered telling her he loved her in her yearbook. Then he quickly discarded the idea. Everybody who signed her annual on Catalina would see it.

It was not going well. There was a gloom in the air that matched the gloom in his heart. He was probably the cause of it. His gaze strayed to the bathroom. A wet black brush sat on the counter beside the sink. There were a few hairs tangled up in its bristles. He leaned closer.

They were short blond hairs.

Bill's sweater had been wet.

Bill had been heading up the hall, away from Jessica's room.

Bill had just been here.

They had taken a shower together!

Michael closed his eyes and rolled into the wall, feeling sick to his stomach. The image of them naked together under the hot water stabbed into his mind like a needle. He had never known such pain. A hard knot formed in the centre of his chest and choked off his air. There was poison in his mouth. He couldn't swallow. *His* Jessie in Bill's arms – he simply could not bear the thought.

Not here! Get out! Get away!

He was going to cry, but he couldn't cry – not in front of her. He had sworn that to himself in Alice's studio after her funeral. He swore it to himself again now with the last fibre of his shattered will. Yet he couldn't move. He couldn't get his head off the wall. And the tears were coming no matter how hard he fought to hold them back. He couldn't stop shaking.

She'll see you! She'll know!

'Michael?' She was standing beside him. She touched his shoulder. 'Michael, what's wrong?'

He tried to speak. He tried to disappear into the wall.

It was not fair. They had been in the shower together in this bathroom having sex when he had been all alone in that other bathroom bleeding to death!

'Michael!' Jessica cried. 'You're bleeding!'

She pulled him off the wall and he fell sitting on the edge of the bed, his arm tightly locked across his eyes, his head down. 'I'm all right,' he managed to get out.

'What happened?' she asked, upset, sitting beside him. Her fingers touched the side of his head, cool and soft. He was able to draw in a breath, clamp down on the tears. He let his arm down, lowered his head further.

'Michael?' she said.

'It's nothing. I slipped and bumped my head.' He tried to get up, not looking at her. 'I'll go find a bandage.'

She stopped him and examined his scalp gently. He shouldn't have let her. 'You've split open your head! We've got to get you a doctor!'

'No.' He turned towards her, and although he didn't intend it to be so, a cold note entered his voice. 'Don't get me anything.'

She took back her hand, her fingers bloody. She swallowed. 'I can't let you go like this.'

'I'll be all right.' He did not believe it. He did not understand why her eyes were moist. He stood. 'Goodbye.'

She let him go, at least to the door. He had his hand on the knob when she said, 'You forgot your yearbook.'

He came back for it. Her hands trembled as she handed it to him. Then she burst into sobs, grabbing her towel and burying her face in it. 'You can't go,' she moaned.

He sat on the bed and put his hands on her back as she bent over. 'It's not that bad, Jessie.'

'But you're bleeding!'

'It'll stop.' He hadn't seen her this distressed since Maria had been hurt. She let go of the towel, looked at him with tears pouring over her cheeks.

'No, it won't stop.'

He was too hurt, too confused. He had no comfort left to give. 'I've got to go.' He picked up his yearbook. 'I've got to get out of here.'

He halt expected her to grab his hand to stop him, to cry some more. Yet, suddenly, she stopped fussing and stared him in the eye. 'You can go,' she said. 'But you have to read it first.'

'What?'

'What I wrote.'

He opened the yearbook. He had not been passing it around. Few people had signed it so far: Sara, Clair, Bubba, Nick, Bill. Michael found Bill's note before Jessica's – something about getting together for a one-on-one game of basketball. Then he spotted Jessica's small neat handwriting tucked in the corner of a page at the back. It was not a long note.

I love you, Michael.

Jessie

Michael sat down again. People were always writing things like this at the end of the year in people's yearbooks. It meant nothing. 'What does this mean?' he asked.

Her eyes never left his. They were a little red, but they were still pretty eyes. He had always thought so.

'I love you,' she said.

He looked down at the note, shook his head. 'I don't know what you're talking about.' He really didn't. Jessica couldn't love him. Only Alice had loved him.

'I've loved you for a long time.' A tear formed in the corner of her left eye. It was a quiet tear, not like the ones of a minute ago. 'I just wanted you to know.'

He closed the yearbook and stood. 'I have to go.'

'OK. Goodbye.'

'Goodbye.' He made it to the door, had his hand on the knob again. 'Why didn't you tell me this before?' he asked, his back to her.

'I was afraid.'

He understood that fear. He asked anyway. 'Why?'

'Alice didn't want me to meet you. She didn't think I was good enough for you.'

Michael turned to face her. She had lowered her head, hiding her face behind her long curtain of hair. 'That's not true.'

She nodded sadly. 'It is.'

He returned to the bed, to her side. She was crying softly. Setting down his yearbook, he put his arms around her. 'The first day I met you,' he said, 'Alice came to visit me in the computer room during fourth period. She had to leave the campus at lunch to see her doctor, but she told me about this wonderful girl she wanted to introduce me to at the football game. She didn't tell me her name, but that night, when I went to the game and spoke to you, I realised you were the girl.'

Jessica raised her head, sniffed. 'It was you?'

He smiled. 'It was me.'

A look of amazement filled her face. 'I'm glad.'

He brushed aside her hair and kissed her forehead. 'I have something else to tell you about that day.'

He had imagined the speech for almost too long. He couldn't live the moment without the memory of it already before him. On the other hand, nothing he remembered was exactly like this. Nothing was this sweet.

'When I met you at our locker that first day, I thought you were the most beautiful girl I had ever seen. I thought about you all that day, and the next day, and the day after that. Finally, Monday morning, I got up the courage to ask you out. You remember that time we spoke under the tree, when we talked about chemistry? I was going to ask you then.'

'How come you didn't?'

'You asked me first.'

Jessica sat back and put her hand to her mouth. 'No. This can't be. All this time . . . But you didn't ask me out later! Not once did you ask me out. I was the one who kept trying to set up a date.'

'Yeah, but only because you wanted to thank me.'

'Thank you for what?' She began to laugh. 'OK, I wanted to thank you. But I wanted to go out with you, too! Couldn't you tell?'

'No. Couldn't you tell I wanted to see you?'

'No. Every time we talked, you ran away.'

'I didn't want to bother you.'

She stopped smiling. 'Was there another reason?'

He hesitated. 'There was Bill.'

'Did you know that time I cancelled our date, I went out with him?'

He nodded reluctantly. 'Bubba told me.'

'I thought you might have known.' She sighed. 'I'm a bitch.'

'No.'

'Yes,' she insisted. 'I'm not who you think I am. Did you know Bill was just here?'

He honestly didn't want her to talk about it now, not right after saying she loved him. 'It's none of my business.'

She spoke seriously. 'But you should know about me. Bubba's going to tell you about it later anyway. I set up this whole scam to lure Bill here. I was in the shower. I was going to seduce him. I even stopped at a drugstore on the way to the harbour and bought contraceptives. Does this sound like the sweet innocent Jessie you think is cute?'

'Well.' He was beginning to feel a tiny bit sick again. She saw it, and hugged him quickly.

'I did it because I couldn't have you. I don't love Bill.'

'He's a nice guy.'

'He's not so nice.' Her face darkened and she looked towards the brush sitting by the sink. 'He told me I was just like all the other girls, loose. He couldn't get out of here fast enough.'

'Really?' That was excellent news, and he was glad to be hearing it first-hand from Jessica rather than second-hand from Bubba.

She chuckled. 'It happened just before you got here. He started screaming at me! It was so weird. I'm not that repulsive, am I?'

'Oh, no.' A faint idea touched the edge of Michael's mind, an idea so ridiculous and mean-spirited that he would have immediately dismissed it had it not been followed by the memory of a remark Bubba had made in the galley. 'Nothing. Absolutely nothing,' he whispered.

'What?'

'Something Bubba said about Bill.'

'Something Bubba said?' It was Jessica's turn to pause. '"But if I were you, I'd keep Sara's receipt."'

'Did Bubba say that, too?'

'Yes.'

'When?'

She blushed. 'In the drugstore.'

They began to smile together. Then they started to laugh. They laughed so loud it hurt. It was the best laugh Michael could remember. But perhaps Jessica would not have said the same. She was beet red.

'Oh, God,' she cried. 'I've been trying to seduce a gay guy.'

'We don't know for sure he's gay,' Michael protested, trying unsuccessfully to stop giggling.

'Yes, we do! It all makes sense now, the whole year.' Jessica doubled up in embarrassment. 'I am so dumb!'

'Hey, there's nothing wrong with being gay.'

'I know that. It's just that I can't believe it,' Jessica said, still howling.

'We shouldn't be laughing.'

Jessica stopped suddenly, sat up. 'You're right. To each his own.'

'We shouldn't judge.'

Jessica nodded. 'I'm sorry.'

'He really is friendly.'

'He is, yeah.' Jessica kept her straight face approximately three seconds. Then she went into another fit. 'He's always liked you!'

Michael couldn't stop her. So he joined her. He could feel guilty about it later. If the truth be known, he was absolutely delighted with Bill's choice of lifestyle. Jessica's shower scheme might have ended a lot differently if Bill hadn't been gay.

But Michael preferred not to think about that.

Somewhere in the midst of their laughter, they began to kiss. Jessica started it; Michael had *never* kissed a girl before and would not have known how to begin. He was pleasantly surprised to discover it was easy to do. He had to assume he was doing it well; he was getting no complaints from Jessica.

They lay back on the bed, their arms wrapped around each other. He couldn't get over the fact that she cared for him! Or how warm and soft her body was. He seriously doubted any other girl would have felt like this. He ran his hand through her wet hair and she leaned into him, tilting her head back. Her mouth was a wonder, so soft and warm, tasting like – well, she tasted like toothpaste, which was fine with him. From now on, he knew, whenever he brushed his teeth, he would remember this moment. It was almost too much for him. He could see a *lot* of her legs. The knot in her robe was about to fall apart. He pulled back slightly.

'What's the matter?' she asked.

'Nothing.'

She smiled. 'I'm not too aggressive for you, am I?'

'No, it's not that.' He twisted his head around. 'I think maybe I'm bleeding on your sheets.'

She sat up with a start; leave it to him to put a halt to the happiest moment of his life. She touched the side of his head gently and grimaced. 'What really happened to you?'

He sat up. 'I can't talk about it.'

'Michael?' she protested.

He raised his hand. 'Not now, Jessie. But later, I

promise, I'll explain everything.'

She continued to worry. 'Does it hurt?'

'No.'

'Liar. We should clean it at least.'

'I can't run water on the cut. It will only bleed worse.'

She touched a part of his head where the blood had already dried. 'We could wash here, if we were careful. I think it would help.' She slapped him on the back. 'Take off your clothes.'

He laughed. 'What?'

'I can't wash your hair in the sink. You're taking a shower.'

She was serious. 'I don't know,' he said.

She leaned over and kissed him briefly on the lips.

'Don't be shy. I'll join you.' She added hastily, 'We don't have to do anything. I know you're not feeling well.'

'I don't know,' he repeated, feeling a different sort of dizziness. She shoved him in the chest and giggled mischievously.

'Come on, Michael Olson, make my night.'

He had a sudden horrible thought of being eighty years old and looking back on this night with a feeling of profound regret. He took her hand. 'I'm not feeling that bad,' he said.

It turned out to be the best damn shower he'd ever had.

Later, when they were dry and dressed, he asked if she knew Polly's whereabouts.

'She's probably in her own room,' Jessica said, sitting on the edge of the bed, brushing her hair, a slight smile on her lips.

'She has a room, too? What number is it?'

'Twenty-eight, I believe. Why?'

'Stay here. I'll be back in a minute.'

When he knocked on cabin twenty-eight, no one answered. He tried the door without calling out Polly's name. It was unlocked.

The room was larger than Jessica's, far more plush. Polly had left all the lights on. An unopened grey overnight bag sat at the end of the undisturbed bed. No one had been sleeping in this room.

He checked in the bathroom. The bath was full. A double-edged razor blade lay in the corner soap tray beside several drops of bright red blood. Michael took a step forward, the joy of his time with Jessica fading rapidly. Sitting at the bottom of the warm bath – the hot water had been left trickling – was a hair drier. Its plug rested less than two inches from a nearby socket.

'The man with the electricity.'

Had she accidentally dropped the drier into the water while blow-drying her hair during a bath, she would have received a terrible shock. Yet what did any of that mean next to a bloody razor? That nothing had been an accident?

'I have to warm my blood.'

She had given Clark the form.

Michael reached down and touched the red drops beside the blade, rubbing them between the tips of his fingers. A strange sensation swept over him, similar to déjà vu but far more disturbing. It was a feeling of stumbling across the obvious and finding it utterly alien, a nightmare of staring into a mirror and seeing someone else. The realisation that had hit him on the deck at the end of his conversation with Polly returned. And this time it remained. He finally understood what Polly had been trying to tell him.

Russ had followed Sara's advice and was jogging laps around the deck in order to stay awake. Not being much of an athlete, Sara had decided to wait in the hall near Jessica's room. When Michael exited in a rush, Sara immediately ran to Jessica's door. She didn't knock; she just barged in.

'I knew you'd show up soon,' Jessica said, brushing her hair in the mirror on top of the cabin's built-in chest of drawers. Sara couldn't help but note Jessica's *glow*. She immediately felt insanely jealous.

'So how did it go?' Sara asked.

'Wonderful.' Jessica beamed. 'How about you?'

'It was great.'

'Did you and Russ *do it*?'

'Of course. How about you and Bill?'

'Three times,' Jessica said.

Sara leaned against the wall. 'How come I just saw Mike leaving?'

'He wanted to talk to Polly.'

'Yeah, but why was he here? I mean, what happened to Bill?'

'Nothing. Bill left, and then Michael stopped by.'

Sara thought a moment. 'He just stopped by to talk?'

Jessica grinned slyly. 'We didn't talk that much.'

Sara was shocked. 'You didn't screw both of them?'

'What's wrong with that?'

'That's disgusting!'

'No, it was fun. I had a great time. Especially with Michael. Bill just got me kind of warmed up.'

Sara almost choked with envy. Then she noticed the blood on the sheets. 'Was it painful?'

Jessica shrugged nonchalantly. 'It's sort of like having an itch. It bothers you at first, but then, when you scratch it, it feels great.' She set down her brush. 'You know what I mean.'

'Oh, yeah. Sure, yeah.'

Jessica laughed. 'I'm only kidding! I didn't have sex with Bill.'

'What happened to him?'

'Nothing. Absolutely nothing.'

Sara felt a small measure of relief. She hated to think she was missing out entirely. 'How about Mike?'

'Awesome.'

'If you're lying to me . . . how many times?'

'Simply awesome.'

'How many times?'

Jessica began to count on her fingers, then threw up her hands. 'I ran out of all the stuff we bought.'

Sara let her head drop against the wall. 'And I thought I was amazing.'

Michael reappeared a minute later. He looked a little pale. Sara didn't have a shred of sympathy for him. 'Hi, Sara,' he said.

'Hello,' she snapped. He paid her no heed.

'Could you two do me a favour?' he asked. 'Could you help me find Polly?'

Jessica sat up. 'Why? Is something wrong?'

'No, I don't think so,' he replied, his voice odd. 'But I want to find her. She's on board.'

'Of course she's on board,' Jessica said, concerned, watching him closely.

'Yeah,' he muttered, thoughtfully.

'What do you want with Polly?' Sara asked. He shook himself. His eyes cleared. 'I want to have a meeting of everyone who was at the party when Alice died.'

'Michael,' Jessica said, anguish in her voice. 'Don't.'

'Maria wants to have the same meeting,' Sara said, confused. 'I just ran into Nick a few minutes ago. She's sent him around to gather everybody together. She wants to have it down in the hull in half an hour.'

'Maria.' Michael chewed on that a moment. 'Interesting.'

'Why are you doing this?' Jessica asked, upset, striding towards Michael. A look of sympathy touched his features, and he took her hand.

'It's all right. I understand everything a lot better now. It all makes sense to me, almost.' He hugged her. 'She didn't kill herself, Jessie.'

Jessica stared at him in disbelief. 'You don't know that.'

He touched the side of his head. 'You asked what

happened – Clark did this to me.'

'Clark?' Sara muttered, more confused.

'Alice's boyfriend?' Jessica frowned. 'Is he on board?'

But Michael would not say.

CHAPTER 22

In the dark and relatively deserted hull of *Haven*, Polly McCoy, last surviving member of her unlucky family, stood above Clark Halley and watched as he attached a potent charge of plastic explosive to the side of the ship's huge black fuel tank. He glanced up at her as he turned the setting on the timer, his thin, sweaty red hair plastered over the sides of his white bony face like streaks of caked blood, his dry cracked lips pulled back from his huge teeth in a skull's grin of ecstasy.

'I'll set it for an hour,' he said. 'It will be almost dawn then.'

'If the tank goes, hardly anyone will survive,' Polly said.

'It can't be helped.'

Polly was cold, even though she had on her biggest and warmest jacket. It was waterproof, but she didn't know how well it would hold up in a fire. 'When I was coming down here after you,' she said, 'I saw Maria. She told me everyone who was at the party will be meeting here soon.'

The explosive looked like a lump of dirty orange Play-Doh. Twin red and black wires trailed from it to the tiny square clock. Polly had seen similar explosives and detonators at her parents' construction company. Philip Bart had been in charge of the stuff.

'So?' Clark said.

She knelt beside him and put her right hand over his hands. A drop of blood from the incision in her wrist fell on to his clammy skin. 'They are the only ones who matter. Let the rest go.'

He chuckled. He was in a great mood. He loved twisting the blue dial on the timer. 'The boat's going down, babe. Ain't nothing going to change that.'

'It could go down slowly.'

He looked at her, holding her eyes. She had never realised before how similar their eyes were – both green, both red. 'None of them would shed a tear for you,' he said. 'Not a one.'

'Give them a chance. Please?'

He noticed her blood on the back of his hand, and his mouth twisted into a ravenous grin. 'I told you a drop of it seeped through the floor.' He held up his stained hand proudly. 'See, it escaped the room. It's free now.'

'I don't know what you're talking about.'

He licked the drop away with his long tongue and bade her lean close, whispering a single black word in her ear. 'Madness.'

'It's you who's mad,' she replied angrily.

He chuckled and let it pass. 'All right, babe. For you, I'll let the sleeping innocent try to swim back to shore. As long as you swear to keep our party people down here for the fireworks.'

'How can I keep them here if they want to leave?'

He showed her a few minutes later, after he had detached the bomb and dragged her into a small colourless room down the hall from the fuel tank. Here there was a tall metal cabinet pressed against the hull; he opened it, squeezing the plastic explosives into the bottom corner.

'It's always darkest before the dawn,' he sang as he decided on a final setting for the timer. The bomb couldn't have been more than three feet from the ocean water.

His answer to her question about how to keep the others from leaving was already in the cabinet, in the green sack he'd brought to the cemetery – a double-barrelled shotgun, covered with dirt. It looked familiar. He loaded it with fresh fat shells, and then set the weapon on the topmost shelf, almost beyond her reach.

'It belonged to your father,' he said. 'Before he burned.'

'I know.'

He looked at her. 'Sure you do. I've been telling you that all along. But it never mattered what you knew. It only mattered how much you cared. Me, I'm free as a corpse. I don't care about nothing.' He added softly, perhaps even with a note of regret, 'It's too late to start remembering, Polly.'

'Too late,' she agreed.

He climbed into the closet, turned and spread his arms. 'Love me, babe, before they get here. It'll feel good, like old times.'

'If you stay in there, you'll die,' she said. Yet she followed him, into his arms, into the darkness. He was a liar. There were no old times. The door closed at their backs. She could feel his breath in her ear, like the whispering breeze in dreams she had long ago forgotten. But she could not feel his arms, only the cold steel of the closet, surrounding her on all sides, like a metal coffin.

'We'll die together,' he promised.

Kats strode *Haven*'s deck alone, wearing the thick fog as if it were a cloak personally given to him by the night. The lounge was crammed with unconscious bodies. The few kids still awake had gathered in the galley to await the dawn. Kats felt as if he had the ship to himself, and the thought of it made him giggle. It was true what they said about the taste of revenge being sweet. He had a natural buzz singing cool music between his ears.

Kats knew about Maria and Michael's desire to have a meeting below deck for all those who had been at Alice's party. Both of them had told him to be sure to come. They hadn't asked him if he wanted to come; they had simply given him the order. It was just like those jerks. Well, he had no intention of attending – at least, not until his plan was fully hatched. Then he might swing by, if only to see them squirm. He could get into that.

Kats leaned over the rail and spat into the fog. The foam tip of a swell caught his eye as it broke against the side of the ship. The waves were riding high; solid five-footers. It would be rough out there on the water.

Kats whirled and headed for the stern. He needed his bag, his equipment. It was almost time to set the trap. He'd hidden his materials well. He knew they'd be waiting for him, safe and ready.

He poked a lifeboat along his way and howled at the invisible sky. He loved it.

CHAPTER 23

The reason Jessica wore glasses instead of contact lenses was because of the unusual sensitivity of her eyes, and this, in turn, was largely the result of allergies. When she was a little girl, she had suffered terribly with a runny nose and itchy eyes, particularly in the spring when Southern California's many olive trees bloomed. Occasionally she had even been bothered with asthma. As she had grown older, she had left the majority of her symptoms behind, but her eyes had continued to remain easily irritated by dust and pollen. Also, probably as a psychological carry-over from her few childhood asthmatic attacks, she had a strong dislike of closed and stuffy places. On several occasions during her high school days, she had left an exciting movie right in the middle simply to get a breath of fresh air.

Haven's lower deck was as bad as a submarine as far as

Jessica was concerned. It was not only cramped, it had an overall battleship look. There were huge thick pipes running along the grey walls and ceiling, and the door to the room Michael had chosen to meet in had a *wheel* on it. Michael had closed the door a second ago and turned the wheel. He had locked them in. Jessica could feel the tightness in her lungs and had to consciously remind herself to relax.

Why am I afraid? I am surrounded by my friends.

With the exception of Kats, everyone who had been at the party when Alice had died was present. Maria in her wheelchair sat near the door. Nick stood behind her – it was Nick who had carried Maria and her chair downstairs. To their left were Sara and Russ, sitting on what appeared to be a huge toolbox. Clair and Bubba stood opposite the door, leaning against the steel hull and looking sleepy. Bill was in the corner with The Rock, and he wasn't giving Jessica a lot of eye contact, which was fine with her. Jessica didn't know how Michael had persuaded Bill to come.

Polly was by herself; she was the only one sitting on the floor, a few feet to the right of a tall metal cabinet. Her bulky navy-blue ski jacket dwarfed her undernourished figure, and she'd tied her dark hair back in a ponytail, making her look all of twelve years old. As Jessica watched her, she noticed Polly's gaze drifting between Michael, a red light above the door and the cabinet to her left. Just these three places, nowhere else.

'Aren't we going to wait for Kats?' Maria asked Michael. Outside the door, a few paces down the hall towards the rear of the ship, was *Haven*'s colossal fuel tank. Beyond that were the engines. Coming down the ladder, they had passed the engineer on duty, a big bearded gentleman taking an open-mouthed nap against a control panel. They pretty much seemed to have the space to themselves.

'He won't come,' Bubba said.

'I could go look for him again,' Michael said to Maria, apparently not bothered by Kats's absence.

'I'd like everyone to be here,' she said.

'He won't come,' Bubba repeated.

'How do you know?' Michael asked, the white gauze strip Jessica had obtained from the captain wrapped in a single strip around the top of his head. But Bubba simply waved his hand, as he often did when asked a question that wasn't in his self-interest to answer. Although he was being sensitive to Maria's desires, Michael obviously wanted to get on with things. 'It's up to you,' he said to Maria.

'Maybe he'll show up,' she said, glancing up at Nick.

'I told him twice about the meeting,' Nick said.

Michael turned and paced in the centre of the room, collecting his thoughts. The room fell silent. Watching him from her position in the corner behind the door, Jessica felt both love and fear. She was still sailing the sky from their time together in cabin forty-five. Of all the strange and wonderful things in the universe that could be true – he liked her! In the shower she had been amazed at how excited she had been, and at the same time, how comfortable; it was as if they had known each other intimately for ages. Yet there was still much about him that she did not understand.

Why didn't he tell me he loved me?

It didn't matter, he'd told her enough to let her know she was important to him, even if perhaps he meant more to her than she meant to him. You couldn't have everything. Yet that was exactly Michael's problem. He wanted the impossible. He wanted to change the past.

'I had a reason for calling this meeting,' Michael said. 'But before I begin, I'd like to know your reason, Maria?'

'You go first,' she said.

'I would appreciate it if you could give me some idea?'

'So would I,' Nick said. But Maria never could be hurried.

'Later,' she said.

'All right,' Michael replied, pausing and scanning the room. 'My purpose in gathering you here is to prove that Alice did not commit suicide. I know most of you have heard me say that before, but this morning I hope – with your help – to put together a number of clues I have gathered to show that suicide had nothing to do with it. I'll start by explaining a couple of alternative theories I gave to the police a few days after the party. I won't spend a lot of time on them, though, because I now realise they are fundamentally flawed.'

He returned to pacing, and Jessica noticed he was leaning slightly to the right. She continued to worry about his head wound, and exactly how he had received it.

'I told the officer in charge of the investigation that Alice's murderer could have hidden in the bathroom after killing her, and stayed there until after we left the bedroom. Looking at it from a slightly different angle, I also suggested that the murderer could have stepped out of the bathroom and secretly slipped into our group moments after we found the body. But both of these scenarios have major problems. The murderer would either have had to enter the bedroom – with Alice – immediately after Nick had been in there, or else the murderer would have had to have been in the bedroom with Alice when Nick got there. With the first possibility, the time would have been incredibly tight. Nick was back outside the bedroom only a few seconds later. And with the second – I just can't imagine Nick not knowing someone was in the room, even if it was dark.'

'I didn't hear anyone, that's for sure,' Nick said.

Michael nodded. 'Because that isn't what happened. Let's get into that now. Let's back up. Let's go downstairs before the gun went off. There were three of us in the living room: Maria, Nick and myself. Then Jessica and Sara entered. Sara, what was the first thing you did?'

Sara thought for a moment. 'I don't remember.'

'You complained about how loud the music was,' Jessica said. 'Then you turned it down.'

'That's right,' Sara said.

'The music was loud,' Michael said. 'I find that interesting. For all practical purposes, the party was over. But let's not dwell on this point right now. Just remember it. Anyway, Sara lowered the volume on the stereo, Jessica and Sara sat down and the five of us talked a bit. Then Polly came in.'

'I remember,' Polly said softly, her eyes big on Michael. He crossed the room and stood above her.

'You turned the stereo off,' he said. 'You said your head hurt. Then you went outside to check on the chlorine in the pool. Isn't that right?'

'Yes.'

'On your way out, you shut the sliding glass door to the patio. I saw you walk over to the pool.'

'It needed chlorine,' Polly said.

'So you tested the water?' Michael asked.

'Yes.'

Michael resumed his striding back and forth. 'Let's pick up Nick's story. He asked where the bathroom was. Sara said there was one in the games room, but that she thought someone was using it. She, in fact, said somebody was in there throwing up. Why did you say that, Sara?'

'When I passed it a couple of minutes before, I noticed that the door was closed and the light was on.'

'But you didn't actually hear anyone throwing up inside, did you?' Michael asked.

'I was speaking figuratively.'

'Did you hear *anyone* in the bathroom?' Michael asked.

'Not really,' Sara admitted.

'Was I in there?' Russ asked Sara.

'Shh,' she said, and patted his arm. 'Stay out of trouble.'

'Jessica told Nick to try one of the bathrooms upstairs,' Michael said. 'So Nick headed for the stairs. Tell us, Nick, about that little walk you took, step by step.'

Nick cleared his throat. 'I went to the stairs. I saw Bill in the kitchen. He was bent over the sink. He looked sick or upset. He didn't look good.'

Bubba glanced at Clair, who took the occasion to stare at the floor. 'What was wrong, Bill?' Sara asked.

'I was . . . I'd had too much to drink,' Bill said.

'You hadn't drunk that much,' The Rock said. 'What was bothering you, buddy?'

'Nothing,' Bill mumbled.

'Come on, Mr Treasurer,' Sara insisted. 'Tell us what the problem was?'

'This isn't important,' Michael interrupted.

'How do you know it isn't important?' Sara asked.

'It's not,' Clair said.

'But I want to know,' Sara said.

'Sara,' Jessica said, not exactly sure how this related to Bill's homosexuality, but knowing it must. 'Shut up.'

'Go on, Nick,' Michael said.

'I went up the stairs, both flights. In the first part of the hall there were four doors: three on the left, one on the right. I didn't know which one led to the bathroom, but Jessie had said it was halfway down the hall, so I skipped the first door on the left.'

'Let me interrupt just a sec,' Michael said. 'The police later checked that door. It was locked from the inside.

I'm sorry, Nick, go on.'

'I tried the second door on the left. It was locked. I thought I heard water running inside.'

'I was in there,' The Rock said. 'I was taking a shower.'

'You come to a party and you take a shower?' Sara asked, still smarting from the rebuff over Bill.

'I was washing out my eyes,' The Rock said defensively, glancing at Polly, who gave no sign that she remembered the chlorine she had thrown in his eyes.

'I tried the door on the right,' Nick continued. 'It led on to a porch that overlooked the backyard. Kats was out there.'

'Did he see you?' Michael asked.

'I don't think so.'

'But you could see him clearly?' Michael asked.

'Yeah. There was some light from the pool. It was Kats. I didn't say anything to him. I tried the last door on the left. It was locked, too. But I thought I heard someone inside.'

'Was I in there?' Russ asked.

'Were you?' Nick asked.

'He doesn't have to answer that,' Sara said. 'Not when our quarterback won't tell us why he was crying in the kitchen sink.'

'I crashed somewhere upstairs,' Russ said.

'You were in that room,' Michael said confidently. 'Please continue, Nick.'

'The hallway turns. There were another two rooms, both on the left. I tried the first door. It was locked. There were people inside. I heard someone groaning.'

'That was Clair and me,' Bubba said without hesitation. 'She was acting out a role in a play for me.'

'You told the police the two of you were outside looking at the stars,' Sara said.

'That was a misunderstanding,' Bubba said with a straight face.

'You're not an actress,' Sara told Clair.

'So what?' Clair said.

'This isn't important either,' Michael said. 'All that matters is that Clair and Bubba were together in that bedroom and that they were so occupied that they couldn't hear what was going on in the next room.'

'Why couldn't they hear?' Sara wanted to know. This time everybody simply ignored her. Nick went on.

'I went to the last room. The door was wide open. It was dark inside. I tried the light switch, but the light wouldn't go on.'

'What was wrong with the light, Polly?' Michael asked.

'It was broken,' Polly said, taking her wrist away from

her mouth. She'd been holding it to her lips for the last minute. She looked exhausted.

'Had it been broken long?' Michael asked.

'I broke it when I tried to fix it.'

'When? How?' Michael asked.

'That night.' Polly shivered. 'My hands were wet. I turned it, and it went on. Then it broke.' Polly lowered her head. 'I fell off the ladder.'

Michael stopped dead. 'You fell off the ladder?'

Polly nodded, her head still down.

'Did you get a shock, Polly?' he asked, his voice falling to a whisper.

'Yes.'

'Did it hurt?'

She looked up, her face sad. 'Yes.'

Michael stood staring at her for a moment and something in his expression softened. Then he seemed to shake himself inside, throwing off whatever troubled him about Polly's remark. He turned back to Nick. 'Go on, and please give us as much detail as you can.'

'I stepped into the room,' Nick said. 'It was cold, dark. The east-facing windows were wide open. The blinds were up. But the other windows – the ones that faced the backyard – they were closed. The blinds were down at least. I could hardly tell there was a window there. Polly must have turned off the pool light. I went into the bathroom and closed the door. I didn't even try to turn on the light. My eyes were beginning to adjust a bit. I could see what I was doing. I wasn't in there but a minute.' He shrugged. 'Then I came back out into the hall.'

'Stop,' Michael said. 'You skipped something. The day of Alice's funeral, you told me that while you were in the bedroom, you felt something. Tell us about that.'

Nick hesitated, and it was obvious to Jessica that he would have preferred not to have been pressed on this point. Jessica did not like the course of Michael's analysis. It was too *real*. It brought it all back, the whole night. The claustrophobic dimensions of the room were not the only thing pressing down on her chest. She was beginning to feel – it frightened her as much as it gave her hope – that perhaps Michael *had* uncovered a truth beneath the obvious. A suicide was horrible to contemplate, but a murder – that wasn't something she could simply forget.

Especially if the murderer was in the room with them.

'I felt scared,' Nick said.

'Of what?' Michael asked.

Nick moistened his lips. 'I don't know.'

'You didn't see anything? You didn't hear anything?'

'No.'

'What exactly were you thinking when you were scared?'

'What?'

'People don't just feel scared when they're scared. They have scary thoughts. What were you thinking?'

Nick had to stretch his memory. 'I was thinking of Tommy. He was a friend of mine. He died in a gang fight.' Nick glanced at The Rock. 'Stanley killed him.'

The Rock scowled. 'That bastard.'

'Who's Stanley?' Sara asked, for all the good it did. They ignored her again. Something in Nick's remark had made Michael pause once more.

'Were you with Tommy when he died?' he asked.

Nick fidgeted. It must have been a painful memory. 'He died in my arms.'

'How did Stanley kill Tommy?'

Nick took a breath. 'He got him in the heart with a switchblade.'

'I'm sorry,' Michael said. 'I had to ask.'

'It's OK,' Nick said. 'Should I go on?'

'Please.'

'Should I tell . . .' Nick glanced down at Maria.

'It'll be OK,' Michael said. 'Honestly, Nick, you can trust me on this.'

'I trust you,' Nick said, uneasy. 'Like I said, I left the

room and went into the hall. I got all the way back to the top of the stairs. Then the gun went off. I . . . I froze, for a second, and then ran down the stairs.'

'*Down* the stairs?' Sara asked.

'Yes, he *instinctively* ran *down* the stairs,' Michael said. 'This is very important. He wasn't the only one who ran down the stairs. Kats did the same.'

'How come we didn't run into Kats then?' Sara asked. She was intrigued with the way things were unfolding, Jessica could tell. Bubba, also, seemed very interested in what Michael was up to.

'Before starting down,' Michael said, 'Kats checked out the backyard from his vantage point on the second-storey porch. The only one he saw was Polly, running towards the back door. Go on, Nick.'

'I bumped into Maria on the landing. I knocked her down. I had to help her up. Then we went back up the stairs. All of you know the rest.'

'Not quite,' Michael said. 'When the four of us – Jessie, Sara, Polly and me – came up the stairs, we heard you and Maria talking around the turn in the hall. That's why we went straight to the last bedroom. But you also went straight to that room. Why?'

'I'm not sure I understand your question,' Nick said.

'You had five doors between you and the last bedroom,

four rooms. How come you didn't stop to check any of those rooms?'

Nick was perplexed. 'I don't know.'

'How come you ran down the stairs?' Sara asked.

'I don't know,' Nick said.

'Do you know, Mike?' Bubba asked.

'You'd better,' Clair said, nervously rubbing her hands together. 'The suspense is killing me.'

'I do know,' Michael said, stopping beside Polly. 'The shot we heard that night did not come from the bedroom. It did not kill Alice. It came from outside, from a spot in the backyard on the east side of the house directly beneath the bedroom window.'

No one spoke for a long time. Yet it was interesting, Jessica noted, that everyone in the room appeared to believe Michael. He sounded so sure of himself. Even Bubba, who spoke first, had no doubt in his voice when he made his one-word request.

'Explain,' Bubba said.

'Nick and Kats were upstairs,' Michael said. 'They were the only ones upstairs who were . . . fully functional. They were the only two people in the house familiar with guns. And when the gun went off, they *instinctively* thought the shot came from *beneath* them. Think about it for a minute. Then think about how the group of us downstairs would have heard a sound originating from the side of the house. The sliding glass back door was shut. The games room and the aunt's bedroom windows were all shut. But the east-facing windows in the upstairs bedroom were open. The bulk of the sound from a shot fired beneath that bedroom would have reached our ears via the second-storey hallway. It was no wonder Sara and Jessie and me – and even Maria – thought the shot came from upstairs.'

'Interesting,' Bubba said, thoughtful.

'There's more,' Michael said, getting excited, pulling a folded square of white paper from his back pocket. 'Alice was supposedly killed by a twenty-two shell. Now I'm not a gun expert, but a twenty-two is a pretty small bullet. The shot we heard was loud.'

'Fire any gun in a quiet house and it will sound loud,' Nick said.

'Yeah, that's what the police told us,' Michael said, unconvinced, stepping towards Nick and carefully holding his paper. 'Look at this.'

Nick studied Michael's secret evidence without fully unwrapping it. 'Where did you get these?' he asked Michael.

'What is it?' Sara demanded.

'Shotgun pellets,' Nick said.

'Fascinating,' Bubba said.

'I removed them from a torn wooden shingle,' Michael said. 'A shingle located at the edge of the overhang of the roof directly outside the bedroom where Alice died.'

'How was the shingle torn?' Bubba immediately asked.

'It was splintered upwards,' Michael said.

'But she had the gun in her mouth,' Jessica said, her voice shaky. Suddenly she wished he would stop. Alice was dead. Nothing was going to bring her back. The feeling belonged to a coward, and that was exactly how she felt – as if she wanted to run away and bury her head in the sand. Yet that was only half of it. As Bubba had said, it was *fascinating*. 'We all saw it,' she insisted.

The reminder of how they had found Alice appeared to dampen Michael's enthusiasm. He leaned against the tall metal cabinet off to Polly's left, and Jessica could not remember when he had ever looked so frail. She wished to God they had a doctor aboard who could examine his wound. He was white as a sheet.

'That's true,' he said. 'But the question is, how did the gun get in her mouth? Let's look at Nick's account just before we heard the shot. He went into the bedroom. It was dark. It was quiet. He couldn't see or hear anything. Yet he was scared. Now why was he scared? He's no chicken. It wasn't the dark that was bothering him. It was something else. There was something in that room that made him think of a stabbing years ago. What was it?'

'He smelled something,' Bubba said suddenly.

'Exactly,' Michael said. 'Nothing was coming to him from his eyes or his ears. But his nose – the dark doesn't affect your nose. He thought of Tommy dying in his arms from a knife wound to the heart because he smelled blood.'

'And that's why he ran to the last bedroom instead of checking the others,' Bubba said, nodding to himself, enjoying the intellectual puzzle.

'Does everybody understand?' Michael asked.

'No,' the others said.

'It is clear,' Michael said. *'Alice was lying dead in the room before Nick even got to it.'*

More silence followed, longer and deeper than the previous spell. And again it seemed that everyone believed Michael. Jessica sure did, and yet she did not know what it meant, other than that everything they had believed about that night had been built on a faulty foundation.

Michael glanced down at Polly, and she stared back at him, or so Jessica thought at first. But Polly's eyes were focused slightly to the side, behind Michael, on the cabinet. Her red lips trembled. She must have had lipstick on – Jessica had never seen them quite so red. Polly was suddenly the centre of attention.

'You fired the shotgun,' Michael said.

'Yes,' Polly replied softly.

'Then you threw the shotgun into your garden and ran into the house.'

'Yes.'

'Why?'

'Clark told me to.'

Jessica jumped from her position in the corner. 'Did he shoot Alice?'

Polly nodded.

'Oh, God,' Clair said.

'No,' Michael said.

'But, Mike, maybe she saw him do it,' Nick said.

'No,' Michael repeated, still watching Polly. Now she was looking at him, and she may have been looking to him for help.

'I didn't,' she whispered.

'How did Clark get the gun in Alice's mouth?' Michael asked. Polly only shook her head. He came and knelt beside her. He wasn't there to help her. His tone hardened. 'Where did he go after he pulled the trigger?'

'I don't know.'

'How did he get her fingers on the trigger of the gun?'

'I don't remember,' she said, begging to be believed.

'Where did he go after he did all these things?' Michael demanded, grabbing her arm. 'How come *none* of us saw him?'

'Michael!' Jessica cried. 'She didn't shoot Alice!'

Polly had closed her eyes. She was not crying, but Jessica could hear her breathing, shallow and rapid. It was the damn room. No one could breathe in here. It was almost as if they were back in the bedroom with the body. Michael let go of Polly's arm and sat back. His next words went off like a silent bomb.

'Alice was dead before anyone shot her,' he said.

Polly pressed her wrist to her mouth. Jessica could have sworn she was sucking on it; a child in desperate need of a bottle. They were all going nuts. Jessica looked again to the locked door with longing. If only there was a window they could open that wouldn't let the ocean in. Michael had finally lost them all with his last remark.

'Did she have a heart attack or something?' Nick asked.

'No,' Michael said.

'A stroke?' Sara asked.

'I read the coroner's report,' Michael said, his eyes never leaving Polly's. 'I talked to the coroner. That night someone broke Alice's nose. They broke it badly. She had brain damage the bullet didn't cause.'

'You'd have to hit someone just right to kill them that way,' Nick said doubtfully.

'How about it, Polly?' Michael asked. 'Did Clark do it?' When she didn't respond, he reached over and grabbed her hand away from her mouth, yanking up on the sleeve of her jacket. Jessica felt dizzy.

Polly's wrist was all red. She had been sucking on her own blood.

'Did Clark do this?' Michael yelled.

She nodded wearily. 'He does whatever he wants.'

Michael threw her arm down. 'Liar.'

'He's not here, is he?' Clair asked anxiously.

'He is,' Polly said.

'Really?' Michael asked. 'Let me see him.'

'I can't,' Polly whispered.

'Let me see him,' Michael insisted.

'Let me see if I can find him,' Polly said, giving up, trying to get up.

The madness was still a few heartbeats in the future, but even before it arrived, Jessica felt the brush of the razor's edge. It was not the same blade that had cut Polly's wrist. It was a sharp point in time. As Polly stood and walked towards the metal cabinet Michael had been leaning against, Jessica felt the weight of the entire year behind her, focusing down on this one moment. That was why the air in the room felt so heavy, she realised, so hard to breathe. Polly started to turn the handle on the cabinet.

'What is that?' Clair suddenly cried.

'What?' Michael asked, jumping to his feet.

'People are shouting,' Nick said, frowning. 'Something's happening.'

Michael strode towards the door. He was halfway there when the red light above the door suddenly began to blink off and on and a screaming alarm pierced the air.

'The ship's sinking!' Sara cried.

With the exception of Maria, Polly and Bubba, they all converged on the door. Nick took hold of the wheel and turned it counterclockwise. It didn't open. He spun it the other way.

'It's stuck,' he said, pounding the metal with his fist.

'Oh, God,' Sara said.

'Let me try it,' Russ said, shoving Nick aside.

'No, I'll do it,' Michael said, pressing Russ out of his way. He pulled up on a metal lever beneath the wheel and spun the wheel counterclockwise again. The siren continued to wail. The door cracked open. In a tangled knot, the group pressed forward.

'Stop,' someone ordered at their backs. Jessica turned

to see who it was. She didn't recognise the voice. She did not know why; it was only Polly, good old Polly, closing the door on the cabinet with her right hand, holding a double-barrelled shotgun in her left. She had her finger on the trigger. They were her target.

'Polly!' Jessica cried. 'Put that down.'

Bubba, standing quietly off to Polly's right, made a sudden lunge for the shotgun. He didn't make it. Even though she was bleeding from her wrist under her jacket, and floating above a space mountain between her ears, Polly was still mighty quick. Bubba caught the tip of the barrels on the bulge of his gut. He froze in midstride and slowly raised his hands, giving Polly his warmest smile.

'Never mind,' he said.

Polly's face was dark. She herded everyone into the corner of the room opposite the door with a few silent gestures of her gun. Then she reclosed the door with her shoulder and locked it. Trapped in her wheelchair a few feet away, Maria watched calmly, unmoving. Polly slumped against the door, clasping the shotgun with both hands as if it might suddenly vanish into thin air.

'We have to stay,' she said finally, her voice barely audible over the panicked shouts from the decks above. Jessica could hear people running, screaming. She would scream next. She smelled smoke. Michael took a step forward.

'Why?' he asked.

'Clark,' Polly said. 'He'll kill them all if you don't stay.'

'But we have to get out of here!' Clair pleaded. 'The ship's on fire!'

'No,' Bubba said, reaching a hand out to comfort Clair. Then he hesitated, glancing at Polly. He let his arm drop to his side. He had not finished what he was going to say.

'What is it?' Michael asked Bubba.

'Nothing,' he replied.

Michael turned his attention back to Polly, took another step forward. 'Where's Clark?' he asked.

'Near,' Polly said.

Another step. He was practically daring her to shoot. 'Tell him I want to talk to him.'

'He won't talk,' Polly whispered, perspiration pouring over her face. 'Stay.'

Michael circled to the left, putting the cabinet at his back and drawing the barrel of the gun away from the others. Jessica could not bear to watch.

He'll sacrifice himself to get us out of here.

Jessica stepped out from the group. The Rock tried to grab her hand, but she shook him off. Michael didn't notice; he was too preoccupied.

'I don't really want to talk to him anyway,' he said. 'It's you I want to talk to. Do you want to talk, Polly?'

'About what?' she asked. Her wrist appeared to be hurting her. She stopped supporting the barrel of the gun with her right hand and hugged the cut to her side. The red light continued to flash above her head like an unholy halo. The smell of smoke kept getting stronger. Jessica decided to circle to the right, towards Maria's side of the room.

'Alice,' Michael said, taking another step towards her.

'No,' Polly pleaded. 'Stop there. He pushed . . . He told me – I'll have to shoot you!'

'I don't think so,' Michael said, ignoring her order to halt.

'But you don't understand,' she cried, pulling back on the trigger with her left index finger. 'You must stay here.'

'All right, Polly,' Michael said, stopping less than a yard from the tip of the shotgun. 'Whatever you want.'

What followed next happened quickly and was confused. Jessica had closed to within approximately six feet of Polly's left side. When Michael paused and began to reassure Polly everything was all right, Jessica took that as a sign that he was about to try for the gun. Since he had to cover three feet in the time Polly had to squeeze her finger a fraction of an inch, Jessica did not believe he would survive such an attempt. She decided to make a dive for the gun.

Jessica had barely begun to move when Polly swung the gun towards her face. The twin holes at the end of the double barrels were wide and black – very frightening. Jessica froze. Then Michael made a try for the gun. His heroic attempt was also stopped short. Polly was simply too quick for the two of them. She snapped the gun again on Michael, then on Jessica, back and forth, holding them both at bay.

Then something incredible happened.

Jessica did not see Maria stand from her wheelchair. Maria was just there, up on her two feet, at Polly's side, forcing the gun down. Unfortunately, whatever magic had suddenly given the small girl the ability to walk had not given her an extra dose of strength. Polly threw her off easily. Maria hit the side of her wheelchair, letting out a cry and falling on her side.

But by then Michael had reached Polly.

He probably could have got the gun from Polly more quickly if he hadn't been so overly concerned with where it was pointed while he wrestled with her. It was good he took his time. Whether Polly did so intentionally or accidentally, the trigger was pulled.

The shot hit the side of the tall cabinet, ripping through the metal. Jessica thought she screamed. Maybe the whole room did. Except for Michael. He was in control. He had the gun in one hand, Polly's bloody wrist in the other. Jessica noticed for the first time that the shotgun was caked with dried mud.

'Now you stop,' he said.

'I can't,' Polly moaned, nevertheless collapsing into him as if he had just come to her rescue. Michael tossed the gun to Bubba and wrapped his arm around Polly.

'Let's get out of here,' he called.

'You can walk!' Nick exclaimed, helping Maria up.

'Mike, there's something I've got to tell you,' Bubba said.

'Later,' Michael called, spinning the wheel on the door.

'I *can* walk,' Maria said calmly as Nick hoisted her into his arms on the off-chance that her reclaimed legs might disappear.

'Did that goddamn Clark light the goddamn ship on fire or what?' Sara yelled over the din as once again they pressed towards the door.

'No!' Bubba shouted.

Everybody stopped. Bubba never shouted. 'What is it?'

Michael demanded. Before Bubba could respond, the heavy metal door swung open. It was Kats, grinning the full length of his greasy moustache. He stepped into the room as if he were captain of the ship.

'Are the kids all right?' he asked, pulling the door closed at his back.

Had he been expecting a royal reception, Kats was in for a big disappointment. Michael leaped to a quick conclusion. 'You bastard,' he swore, throwing Polly to Jessica and drawing back his fist. 'What have you started?'

'Hey, Mike, it was only a prank,' Bubba said, jumping in front of Kats, the dirty shotgun still in his hands. 'Kats just let off a few smoke bombs to scare everybody into the lifeboats. There's no fire. The ship isn't sinking. There's nothing to get shook about.'

'We have to stay,' Polly moaned softly in Jessica's arms.

'Why?' she asked, repeating Michael's question. Polly's head sagged back on Jessica's shoulder. She looked up at Jessica with eyes both sad and angry.

'You talked me into it.'

'Into what?' There was a hard lump inside Polly's jacket. Jessica wondered what it could be. It didn't feel like a gun. Polly's gaze slipped past Jessica to the cabinet where she had got the shotgun.

'Go look, Jessie,' she said. 'You'll see, it's dark in there, like the tunnel we got lost in when we were small.'

The shotgun was in safe hands. The fire apparently didn't exist. Yet the fears of the whole night suddenly coalesced above Jessica and fell over her in a smothering wave. Polly's gaze had been moving to the cabinet since they had come down to this wretched room. Had Polly been pointing to something worse than a hidden weapon?

Jessica pulled a handkerchief from her pocket and handed Polly over to Russ, telling him to bind her wrist. Sara quickly moved to help. Everybody seemed to be talking at once. The alarm continued to blare. Jessica hardly noticed. The tall grey cabinet, its side ripped and twisted from the blast of the shotgun, held her attention. She stepped towards it.

The world exploded in her face.

CHAPTER 24

Orange fire. Black water. And a naked fist of thunder. Time could have come to the Bible's cataclysmic end. Except there came pain – terrible pain.

Since she was closest to the cabinet, the shock wave hit Jessica the hardest. Her eyes had no chance to absorb the blinding flash when she was literally swept off her feet and thrown backwards. Her moment in the air existed in her mind all out of proportion to reality. It lasted for ever, and yet it remained incomprehensible to her. She couldn't fly. *Haven* didn't carry nuclear warheads. What was going on?

Then she hit the far wall, and the agony almost consumed her. It pulsed throughout her body, shrieked inside her right arm. A long thick pipe had whipped loose from the ceiling and pinned her to the wall.

Flames danced in short-lived fury and tried to claim

the ceiling. But the blaze could not go down. The ocean was pouring in. Jessica tried to draw in a breath and gagged on fumes. Dark numbing water swam around her ankles and up her calves. Cries wailed in her ears. Everyone was trying to open the door again, and this time they were in a hell of a hurry.

Jessica could hardly see. She had lost her glasses. There was a lot of smoke and the blast had knocked out the overhead lights. Yet the red light above the door remained functional, throbbing like a maddened heartbeat in the closing darkness. The fire was going out already. The water was rising. A shadow stumbled against her, grabbing on to the wall for support.

'We have to get out of here,' Michael said, taking her left hand and giving it a tug. Jessica screamed.

'I'm stuck,' she gasped. Out of the corner of her eye, she saw the group manage to force the door open against the pressure of the rising water. For a few seconds, the water around her knees dropped. Then something crashed outside the hull and it quickly rose again, faster than before. The cabinet was gone; a gaping hole into the underworld had taken its place. She realised then how close she was to dying.

Michael pulled himself past her and tugged on the pipe pinning her right arm to the wall. It didn't budge at all, and yet the effort somehow shot the pain in her arm into the region of the unbearable. She teetered on the edge of blacking out. It was only the swelling current, and the horror of drowning beneath it, that kept her conscious. Michael called to the others.

'Jessie's stuck. I need help.'

Several had already escaped out the door, if it could be called escape; the flood was sweeping away everything that stood in its path, and who knew where it was taking them. Jessica could not find Bill or Clair or Bubba. But Sara and Russ were in the corner to the right of the door, fighting to hold up what might have been an unconscious Polly, and Nick was still hanging on to Maria, trying not to go under. It was only The Rock who seemed to hear Michael. He splashed towards them. Michael pointed to the pipe.

'We've got to bend this back,' he said.

The Rock grabbed hold of the pipe with his thick hands and pulled with everything he had. The pipe creaked. Jessica screamed again. The blood must be squeezing back over her shattered bone. She knew it was broken; it felt like a meaty pancake beneath the hard metal. The Rock leaned his head close to her face.

'Can you pull it out?' he shouted.

'No!'

'Can you try?'

'It hurts!'

'Mike,' Nick called, one arm wrapped around Maria, the other hugging another steel pipe that had fallen from the ceiling. 'Can you get her loose?'

Maria must have taken in a lungful of salt water; she was coughing horribly. Michael looked to The Rock, and to Sara and Russ struggling to save Polly. 'I don't know!' he called back.

'Theodore?' Nick shouted.

Who in God's name is Theodore?

'I'm working on it!' The Rock replied.

'Tell them to go,' Jessica said.

'Not yet,' Michael said, fighting to get around The Rock in order to grab the pipe from above. 'Not till you're free.'

'Go!' Jessica screamed at Nick and the others. 'Get out!'

'Jessie!' Sara called, flailing in the river flowing through the door. Russ had finally got a handle on Polly; he had her swung over his back. He looked as if he could get her to safety, but he glanced over at Jessica before he left.

'Just go!' Jessica yelled. 'I'm almost free.' Her brave lies amazed her. She had always thought brave people were not afraid. The water was now up to her waist.

Russ left with Polly and Sara. Nick got out with Maria a few seconds later. It was down to the three of them. *Haven*'s alarm cried on. It was a death cry. The floor lurched to the side. Jessica could not bring herself to tell The Rock and Michael also to flee. She almost wished Polly's shotgun blast had caught her in the head. The thought of coming to the end choking beneath the sea was too much for her. She had to fight not to faint.

'We have to pull at the same time!' Michael said. He was to her right, his hands on the pipe above her head, while The Rock was directly in front of her, gripping the pipe inches below her trapped arm. The Rock had decided on a strategy. He had his feet planted to either side of her waist; he would be able to use the strength in his legs to pull harder.

'Let's do it!' The Rock shouted back. 'One! Two! Three!'

They pulled. The pipe creaked again, and she screamed again. It made no sense – freezing on the outside like this while she burned on the inside. The water level passed her breasts, heading for her mouth.

'You must pull, too!' Michael yelled at her, probably not knowing he was asking her to pull her bones apart.

'I can't,' she wept. 'It hurts.'

He let go of the pipe and grabbed her chin. Through

the pain, the smoke and the haunting red light, she hardly recognised him. 'Please, Jessie,' he said.

He was begging her. She couldn't let him down. 'I'll try.'

Michael repositioned himself. They counted to three again. The Rock leaned back and howled as if he was on a football field. The pipe squealed. Jessica closed her eyes and prayed for it to end. She pulled.

My God.

The pain was not natural. It soared upwards like a light beam fleeing the spectrum. Perhaps it momentarily yanked her soul out of the top of her head. She might have blacked out. She didn't feel her arm snap free. The next thing she knew, she was bobbing loose, with Michael holding on to her. She opened her eyes.

'We'll be all right,' he said.

'Honestly?' she asked.

They had outwitted the pipe none too soon. Even as they turned to leave – holding on to the wall to keep from being sucked down – the water level passed the top of the door. That was a problem. Not only did she not know how to swim, she did not know how to hold her breath underwater. She was really a pathetic girl to have to rescue. She stopped.

'What is it?' Michael asked behind her. While freeing

her, The Rock had accidentally taken in a mouthful the wrong way; he was caught in the throes of a coughing fit.

'I'm afraid,' she said. Her one healthy arm was hardly able to hold on against the power of the current pouring through the submerged door. The ceiling was less than two feet from the tops of their heads and getting closer. The red light would go under next and then it would be pitch black. The Rock continued to choke. Michael spoke with amazing patience.

'There is nothing to be afraid of. This is a big ship. It will take a while to sink. Once out of here, we'll be halfway home. Go on, just hold your breath, let go and duck down. It might even be fun.'

'All right,' she said. But she didn't move. Michael turned round to The Rock and patted him on the back as if he were a baby needing burping.

'You OK?' Michael asked.

The Rock nodded, although he was obviously far from OK. He had taken in a lot of water. She was killing them all. The Rock motioned for them to get going. Michael reached for her hand that was holding her in place.

'Michael,' she said anxiously.

'I'll go with you,' he said.

'No. You go first.'

'Close your mouth, Jessie.'

'But—'

'Close your mouth.' He pulled her protesting fingers loose. She did close her mouth, but forgot to duck down. It didn't make much difference. The current took hold of her and pulled her under. She was in a washing machine set to black and tumble. Water shot up her nose. *Nothing* could have been worse, not even burning at the stake. Panic consumed her reason. She was smothering! She had to take a breath! Not even the knowledge that she would drown if she did could stop her. She opened her mouth, tasting the salty cold, her bitter death. It was over. She couldn't believe it. She started to suck in.

Then she burst to the surface riding a foaming wave towards the huge fuel tank.

'Eeh!' she screamed.

Michael had caught the same wave. He grabbed her uninjured arm, and the wall, preventing her from a nasty collision.

'The ladder's around this room,' he said, pulling her to her feet. 'We're going to be fine.'

There were more red lights on in the hall. Fortunately they were not blinking, nor were they about to go under. The water level was about three feet. It was, however, a torrential three feet; it was hard to stand. Glancing back the way they had come, Jessica noticed an equal amount of water rushing from the room beyond the one that had held them prisoners. The blast must have torn through the wall and the hull. *Haven*'s crew was at a minimum. Those on duty must have raced to the top deck the instant the smoke bombs had gone off to help evacuate everyone; obviously, none of the crew had had a chance to return to the hold and seal off the flooding section. Michael was wrong. This ship was going under soon. The floor lurched again as they began to round the corner.

'I hate ocean cruises!' she complained.

'They're usually not this bad,' Michael said philosophically.

Someone had forgotten to turn off the engines. The turbines were freezing up and were not happy about it. The grinding noise vibrated the insides of Jessica's skull. It was as if a whale had swallowed them whole and then been harpooned.

'Up you go!' Michael yelled over the noise when they got to the ladder. Every other deck on the ship had stairs except this one. The pain in her arm had not gone away with the pipe. The ladder looked as insurmountable as Mount Everest.

'I'll follow you!' she gasped, trying to hold up her right arm.

'You can do it with one hand,' he insisted. 'I'll be right behind you if you fall.'

The rungs were smooth and wet. Her foot slipped before she had got halfway up and she banged her nose. It was a good thing Michael had his hand on her butt.

The next deck was dry. But their pace didn't improve. *Haven* had gone beyond lurching to shaking. Twice they stepped on to the companionway only to be thrown off. Both times Jessica landed on her broken arm. She could actually feel the bones grinding against each other. All around them, the lights went out, including the emergency lights. Tears poured over her face. She couldn't bear to move another inch. In the black, Michael pulled her off the floor.

'Think of the story we'll have to tell our grandchildren,' he said, trying to give her courage. She clung to him. She couldn't talk. He dragged her back on to the stairs.

As Bubba might have said, the gods were finally kind. They escaped the darkness, and the lower decks. Stepping on to the top deck, tasting the fresh air, and watching her close friends preparing to launch a lifeboat, Jessica almost forgot her pain.

They almost forgot something else. They were all aboard and lowering the small boat off the davit and over the side when Michael suddenly leaped to his feet.

'The Rock!' he exclaimed. 'He's still aboard!'

They were approximately twenty feet beneath the topdeck, bobbing against the hull. The fog had cleared somewhat, and there was a hint of dawn in the misty night, but the bow of the ship was still invisible. Working the ropes together, Russ and Nick looked up and shook their heads.

'We can't pull this thing up with everybody on it,' Russ said.

'And we're going to have to get clear soon or we'll get sucked under,' Nick said.

Michael caught hold of one of the ropes, the side of his head plastered with blood. 'I'll climb back up. I can't leave him.'

'When did you last see him?' Bubba asked, sitting beside Clair.

'In that room,' Michael said.

'You can't go back down there,' Bubba said.

'I can do it,' Michael said confidently. Jessica grabbed his leg with her good arm.

'No!' she yelled, feeling instantly selfish. The Rock had, after all, saved her life.

'I'll get him,' Nick said. But Maria grabbed him.

'It's going to go under any second,' she said.

'I'll get him,' Russ said, gripping the rope and preparing

to hoist himself up. It was Sara's turn to stop her man.

'The hell you will,' she said.

'I'll save him,' Bubba said gallantly. Everyone stared at him. He waited for a moment without budging an inch, then turned to Clair. 'Aren't you going to stop me?'

'You're not that dumb,' she replied between chattering teeth.

'Don't look at me,' Kats told everybody.

'I'll go,' Bill said, getting to his feet.

'If he got caught in that room, he's dead,' Bubba protested.

'He's my friend,' Bill said quietly.

'I'll go with you,' Michael said, undoing Jessica's hold on his leg. But Bill stopped him.

'I can do this one,' Bill said.

'You might drown,' Michael said, looking him straight in the eye.

'Maybe,' he said. 'Maybe not. Stay here, Mike, you can't do everything.'

Michael held his eyes a moment longer, then nodded. Before Bill climbed up the rope, he leaned over and hugged Jessica.

'I'm sorry,' he said in her ear. She kissed his cheek.

'I'm sorry, too,' she said. 'Come back to us quick.'

Bill had strong arms. He was up the rope and over the

rail in a few seconds. Nick and Russ continued to lower the lifeboat. They hit the water a moment later. The swells of an hour ago had vanished. Yet the ocean beside the ship was in turmoil, bubbling like a steaming pool above a geyser about to burst. Nick and Russ disengaged the ropes and shoved off.

'We have to wait for them!' Jessica protested. Michael sat down across from her and shook his head.

'We can't wait this close,' he said.

The lifeboat came equipped with two oars. Nick and Russ took them out fifty yards off the stern. No other lifeboats were visible through the fog. They could hardly see the ship. Without her glasses, Jessica was particularly handicapped. Yet five minutes later even she saw enough to know when the *Haven*'s tail suddenly dropped.

'No!' she cried.

It happened unbelievably fast. The nose rose up like a great white whale readying to launch towards the heavens. Only this whale had a grievous wound. As they watched in horror, it began to slide backwards, bellowing loud blasts of spray as if it, too, felt the pain of drowning.

Then it was gone, and they were alone on the water.

CHAPTER 25

They drifted aimlessly through the strange night. They could have been trapped in the centre of an underground lagoon. The water was *flat*, and the fog seemed a thing risen from below, possessed of evil purpose. It would unfold far enough to tempt their eye, and then suddenly close over, as if it were playing a game of hide and seek that only it could win. Yet the hint of dawn continued to gather strength in the mist. It was now no longer completely dark. Far away, Jessica could hear the faint sounds of people shouting to one another. She hoped most of the class had had a chance to get clear. It was Bubba who spoke first.

'Those were pretty powerful smoke bombs you had there,' he said to Kats.

'My stuff didn't blow open that hole. Mine only made smoke,' Kats said defensively, casting a worried eye on Michael.

'I suppose,' Bubba said, frowning, perplexed at the cause of the explosion.

'Could either of them have escaped?' Michael asked Bubba.

'Don't ask me to quote odds.'

Jessica was sick with grief, cold and pain. The Rock and Bill both gone – she couldn't grasp it. She couldn't stop shivering. The lifeboat didn't come equipped with blankets. Her arm hung limply on top of her trembling knees. It was no longer straight. Looking at it made her nauseated.

'What the hell *did* you do?' Michael asked Kats.

'It was just a prank, like Bubba said,' Kats replied uncertainly. 'I just wanted to scare everybody off the ship.'

'Why?' Michael demanded.

'I thought it would be funny,' Kats said with a trace of bitterness.

Michael scowled, before turning to Jessica. 'How's your arm, Jessie?' he asked.

'It's all right,' she lied.

'It looks like it could be broken,' he said.

'I'm all right. Don't worry.'

'How many life jackets do we have?' he asked the group.

They had four. They were stored in small compartments spaced around the inside of the lifeboat. Clair, Maria and Sara each put one on. Michael tried to get Jessica into a jacket but she just shook her head; she wasn't sticking her arm through any strap for anything. Michael then tried Polly; she ignored him altogether. She didn't appear completely recovered from whatever blow she had received when the bomb had gone off. Nick took the last life jacket. Apparently he couldn't swim either. Nick still had his big question.

'Since when can you walk?' he asked Maria.

'Since my back healed,' she said.

'But you were paralysed,' Jessica said.

'I was, yes, but it was temporary. The fall didn't cut my spinal cord. It merely bruised it. There was a lot of swelling and pressure near where the vertebrae broke. The feeling did not begin to return to my legs until I got to the rehabilitation clinic.' She put her hand on Nick's knee. 'I'm sorry I couldn't tell you.'

'Why couldn't you?' Nick asked, hurt.

She glanced at Michael. 'I wanted what Mike did. That's why I called the meeting.'

'How could you be sure the person who killed Alice was the same person who tampered with the float?' Michael asked.

'What were the chances Tabb High had two psychotics?' she asked.

'That's logical,' Michael said.

'How did you know – how *do* you know someone killed Alice?' Sara asked.

'I knew her for only a short time,' Maria said. 'But I knew her well enough to know she wouldn't have taken her life.'

'What was your plan?' Michael asked.

'I wouldn't actually call it a plan,' Maria said. 'I thought I'd have you all together in a room, and then I would stand and walk across the room. I would be watching all your faces, and in one of them, I knew, I would see the disappointment, maybe even the guilt. But only if I took you completely by surprise.' She spoke to Nick. 'You see why I kept silent. I was afraid the truth of my injury would leak out, and then I could never have my surprise, and catch the person who hurt me.'

'I would have kept your secret,' Nick said.

'I'm sorry,' Maria repeated. 'I felt I would only have the one chance. And I must apologise to you also, Jessie, for what I said the morning after the dance. I have no excuse – except I couldn't feel anything below my waist. The doctors hadn't explained to me yet that the paralysis might pass. I was scared. I just needed someone to blame,

I guess.'

'I understand,' Jessica said. 'But why didn't you write me later?'

It was hard for Maria – who had always been as proud as she was kind – to answer the question. 'I was too ashamed,' she said miserably.

'But now you've lost that one chance you wanted,' Nick said.

Maria looked at Polly, who sat with her head bowed at the end of the raft, holding on to her wrist, silent and unmoving. 'Maybe not,' Maria said.

'But what about Clark?' Sara asked, confused. She wasn't alone in her confusion. *Haven* had sunk. It may have taken some of them with it. But they had unfinished business to complete. They looked to Michael, thinking he would take them back to the party to finish the investigation. But he went back further, to many years earlier.

'Polly,' he said. 'We need to talk some more.'

She pulled her jacket tighter and did not look up. 'I'm cold.'

'I want to talk about your parents,' Michael said.

Now he had her attention. Polly slouched deeper. 'You have the same name,' she said.

'That's right,' Sara said. 'Michael McCoy.'

'Does that matter?' Michael asked.

'No,' Polly said.

Jessica understood. Polly had idolised her father. She – and not Alice – had been the light of her father's life. Polly was trying to tell Michael to help her, not hurt her. Jessica doubted that Michael cared. It was clear who he thought was responsible for Alice's death.

'You were in the car with your parents when they crashed,' he said. 'Tell us what happened?'

Polly fingered her cut wrist nervously. 'They died.'

'Why did the car go off the road?' he insisted.

'I don't know.'

'Did you start an argument in the car and distract your dad?'

How could he know that?

Michael was probably using simple deduction. He knew Polly and her parents had been on a deserted road. If a tyre hadn't blown, then the father must somehow have become distracted. Michael had hit the bullseye. Polly's face crumpled.

'I just wanted another soda from the cooler. That's all I wanted.'

'It wasn't your fault,' Jessica said quickly.

'They burned,' Polly said, distraught. 'And I got away. I didn't even get scratched.'

'Then why did the doctors keep you in the hospital?' Michael asked.

Polly's head snapped up angrily. 'To hurt me! They taped me up with wires. They gave me shots. They tried to make me go to sleep and forget. But I didn't go to sleep. I remember everything that happened!'

Michael apparently had her where he wanted. He pounced hard. 'Was Clark in the room with you and Alice?'

'Yes.'

'There was a ladder in the room. There were Christmas lights hanging out of the closet. Alice told me you wanted her to find some paper cups. Was she up on the ladder getting the cups from the closet?'

'Yes.'

'Were the wires in her way?'

'Yes.'

'What happened?' Michael asked.

'Clark pushed her! She fell! She landed on her nose!' Polly stopped, horrified with what she had just said, or maybe at the memory of what had happened. Tears filled her eyes. 'It made this terrible cracking sound.'

'So that's what happened,' Sara gasped. 'That bastard.'

'Wait a second,' Clair said. 'Who shot Alice?'

'Clark did!' Polly said.

'What else did Clark do?' Michael asked in a mocking tone.

'He took Sara's money!'

'Huh?' Sara said.

'He took it. He hated you and Jessie. He blamed you for making me have the party. He tried to kill Jessie. He tampered with the float!'

'Did he chop down the tree?' Russ asked, interested.

'Yes! Then he went home and smothered Aunty!'

'That's gross,' Sara said. 'How did he get my money?'

'He can do anything! He's a sorcerer! He has the spirits of dead Indians do whatever he wants!'

'I've got to meet this guy,' Bubba said.

'You've already met him,' Michael said. He leaned towards Polly, obviously unimpressed with her outburst of information. 'Let's go back to the bedroom, Polly. Before Clark shoved Alice off the ladder, was he arguing with her?'

'Yes.'

'About what?'

'She wanted him to come to the party, but he came . . . No, she *didn't* want him to come, but he came anyway.' She nodded to herself. 'That's it.'

'Did you want him to come?'

Polly regarded him suspiciously. 'No.'

'Polly?'

'Well, he was mine at first. She took him away from me, you know.' She added softly, 'I just wanted to see him again.'

'Did Clark take the form I wanted your aunt to sign?'

Polly hesitated. 'I told you he did.'

'Did Clark set the bomb on the ship?'

'Yes.'

Michael reached into his back pocket and removed a soggy piece of paper. He handed it to Polly. She could not look at it. A strange light had entered Michael's eyes. Jessica didn't like it. He was a hunter closing in on his prey.

'That's the form, Polly,' he said. 'I found it in your backyard yesterday.'

Polly winced, putting her hand to her head as if it hurt. 'He must have dropped it.'

Michael got on his knees, rocking the lifeboat, moving close to Polly. 'No, Polly. You didn't give it to him.'

'Yes, I did.' She swallowed painfully. 'I did.'

'He didn't push Alice off the ladder.'

'He must have!'

'Where is he, Polly? Where's Clark?'

'He's there!' she cried, pointing desperately into the fog. 'He's there on the ship!'

Michael grabbed her by the shoulders and shook her. 'The ship's gone. Clark's gone. He's been gone all along. He never came to the party. He never came to see you after the party. He didn't push Alice off the ladder. It was you, Polly, it was you who pushed her!'

He's been gone all along?

Jessica's brain did a double take. What Michael was saying was preposterous; it made no sense. It was insane . . . yet he was talking about insanity. Something inside Jessica suddenly clicked. Polly had been going on about all the evil things Clark had done, and yet not one person had seen him at the party. No one had seen him at the homecoming dance. And yet Clark *had* to exist. He had to be real. Michael had said Clark was the one who had hit him on the head.

He is saying there are two Clarks: the real one, and the one Polly talks to – an imaginary Clark.

He was saying Polly was insane.

'No,' Polly moaned, collapsing in his arms. He would have nothing to do with her. He threw her back into the side of the lifeboat, almost throwing her overboard. A year of pain and bitterness twisted his face and voice.

'She was up on the ladder,' Michael said. 'You were arguing about Clark. She was trying to get the paper cups down for you. There were the Christmas lights, a bunch of wires. Her hands must have been tangled up in them. She wouldn't call Clark and ask him to come. You were mad. You shoved her. She wasn't able to get her hands out in front of her to brace her fall. She hit the floor with her nose, the hard wooden floor. She died, Polly, and you snapped. You couldn't take it. You had to make it look like she had killed herself. Or maybe you thought you would make it look like Clark had killed her since he was the one that had made you lose your temper. You went to the garage and got your father's shotgun and hid it around the side of the house. But you needed another gun. You knew where to get it. You knew Kats. You used to get petrol at his station. You knew he always carried a gun. You went out to his car and stole the gun from his glove compartment. You turned up the music in the living room. You went back to the bedroom. You put on gloves and you stuck the gun in Alice's mouth. You wrapped Alice's fingers around the trigger. But you made a mistake there. You put the gun in her right hand. You should have put it in her left. It didn't stop you, though, that mistake. You got a couple of pillows or something and held them around the gun to smother the noise. Then you pulled the trigger, Polly. You blew a hole in your sister's head. But you weren't half done. You hid the pillows or whatever in the first upstairs bedroom. They probably had gunpowder stains on them. You locked the first bedroom door. Then you came downstairs and turned off the stereo. You wanted to be sure we heard the shotgun. Then you went around to the side of the house after checking the pool and fired it off. I noticed on the boat the shotgun had dried mud on it. You must have thrown it into the garden where no one could find it, and left it there. You're pretty clever. When you ran inside, you had the whole house fooled. Is this what happened? *Do you remember, Polly?*'

Polly had listened to Michael's speech with her face buried in the side of the lifeboat. But now she sat up and brushed her dark hair from her green eyes. The gesture seemed symbolic; it was as if her inner vision had just cleared. She looked at Michael.

'I remember,' she said calmly. 'You're right.'

The admission took the wind out of Michael's sails. He was right – it was over. There was no mystery left to drive him on, Jessica saw, and also, perhaps, no reason to be bitter over what had befallen his Alice. He sat back on his heels and touched his head much the way Polly had a minute earlier. It was still bleeding. He was in worse shape than any of them.

Jessica also knew that he was wrong.

'Why?' he asked.

'I have no excuse,' Polly said, unzipping the front of her bulky navy-blue jacket. She had something hidden inside in a clear plastic bag. 'I'm a bad girl.'

You can't have a soda, you're a bad girl.

He had been so quick to condemn her a moment ago, but now Michael appeared no longer interested in confessions or revenge. He glanced at Jessica, and she believed he was remembering back to the day of the funeral when he had yelled at her in Alice's studio. He had been looking for someone to blame then. He had been through a lot since then. He was wiser. 'It was the light bulb,' he said to Polly. 'The electrical shock. It was – a mistake.'

He was referring to the doctors who had treated Polly years ago. Polly heard him, but wasn't listening. Too late Jessica realised what was in the plastic bag: red and black wires, a timer, a lump of orange dough, a detonator. Another bomb. Polly pulled it out and flipped a switch. 'It was a mistake,' she said.

'Oh, no,' Bubba said, sitting up.

'I don't deserve to live,' Polly said, her attention on Michael. 'I *can't* live with what I remember.' She turned the dial on the timer. 'You have five minutes. Leave while you can.'

'Polly,' Jessica said. 'Don't do this. You have your whole life in front of you.'

Polly was not spaced. She was resolved. 'I died in that room when Alice hit the floor. I've been killing time since.' She coughed. 'I am going to do this. Nothing will stop me. Leave.'

'How about you leave,' Bubba suggested hopefully. Clair elbowed him in the side.

'Shut up and let Mike handle this.'

'Polly,' Michael said. 'We don't have anywhere to go.' He held out his hand. 'Give me that thing.'

Polly nodded to the fog, to the faraway voices. 'There're other kids out there. You can find them.' She glanced down at the timer. 'You have four and a half minutes.'

There was something in her voice that made Michael take back his hand. He looked at Bubba, who in turn leaned forward and took a closer look at the mechanism Polly held. Michael's unspoken question was clear: *If I pull it out of her hand, will it go off?* Bubba considered a moment and then shook his head.

'Don't try it,' he said.

'I don't want to spoil the party,' Russ said. 'But we should get the girls off the lifeboat now. That thing could blow any second.'

'I'm not leaving without you!' Sara cried.

Russ frowned. 'Who said I was staying?'

'Oh.' Sara turned to Jessica. 'You don't have a jacket?'

Jessica gestured vaguely towards her butt. 'There's one under my seat.'

'Russ is right, Mike,' Nick said. 'It could blow any second.'

It was seldom Michael appeared lost. He quickly scanned the ocean. Then he slapped the side of his leg with his fist. 'Dawn's coming and the fog's lifting, but we could be in the water an hour.'

'I'd rather tread water that long than be spread all over it,' Kats said.

'Bubba?' Michael asked.

'I can float till the Coast Guard gets here.' Bubba stood and grabbed Clair. 'Let's go for a swim.'

'Mike?' Clair asked, tightening her life jacket. They were all waiting for him to tell them what to do. He threw his hands up.

'Go then, get away. Swim towards the voices. There have got to be other lifeboats out there.'

The gang jumped overboard almost as one, sending the lifeboat rocking. Nick didn't even stay. Jessica understood. He had to take care of Maria. They disappeared within seconds in the fog. Michael sat back down across from Jessica. 'Get out that jacket.'

'There's no jacket,' Jessica said.

He did a double take. 'You're kidding?'

'No.'

He glanced anxiously at Polly. She had the bomb hugged to her chest, her eyes half closed. 'It doesn't matter,' he said. 'You'll be OK. Just swim after the others. You can catch up.'

'You're not staying,' she said.

'I'll be along in a few minutes.'

He was a lousy liar. The minute she was gone, he was going to try to talk Polly into giving up the bomb. And if that failed, he would attempt to take it from her by force. He would risk his life in order to save Polly's. 'You go after the others, and I'll be along in a few minutes,' she said.

His anxiety increased. 'This is no time for games. Get out of here, Jessie!' Holding on to her right arm, she came and sat beside him. He was so beautiful; it made her heart ache to think she'd only been given one night to love him. 'My arm's broken,' she said.

'*What?* Why didn't you say something?' He whirled in the direction the others had disappeared. 'All right, it doesn't matter. I'll go with you. We can still catch them. You can swim with a broken arm.'

'No.'

'Yes, you can! I'll help you.' He stood and tried to take her hand. 'Come on.'

'I can't swim.'

He dropped back down. The life went out of his eyes. 'No?'

'No. I have to stay. *You* have to go.'

He turned away from her and stared at Polly. A minute went by and he didn't say anything. Then he burst out crying. 'I *can't* leave you,' he whispered.

She pressed her left hand to the side of his cheek. He was shaking with fear, and she was suddenly calm. The fear was still there, but it was as if deep inside she understood that it was supposed to end this way. Her destiny had come to her. It was a relief in a way.

'She's my friend,' she said. 'We've been together since we were children. I can't leave her.' She wiped at his tears. 'It's all right. I love you, and I got to tell you that. I remember the night we went out. You told me you sometimes swim around the pier in the morning for exercise. You're hurt, but you're still a swimmer. You'll catch the others. Now go ahead, get out of here.'

He bowed his head and covered his eyes. 'You're going to die.'

'Nothing's decided yet.' She hugged him as best she could. 'Please, Michael, before it's too late.'

'I can't.'

'Yes, you can. You can do it for me. For us. Please, go.'

He shook his head. He wouldn't look at her. And she suddenly realised he wouldn't leave. Not Michael. Not for anything.

Except possibly to give her some kind of chance.

Polly was watching them. She caught Michael's eye, subtly shifting her hold on the bomb's wires. Polly didn't have to speak the threat aloud. It was there in the air. If he didn't leave, she would blow the three of them up right then.

'Damn,' Michael whispered. Beaten at last, he did turn to Jessica, looking at her for the longest time. And she remembered the first time she had seen his face, how she had admired the warmth and intelligence in his eyes. From that point on, the whole year, she had wondered what he thought of her.

'I love you,' he said.

She smiled. 'That is good.' He kissed her goodbye once. Then he was in the water and swimming away. The fog swallowed him up as it had the others. She turned her attention to Polly.

'Do you want to talk?' she asked.

Polly had seen everything. 'You could have taken Sara's life jacket. Sara can swim like a fish.'

'I could have.'

'Why didn't you?'

'I wanted to talk to you alone.'

Polly looked away. 'Oh, Jessie.'

'What happened to your wrist?'

'I cut it with a razor blade. I'm crazy.'

'You seem sane enough now.'

'I suppose I have Mike to thank for that.'

'He doesn't know everything. How come you didn't defend yourself?'

'I used Clark for that. But Mike is right. Clark never came back to see me after Alice died. No one came.'

Polly shrugged. 'Mike knows enough.'

'You didn't smother your aunt. You'll never convince me of that.'

'When I came home, after I chopped down the varsity tree, I thought I saw Clark leaving my house. And then I went inside . . .' Polly drew in a weary breath. 'She was hard to take care of. There were so many times I wished she was dead.'

'That doesn't mean you smothered her. She was old. She just died.'

Polly paused. 'I suppose that's true.'

'And you didn't take Sara's money.'

'Yes, I did do that. I remember she had just got it out of the bank. She had to run back inside for a receipt or something. She had it less than five minutes when I took it.'

'Did you have a reason?'

'I was afraid she'd lose it. She had all cash.' It was coming back to Polly in bursts of clarity. 'Yeah, I took it out of her bag and put it in mine. And then, when I got home, I put it in our safe.' Polly chuckled without mirth. 'And then I forgot about it. I forget my name sometimes. I'm crazy.'

'Stop saying that.'

'It's true.'

'You didn't kill Alice.'

Polly looked away again, hugging the bomb closer. Jessica wondered how much time was left. She supposed she wouldn't feel anything when it went off. But that remark Kats had made about being spread all over the water . . . She couldn't go out this way – torn to tiny red pieces. She couldn't help thinking of her mother receiving the news. Not everything that was left of them would sink. The calm and silence of the surrounding sea remained, but her internal calm began to waver.

'Get out of here,' Polly said.

'I have nowhere to go.'

'Well, it's your own fault.'

'I don't care how mad you were at Alice. I don't care if everything else Michael said about that night is true. You didn't push her off that ladder. You loved her.'

In response Polly yanked open a compartment on the side of the lifeboat. There was a life jacket inside the compartment. She threw it to Jessica. 'Get out of here.'

'No.'

Polly checked the timer, tension spreading across her face. 'There's less than a minute left.'

'I don't care.' Jessica set the life jacket aside.

'What are you doing? Go!'

'Did you push Alice off the ladder?'

'I'm not bluffing!'

'Did you push Alice off the ladder?'

Polly blinked. 'No. We were arguing about Clark. Her hands got all tied up in the Christmas lights like Mike said. And then, she slipped. She fell forward. She landed on her nose.' Polly closed her eyes and grimaced. 'I was always arguing with her about something.' Then her eyes popped open. 'Oh, Christ.'

'That's it. It was an accident. It was an accident your father drove off the road. You didn't do anything wrong.'

The immensity of the revelation had Polly stunned. Yet she would not easily abandon her madness. It had a hold on her stronger than the most potent drug on the most hopeless addict. 'I sunk the ship,' she said.

'The Rock probably got out some way. And Bill's an

athlete. I bet he was able to swim clear. What's one old boat? You've got millions. Buy the captain a new one.' Jessica paused. 'You didn't do anything wrong.'

Polly began to cry. '*You're* wrong. I did tamper with the float. I thought you would be elected homecoming queen. I blamed you for making me have the party.'

'I forgive you.'

'I tried to hurt you! I was jealous of you!'

'Why?'

'Because everybody loves you! I heard what Mike just told you! No one's ever told me that!'

Jessica picked up the life jacket and threw it overboard. Immediately it began to drift away from the lifeboat. 'Does this tell you something? You're my friend, Polly.'

Polly stared at her in utter amazement. 'You'll die.'

'Maybe we'll both die. But we don't have to.'

'You would do this to Mike?'

'No.' Jessica got to her knees and slowly crawled towards Polly, wincing with the pain in her arm, the fear in her heart. 'If I die, *that* will be your fault. You're not crazy now. You know what you're doing.' Jessica stopped and stuck out her left hand. 'Give it to me, Polly.'

Polly held her eye. 'Alice told me you would end up with Mike.'

'Let's not disappoint her. Give it to me.'

'I don't even know how to turn this thing off!'

'That is not a problem,' Jessica said, losing patience. 'Give it to me!'

Polly's anxiety evaporated, being replaced by an indignant expression and tone that was almost comical given the circumstances. 'Really, Jessie, you've got a broken arm. I can get rid of it myself.' And with that Polly stood and – holding on to the detonator and the plastic explosives as one unit – threw the bomb as far as she could into the fog. Polly's choice of direction seemed commendable; she had thrown it opposite the direction towards which the gang had disappeared. Of course, it was always easy to end up going in circles in the fog.

The bomb exploded. A couple of seconds later they felt the spray. A couple of seconds after that they heard an irate shout. It was Bubba.

'Hey, girls! Lighten up!'

'Come back!' Polly yelled happily. 'Come back! Everything's OK! I'm OK!' She plopped down beside Jessica and the two girls laughed and cried together as they used to in the good old days before time had made them into terrible teenagers. But there was one thing Jessica still didn't understand. 'Why did you chop down the varsity tree?' she asked.

'I used to hate seeing all those jocks and cheerleaders

gather under the tree every afternoon at lunch. They're such a bunch of snobs.' Polly smiled. 'That's one thing I don't regret.'

There was a reason the ocean had been so flat. *Haven* had sunk less than a quarter of a mile off Catalina. The swells that had rocked the ship earlier had been effectively blocked by the proximity of the island.

This was fortunate. Not a single passenger or crew member drowned as a result of the bomb. When the sun rose half an hour later and the fog cleared, all of Tabb's senior class – including The Rock and Bill – could be found either drying out on the beach or floating about on a lifeboat offshore. Some called it a miracle. *Haven*'s captain, though, was quick to credit one passenger with keeping his head in the middle of the crisis and hurrying everyone into the lifeboats. He was Mr Carl Barber, better known as Kats.

Very few people realised that Kats had started evacuating the ship *before* the bomb went off. From then on, he was considered something of a hero.

EPILOGUE

It was a different morning from the previous one. There was no fog. There were no bombs. There was nobody on the beach. Michael was glad the school year was finally over.

It was Sunday. He could hardly remember Saturday. He had spent the whole day – and night – in Catalina's small but efficient hospital. The diagnosis had not been too bad. Twenty-four stitches in the scalp and 'a moderate concussion'. Michael would have hated to have seen a serious one. He still had a slight headache. They hadn't wanted to release him so soon. Then he had told them how poor he was.

The sun was an hour into the clear sky, dazzling on the gentle blue Catalina water; he was still on the island. Michael sincerely believed the morning shore was the best place in the world to sit while waiting for someone.

He had recently adopted that belief. He stretched his bare feet through the cool grainy sand. Jessica was supposed to meet him soon.

He had a girlfriend. He had a sister. He had vindication.

A good day to be alive. I need a lot more of these.

Lieutenant Keller had called him and asked if he could interest him in pursuing a career as a detective. Keller had sounded properly chastised, but to his credit, he had also seemed happy to be proven wrong.

Michael had a visitor before Jessica arrived. The fellow seemingly came out of nowhere. He wore black leather as if he had been born with it on. His red hair shone in the morning light. He carried a brown paper sack in his left hand.

'Hi, Clark,' Michael said, not getting up to greet him.

'Hello.' Clark glanced at the white bandage wrapped around Michael's head. He apparently decided to remain standing. Michael felt no fear, not even when Clark removed a gun from his coat pocket. 'This is yours,' Clark said.

Michael accepted it. Clark had removed the bullets. 'Thanks. Just what I need.'

Clark gestured to Michael's bandage. 'Did I do that?'

'Yeah.'

Clark chuckled. 'You should have known better than to come to my door in a hundred-degree heat with a sports coat on.'

'You knew I had the gun?' Michael wondered what Clark had in the bag.

'Sure. But I didn't know what you were going to do with it.'

In his own way, Clark was apologising. Michael decided he had no reason to hold a grudge since he had been the one who had brought the gun. 'I wasn't going to shoot you,' he said.

'Should have told me before I clobbered you.'

Michael studied Clark's face. He wanted to make sure he had the real one. 'I chased you the whole year.'

'I knew you followed me from the petrol station that one day.'

'You were on a fast bike. Why didn't you ditch me?'

'I wanted to know why you were following me,' Clark said.

'Were you really stoned that night I met you at the game?'

'Probably. Why?'

'Honestly? You're a weird guy, Clark. I followed you because I thought you might have killed Alice.'

'Why would I kill Alice?'

The proverbial question. It was good to finally understand there was no answer to it, that it had been an accident. 'It doesn't matter. How come you're here?'

Clark's green cat eyes brightened. 'I heard about what happened on the radio. I called the hospital to see how Polly was doing. They referred me to her doctor. He wants me to come and meet with him and Polly. He told me she was starting therapy. He thought I could help her.' Clark shifted his paper sack into his right hand. 'What's the dude talking about?'

Polly must have been placed into the hands of an innovative psychiatrist. Michael approved. Confronting a flesh-and-blood illusion couldn't be any worse than being struck by lightning.

Clark hadn't actually answered his question. 'I don't want to spoil the surprise,' Michael said. 'But you definitely should go. You'd find it fascinating.'

Clark showed interest. 'How's she looking these days?'

'Thin and sexy.' Michael had to shake his head. 'What did Alice ever see in you?'

Clark was not offended. When he spoke next, though, there was a strange authority in his voice. 'She used to talk about you. She thought you were all right. I guess you thought the same about her. But your Alice was not mine. She was an artist. She could have been great. She had my passion.' He wiped his nose with the back of his arm. 'She couldn't stand me most of the time, but she saw something in me most people don't.'

'What was she to you?'

Clark handed him the bag. Inside was an achingly beautiful painting of Alice walking alone on an ocean shore beside a wide desert, wearing a long white dress, a string of jewels around her neck. It was on the small side, twelve inches by twelve inches, and had yet to be framed, but the colours pulsed with life; they literally took Michael's breath away. He understood. Alice had meant a great deal to him.

'You cleared her name,' Clark said.

'So you came all the way over here to give me this?'

Clark nodded. 'You're right, I'm a weird guy.'

He walked away before Michael could even thank him. Michael stood and threw the gun into the ocean. A few minutes later he heard Jessica call his name.

The doctors had put a pin in Jessica's arm. It was a nasty break, they said, but they were optimistic she would have a hundred per cent recovery. With her cast in its sling and the wide black-rimmed glasses her mom had brought her from home on her nose, she was a fine sight. She even had her hair pinned up; she hadn't been able to wash it since – well, since she had taken a shower with Michael. But she didn't care how she looked because she knew Michael wouldn't care.

He was sitting on the beach near the water and looking at a paper or book or something. She was amazed at the pleasure it gave her simply to watch him and know that she was going to see him tomorrow, and the day after that. Although they had been in the same hospital, with rooms down the hall from each other, they had hardly spoken since the lifeboat. She raised her left hand and waved.

'Michael!'

Putting away his object of interest in a brown sack, he stood and walked towards her. She was relieved to see he had got over his slight limp. She met him halfway. It was cute – the awkwardness in his greeting. He gave her a light pat on the shoulder. She gave him a sloppy kiss on the lips.

'Hi,' she said. 'Love your hat.'

He touched his bandage. 'Bubba wanted to sign it.'

'How do you feel?'

'Great. How about you?'

'Fantastic.'

'You look good.'

'Liar. But it's OK – I'm a liar too. My arm is actually

killing me. And I just swallowed two of those yellow pills the doctor gave me.'

'I hope they weren't Valium.'

'Me, too! My mom dropped me off, but how did you get out here?'

'Hitchhiked. It's easy to get a ride when you look like a war vet.'

They began to walk down the beach, holding hands, Michael carrying his brown bag. *Haven* was underwater but not forgotten. They passed three plates, a chair, one soggy pillow and a dozen beer cans before they had gone a hundred yards. A gentleman from the Coast Guard had said debris from the sunken ship would wash ashore for a long time.

'I suppose your trip to Hawaii is off?' Michael asked.

'Postponed,' she corrected. 'Sara and I are going later in the summer. In a way, I'm glad we have to wait.'

'Why?'

'It will give you a chance to arrange your schedule so you can come with me.' She added quickly, 'Sara's bringing Russ.'

'Oh, yeah, he's a free man now. How are those two getting along?'

'They're at each other's throats. They're in love. He's helping her with her PPB – Post Presidential Blues. She doesn't know what to do with herself now.' She smiled. 'You haven't said yes yet.'

'What would your parents say?'

'Nothing. I won't tell them you're coming. What would your mom say?'

'That you only live once. To tell you the truth, Jessie, I don't know if I could afford it.'

'Do you *really* want to come with me?'

'Absolutely.'

'Then it'll be my treat. And don't say no. My parents gave me a bunch of cash for graduation that I've got to get rid of immediately, before I get materialistic.'

'I don't know. That's a lot of money.'

'Michael!'

'I'll come.'

She laughed. 'Had to twist your arm, didn't I? That's great. I'll have my cast off. You can teach me how to swim. But you're sure getting the time off won't be a problem?'

'I'm quitting my jobs at JPL and the 7-Eleven. I'm going to bum around all summer and write a book.'

'Can you write?' she asked.

'I hope so.'

'What's it going to be about?'

'This year.'

'Hah! No one will believe it.'

'I'll turn it into a novel,' he said. 'Where did you say you were going to go to school next fall?'

'I'm not. I've been thinking about what you said about my awesome voice. I'm starting a rock-and-roll band. What are you laughing at?'

'I'm sorry. It's such a coincidence. I told Clair on Friday morning I was going to start a band. She told me to get you for a singer.'

'*Clair* said that?'

'Yeah. Can I be in your band?'

'Can you play an instrument?' she asked.

'No.'

'It doesn't matter. I'll teach you piano if you promise to put me in your book and make me real sweet.'

'I wouldn't know how else to make you.'

'Hang around with me for a while. You'd be amazed.'

They had company – half a dozen seagulls hunting for lunch in the leftovers from *Haven*'s galley. And far off, perhaps half a mile up the beach, somebody was scouring the sand with a garbage bag in hand.

'Is that The Rock?' Jessica asked, squinting through her glasses.

'Yeah. I spoke to him earlier. He had a story to tell. Right after we swam out of that room, the door closed on him. He had to go out the hole in the hull. I don't know how he did it.'

'He deserves his nickname. What about Bill?'

'He says he was still on the top deck when the ship suddenly went belly-up. He was thrown clear.'

Jessica pointed down the beach. 'What's The Rock doing?'

'He doesn't want a cameraman from a news station coming over to Catalina and seeing what drunks we have for a senior class. He's picking up all the beer cans. Did you know that yesterday when the tide was out people were able to spot the *Haven*'s antennas sticking from the water?'

'Really?'

Michael looked wistfully out to sea. 'I'd like to rent scuba equipment and check her out.'

'For something in particular?'

'Well, I'd like to find my yearbook for one thing.'

She poked him. 'Why?'

He blushed. 'No particular reason.'

'Liar!' she called him again, bouncing away to the water's edge. 'I'll write it in the sand with my toes.' She kicked off her shoe. 'Michael Olson is the greatest *lover* Jessica Hart has ever—'

He stopped her. He was easy to embarrass. They

continued their stroll, the sun warm on their faces. They found a yearbook a few minutes later. Talk about coincidences – it was Sara's, and it was sitting next to Bubba's sombrero. Jessica picked it out of the foam and shook it off. The paper Sara had glued over the inside cover had come loose. The handwriting beneath was smeared but still legible.

'Listen to this,' Jessica said. '"My dearest Sara. My heart patters at the thought of us making love tonight above the deep ocean swells, our bodies locked in passion, the salty sweat on the burning flesh of our entangled limbs mingling like oil and wine, ready to burst into flaming ecstasy. My head swoons . . ."' She read all the way through, giggling like a schoolgirl by the time she came to the last line. '"Love you always, in so many different positions. Bubba!"'

'Now there's someone who knows how to write.'

'Do you think he slept with her?'

'She's your friend.'

'I doubt it. She says she did it with Russ when it's obvious she didn't even untie his shoes. Then again, Bubba is *your* friend. What do you think?'

Michael started to scratch his head, but ran into his bandage. 'Ordinarily I would say yeah. But Bubba and Clair are getting married tonight in Las Vegas.'

'*What?*'

'Bubba has a ticket waiting for me at Los Angeles airport. I'm flying out there this afternoon. I'm going to be his best man. You should come. Maria and Nick are getting married also.'

'This is a joke.'

'No. If Nick marries Maria, she is automatically allowed to remain in the country. They're all eighteen. I think it's great. Nick said Maria wants you to be her bridesmaid.'

'You're serious? Who's going to be Clair's bridesmaid?'

'It might be you. As you can imagine, this is all sort of short notice.'

'But Clair and I hate each other.'

'Pretty girls always hate other pretty girls. It's biological. That's what Bubba says. Maria's counting on you.'

'Then I'll come. Clair must be pregnant again.'

'Bubba says no.'

'I don't believe it.'

A smile lit up Michael's face. 'I can tell you someone who's not pregnant any more.'

'Your mom! What did she have?'

'A seven-pound six-ounce girl.'

Jessica dropped Sara's yearbook and hugged him. '*Brother* Michael! Are they both OK?'

'Yeah, they're fine. Mom had the baby about the same

time we were in the lifeboat.'

'What did she name it? No – let me guess. Alice?'

'Mom wanted to, but I said no.'

'Why?'

It might have been a delicate question. Michael let go of her hand and looked down at the paper sack he carried. 'Life has to go on.' He shrugged. 'I'm still learning to let her go.'

'I understand. I shouldn't have . . . What's in the bag?'

He showed her, and it brought tears to her eyes, and not just because it was so beautiful. 'I had this dream,' she said, staring at the painting in her hands. 'It was the morning we were together at the hospital waiting to hear about Maria. There were four of us in a black tunnel. You, me and these two little girls. One of the girls was Alice. When we got to the end of the tunnel, we were in a place like this. Who did this painting?'

'Clark.'

Jessica made a face. 'The *real* one. Not Polly's imaginary one.'

'Yeah,' Michael muttered, a faraway look in his eyes. 'What is it?'

He didn't seem to hear her question at first. 'I had this dream,' he said finally. 'I had it many times this year. It started a couple of days after I met you. In it I'm standing on a bridge over a roaring river. There's a desert in front of me and a forest behind me. And there's this girl – I never see her face. But she tells me to go forward, that she will follow.' He glanced at the sky. 'I always used to wonder if it was Alice.'

'Who do you think it is now?'

'My sister.'

'How did you feel in your dream?' she asked.

'Happy. But also sad. I felt I was leaving paradise.'

'I felt very happy in mine. I didn't want to wake up. I felt like I was being reborn.'

Michael was impressed. 'Maybe that's how it really was.' Then he shook his head. 'We'll never know.'

She took his hand. '*I* know. I was supposed to meet you. Alice knew it. That's why she wanted you to meet me. She was wise.' Jessica smiled. 'She knew how far out I am.'

Michael smiled, too, briefly. The sadness of leaving paradise, however, was still there. 'If there is a design to our lives, and Alice was sensitive to it, then maybe I messed things up. The night of the party, she was upset she didn't get to introduce me to you. I could have let her, you know. She felt as if somehow a wrinkle had been put in the canvas.' He took the painting back and put it in the bag. 'I don't know why it bothered her then, or why it bothered me later.'

'She didn't die because you avoided me. You don't think that, do you?'

He shrugged again. 'I shouldn't have brought it up.'

'Michael, you have a guilt complex. You've done more good for more people than anyone I know. I grew up with Alice, but I deserted her the night she died like everyone else. I went by the obvious facts. You went by your gut feeling, and you used your head. You saved her memory.'

'I was late doing it.'

'Not at all. The truth is coming out. It hurts Polly's image, but that's OK. Polly's got something out of all this. Her memory was saved. You gave it back to her.'

Michael was doubtful. 'I was hard on her.'

'You had to be hard.' Jessica paused. 'She told me to thank you.'

'You spoke to her?'

'Late last night, on the phone. She's in another hospital. This one's supposed to be the best.' Her voice faltered. 'We had a long talk.'

'Was it painful?'

Jessica nodded. 'But I'm glad we had the chance. Her doctor arranged the call. I understand her a lot better now. We're going to talk again soon.' A seagull ran across their path with a Ritz cracker in its mouth, fleeing from another almost identical bird. Jessica smiled at the sight, although it touched her with strange sadness. Birds of a feather, and best friends – they were sometimes each other's worst enemies. 'I asked her why.'

'Why?'

'Why Clark. Of all people to dream into her life, why him? Her response really hit me. She said she just needed someone to love her, but that any time she ever did love someone – in real life – it always brought her pain. She couldn't help who she invented. Her lover had to be her tormentor. Clark was just someone who fitted the bill.'

'She said that?'

'Yes.'

'It sounds to me like she's on the road to recovery. She has you to thank as well. You saved her life. It was you who got the final truth out of her.'

Jessica took his hand and pulled him close. 'OK, we're both heroes. Now let's talk about happy things or I'll leave you and go out with Bill again.'

'That isn't much of a threat.'

She shoved him away. 'Hey, he's as big a hero as they're making Kats into.'

Michael groaned. 'Don't remind me.'

'Oh, you never answered my question. What—'

'Ann,' he interrupted. 'We chose it together.'

'Why Ann?'

'Why not? It's a nice name. It's easy to spell.'

'Ann was Alice's middle name.'

He was amazed. 'I didn't know that.'

'Are you sure?'

'Positive.'

She smiled. 'What's in a name? Maybe everything, huh?'

'Let's wait and see who she grows into before we try to answer that one. But speaking of names . . .' He set the painting down and pulled a heavily wrinkled envelope out of his back pocket. 'Last autumn I built a telescope. I used to take it out to the desert a lot. Anyway, to make a long story short, I discovered a comet.'

'You what?'

'A comet. They're these big balls of ice and dust that—'

'I know what a comet is. That's incredible. Are you going to win the Nobel Prize?'

'If Bubba uses his influence.' He handed her the envelope. It looked as if it had been underwater. Jessica realised it was the sealed envelope his mother had given him before the graduation ceremony. It *had* been underwater. 'This is the confirmation of the sighting,' he said.

'How come you haven't opened it?'

'I spoke to the observatory on Thursday. I already know what it says. Besides, I wanted you to open it. That's why I brought it to the all-night party.'

She let go of his hand and got to work; it was a lot harder getting to a sealed letter with only five fingers. 'When will it be visible?'

'It won't, not without a telescope. In fact, it's already passed its closest approach to the earth. It's heading back out into space. But if you want, I can take you out to the desert and show it to you in my telescope.' He watched her fumbling. 'Need help?'

'I can manage, thank you. Is it like Halley's comet? Will it come back?'

'Sure.'

'When?'

'In a couple of thousand years.'

'Then you had better take me to the desert soon.' She finally got the paper out. There was an official seal on top, and words of congratulation and numerous astronomical notations below that made about as much sense to her as did the name given to the comet. She frowned. 'I don't understand.'

'They always let the person who discovers a comet choose its name.' He stopped. 'What's the matter? I thought you would be flattered.'

'I am. It's just the way you put our names together—'

Michael snapped the letter from her hand. He quickly scanned it and his forehead wrinkled. 'I told them to name it Jessica-Michael not Jessica-Olson.'

She nodded. 'Uh-huh. Are you sure you're not trying to tell me something?'

'No, honestly. It's a mistake.'

'Right. Who's getting hitched tonight in Las Vegas? And why is it *I* have to be there?'

He turned red. 'I didn't mean that.'

'I believe you.'

'Jessie!'

'The nerve of the guy. He washes my back in the shower once and he thinks I've got to marry him.'

Michael started to protest again. Then he stopped and grinned. 'I washed a lot more than your back, sister.'

'I haven't forgotten.' She kissed him shyly. 'Maybe I should marry you.'

Chain Letter

TWO BOOKS IN ONE

Chain Letter

When Alison and her friends start receiving chain letters demanding dangerous and impossible deeds from them, they figure it is just a sick joke. Until one by one they start to go missing …

Chain Letter - The Ancient Evil

Just when they thought they were safe, the letters start being delivered again. This time demanding even more horrific tasks from them in return for their lives. Can they survive long enough to uncover the sender?

www.bookswithbite.co.uk

Sign up to the mailing list to find out about the latest releases from Christopher Pik

The Last Vampire

THE LAST VAMPIRE
BLACK BLOOD

Alisa Perne is the last vampire. Beautiful and brilliant, for five thousand years she has hunted alone, living among humans, living off humans. But somebody knows her secret – and they want her dead ...

www.bookswithbite.co.uk

Sign up to the mailing list to find out about the latest releases from Christopher Pik

the Vampire Diaries
The Awakening & The Struggle

itv 2 Now a major itv2 series
the Vampire Diaries
The Awakening & The Struggle
L. J. SMITH